MISTAKEN REALITY

OTHER BOOKS AND AUDIO BOOKS
BY TRACI HUNTER ABRAMSON

UNDERCURRENTS SERIES

Undercurrents

Ripple Effect

The Deep End

SAINT SQUAD SERIES

Freefall

Lockdown

Crossfire

Backlash

Smoke Screen

Code Word

Lock and Key

Drop Zone

Spotlight

Tripwire

ROYAL SERIES

Royal Target

Royal Secrets

Royal Brides

GUARDIAN SERIES

Failsafe

Safe House

Sanctuary

STAND-ALONES

Obsession

Deep Cover

Chances Are

Chance for Home

Kept Secrets

Twisted Fate

Proximity

Entangled

Mistaken Reality

MISTAKEN REALITY

A NOVEL BY

TRACI HUNTER ABRAMSON

Covenant Communications, Inc.

All statements of fact, opinion, or analysis expressed are those of the author and do not reflect the official positions or views of the Central Intelligence Agency (CIA) or any other U.S. Government agency. Nothing in the contents should be construed as asserting or implying U.S. Government authentication of information or CIA endorsement of the author's views. This material has been reviewed by the CIA to prevent the disclosure of classified information. This does not constitute an official release of CIA information.

Cover image: *Apple on White Background* © glasslanguage, *Hand Grenade in Green* © ilze79, *Red Apple* © blackred; courtesy of Istockphoto.com.

Cover design copyright © 2019 by Covenant Communications, Inc.

Published by Covenant Communications, Inc.
American Fork, Utah

This is a work of fiction. The characters, names, incidents, places, and dialogue are either products of the author's imagination, and are not to be construed as real, or are used fictitiously.

Printed in the United States of America
First Printing: October 2019

26 25 24 23 22 21 20 19   10 9 8 7 6 5 4 3 2 1

ISBN 978-1-52440-941-8

For Luke

Always remember
nothing is impossible

ACKNOWLEDGMENTS

THANK YOU TO THE WONDERFUL people at Covenant who continue to support me in doing what I love, especially Robby Nichols for your constant support and my wonderful editor, Samantha Millburn. Truly, I am so grateful that you continue to nurture my writing abilities and always encourage me to improve. Thank you to my critique partners, Paige Edwards and Ellie Whitney, and the members of my writing group, Nicole White and Kyla Beecroft. You all help me so much more than you know.

Thank you to real Hadley Baker for sharing your dreams with me as well as lending me your name. Oh, and thanks for naming your fictional cat in this book. Thanks also to Jake Turner for sharing your hopes and ambitions and for letting me use some of those within these pages.

Thanks to my husband, Jonathan, for supporting my crazy career, even when it takes me all over the world. Thanks also to my children for all you do to help me in my writing endeavors.

Thank you to the Central Intelligence Agency Publication Review Board for your efficient service in helping review my manuscripts.

Finally, thank you to the many readers who have supported me on the journey as we discover what happens next.

CHAPTER 1

HADLEY FOLLOWED THE MAÎTRE D' THROUGH the elegant restaurant, Spencer and their three dining companions falling into step behind her. White table-cloths, fresh flowers, dripping chandeliers. Across the room, tall windows framed the Occoquan River, sailboats visible in the distance. Hadley soaked it all in.

Her gaze wandered as she recognized several familiar faces. Was that James Whitmore, the senator from Virginia? And Richard Lincoln from Channel 9 News two tables over? And the woman in the corner—where had Hadley seen her before?

The maître d' stopped at a round table in the corner. He leaned down to light the candle in the center before pulling Hadley's chair out for her.

"Thank you." Hadley took her seat, Spencer sitting on one side of her and his boss, Carlos, sitting on the other.

After the maître d' passed out menus, Spencer immediately set his aside and took Hadley's hand in his. "Hadley, you look stunning tonight."

Hadley's cheeks flushed at the compliment. "Thank you."

"I have to say, Spencer, you are a very lucky man," Carlos said. "Hadley is every bit as beautiful as you claimed."

Her blush deepened. Though she had met a few of Spencer's coworkers once before, this was the first time she had met his boss.

One of the two clients sitting across from them nodded his approval. "How long have the two of you been together?"

"Long enough," Spencer said. He squeezed her hand, his eyes meeting hers briefly before he continued. "Long enough for me to know I want to spend the rest of my life with her, just the two of us."

The mention of a life together sent a bevy of butterflies fluttering in her stomach, though the wings turned sharp as she contemplated the end of

Spencer's sentence. She wanted to question him, but she felt too uncomfortable having such a private conversation in front of men she had just met; instead, she fixed a neutral smile on her face.

Carlos kept the conversation going. "Better be careful there, Spencer, or you're going to find yourself spending all your money on diamonds and diapers."

"Diamonds maybe," Spencer countered. "I'm passing on the diapers."

Hadley's eyebrows drew together, and she pulled her hand free. In an attempt to hide her discomfort, she cast her gaze at her water glass, where a cloth napkin had been folded in the shape of a fan and placed inside. She removed it and laid it in her lap.

No one spoke until she looked up at Spencer. He put his hand on hers again. "You'd rather have diamonds than diapers, wouldn't you?"

Trapped by the direct question, she said, "Actually, family is more important to me than jewels."

Something flashed in Spencer's green eyes. "I'm sorry, but children aren't in my plans."

Heat flushed up her neck and into her cheeks. She didn't want to make a scene, so she lowered her voice. "Maybe we should talk about this later."

"Hadley, you should know I'm not budging on this. I've given my life to my career. I don't want to be a father. Ever."

Shock, disbelief. Hadley absorbed both emotions, searching for some sense in Spencer's words. He couldn't mean it. Her focus solely on Spencer, she shook her head. "You never said anything before about—"

"I'm saying it now," Spencer interrupted. "I don't want children. If you do, then maybe we don't have a future after all."

"Maybe we don't." Tears burned in the back of her eyes, but Hadley refused to let them surface. She wouldn't give these men the satisfaction of seeing her cry. Instead, she stood. "Gentlemen, if you'll excuse me, I need to go to the ladies' room."

With silence hanging over the table, Hadley headed for the privacy of the restroom walls.

* * *

A blue pickup, a white van, and three men standing between them. Three terrorists, JD corrected as he took position at the rear corner of the upscale hotel in northern Virginia.

JD glimpsed a sailboat on the Occoquan River a few hundred yards away. The white sails against the blue sky should have evoked a sense of calm, but if intel was right, calm wasn't what these men had in mind. Rabell's men.

JD knew the man's file well. Over the past few years, Rabell had expanded his empire, his fingers reaching into all manner of chaos and terror. Arms deals, smuggling, terrorist attacks. Rabell's attacks didn't follow the usual pattern of religious extremism or fighting for political dominance. Instead, he attacked anyone who stood in his way. His primary goal: profit.

Noah Cabbott's voice came over JD's communication headset. "Any sign of the bomb?"

"Negative. It's got to be inside the van," JD said. "If they already had it planted, these guys would be long gone."

"Maybe the bomb squad will get here in time after all."

"What's their ETA?"

"Fourteen minutes."

One of the suspected terrorists made a sweeping motion with his hand, spurring another man into action. The youngest of the three crossed to the van parked to the right of the service entrance. He opened the back door while the other two men climbed into the pickup. A minute later, he reemerged and started toward their apparent escape vehicle.

JD's hand flexed on the grip of his pistol. "They're on the move." He gave the make and model of the pickup, along with the license plate number.

"On my way."

The truck engine started, but before the third man could reach the vehicle, Noah whipped around the corner behind the wheel of a full-sized SUV.

Panicked voices spoken in a foreign tongue echoed through the air.

JD lifted his gun and peeked around the corner of the wall where he had taken cover. "Federal agents!" he shouted.

An instant later, gunfire sounded, and plaster sprayed into the air as the bullets impacted the wall inches from JD's head.

JD ducked and took aim. "Drop it!"

The warning fell on deaf ears, and JD fired, his bullet striking the man who had been caught in the open space between the van and the pickup.

Even as the truck went into motion and headed for the narrow piece of driveway between the SUV and the trees to Noah's left, more bullets sprayed the air, this time originating from the passenger side.

Noah stepped out of his vehicle and used the door for cover. He squeezed off two shots, the splatter of blood on the windshield indicating he'd hit the driver.

The truck swerved, now heading directly for where Noah had taken cover. The passenger-side door opened, and the only uninjured man jumped out and came up shooting.

He fired at Noah, forcing Noah to face the danger of the oncoming vehicle to avoid the spray of bullets.

With no angle for a shot, JD sprinted forward. The truck was within fifteen feet of Noah's SUV when he fired, and his bullet hit the last terrorist in the chest.

"Clear!" JD shouted.

Noah abandoned his position and raced toward the line of trees bordering the service area parking lot. He ducked behind a thick oak as the truck smashed into Noah's government-issued vehicle.

Metal crunched. Glass shattered. Debris exploded into the air.

"You okay?" JD shouted to Noah.

"Yeah. Check the two over there." Noah approached the truck to evaluate the driver, and JD headed for the last man he had shot.

JD kicked the fallen pistol clear before leaning down to find a weak pulse on the man. After checking him for additional weapons, he confiscated a knife and a second gun. When he checked the other terrorist sprawled on the ground, he quickly ascertained that the man hadn't survived his wounds. After removing the man's weapons, he retrieved the keys to the van.

Noah stood beside the pickup, a shake of his head indicating the driver was also dead.

JD pulled out his cell phone and dialed. "I need an ambulance." He proceeded to give their location before he hung up and looked at Noah. "You sure you're okay?"

"Yeah." Noah drew an unsteady breath when he glanced behind them at the two vehicles, their hoods crumpled, glass glittering on the surrounding pavement. "Thanks."

JD nodded, heading for the van. He checked the doors for booby traps before unlocking the back. He pulled the doors open and stared. Plastic explosives filled the entire cargo compartment. The old-fashioned red numbers counted down: 13:44. 13:43. 13:42.

"What's the ETA on the bomb squad?" JD called out.

Noah relayed the question to dispatch before responding. "Eight minutes."

"Better tell them to step on it."

Noah passed on the message, along with the request to evacuate the hotel through the front entrance. Noah rounded the back of the van and came to an immediate stop. "I guess intel was right on this one."

"Yeah." JD pushed the van's back doors open wider. "But none of these guys were Rabell."

"Which means he'll try again."

"Exactly." JD let out a sigh. "The question is, Who is his target?"

* * *

Kelsey Cabbott waited by the phone, eager for the latest update. Her group at the CIA had identified the bomb threat in Occoquan, Virginia, and she had personally passed the information on to the FBI, knowing her husband would likely be one of the agents involved.

Sure enough, Noah had texted her shortly after the intel had been shared to let her know he had to go in for a weekend assignment. She looked at the clock. If the agency's source was correct, the bomb would be going off any minute.

Kelsey had conducted the phone interview of Jenetta Blaese, the twenty-six-year-old woman who had called a tip in to the CIA hotline. Jenetta's boyfriend, one of Rabell's men, hadn't known she was home when he'd gone over his plans with his two partners, plans that would destroy The Waterfront Resort and kill everyone inside.

Eli, a CIA analyst in Kelsey's division, knocked on her open office door before walking inside. "Hey, Kelly. Any word yet from the FBI?"

"Not yet." Even after a year working at headquarters, Kelsey's coworkers still didn't know her real name or the fact that she was married to an FBI agent. Safer that way, she reminded herself. After spending more than two years deep undercover, using an alias was now second nature. "Have the U.S. Marshals secured our source yet?"

"Yeah. They picked her up an hour ago."

Jenetta had provided an incredible amount of detail, enough so that the agency had agreed to relocate her under the witness protection program to ensure her safety.

Kelsey's phone rang. "Kelly Park."

"Kelly, this is Burt Powell with the FBI. A bomb has been located at The Waterfront Resort in Occoquan."

"Status?" Kelsey asked.

"Agents are on scene, three suspects have been contained, and the bomb squad is on the way."

"You'll keep me updated?"

"Yes, ma'am."

"Thank you."

The moment Kelsey hung up, Eli asked, "Well?"

Kelsey repeated the information.

"How much time is left?"

She looked at the clock. "Five minutes."

"I hope the bomb squad is close."

"Me too." Kelsey's gaze remained on the clock face. She sent up a silent prayer, frustrated that she was powerless to do anything besides watch the seconds go by and hope her husband stayed out of harm's way.

CHAPTER 2

HADLEY DABBED AT THE MASCARA pooling beneath her eyes, grateful the restroom was empty. She had been so certain this time would be different. Spencer moved in the inner circle of DC society and had an exciting job with a Capitol Hill PR firm. His manners were impeccable, not to mention he looked amazing in a tux.

When Spencer had first asked her out, she had been delighted to discover he shared her old-fashioned values, as well as her active lifestyle. How could she have known he didn't care for children—something she loved so dearly?

For that matter, how had Spencer missed her desire to have a family of her own someday? She was a third-grade teacher, for heaven's sake. And to break up with her in front of a table full of strangers . . . Apparently his PR skills needed some honing when it came to his personal life.

Hadley reached for another tissue only to find the dispenser on the bathroom counter empty. She pressed her lips together and dropped her black-streaked Kleenex into the trash can before turning toward one of the bathroom stalls.

She had been so excited about this dinner. Hadley had even suspected that after six months together, Spencer had been ready to explore a more permanent future. But instead of contemplating whether she wanted to someday have him put a ring on her finger, she was now left to pick up the shards of her heart after yet another breakup.

Drawing a deep breath, she straightened her shoulders and willed the tears to stop.

She hated crying. It wasn't going to solve anything. Besides, it was better to know sooner than later that Spencer wasn't the man of her future.

She retrieved a piece of toilet paper and dabbed her eyes again. The bathroom door opened, and she stayed where she was, opting to hide rather than face the new arrival.

"Anyone in here?" a woman's voice called out over the sound of someone's car alarm.

Hadley opened her mouth to answer, but no sound came out. She took a breath and tried to speak again, but before she could, the door closed, and she was left alone. The irritating shrill of the alarm continued, and Hadley tried to block it out.

She used the toilet paper to wipe the last of the mascara from her eyes before digging through her purse for her makeup. If she was going to walk back into that room full of strangers, she was determined to face them with her head held high.

* * *

JD watched the timer count down as the bomb techs took their first look at the device in the back of the van. 4:23. 4:22. 4:21.

Casey, the junior of the two bomb techs, pointed at a cluster of wires near the wheel well. "Am I seeing this right?"

"Yeah." Leo turned to JD and Noah. "We've got a problem. This bomb has a dead man's switch. We go to disarm it, and it explodes."

"Then we need to move it away from the hotel."

"Negative. It's wired into the wheel well. If the tire turns, it goes off," Leo said. "Best thing we can do is clear everything out of the blast radius and make sure the hotel is evacuated."

"I'll move the dumpsters," Noah said.

"I'll double-check the hotel." JD glanced at the timer and hit the stopwatch function on his cell.

"The police are out front to make sure everyone stays in the front parking area where it's safe," Noah said.

"Got it." Leaving his partner to help the bomb techs, JD sprinted toward the back door and the screech of the fire alarm.

He cleared the kitchen, freezer, and storage room in thirty seconds. The main banquet hall, lobby, and front desk took thirty more. His heart racing, he checked the indoor pool, exercise room, business center, and three conference rooms. All empty.

His cell phone buzzed. Heading for the front door, he read the message from Noah.

Forty seconds. Clear the building.

JD opened the door to the men's restroom and confirmed it was vacant. Seconds ticked by in his head. Twenty seconds. Nineteen.

One more room to go. He yanked open the women's restroom, and a shriek pierced the air.

Surprise stole two seconds from him while he stared at the stunning brunette in the doorway. "Is anyone else in there?" he asked, raising his voice to be heard over the alarm.

"What?"

He pushed past her into the women's restroom. "We're evacuating the building. Go out the front entrance."

The woman didn't move. Instead, she stared at him like he was completely insane.

Eight seconds. Seven.

With no time to spare, JD grabbed her around her waist and hoisted her over his shoulder. She gasped as he gripped the back of her thighs to hold her in place. An instant later, fists pounded on his back.

"Put me down!" she shrieked. "What are you doing?"

Ignoring the abuse and her question, JD sprinted for the front entrance.

The automatic glass doors opened on his approach, and he slowed down only long enough to make sure they could fit through the opening.

He was barely outside when the ground shook and an explosion echoed through the air. He stumbled forward, the weight of the woman preventing him from regaining his footing. In an instant, the woman fell onto the grassy area by the hotel's driveway, and JD crashed into a bed of petunias. Glass shattered, and the ground shook again. JD reached over and put his hand on his companion's head, shifting his body to shield her from the flying debris. They lay there for a full minute before JD asked, "Are you okay?"

She stared at him, bewildered. "What—? Was that a—?"

"A bomb? Yeah."

Shock replaced surprise, and the woman's mouth opened twice before she managed to form a complete sentence. "Why were you inside if you knew there was a bomb?"

"I was doing my job." JD sat up and gripped her elbow to help her up as well. "JD Byers. FBI."

"Hadley Baker." She drew in a deep breath and immediately coughed on the lingering smoke. Her gaze shifted to the hotel, where the windows of the first two floors had shattered and flames licked through the openings.

JD could almost see her mind working through the shock, her dark-brown eyes finally meeting his once more.

"You saved my life," she finally said.

"Like I said, I was doing my job." He started to stand, but Hadley put her hand on his arm. The contact and the jolt that shot through him beneath her touch kept him in place.

Hadley blinked several times, and her voice was husky when she managed to speak again. "Thank you."

"You're welcome."

* * *

Hadley sat in the back of the ambulance and watched the buzz of activity in front of her. The acrid scent of smoke hung in the air. Lights flashed from dozens of emergency vehicles. Firefighters sprayed water on the smoldering fire. Police cars blocked the nearest intersection, where an officer was diverting traffic.

A crowd of people from the hotel stood clustered in the parking lot, various law enforcement personnel interviewing them in turn. Even from a hundred feet away, the buzz of activity carried toward her.

The shrill ringing she had mistaken for a car alarm had actually been the fire alarm signaling everyone to evacuate. She wasn't sure why it had sounded so muffled in the restroom.

Her heartbeat stuttered when her gaze landed on the front doors. She had been twenty feet from there only seconds before the bomb had gone off. Had that FBI agent not arrived when he had, she wouldn't still be here. JD Byers had literally saved her life.

A shiver worked through her as she looked down at the cuts and scrapes on her arms and legs and the rip in the left sleeve of her dress.

"Here." The paramedic draped a blanket over her shoulders. "Keep this around you."

"Thanks." Hadley gripped the lightweight fabric, pulling it more firmly around her, even though she could still feel the waves of heat coming from the fire.

A handful of hotel guests climbed into their vehicles and joined the throng of cars trying to clear the area. For the first time since she had been carried out of the hotel, she remembered Spencer. Where was he? Had he really evacuated the building without any concern about her whereabouts? Or maybe he'd assumed she had left the hotel completely when she had gone to the restroom.

Footsteps approached from the side of the ambulance. JD moved into her view, his chiseled features etched with concern. She guessed he wasn't much older than her, maybe thirty years old, but he carried with him an air of authority and experience, as though he had been through this kind of situation before.

"How are you doing?" JD asked.

"Okay."

"Are you up to answering a few questions?"

"I think so."

JD pulled a small notepad and pen from the inside pocket of his suit jacket. "Where were you before you went to the restroom?"

"I was in the restaurant having dinner."

"Alone?"

"No. I was with my boyfriend and some of his clients." Hadley hesitated before adding, "Actually, he's my ex-boyfriend now."

JD glanced at her, his pen hovering over the notepad. "Can you give me their names?"

"Spencer Andrews is my ex. His boss is Carlos Hernandez. The other two were Keith and Drake, but I don't know their last names."

"Where are they?"

She looked past JD, taking a moment to orient herself with where Spencer had parked when they'd first arrived. Her eyes narrowed when she saw the empty parking space. She looked around again. Surely Spencer wouldn't have left her, would he? In her mind, she mapped the route they had taken when they'd walked into the hotel and again faced the same results.

"He was parked right over there." Hadley pointed at the empty space in the row of parked cars by the hotel, debris on the sidewalk. "He was in that spot, three from the end."

"When did he leave?"

"I don't know. I didn't see him after I left the table and went into the restroom."

JD stared at her, looked back at the parking lot, and returned his attention to her again. "I may have some more questions for you."

"I'm not going anywhere."

"Actually," the paramedic interrupted, "you need to go to the hospital to get checked out."

JD took down her personal information before retrieving a business card from his wallet. "Here's my number. I'll be in touch."

Hadley watched him as he started toward a man around his age who was also dressed in a business suit. She noticed a rip in JD's sleeve and turned to the paramedic. "Shouldn't he go to the hospital too? He was just as close to the hotel as I was when the bomb went off."

"He should, but I doubt he'll go unless someone gives him an order." He motioned to the gurney in back of the ambulance. "Let's get you out of here."

Hadley nodded, but her attention remained on the man responsible for saving her life.

CHAPTER 3

JD GLANCED BACK AT HADLEY, his curiosity humming. His professional curiosity, he amended. Had her ex-boyfriend been involved with tonight's bombing? And if so, why would he have brought her with him if she wasn't involved? JD approached Noah and held up his notepad. "I may have a lead."

"What have you got?" Noah asked.

"A couple of people who might have left right before the bomb went off," JD said. "Could be they knew to get out of there."

"It's worth tracking down, but first you need to go to the hospital."

"I'm fine."

"It's either the hospital or witness statements. There's a party of ten over there who still need to be interviewed."

JD glanced in the direction Noah pointed, to a group of elderly couples, at least two wearing hearing aids.

"Fine. I'll go to the hospital, but I'm driving myself."

"Are you sure . . . ?"

"Yes, I'm okay to drive." JD took several steps before he remembered Noah's vehicle wasn't drivable. He turned back. "Do you need me to come back for you?"

"Don't worry about me. I'll have one of the black-and-whites drop me off at the office."

"I'll see you later." Once in his car, he followed the ambulance transporting Hadley out of the parking lot. Figuring the paramedics would know the closest hospital, he took position behind them. They were only a few blocks away when he realized where they were going.

He turned onto the hospital access road, his stomach tightening when he thought of the last time he had been here. Absently, he rubbed his chest where three scars provided a constant reminder that he was a walking miracle.

The ambulance circled to the rear entrance. JD veered off to the emergency room parking lot. To his right, he could see the main entrance. All he had to do was close his eyes to relive that moment when a car had come screeching around the corner and Noah had yelled out a warning that was followed by gunfire.

JD shook his head, pushing the memories aside. It had been nearly a year since he had been released. Today was different. He would go in, let the doctor confirm he was okay, and then go back to life as usual.

Refusing to show weakness even to himself, he made his way inside and approached the receptionist.

The woman behind the desk looked up. "Agent Byers. What can I do for you?"

JD studied the woman in her early thirties. She looked vaguely familiar, but he couldn't place her. Rather than admitting he didn't remember her, he answered her question. "Had a little incident today. My partner wants me to get checked out." JD looked at the handful of people in the waiting room. "How long is the wait?"

She handed him a tablet. "Fill this out, and I'll get you right back."

"Thanks." He stepped to the side and proceeded to enter his information. He returned it to the receptionist, and a moment later, his name was called.

Resigned to his fate of being poked and prodded for the next few minutes, he followed a nurse through the indicated door, wanting nothing more than to regain his freedom.

* * *

Hadley followed the doctor's instructions, looking one way and then the other while he shined a light in her eyes. He had already asked her a bunch of questions, obviously checking for signs of a concussion. "How close were you when the bomb went off?"

She was certain she had answered this question a dozen times already. "We were about fifteen feet from the hotel entrance."

"You were very lucky." The doctor clicked the light off and stepped back. "Everything looks okay, but if you start feeling dizzy or your headache gets worse instead of better, come back in." He reached for a flyer hanging in a plastic holder affixed to the wall. "Here's a list of other signs of a concussion."

"Thank you, Doctor." Hadley took the paper from him. "Can I go home now?"

"As soon as the paperwork is finished, you're good to go."

Another fifteen minutes passed before Hadley was finally released to leave. She walked by the nurses' station, debating which of her coworkers might be willing to give her a ride home. She didn't look forward to explaining how she'd ended up here on a Saturday night, but it was better than getting in a vehicle with a cabbie or Uber driver she didn't know.

She scrolled through her favorites list on her phone, glancing up when she heard someone approaching.

Agent Byers closed the distance between them. "Are they letting you go?"

Hadley nodded. "I didn't realize you were here."

"My coworker insisted." He glanced around before his gaze came back to her. "Is anyone here with you?"

"No. I was just debating who to call for a ride."

"I can give you a lift," he said. "Where do you live?"

"Lake Ridge."

He motioned to the door leading to the lobby. "Come on. Let's get out of here."

Hadley considered her decision not to ride with a complete stranger but relented. After all, the man had saved her life.

The moment they entered the lobby, the woman behind the desk stood. "Agent Byers, I wanted to thank you."

"Thank me for what?" he asked.

"You don't remember me, do you?"

JD's eyes narrowed momentarily before widening with recognition. "You were here the day of the shooting."

"Yes. If you hadn't pushed me out of the way, I doubt I would be here right now."

"I was just doing my job."

"We both know you went above and beyond that." She extended her hand, and JD shook it. "I'm glad to see you walking out of here on your own two feet this time."

"Me too." JD put his hand on Hadley's back to guide her forward. "Have a good night."

Hadley waited until they passed through the sliding-glass doors before she asked, "What was that all about?"

"I happened to be there when she was in the wrong place at the wrong time."

Though curious about the details, when JD fell silent, Hadley didn't press.

He pulled his keys from his pocket and led her to a silver SUV in the far corner of the parking lot. He opened the passenger door.

"Thank you." Hadley slid into the seat, glancing up at JD, who still stood beside the car, waiting to close her door. Spencer never did that for her.

As soon as JD took his place behind the wheel, he asked, "Where to?"

Hadley rattled off her address.

"Have you heard from the ex-boyfriend yet?"

"No." Hadley glanced at him, uncertain whether he was making conversation or conducting an interview. "I still can't believe he left me."

"What does he do for a living?"

"He works for Opinions Matter."

"The PR firm in DC?"

"That's right."

"Any idea who his current clients are? You mentioned the two at dinner with you tonight."

"All I know is he was working a lot up on the Hill." She shifted in her seat, so she could see him more clearly. "You don't think Spencer was involved with the bombing, do you?"

"I doubt it, but I have to look into everyone who was there." He pulled up to a red light and glanced at her. "Were you together long?"

"Six months." This time, when she thought of the breakup, anger surfaced over the hurt. "I thought I knew him, but I was so wrong."

"It can happen to anyone."

"Maybe, but it's the last time it's going to happen to me."

JD fell silent for a minute before the questions started again. "Did you go out with Spencer's clients often?"

"No." Both physically and mentally exhausted, Hadley leaned her head against the headrest. "I'm sorry, but I really don't want to think about Spencer right now. Can this conversation wait until tomorrow?"

"Yes, of course." They drove in silence for several minutes before JD asked, "Is there a time I can come by tomorrow? Or if you'd rather, you can meet me at my office."

Tonight's experience had already caused her to change her plans for tomorrow, but still, she resisted. "Could we do it in the afternoon?"

"Two o'clock work for you?"

"That's fine."

JD pulled into a parking space near her apartment and turned off the ignition. He climbed out and circled the car, opening the door for her. "I'll make
sure you get inside okay."

"Thanks." She led the way to her apartment, trembling when she slid the
key into the lock. Her hand closed over the knob, a wave of panic crashing over
her.

She looked at JD.

"I know you've been through a lot today. Do you want me to check out
your apartment?" he asked.

The offer alone calmed her. Her hand dropped to her side. "I feel silly for
asking, but would you mind?"

"Any roommates I should know about?"

"Only my cat."

JD opened the door and slipped inside. A few seconds passed in silence
before the light flipped on.

Hadley glanced through the doorway at her simply furnished living room.
Her hiking boots lay next to her couch covered in throw pillows. To her left,
her teaching bag leaned against a kitchen chair, the stack of papers she had
been grading this afternoon still scattered on the table's surface.

JD emerged from the short hallway leading to her bedroom and bathroom.
"All clear. The cat must not like strangers, because he's hiding under your bed."

"She," Hadley corrected. "Lucy isn't a fan of new people."

"Can't say I blame her," he said. "I'll see you here tomorrow afternoon."

Hadley walked inside and put her hand on his arm. "Thank you again.
For everything."

"You're welcome." He pointed at the dead bolt. "Don't forget to lock up."

As soon as JD closed the door between them, Hadley flipped the dead
bolt. She leaned back against the door and closed her eyes. Maybe in the
morning, she would wake up and discover this day had all been a bad dream.

* * *

JD navigated through the maze of cubicles until he reached Noah's desk.
"Anything new?"

"I tried tracking the names you gave me. Spencer Andrews's cell phone is
off, and Carlos Hernandez isn't answering."

"Do you have a location on either?" JD asked.

Noah waved at one of the two computer screens on his desk. "Both the GPS signal on Carlos Hernandez's cell phone and his car put him at home. Mitch and Cooper are on their way over there to question him."

"And Andrews?"

"He drives a '67 Corvette. No GPS to trace."

"That doesn't make sense. The way Hadley was talking, I thought they all drove to dinner together."

"Better give her a call."

"Yeah." JD crossed to his desk opposite Noah's. He retrieved Hadley's number from his notes, a ripple of irritation surfacing. It didn't seem fair that he was calling a beautiful woman on a Saturday night, and it was strictly business.

The phone rang three times before Hadley answered with a tentative, "Hello?"

"Miss Baker, this is Agent Byers," JD began. "I'm sorry to bother you, but what car was Spencer Andrews driving tonight?"

"His company car," Hadley said.

"Do you know the make and model?"

"It's a black Cadillac Escalade," Hadley said. Apparently anticipating his next question, she added, "It's new. He's only had it about three months. I don't know the license plate number or anything, but I remember it has DC plates."

JD added the new information to his notes. "What about the other men at dinner? Did they drive with you?"

"Yes. Spencer picked them up on his way to get me."

"Do you know where he picked them up?"

"I'm sorry. I don't."

"That's okay. I appreciate your help." JD started to end the call, but instead, he asked, "How are you holding up?"

"Honestly, I have every light on in the house, and I'm afraid to go to bed."

"I'm sorry. Do you have any friends or family you can stay with tonight? I should have asked you that before I dropped you off."

"My folks live across the country, and I don't think I'm ready to talk to anyone else about this yet," Hadley said. "I'll be fine."

"Call me if you need a friendly voice. Anytime, day or night."

"I appreciate that." Hadley's voice trailed off, silence humming between them for several seconds. "I guess I'll see you tomorrow."

"Yeah, I'll see you then." JD hung up and tapped on his computer keyboard, pulling up the list of vehicles registered to Opinions Matter. When he came up empty, he began a search for the company itself to determine if there was another level of ownership that would mask his search. Again, nothing.

Noah ended a call and swiveled in his chair to face him. "Any luck?"

"Hadley said Spencer was driving a company car, but there's no record of it being registered to the company," Noah said. "What about you?"

"That was Mitch on the phone. According to Hernandez, he's been home all night."

"Could he be lying?"

"Not likely. He and his wife had a couple neighbors over to watch the ball game on TV."

"Then who was with Spencer Andrews?" JD asked.

"That's an excellent question."

CHAPTER 4

KADE SLOWED TO A WALK beside his wife as they approached the cottage in the woods they had made their primary residence. Beyond keeping them in shape, their early-morning run also served as a regular security sweep of their property and the surrounding area.

"You know what you should do today?" Kade asked.

Renee slanted a suspicious look in his direction. "What?"

"You should go to that little bakery we like and pick up some brownies."

"We just ran five miles." Renee stopped at the edge of their front porch and put one foot on the bottom step to stretch her calf. "Doesn't it seem counterproductive to already be thinking about brownies?"

"I thought we ran so we can eat brownies."

"I think it's more accurate to say we run so we're ready in case anyone is ever chasing us."

Kade acknowledged his defeat. Though Renee was a member of the support staff for the secret government program known as the guardians, she had stepped into an operational role more often than he liked.

"You could pick up some ice cream and hot fudge when you get the brownies, and we can make sundaes for dessert tonight."

"Or you could do the shopping," Renee suggested.

"But I'm a ghost," Kade pointed out. "I'm supposed to be invisible."

"And you're good at your job." Renee stretched her other leg. "You can put on one of your disguises, and no one will even know you're there. Besides, I need to work through a kink with our FBI interface. We stopped getting intel reports yesterday."

"That's not good." Kade let out a sigh. "I really hate it when national security gets in the way of dessert."

"It's a challenge." Renee led the way inside. "Tell you what. I'll make you one of those peanut butter smoothies you like."

"That would be great. Thanks."

"Can you check the database and see if there are any updates?"

"Sure." Kade crossed the living room to the long table they had converted into two work stations. He leaned down and logged on, taking a moment to enjoy the view of their wooded lot through the window.

When he glanced back at the laptop, an alert filled the screen. "Hon, you'd better come take a look at this."

"Be right there." The blender turned on, and three minutes later, Renee entered carrying two large cups. "Here you go."

Kade took the cup from her but set it aside. "Looks like that FBI interface is more critical than we realized. They were on scene for a bombing last night."

"What? Where?"

"A resort in Occoquan."

"Any casualties?" Renee asked.

"Looks like the FBI killed two of three suspects."

"What about the third?" Renee set her drink down and sat at her computer.

Kade scanned farther down on the news summary. "In critical condition."

"Any indication of the motive?"

"Nothing listed in the news." Kade typed a note into the guardian message board to the operative most closely associated with Rabell's program.

"You think you'll need to go up there?"

"I'm not sure yet, but with the recent CIA report about Rabell, my money's on him." Kade picked up his smoothie and took a sip. "I'm going to hit the shower."

"I'll see what I can do about getting our link reestablished."

"Thanks." Drinking his smoothie on his way, Kade headed upstairs. Though he preferred to keep Renee close when on assignment, if Rabell was involved with this case, he wanted his wife safely tucked away. That man was pure evil.

* * *

Hadley opened her eyes, her gaze landing on the chair in the corner of her bedroom where she had tossed her torn dress. It wasn't a dream.

She rolled onto her back and winced when her weight aggravated the cut in her shoulder. She was lucky she hadn't needed stitches.

Gingerly, she sat up and grabbed her cell phone. No new messages. She opened her news feed, a photo of the hotel bombing topping the headlines.

A worm of doubt crept into her mind, right next to the dull headache forming. Last night when JD asked about Spencer, Hadley had been 100-percent certain Spencer wasn't involved in anything illegal. The man was a pillar of society, someone who rubbed elbows with some of the most powerful men and women in the country.

Now, she couldn't help wonder why he hadn't at least had the courtesy to make sure she was all right after last night's bombing. And why had he abandoned her at the hotel in the first place? He might have been a complete jerk when they'd broken up, but until that moment, he'd always been a gentleman. And a gentleman didn't abandon his date, even if his date was now his ex.

A well of nervous energy bubbled inside her, her mind refusing to calm. She climbed out of bed and crossed to the dresser. Maybe a run around the neighborhood would help her clear her head before JD arrived for another round of questions.

* * *

"Did you get it working?" Kade asked as soon as he walked back into the living room.

"Yeah, and get this." Renee pointed to her screen. "Jim and Katherine Whitmore were among the guests at the hotel when the bomb went off."

"What was the senator doing there?"

"It was the engagement party for Makenna Burke. I pulled the guest list from the FBI reports and loaded it into the guardian database, along with the interview notes." Concern lit Renee's features when she asked, "You don't think the senator was the target, do you?"

"I don't know, but that's going to be my focus today." He sat beside her. "Any new updates from the other guardians?"

"Nothing, which is odd. I thought you had a man inside of Rabell's organization."

"We do. He must not have been able to get a message out yet."

"I hope we hear something soon."

"Me too. I don't like being in the dark." Kade sensed Renee's gaze on him. He turned to meet it. "What?"

"Maybe we should relocate closer to Occoquan for the next few days. Your new rig is waiting to be broken in," Renee said, referring to the tractor-trailer that had been converted into a luxury mobile home.

"I don't want you anywhere near Rabell's operation," Kade said. "I wouldn't feel comfortable leaving you alone in the rig if I have to take off."

"It sounds like the Whitmores may have ended up in the middle of this thing. Maybe they would be up for a houseguest."

"Maybe." Kade's cell phone rang. He glanced at the screen. "Speak of the devil." He hit the talk button. "Hey, Senator. We just heard about last night. Are you and Katherine okay?"

"Yes, but I was hoping for a favor."

"What's that?"

"I have an FBI agent coming over to interview me today," Jim said. "I was hoping you could run a background for me."

"Sure. What's the name?"

"Noah Cabbott."

"It'll take me at least an hour if you want me to go deep."

"Anything you can get me would be appreciated. I need to know how much I can share with him," Jim said. "I also have to ask: Do you think it's possible I was a target because of my involvement with the guardians?"

"I don't know who would be able to make the connection. That information has been tightly held."

"Yes, but after the trouble the guardians have had the last couple years, the question is worth asking."

"We'll look into it and get back to you." Kade hung up and spoke to Renee. "Looks like we both have work to do today."

"I'm done for now. What can I do to help?"

"Dig into the CIA files and see what you can find on Noah Cabbott."

"Noah Cabbott? FBI?"

"Yeah. You know him?"

"No, but I know his wife." Renee's eyebrows lifted. "According to the guardian files, so do you."

"What do you mean?"

"Remember the rescue operation last year when the guardians sent the Saint Squad in after a deep-cover operative? A woman who had been taken captive in Abolstan?"

"Yeah. She'd been shot by Salman Nassar."

"Taja Al-Kazaz, also known as Kelly Park. Her real name is Kelsey Cabbott. She's Noah Cabbott's wife."

"Sounds like this guy's already been thoroughly vetted."

"Oh yeah."

"I'll let the senator know Noah's background and see if the senator's up for some visitors."

"When do we leave?" Renee asked.

"Give me an hour or so. I still have a few things I want to pack," Kade said.

"I'll be ready. We can pick up some brownies on the way."

"Now you're talking."

CHAPTER 5

Noah studied the palatial home of Senator James Whitmore as he walked up the driveway. Though he had four members of congress he needed to interview regarding the bombing on Saturday night, all the others had set up appointments with him for tomorrow in their offices on Capitol Hill. Senator Whitmore had invited him to his home.

Noah rang the doorbell. Less than fifteen seconds passed before the door swung open. Noah flashed his badge. "Senator Whitmore, I'm Special Agent Noah Cabbott."

"Yes, of course." The senator shook Noah's hand. "Please come in."

"Thank you." Noah stepped through the doorway and saw the large picture of the Washington D.C. Temple. He'd forgotten the senator was also a member of The Church of Jesus Christ of Latter-day Saints. "I have that same photo in my house."

"You're a member of the Church too, then."

"I am." Noah followed the senator into the living room, where an elegant, dark-haired woman sat on a couch. "I appreciate your willingness to meet with me, especially on a Sunday."

"I know how important it is to get information quickly in the investigative process." The senator motioned to the woman. "This is my wife, Katherine. Katherine, this is Agent Cabbott."

Katherine stood and offered her hand. "It's good to meet you."

"You too." They all sat, and Noah retrieved a notebook from his pocket. "I'm following up with everyone who was at the hotel last night. We're trying to ascertain who might have been a target."

The senator reached for his wife's hand. "I'm afraid it might have been me."

"Why do you believe that?"

"I hate to say it, but there are a few reasons," Senator Whitmore said. "Several of them are classified, and everything I can tell you is confidential."

"I assure you, any information you give me will be treated strictly as need-to-know."

"First, what questions do you have for my wife and me?"

Noah stared at the couple for a moment before he comprehended the senator's underlying message. His wife wasn't privy to classified information. That conversation would have to wait until they were alone.

"Why were you at the hotel last night?"

"We were attending an engagement party," Senator Whitmore said.

"Congressman Burke's daughter is getting married next spring," Katherine added. "Over half of the people at the restaurant were there because of the party."

"I would think the congressman would have reserved the entire venue for such an event, especially since so many high-profile guests were in attendance."

"Actually, they did try to reserve the whole restaurant," Katherine said. "The hotel manager called Francine last week to let her know there had been a mix-up. They had accidentally double-booked a smaller event."

"Francine?" Noah asked.

"Francine Burke," Katherine clarified. "She's the mother of the bride."

"Do you know what the smaller event was?"

"I think it was some sort of dinner for a public relations firm." Katherine's lips pursed as though she was contemplating saying something else.

"Is there something else, Mrs. Whitmore?"

A little sigh escaped her. "I don't like to speak ill of others, but Francine's claim struck me as odd. A small dinner party that took up only a few tables could have easily been rescheduled or moved to another location."

"I agree, but why would she lie about something like that?" Noah asked.

"The congressman was represented by the same public relations firm hosting their dinner party. It's possible he granted a favor to the firm," the senator suggested.

"To what end?" Noah asked.

"It could be for any number of reasons," Senator Whitmore said. "Congressman Burke has built his career on championing causes that are headline grabbers. This might have been a subtle way to get potential supporters into the room, his way to connect with people he wouldn't normally have easy access to."

Noah rolled this new possibility over in his mind, grateful he didn't have to deal with such things in his own career. "What issues is he currently the most vocal about?"

"School safety, immigration, and human trafficking."

"All hot topics." Changing the subject, Noah asked, "Does the name Spencer Andrews mean anything to you?"

"I can't say that it does."

"Have you ever dealt with the company Opinions Matter?"

"I've never had any personal association with them," Senator Whitmore said, "but that's the firm that was having the dinner party at The Waterfront Resort last night."

"Can you think of anyone in attendance last night who was their client, besides Congressman Burke?"

"Several of my colleagues have used their services, but I'm not sure who currently employs them."

A buzzer went off in the kitchen. "That's my cue," Katherine said. "If you'll excuse me . . ."

Noah stood. "Yes, of course."

Senator Whitmore also rose to his feet. He motioned in the direction of the entryway. "Let's continue this conversation in my office."

Noah followed him through the entryway and into an office located to the right of the front door. He caught a glimpse of a family photo and a familiar face.

"Are you related to Charlie Whitmore?" Noah asked.

"He's my son." Senator Whitmore took the seat behind his desk. "How do you know Charlie?"

"We were in the same class at the FBI Academy."

"Small world."

"It certainly is." Noah took a seat across from the older man. "You mentioned you might have been a target last night. Can you tell me why?"

"I am involved with a highly classified project that has gone through some challenges over the past couple years. We think we plugged the leaks, but it's possible someone came after me to try to shut down the program."

"What can you tell me about this program?"

"Only that it could be a motive." The senator laced his fingers together, his arms resting on his desk. "I wish I could give you more information, but the risks to the others involved are too great."

"I don't know how I can help without at least some clue about who might be after you."

"I'll work the possibility that the program is involved from my side of things. What I hope the FBI will investigate is the other reason I could be a target."

"And what reason is that?" Noah asked.

"I'll be testing the waters this fall regarding my upcoming candidacy for president."

"How many people know about this?"

"Beyond my family, not many, but as we draw closer to going public, the likelihood of the news leaking prematurely increases." Senator Whitmore opened the desk drawer to his left and retrieved a manila folder. "I compiled a list of those who are in my inner circle. I doubt any of them are involved . . ."

"But it's possible someone learned of your plans through them," Noah finished for him.

"Exactly."

Noah took the folder and opened it. He browsed through the names, discovering that all those listed were influential members of the senator's political party. "I'll certainly look into this."

Senator Whitmore stood. "If I receive any pertinent information about my classified programs, I'll let you know."

"I appreciate it." Noah pushed out of his seat and headed for the door. "Thank you again for making time to meet with me."

"I'm happy to help in any way I can."

Noah shook Senator Whitmore's hand. "Enjoy the rest of your Sunday."

"You too."

Noah walked outside and climbed into his car. As he started the engine, he looked back at the stately home. Was it possible someone had tried to kill the senator? Or was there another target he didn't know about? And what was this program the senator refused to talk about?

With more questions than answers, Noah started the car. He hoped JD was having more luck than he was.

* * *

JD rounded the corner and turned into the familiar parking lot. He and Noah had come up empty last night when searching for Spencer Andrews's company car. This morning in the shower, JD had remembered the security cameras in the common area outside Hadley's apartment. Not sure how frequently the images recycled, he had called the manager and set up an appointment to pick up copies of the feed this morning.

He pulled into one of the visitors' spots and made his way into the office. A currently vacant desk occupied the space inside the main entrance, an open door leading to a private office.

"Be right there," a male voice called out. A moment later, a man in his late twenties emerged.

JD flashed his badge. "Agent JD Byers. Are you Chad Hicks?"

"That's right." He shook JD's hand before giving him a flash drive. "I downloaded the images you asked for onto this. The camera recycles every forty-eight hours, but I gave you all I've got."

"How many camera views do you have?"

"Four total: three in the parking lots, and one aimed at the office in case of a break-in."

"Do you have trouble with break-ins here?"

"I'm sure you know as well as anyone that gang violence has been on the rise in this area. We have to be careful not to leave money in the office after our promotion weekends."

"Smart." JD held up the flash drive. "Thank you for this."

"No problem. Let me know if you need anything else."

"There is one more thing. How well do you know Hadley Baker?"

Chad motioned toward the parking lot. "I see her coming and going, but when she's not out hiking or going for a run, her boyfriend is usually with her."

"Have you met Spencer?"

"Other than waving when he comes and goes with Hadley, I've only talked to him once," Chad said. "He came in a couple weeks ago to ask about Hadley's lease."

"What about Hadley's lease?"

"He wanted to know how soon it was up and what our policies are about subleasing," Chad said. "I wasn't able to give him details about her lease, but I gave him the policy info."

"Any idea why he was asking?"

"Best guess, he's planning to propose."

"Thanks again for your help."

"No problem."

JD walked outside, the humidity hanging thick in the warm air. The dogwood tree to his right had started to lose its blossoms, and new leaves were competing with the delicate white flowers.

He headed for his car, his eyes sweeping the parking lot. A young couple strapped a toddler into a car seat before climbing into their car. JD watched them pull away before turning his attention to a woman jogging toward the complex, her dark hair pulled back in a ponytail. White bandages on her bare arms caused him to take a closer look. Hadley.

He started toward her apartment. Maybe she would talk to him now and save him a trip this afternoon. He noticed the way her steps slowed when she saw him, as though she needed an extra second to recognize him as the person she had met the day before.

He continued forward, both of them heading toward her apartment from opposite directions. He was nearly to the corner of her building when he noticed the black Cadillac SUV parked in the side lot. He glanced down. DC plates.

Changing direction, he approached the vehicle and saw a figure in the driver's seat. He lifted his hand to rest it on the handle of the weapon holstered in the back of his waistband.

Everything about the scene before him screamed that something was wrong. Windows up on a warm day, engine turned off. The pollen coating the windshield indicated the vehicle had been there for at least a few hours.

JD approached cautiously from the rear and knocked on the driver's-side window. No response. Then he got his first good look at the man inside. Eyes open but unseeing, a splatter of blood on the inside of the glass.

JD quickly tugged a pair of crime-scene gloves out of the pouch beside his holster. After he put them on, he pulled on the door handle. The vehicle was unlocked. He checked for a pulse, not surprised that he didn't find one.

Footsteps approached, and JD turned to wave off the newcomer, but it was Hadley standing behind him.

"That's Spencer's car," she said, then as though gathering her courage, she straightened her shoulders and stepped forward.

"You don't want to see this."

Hadley looked past him and gasped. "Spencer."

CHAPTER 6

HADLEY GULPED IN AIR, BREATHING in the cloying aroma of spring blossoms and the underlying scent of death. In front of her, JD had his phone to his ear. His conversation could have passed for a rerun of an *NCIS* episode.

JD hung up and faced her, his expression grim. "Did you hear from Spencer after I dropped you off last night?"

"No." Hadley's attention fixated on Spencer's lifeless figure. "I can't believe this is happening."

"Any idea who might have done this?"

She shook her head. The turmoil of emotions that had swirled within her since dinner last night surfaced once more, only this time she viewed them with new clarity. Spencer's sudden lack of decorum had been so unlike him, and yet . . . "He wanted me to break up with him."

"What?"

Hadley tore her gaze away from Spencer, from the future they could have shared. "We broke up because Spencer said he didn't want to have children."

"That's an odd conversation to have with an audience," JD said.

"I thought so too, but now I think he must have known something was wrong. He must have wanted me to leave."

"You said he picked up everyone else before he picked you up?"

"That's right." Her eyes strayed to the open car door, and tears threatened.

A police car arrived, lights flashing.

JD stepped into her field of vision. "You don't need to be here for this. I can talk to you after the coroner is done."

Though part of her wanted to wait and see if this whole thing was a big mistake, she found herself nodding.

JD turned his attention to the approaching officer. "Cordon off this area."

"Yes, sir."

"Do you need me to walk you back to your apartment?" JD asked Hadley.

"No." Again, she glanced in Spencer's direction, but this time she could see only his company car.

She took a step back, but before she could leave, JD put his hand on her arm. "I'm sorry for your loss."

Pressing her lips together, she fought against the new wave of emotions. Unable to speak, she headed for her apartment. Another police car turned into the lot, reminding Hadley once more that her life had taken a turn into a different world, one she had yet to learn how to navigate.

* * *

JD watched Noah park beside the coroner's vehicle. JD had spent over an hour searching the car and the surrounding area for clues as to why Spencer Andrews had been killed and who was responsible. All the while, the image of Hadley continued to creep into his consciousness.

Noah's arrival was a welcome distraction to his current work challenge. He needed to think about something besides the intriguing woman who kept finding herself in the middle of bad situations.

JD glanced briefly in the direction of Hadley's apartment before speaking to Noah. "Thanks for coming."

"This isn't a case we want to leave on our desks until Monday." Noah motioned to the scene of Spencer's murder. "I didn't expect you to find the missing car like this."

"Neither did I," JD admitted. "I ran the plates. The vehicle is registered to Voice Today."

"I've never heard of it."

"Me neither. The website didn't give much info. Looks like some sort of consulting firm on Capitol Hill."

"We can run a deeper background on Monday."

The coroner finished his external examination and approached them.

"Do you have an estimated time of death?" JD asked.

"Best guess, between eight and ten o'clock last night."

"Thanks, Doc," Noah said.

"I'm going to transport the body. I'll let you know when I'm done with the preliminary autopsy."

"Thanks." JD waited for the coroner to return to the SUV before speaking again to Noah. "The bomb at the hotel went off a few minutes before eight."

"That suggests he was probably killed shortly after he left."

"He must have been here when I dropped Hadley off last night." JD looked out over the parking lot.

"The question is, Why was he here?"

"He lives in the District. I have to think he came to check on Hadley and make sure she survived the bombing."

"Wait, you think he was involved and then came to check on his girlfriend?"

"Hadley thinks he deliberately cornered her into a breakup so he could get her to leave without alerting the men they were with."

"Then we know who we're looking for."

"Sort of. If the man pretending to be Spencer's boss was using an alias, it's possible the other two were as well. Not that first names were going to give us much anyway."

"Better see if we can get Hadley to work with a sketch artist," Noah said.

"Yeah. I'm going to interview her as soon as we're done here."

"I can finish up," Noah offered. "Go talk to her. She's our best lead so far."

JD didn't have to be told twice. "I'll catch up with you later."

"If you aren't done before I leave, I'll meet you at Spencer's apartment. The search warrant just came through."

"Kelsey must be cooking dinner tonight if you're not going to wait around for me to finish."

"Butter chicken and Indian fry bread."

"You could bring me some leftovers on Monday," JD suggested.

"What are you talking about? You're going to show up tonight for dinner anyway."

"Why do you say that?"

"Because it always happens at some point on the weekends."

"I need to find a girlfriend."

"Yeah, one who can cook." Noah chuckled. "Kelsey is already planning on you joining us."

His spirits lifted when he thought of Noah and his wife, but the prospect of facing Hadley sobered him. If she was right, Spencer had died trying to protect her. Now it was JD's job to not only protect her but also determine the extent of Spencer's involvement in the bombing. Though dozens of questions buzzed in his head, one dominated all others: Why had Spencer taken Hadley to a restaurant only minutes before a bomb had gone off?

* * *

Spencer couldn't have known. Hadley paced her living room, so many scenarios rolling through her head, none of them making any sense. She had showered and changed out of her workout clothes, the soothing hot water opening her mind to even more possibilities.

Was it really possible Spencer had broken up with her to get her to leave before the bomb had gone off? And if so, why would he have taken her to the restaurant in the first place if he'd known of the danger?

Had the men with them last night left because they were involved in planting the bomb? Were they the ones who had killed Spencer? And why?

She wanted to think Spencer was the man she had fallen for—the thoughtful, caring man who could have stepped right off the screen of a Hallmark movie. The reality that Spencer would never be part of anyone's happily ever after, including his own, only served to heighten the contrast between her six months with Spencer and the past twenty-four hours.

Hadley tucked her damp hair behind her ears and began another lap around her living room. A knock at the door diverted her path. Though she'd anticipated JD's arrival, she moved cautiously to the door and looked through the peephole before unbolting the lock.

Her thoughts spilled out in her words the moment she opened the door. "None of this makes any sense. Why would Spencer invite me to dinner if he knew there would be a bomb?"

JD waited until he was inside, the door closed behind him, before he spoke. "Tell me more about the other men at dinner with you."

Hadley led the way to the couch and dropped onto one side. "It was the first time I'd met any of them."

"Even his boss?"

"Yeah."

"What was the purpose of the meeting?" JD asked. "New clients? Celebrating something?"

"Spencer said he had a couple clients coming into town and was asked to take them out," Hadley said. "I didn't even find out about them joining us until an hour before he picked me up."

"Does he do this kind of thing often?"

"All the time, but usually, it's in DC, and this is only the second time I've ever met anyone he worked with." Hadley laced her fingers together. "Since I live so far away from him, he usually didn't want to have to come pick me up and take me back home here in Lake Ridge when they were eating in DC, and he didn't want me driving into the city by myself at night."

"Tell me about Keith and Drake."

"There's not a lot to tell. Neither of them said much."

"Can you describe them?"

"They were both a bit taller than average, maybe six feet or so. Blake had dark-brown hair and dark eyes. Keith's hair was also brown but lighter."

"And Spencer's boss?"

"He wasn't much taller than me. I'd guess around 5'9. He looked Hispanic, which makes sense, considering his last name is Hernandez."

"Actually, we don't know what his last name is." JD leaned forward and rested his elbows on his knees. "Spencer's boss was home all night and has several witnesses to prove it."

"What?" Hadley absorbed the latest shock.

JD tapped on his cell phone and showed her a photo. "Have you met this man before?"

Hadley looked at it briefly before shaking her head. "No. Why? Who is he?"

"The real Carlos Hernandez."

"Why would Spencer say . . . ?"

JD apparently sensed her need to let her mind catch up with the latest deception because he waited a moment before he said, "I'd like for you to come with me into the office and work with a sketch artist."

"I can try."

"You said you were with Spencer one other time for a client dinner. When was that?"

"Three weeks ago."

"Where?"

"It was at the same restaurant."

"But with different people?"

"Yeah." Hadley struggled to recall that evening. "Three men were there. Julio, Wyatt, and someone else. I can't remember his name. I think two of them were brothers."

"Three men?" JD retrieved his cell phone from his pocket and tapped the screen several times. Finally, he turned it toward her. "Was he one of them?"

Hadley stared at the familiar face, the eyes closed, the pavement his head rested on the only background visible. "That's Wyatt." She swallowed hard. "Is he . . . ?"

"He's dead. He was one of the men who planted the bomb."

"Then Spencer was involved."

"It appears so."

CHAPTER 7

JD stepped through the door of the Georgetown condominium and announced himself. "Federal agent. Anyone home?"

No answer. He headed for the hall while Noah walked into the living room. After JD confirmed that both bedrooms were indeed empty, he returned to the expansive living room and let out a low whistle. "Whether Spencer was working for Opinions Matter or Voice Today, someone was paying him well."

"We'll see soon enough. Mitch already put in the request for his bank records," Noah said.

"How much do you think a place like this goes for?" JD asked. "Six, seven hundred thousand?"

"In this neighborhood, I'd guess closer to a million." Noah crossed to a set of french doors on the far side of the room. "Especially with this view."

JD stepped next to him. "This guy had his own balcony?"

"Like you said, someone was paying him well."

"I think I went into the wrong career."

"I wouldn't say that. You're still alive."

"Good point." JD took another look around. The décor had the earmarks of a professional decorator, and the lack of dust and clutter suggested a regular cleaning service.

"I'll start in here."

"Then I'll take the bedrooms." JD walked to the end of the hall and entered the master. The king-sized bed accented rather than dominated the room, and a flat-screen television hung on the wall where it could be seen easily from either the bed or the two armchairs in the corner.

His hands already clad in crime-scene gloves, JD opened a dresser drawer, methodically searching each one but finding nothing beyond clothing. The closet boasted designer everything, from Savile Row to Armani. Built-in drawers and cubbies displayed an assortment of expensive ties and even more expensive shoes. JD doubted a single item here cost less than a hundred dollars. He pulled open another drawer. Okay, maybe his socks were in the affordable range. Barely.

JD removed drawers, checking underneath each one as well as inside the tracks to make sure nothing had been hidden. After discovering nothing out of place, he moved back into the bedroom. His eyes were drawn to the single photograph on the bedside table. Hadley. Based on the snowy background, the Washington monument visible in the distance, JD guessed it had been taken last month. Except for the big snow storm in early March, DC hadn't experienced much in the way of snowfall.

Had Spencer waited five months before he put Hadley's photo in his apartment? Or was this a replacement for an earlier image?

He opened the top drawer of the bedside table to find a few folded bills, a handgun, and a small black box. After slipping the gun into an evidence bag, he picked up the box and flipped the lid. Staring back at him was evidence of exactly how much Spencer Andrews had cared for Hadley. He had hoped to marry her.

JD bagged the ring. He hadn't yet uncovered Spencer's next of kin, but he guessed they would want Hadley to have the jewelry that had been intended for her.

After completing his search of the master bedroom, JD moved into the second bedroom, which had been fashioned into an office. A simple cherry desk faced the window, the surface bare. The two bookshelves revealed an eclectic collection of biographies, political thrillers, classic novels, and nonfiction books.

"Anything?" Noah called out.

"Nothing yet," JD said as Noah entered.

"Me neither. I'll dust for prints." Noah's gaze landed on the two evidence bags JD had left on the desk. "Want me to run the gun ownership too?"

"We can do that when we get back to the office," JD said. "Hopefully, Hadley will be done with the sketch artist by the time we're finished here."

"Someone else can take her home."

"I'd rather do it myself. She's been through a lot."

"Yes, she has."

Silence filled the room.

JD looked up to see Noah staring. "What?"

"I'm trying to decide if I should caution you about getting involved with someone who's recently been through a traumatic experience."

"I vote no."

"She did just lose her boyfriend," Noah said.

"You don't have any room to give me this kind of advice, considering you met your wife in the middle of a terrorist attack."

"I didn't meet her during a terrorist attack. We went through one after we already knew each other."

"Either way."

"Besides, Kelsey is CIA. She's been trained to deal with this kind of emotional turmoil," Noah said. "Hadley's a third-grade teacher."

"That's a whole different level of warfare," JD said.

Noah chuckled. He retrieved the needed materials from the backpack he had brought with him. While he went about his task, JD searched the office a second time. The clock on the wall read 1:45. Had this morning gone as planned, he would have been heading over to Hadley's apartment right now. He also would have taken the time to eat lunch, which his growling stomach would have appreciated.

JD pulled a random book off the shelf and flipped through the pages. It looked brand new. He selected a second book, finding the same results. "It doesn't look like he's read any of these. What do you think? Did he buy them to impress his visitors, or did he never find the time to read them?"

"Since the books are in the office instead of the living room, I would have to think it's the latter." Noah dusted the desk.

JD pulled a third book off the shelf, this one on Paris. The first few pages turned easily enough, but when he tried to go beyond them, he discovered something entirely unexpected. "Looks like he wasn't using this book to plan a trip to see the Eiffel Tower. Check this out."

Noah finished what he was doing before backing out of the closet. JD set the open book on the table, a hidden safe contained within the binding.

"Can you tell if anything is inside?" Noah asked.

JD shook it, a rattle sounding within. "Sounds like it."

"Bag it. We need to see if he has any more concealment devices around here," Noah said. "Obviously, he was worried about someone looking through his things."

"Are you done collecting prints?" JD asked.

"There aren't any."

"None?"

"None," Noah confirmed. "I think the reason this guy's place is so clean is because someone wiped it down after doing their own search."

"Every time we try to find answers on this case, we end up with more questions."

"I know." Noah pulled out his cell phone and began taking photos. "You search. I'm going to document everything and see if Kelsey can recognize any concealment devices here that we wouldn't think to look for."

"I thought you and Kelsey were trying to keep your work lives separate."

"This will be like a fun puzzle for her. She loves this stuff."

"You two are strange. Very strange."

"Yeah, but we're happy that way."

"Whatever." JD bagged the book safe and started his second search. Another hour was all he was willing to give it. He was ready to get some food and check on Hadley.

* * *

Sitting beside the FBI sketch artist, Hadley rubbed her fingers against her temples. "I'm sorry. Everything is becoming a blur."

"Two out of three isn't bad," Angie said. "We can try to get the third tomorrow."

Hadley nodded, even though she wasn't sure she even knew which direction was up at the moment.

"Did you drive yourself here, or do you need me to find you a ride home?"

A weight came over her at the thought of getting into a car with someone new. "I think Agent Byers was going to take me home."

"I can call and check." Angie picked up her phone and dialed. "Hey, JD, it's Angie. Are you in the office?" She fell silent, and Hadley tried to listen to the voice on the other end. "Yeah." More silence. "Okay, I'll bring her out."

"Is he back?" Hadley asked as soon as Angie hung up.

"He's on his way. By the time I get you signed out, he should be here," Angie said.

"Okay." Hadley stood. "Thank you for all your help."

"Thank you," Angie countered, lifting the images. "Sometimes this is all it takes to break a case wide open."

"I hope that happens soon. I feel like I'm spinning on a merry-go-round that won't stop."

"I know it may sound crazy, but sometimes the best thing to do is go out and do something," Angie said. "It's a beautiful day. Go take a walk, or go for a ride. Get away from your normal, and give your mind the chance to catch up with everything that's happened."

"I might try that." Hadley followed Angie to the door. "Thanks."
"Anytime."

CHAPTER 8

KADE MADE THE TURN ONTO the private road that led to the back of the Whitmores' estate, his tractor-trailer barely able to fit between the trees lining it on either side. He glanced at his wife, who was working in the passenger seat beside him. "Anything new yet?"

"Nothing." Renee logged off and closed her laptop. "The guardian working undercover still hasn't logged in, and the FBI hasn't put anything useful in their latest updates. From what I can gather, they're still in the fact-finding side of things."

"Anything in the CIA's database?"

"Just that the intel on the bombing came from a source they now have in protective custody: a woman named Jenetta Blaese."

"Do you think the source has more to offer?" Kade asked, driving past the barn and making the turn to park his rig under the shade of the trees lining the back of the Whitmore property.

"I doubt it." Renee shook her head. "I read through the transcripts. It looks like Jenetta was dating one of the bombers. I don't think she had enough direct involvement to know anything beyond what she overheard during one of the planning sessions."

"Sounds like we're lucky she knew what to do with what she heard." He turned off the engine.

"The Whitmores certainly benefited from her decision."

"True." Kade pulled out his cell phone and texted the senator to let him know they had arrived.

Renee opened her door and climbed out of the cab. As soon as Kade joined her, she asked, "Do you want me to go into Langley and see if I can find out anything at CIA headquarters?"

"I'd rather you work with the senator on possible targets."

"What are you going to do?"

"I'm going to see if I can find our missing operative. It's time he comes in from the cold."

* * *

JD climbed out of his car and circled to the passenger side as soon as Hadley and Angie walked out the door. His idea to grab something to eat on his way to pick Hadley up had been sidelined when the search for more concealment devices had taken nearly two hours—a search that hadn't revealed anything new.

"How did it go?" JD asked when the women reached him.

"She did great," Angie said. "We have two out of three. We'll try for the third one tomorrow after she's had some time to rest."

"Sounds good," JD said before focusing on Hadley. "Ready to get out of here?"

Hadley drew a deep breath and let it out in a rush. "Yeah."

JD opened the passenger door and waited for her to get in before closing it. As soon as he was seated beside her, he said, "I was going to go grab some dinner. Do you want to join me?"

Hadley didn't respond for a second, making JD wonder if he had made her uncomfortable. Finally, she said, "I'd really like that, but the idea of going into a restaurant right now is pretty overwhelming."

"I think I know just the place. Great food without many people," JD said. "In fact, it's a lot like eating at home."

"I guess . . ." She trailed off. "I think I would like that. I don't really want to be alone."

"Let's see if we can make it happen." JD pulled up his favorites and hit a familiar number. A female voice answered, and JD barely managed to keep the humor out of his voice. "Hey, any chance you can squeeze in a reservation for two tonight?"

"As opposed to your usual reservation for one?" Kelsey teased. "I'm intrigued."

JD glanced at the dashboard clock. "Would five thirty work?"

"I'll have the appetizers ready."

"And fry bread?"

"And fry bread."

"You're the best." JD hung up and asked Hadley, "Do you have to work tomorrow?"

"Actually, I'm on spring break this week." She leaned back in her seat, turning her head slightly toward him. "I can't imagine trying to teach right now. I can barely put together a coherent sentence."

"You're doing extraordinarily well, considering."

"Considering I broke up with my boyfriend, nearly got blown up, found out my ex-boyfriend was murdered, and discovered he might have forced a breakup to protect me?"

"Yeah, considering all that." JD pulled up to a stoplight and glanced at her. "You've had a busy couple of days."

A burst of laughter escaped her only to be swallowed by silence a second later. "How can I laugh at a time like this? Spencer is dead. And he might have been involved with trying to kill hundreds of people."

"It's nervous energy," JD said. "But laughing can be good. It helps you remember that life can get better and that you'll find a way to get back to normal."

"I don't know. This is all new to me."

"I'm afraid it's not new to me."

Hadley shifted in her seat, so she was facing him more fully. "Do you always get so involved with your cases?"

"What do you mean?"

"You took me home last night. You've been driving me everywhere today," Hadley said. "I wouldn't think FBI agents would be this attentive to their witnesses."

"Maybe not, but I want to make sure you're okay." JD kept his eyes on the road. The truth was that he couldn't explain why he kept putting himself in Hadley's path. Their interaction had largely come about because of his job, but he wasn't in the habit of hand-holding witnesses, and he certainly didn't ask them to dinner.

Not wanting to dwell on the thoughts swirling in his head, he said, "Tell me about your class. How many little people do you teach?"

Her expression brightened. "Twenty-four."

"Twenty-four eight-year-olds? Now, that's terrifying."

Hadley's laughter escaped her again, but this time she didn't fight it.

* * *

JD parked in front of a colonial and turned off the car. Hadley stared at JD in confusion. "I don't understand. Where are we?"

"My partner's house."

"I thought we were going to a restaurant."

JD opened his door. "Trust me. This is better."

Her expectations for her meal with JD took a turn. She had thought taking Angie's advice to go do something was a good one, but spending her evening with men who carried guns for a living hadn't exactly been what she'd had in mind. Then again . . .

JD opened her door. "You're going to want to unhook your seat belt."

Hadley didn't move. "But you made a reservation."

"With Noah's wife." His lips curved. "It's been a running joke since Noah started dating Kelsey. The woman is an amazing cook, but she refuses to open a restaurant, so I come to her."

A little more comfortable with the idea that JD did this often, Hadley unclipped her seat belt and climbed out. "You're sure she's okay with a last-minute dinner guest?"

"Of course. That's why I called ahead." JD put his hand on the small of her back and guided her forward. "You said your family lives across the country. Where are you from?"

"Wyoming."

JD rang the doorbell. "How did you end up out here?"

"This is where I found a job," Hadley said. "I didn't expect to stay for more than a year or two, but I fell in love with Virginia. It's so green here."

The front door opened, the scent of curry and something exotic wafted over them. JD's partner waved them inside. "Come on in."

"Hadley, you remember Noah."

"Of course. Thank you for having me over. I hope it isn't too much of an imposition."

"Not at all." Noah led her through the wide hallway to the back of the house. A slender woman with thick, dark hair stood at the stove, a wooden spoon in one hand. Her plain, white apron read, "Your opinion isn't part of the recipe."

"Kelsey always makes more food than we can possibly eat," Noah said. "Right, hon?"

"I have to. Otherwise Devin would starve to death."

"Devin?" Hadley asked.

"It's my middle name," JD said. "I used to go by Devin, but when we had three other Devins transfer into our office, I decided it wasn't worth the confusion."

"Ah."

Noah approached Kelsey and made the introductions.

"It's nice to meet you." Kelsey wiped her hands on her apron before offering one to Hadley. "So glad you could join us."

Hadley took in the warm kitchen and breathed in the Indian spices. "Me too."

* * *

JD leaned back in his chair and blew out a satisfied breath. "Kelsey, you outdid yourself."

"Glad you enjoyed it."

"This was amazing," Hadley said. "I've never had anything like it."

"I keep telling her she should open a restaurant," JD said.

"And I keep telling you that I only cook for friends." Kelsey pushed back from the table. "Speaking of which, I hope you saved room for dessert."

"Baklava?" The single word escaped JD in a reverent whisper.

"Baklava," Kelsey confirmed.

"Wait. You made baklava from scratch?" Hadley asked. "Where did you learn to cook like this?"

"I used to nanny overseas. Cooking was part of the job," Kelsey said.

JD knew he was one of the few outside the CIA who knew Kelsey was really among their best undercover agents. Had one of his cases not spilled into one of hers, he doubted he ever would have suspected Kelsey was anything other than what she claimed to be.

Noah rose and collected their dinner plates. "Should we have dessert out on the deck?"

"That's a great idea." Kelsey retrieved dessert plates and forks from the cabinet. "JD, as much as you like baklava, you really should let me teach you how to make it."

"I'd never be able to make it like you."

"I would love to learn," Hadley said. Her cheeks colored slightly, as though embarrassed that she had spoken her thoughts aloud.

"If you aren't busy next Saturday, you're welcome to come over, and I'll teach you."

"Are you sure?"

"Positive." Kelsey leaned closer. "Noah needs JD to help him stain the deck. I was planning to make some to bribe him."

Hadley lowered her voice. "I think it will work."

"You know I can hear you, right?" JD asked.

"Trust me, if I wanted to keep a secret from you, I'd do a better job than this," Kelsey said, her voice now at a normal volume. She handed the plates and forks to Noah and picked up the pan of baklava. "Come on. Let's go enjoy this gorgeous day."

CHAPTER 9

"YOUR FRIENDS ARE SO NICE." Hadley balanced a paper plate with baklava on top of a larger one that contained the chicken dish they had eaten at dinner. "I can't believe Kelsey sent so much food home with me."

"I live for lunchtime after I eat at their house."

"I can see why. Kelsey is an incredible cook."

"Do you like to cook?"

"I like to bake, but when it comes to regular meals, I mostly cook out of necessity." Hadley looked down at the food on her lap. "Although, if I could cook like this, I might reconsider."

"Saturday will be a good time to try." JD paused and glanced sideways. "How are you holding up?"

"Tonight was nice. A couple times, I was able to pretend this was normal."

"You said you'd been with Spencer for a while. Did you see him a lot?" JD asked. "It couldn't have been easy living so far apart."

"It wasn't," Hadley admitted. "We used to take turns choosing where we would meet. Every other weekend, I went up to DC so we could go out on a Friday night. On the other weekends, he came down to Lake Ridge on Saturday afternoon." Hadley fell silent. How many times had she wished she had a boyfriend who could spend evenings with her, someone who would just be with her instead of always taking her out to some fancy dinner or concert? "I still can't believe Spencer is dead."

"It may take some time to sink in," JD said. "I know it's late, but would you be willing to help me sketch out who was at the restaurant last night?"

"I already told you who I was eating with."

"I'm talking about the other people who were there. Someone was the target for the bomb we found," JD said. "It's possible it was a public figure."

"There were a lot of those." Hadley took a moment, trying to recall who she had seen as she'd walked to her table. "Adam Pratt and Lily Stanton were there, along with some of the other cast members from the movie they're shooting at Occoquan."

"Who else?"

"Honestly, it felt like a who's who of Washington politics. At least two big tables had congressmen and senators at them."

"Do you know which ones?"

"I recognized Senator Whitmore." Hadley's eyebrows drew together. "Don't you have a list of who was there? I thought you guys interviewed everyone after we evacuated."

"We did, but we want to make sure we didn't miss someone else who might have fled the scene," JD said. "One more question."

"Only one?" Hadley asked, annoyance rising as the normalcy of her time with JD faded and she was once again reduced to a simple witness.

"One more for now," JD amended. "Was there anyone who was supposed to go to dinner with you who didn't show?"

"Not that I know of."

JD pulled into the parking spot next to the ancient pickup truck Hadley's father had given her when she was in college. She unclipped her seat belt and opened her own door, anxious to curl up in front of the television and pretend this really was all a dream. "I guess I'll see you later."

JD turned off the car and met her on the sidewalk. "Do you want me to check out your apartment before you go in?"

A bubble of fear rose inside her, but she shook her head. She had to start taking care of herself sometime. Now was as good a time as any. "I'll be fine."

Despite her declaration, JD walked her to her door. "I'm sorry if it seems like I'm constantly questioning you."

"I get it." Balancing the plate of leftovers in one hand, Hadley retrieved her house key and unlocked her apartment. "You're protecting your witness."

"No, that's not the case at all."

Surprising herself, she whirled to face him. "I don't get it. One minute you're the professional FBI agent asking me tons of questions, and the next, you're acting like a friend who cares. I don't know what to think."

JD reached out and laid his hand on her arm. He seemed to search for words, several unidentifiable emotions appearing on his face. Finally, he said, "I'm worried about you, but I'm even more worried that I'm starting to feel personally involved."

"You are?"

"Let's just say that if I hadn't met you at a crime scene, I would be asking you out."

Her emotions did an unexpected somersault. "You did ask me out."

"But I shouldn't have." JD broke contact and stepped back. "I'll wait here until you get inside and lock up."

"Thanks." Her frustration with JD now gone, she pushed open the door, flipped on the light, and gasped. The paper plate fell from her hand, chicken and fry bread spilling onto the carpet. The mess blended with the rest of the scene before her. Her belongings covered the floor, strewn out as though someone had been given thirty seconds to find a hidden treasure. "JD!" She gasped again. "JD, come here."

He was by her side in an instant. Before she could blink, his gun was in his hand. As he had last night, he positioned her beside her door. "Stay here."

Hadley closed her eyes as though doing so would block out reality. Someone had been here. Someone had broken into her home. Had they watched her leave? Or had her absence been pure good luck?

The thought of what might have happened had she stayed home today caused her to open her eyes and face the wreckage and the questions head-on. Her mind continued to churn, everything boiling down to two questions. Who did this? And what were they after?

* * *

JD's heart leapt into his throat when he saw the flash of movement. He aimed his weapon as a terrified meow tore through the air. Hadley's cat streaked out of the bedroom in a blur of black fur.

Willing his heartbeat to slow to normal, he cleared the apartment and returned to Hadley, who now stood inside the apartment beside the open door. She held the traumatized animal in her arms, her face pressed against Lucy's fur.

JD closed and locked the front door before holstering his gun and conducting a second analysis, this time searching for the point of entry. Though the back door was unlocked, he didn't find any evidence of damage. He returned to Hadley, not sure what words of comfort he could offer. Before he could say anything, she set the cat down and threw her arms around him. Her body trembled, but he could sense that she was fighting against the tears that threatened.

His arms came around her instinctively. "Hey, it's okay. Whoever did this is long gone."

He held her in silence, his hand stroking her back. The thought that he wished he could hold her like this under different circumstances surfaced. He didn't try to fight it. Hadley was a beautiful woman, one with an innate kindness and grace he couldn't help but admire.

A minute stretched into two before she finally pulled free. "Why would someone do this?" She looked around the room as though seeing it for the first time. "They didn't take my TV."

"I don't think they were robbing you. They were looking for something," JD said.

"But what?" she asked. "I don't have anything valuable."

"Do you own a laptop?"

"Yeah. It's on my kitchen table." Hadley waved in the direction of the kitchen. She pressed her lips together. "It *was* on my kitchen table."

"Any idea why they would be interested in it?"

She shook her head. "Why is all of this happening to me?"

"I don't know. Yet." JD pulled out his cell phone and called the local police. As soon as he hung up, he asked, "Does anyone have a key to your apartment?"

"No. Well, except for the management office." Hadley looked at him. "Why do you ask?"

"Your back door was unlocked, but there wasn't any sign of forced entry," JD explained.

"I'm sure the door was locked. I checked it at least a dozen times last night, and I never opened it this morning."

"It's possible someone picked the lock on the front door and exited through the back." JD pondered a moment. "Has Spencer given you anything lately? Any kind of gift or something he might have left here?"

"He gave me a necklace for Valentine's Day."

"Where is it?"

"On my dresser." Hadley led the way into her room. "That's it right there."

JD leaned down and studied the simple gold chain, a heart pendant attached. He took a pen out of his pocket and used it to hook the chain and lift the necklace for a closer look.

"Where do you keep your sandwich bags?"

"In the kitchen, top drawer to the right of the sink."

JD left her room and went to retrieve a bag, finding the box of Ziplocs on the floor under a frying pan. Careful not to touch anything, he retrieved a bag and used it to protect the necklace.

Hadley followed him into the kitchen, a squeak of alarm escaping her when a knock sounded at the door.

JD laid a hand on her arm in a comforting gesture. "I'll get it." He moved into the living room and peered out the peephole at a policeman standing on the other side. He opened the door. "Come in." JD flashed the officer his credentials. "Agent Byers, FBI."

"Officer Crandall. Is this your residence, sir?"

"No. It belongs to a witness of yesterday's bombing." JD proceeded to walk the officer through the apartment. "I need you to dust for prints, and I'll need a copy of your report."

"Of course."

While the officer went about documenting the crime scene, JD returned to Hadley. "I think we need to find you somewhere else to stay tonight. I don't like the idea of you sleeping here."

"There's no way I'd be able to sleep here," Hadley said. "I think there's a hotel on Route 1 that allows pets."

"I have another idea," JD said. "Once Officer Crandall is done here, pack some things so you can stay with me for a few days."

"With you?"

"I'd love to set you up in a safe house, but unfortunately, since you aren't classified as a protected witness, that option isn't available to us," JD explained. "Don't worry. It's a big house."

"How far away is it?" Hadley asked.

"It's two doors down from where Kelsey and Noah live," JD said. "Kelsey's parents are on a mission for their church. I've been living in their house since Kelsey and Noah got married."

"I'd need to bring Lucy with me."

"I'll call and double-check with Kelsey and Noah, but I'm sure it will be okay. In fact, there's a litter box in the garage Lucy can use while you're there," JD said. "Do you have a cat carrier?"

"Yeah. It's in the laundry room." She glanced around the disaster area of her home. "Or at least, that's where I saw it last."

"We'll find it."

* * *

Noah retrieved his laptop from his backpack and carried it to the kitchen table.

Kelsey started the dishwasher and crossed to him. "Why do I get the impression that you brought work home with you?"

"Because I brought work home with me." He opened the laptop and turned it on.

She fisted both hands on her hips until he lifted his gaze to meet hers. "I thought we agreed we weren't going to do that anymore, especially on Sundays."

"I know, but didn't we make an exception for when terrorist attacks might happen within a hundred-mile radius of our house?"

Her face remained neutral, a skill she had honed during her years working undercover, a skill Noah couldn't help but admire. A minute passed before she pulled up a chair. "Okay, what have you got?"

He bit back a smile as he angled the laptop toward her. "These are photos of Spencer Andrews's apartment." Noah clicked on an image of the hidden safe. "We found raw diamonds stashed inside this book."

"Diamonds?"

"Yeah. I hoped you could help me identify anything else this guy might be using as a concealment device."

"This could take a while."

"We do still have leftover baklava in case we need a snack break."

Kelsey smiled. "Pull up the first photo. We might as well start at the beginning."

Noah's phone rang, and he glanced at a fellow agent's name on caller ID. He answered. "Hey, Mitch. What's up?"

"We got an ID on our bombing suspects," Mitch said. "The two that died on scene both came into the country illegally."

"And the third?"

"He didn't make it."

"ID?"

"Nothing so far. His prints didn't flag. The lab is running his DNA now."

Noah stood and paced into the living room. "Where are the other two from?"

"Syria, but they've been living in Abolstan for the past five years."

"With Rabell's group?"

The mention of Rabell drew Kelsey's attention, her eyes now fixed on Noah. The concern he read there was enough to raise his suspicion that his case was about to collide with his wife's current project.

"Yeah," Mitch said, interrupting his thoughts. "Intel was able to trace their movements from Abolstan, into Turkey, and on to Lisbon before they boarded a freighter to Baltimore."

"Any clue how long intel has been tracking this?"

"I don't know, but since the CIA gave us the tip about the bomb, I have to think it's been a while," Mitch said. "I'll give you a call if I hear anything else."

"Thanks." Noah hung up and turned to his wife. "What can you tell me about Rabell?"

"The basics. Known terrorist who previously associated with Salman Nassar. After Nassar's organization crumbled, he created his own splinter faction. Over the past year, Rabell's group has been notorious for smuggling contraband of every kind. They're also suspected of a car bombing in Madrid."

"You know more than that," Noah said with certainty.

Kelsey gave him a single nod. "Yes, but you asked me what I could tell you. You know I have to get clearance to discuss classified information with you."

Though he always found it ridiculous that he and his wife couldn't speak freely at home, considering they both had top-secret clearances, he said, "It sounds like we need to meet tomorrow. Your office or mine?"

"Mine, but we'd better make it Tuesday."

"Why Tuesday?"

"I need to gather some intel and permissions before I'll be able to give you anything useful." She motioned at the laptop screen. "But for now, let me tell you where I would hide diamonds if it were me."

"This should be good."

* * *

I can't believe . . .

Hadley didn't want to think about how many variations she could use to complete that sentence right now.

The latest combination regarded her staying with a single man in his house, a single man she hardly knew. What was she thinking? She wasn't, she admitted to herself, but for reasons she couldn't explain, JD made her feel safe. He was also armed, and she trusted him. Otherwise, she never would have handed over her cell phone so he could put some sort of blocking program on it to prevent her from being traced through the phone's GPS signal.

That thought alone brought another level of surrealness to the situation. Who would want to find her?

She glanced at JD carrying her suitcase and a bag of cat litter up the front walk of the brick-front colonial. He had been so patient with her at her apartment, somehow creating a sense of calm as she had struggled to find clean clothes and the other things she would need during her stay.

The cat carrier Hadley held jerked to the left when Lucy moved suddenly. "It's okay," Hadley told Lucy.

JD set Hadley's suitcase on the front porch and retrieved his keys. Once he unlocked the door, he led the way inside, walking straight to the keypad for an alarm system. He punched in the code, a beep signaling that it had disarmed. He picked up the suitcase once more and headed up the stairs. He set her belongings inside the second door to the left. "This is yours. It connects to the bathroom." JD pointed at the door in the far corner of the room. "I'll go get the litter box. There should be enough room on the bathroom floor to put it in there."

"Thanks." Hadley set the cat carrier down. She looked at the thick duvet on the queen-sized bed, tempted to lie down.

JD's footsteps pounded up the stairs, and he entered her room, carrying the litter box and a box of liners. He set them down. "I know you have to be exhausted. Help yourself to anything you can find in the kitchen. I'm going to set the alarm for the exterior doors, so as long as you don't go outside without telling me first, it won't go off on you."

"JD, I don't know how to thank you."

"You don't have to thank me." He retreated a step. "Make yourself at home. I'll see you in the morning."

"Good night." Hadley waited until he disappeared down the hall before she moved to the door and pushed it closed. She looked down at Lucy. "Let's get you settled so we can both get some sleep."

Once Hadley was satisfied Lucy had everything she needed, she changed into a pair of flannel pajamas, pulled back the thick blanket, and crawled into bed.

Lucy jumped up beside her, immediately climbing on top of Hadley. The last thing Hadley remembered was the constant buzz of Lucy's purring as they both drifted off to sleep.

CHAPTER 10

ALREADY DRESSED AND READY FOR work, JD passed the closed guest-room door and debated what to do if Hadley didn't emerge before it was time for him to leave for the office. He hadn't heard a sound from her room since they'd said good night.

She should be safe here. Those words had repeated in his mind last night when he had checked the perimeter of the house and engaged the alarm. But that didn't stop him from getting up several times during the night to make sure they didn't have any unexpected visitors.

They had left her truck parked outside her apartment. It was an older model, one that wasn't equipped with a GPS, but JD hadn't wanted to take the chance that a tracker had been planted, nor did he want to do a search for one in the dark without the proper equipment.

The fact that the break-in at her apartment had occurred while her truck had been outside concerned him. The intruders didn't appear to care what got in their way, and JD could only be grateful that Hadley hadn't been home to find out what they would have done had she been present.

JD made his way into the kitchen, debating what to make for breakfast. After checking out his pantry and refrigerator, he discovered two things: his options were limited to cold cereal and oatmeal, and he needed to go grocery shopping.

He took a moment to mourn the leftovers Kelsey had sent home, left-overs that hadn't survived the events of the evening before. Hadley had dropped hers when she'd seen the state of her apartment, and his had perished underneath a bag of kitty litter. What a waste.

The doorbell rang, and JD went to answer. After glancing out the front window at Noah standing on the stoop, he disengaged the alarm and opened the door.

Noah held up a paper plate holding half a coffee cake. "Kelsey was in a baking mood last night after you left, and we thought you might want something besides yesterday's leftovers for breakfast."

"You're a lifesaver." JD took the offering and motioned Noah inside. "The leftovers were a casualty of war. I was debating whether I had time to run to the store before leaving for work so Hadley would have food in the house today."

"You have plenty of time. Burt approved you working from home today," Noah said, referring to their boss. JD closed the door. "I talked to Mitch this morning. He's going to follow up with forensics about the book safe and go through Spencer's bank and phone records."

"What are you going to do?" JD asked, leading the way into the kitchen.

"I'm going to check out Spencer's apartment again." Noah sat on one of the bar stools at the kitchen counter. "Kelsey gave me some ideas of where to look for concealment devices."

"Let me know if you find anything."

"I will." JD unwrapped the crumb cake and broke off a piece. "Since I'm going to the store today, do you want me to pick up something for dinner tonight? I figure it's my turn to cook for you."

"Thanks, but I promised Kelsey I'd take her to a movie." Noah reached out and broke off a piece of crumb cake for himself. "You and Hadley are welcome to join us."

"Thanks, but I have a feeling Hadley would prefer to avoid public places right now."

"Can't say I blame her." Noah popped the bite of crumb cake into his mouth. "I'd better get going. I'll call you as soon as I have any updates."

"Thanks." JD followed him to the door, securing the dead bolt and engaging the alarm after he left. He turned to find Hadley descending the stairs.

"Are you leaving for work?" she asked.

"I'm working from home today."

"Oh." Hadley's steps slowed briefly, but she continued downward.

"Did you get Lucy all settled in?"

"Yeah." Hadley gave a slight smile. "She had a very restful night, sleeping on top of me."

"On top of you?"

"I think she's still traumatized by the break-in."

"Understandable." JD started for the kitchen. "Noah brought over some crumb cake for breakfast."

"That sounds good. Do he and Kelsey always feed you?"

"They're pretty good to me," JD said. "We usually get together a couple times a week. They're going out to a movie tonight and said we could join them . . ." JD saw the tension come into Hadley's shoulders. "I told them we'd probably want to stay low-key for now."

"Yeah, the idea of being in a dark theater with a bunch of strangers doesn't sound very appealing."

"That's what I figured. I need to head to the grocery store. You can come with me if you want, or you can give me a list."

A line appeared between her eyebrows, and she contemplated. "I think I can handle a trip to the store."

JD opened the cabinet and retrieved two plates. He cut two pieces of crumb cake and handed one to Hadley. "Here you go."

"Thanks." Hadley sat at the kitchen table, and JD took the seat across from her. "How long do you think it will be before you find out who was at my apartment?"

"I'm not sure. It's always hard to shake things loose on the weekends."

"I hope this ends soon."

"I know. So do I."

* * *

Hadley looked around the grocery store parking lot twice before she stepped out of the car. Her gaze swept over the nearby cars again. The crisp, blue sky sparkled above them, a faint breeze stirring the air of the overly warm day.

JD put a hand on her back. She wasn't sure if it was intended as a gesture of comfort or to break through her fear, but regardless, she managed to take her first steps toward the store.

She didn't realize he'd kept his hand in place until JD broke contact to grab a cart. *No one knows I'm here*, she reminded herself. With some effort, she followed JD inside and fell into step with him as he headed for the produce section.

"What kind of stuff do you like to eat?" JD asked.

It was a simple question. She could do this. Hadley repeated JD's words in her mind as she formulated an answer. "I'm not picky."

"How do you feel about hamburgers and grilled chicken?"

"I like both." Hadley watched him select two apples and slide them into a produce bag.

"Good, because that's about the extent of my culinary skills."

"I don't mind cooking. I make a mean lasagna."

"Sold." JD picked up at bunch of bananas and put them in the cart. "What do you need to make it?"

"Let's start with onions and mushrooms." Hadley selected both, and she and JD also gathered what they would need for a side salad.

"What about some berries?" JD asked.

"That's a good idea. We could get some whipped cream and have those for dessert." Hadley picked up some blueberries and raspberries. "What else do you like for dinner?"

"There's a good Mexican place on Route 1. We could order takeout one night," JD suggested.

"We don't have to order out. Mexican food is easy to make."

"Really?"

"Really."

Together they went through every aisle, debating different items. By the time they reached the checkout, their cart was nearly full. Hadley helped JD put everything on the conveyer belt, then reached for her purse. "Here. Let me pay for this."

"I've got it."

"You don't have to do that." She pulled two twenties from her wallet and offered them to him. "Let me at least give you this."

"It's fine." JD retrieved his own wallet and slid his credit card into the machine. "You're my guest."

Realizing he wasn't going to budge on the matter, Hadley put the cash back in her wallet. "Thank you."

"You're welcome." JD loaded the bagged groceries into their cart and signed the signature pad. "Let's go."

She helped JD load their groceries into his trunk. A short distance away, a pregnant woman unbuckled a young child and took the little boy's hand to walk him into the store. Two cars over, a store clerk escorted an elderly man to his car.

Hadley let her gaze sweep over the other patrons coming and going, all of them looking as though they had no concerns. "I almost feel normal."

"You were overdue for that."

"True."

JD opened her door before pushing the shopping cart to the cart return. When he climbed behind the wheel, he said, "Do we need anything else while we're out?"

"I don't think so." Hadley waited for him to start the car. "I know you have work, but I'm not sure what to do with myself today. I don't really want to go out anywhere, but . . ."

"But you're out of your element," JD finished for her.

"Yeah."

"You have a few options. There's a pool table in the basement and plenty of movies to watch, between their DVD collection and my Netflix account," JD said. "And the library at the house is pretty well stocked. There's a computer you can use as long as you don't log in to any of your accounts. We don't want to chance someone looking for you through any online profiles."

"This is so surreal, the idea that someone would care where I am."

"My objective today is to find out why," JD said.

"I don't suppose there's a treadmill or exercise bike anywhere in the house."

"Actually, yeah. The treadmill is in the basement too."

"That might help me burn off some nervous energy." Hadley stared out the window at the businesses and restaurants clustered along the main road. She had often frequented a similar strip near her apartment, usually alone.

She fell silent, the image of Spencer's lifeless form filling her mind. She shook her head to force the image aside. When they entered the residential area, she studied the houses they passed, the tidy yards, the sedans and SUVs parked in the driveways. Wasn't this what she'd hoped for someday? Would she have ever had it with Spencer?

She wanted to think their relationship could have grown into a house in the suburbs, but in truth, she knew it wouldn't have. He might have made up his comment about not wanting kids, but she doubted he ever would have been willing to live in a normal neighborhood with a lawn to mow and soccer games to attend on the weekends. She knew it. Or she would have fought to preserve their relationship on Saturday night instead of accepting it was over.

Though she had anticipated Spencer offering to put a ring on her finger, she suspected it never would have fit.

* * *

JD wasn't sure what caused Hadley's silence, but he didn't have to be a mind reader to know her thoughts had turned to the events of the past few days. "You seem deep in thought."

She tore her gaze from the window and looked at him. "I guess I'm wondering how to get back to normal, if that's even possible."

"I imagine it'll be a different normal, but you'll get there." JD pulled into the driveway, shut off the engine, and popped the trunk.

He opened the garage door, and together they carried the groceries into the kitchen. They were still putting things away when JD's cell phone rang.

He put the milk in the refrigerator and answered the call. "Hey, Noah. Any luck at Spencer's place?"

"Yeah, I found two more concealment devices. I emailed the images to you."

"We just got back from the store. Let me finish putting things away, and I'll call you back."

Hadley put a hand on his shoulder. "You have work to do. I'll take care of it."

"Thanks." JD headed for the office with Noah still on the phone, logged on to his computer, and opened the attachment. Two photos of glittering stones filled his screen. "Are these . . . ?"

"Diamonds? Yeah," Noah said. "One stash was in an outlet, and the rest were in the back of a clock. With the way Kelsey identified them as possibilities, I have to wonder if Spencer had some ties with intelligence somewhere. These concealment devices were a step above what someone could find online."

"Has anything popped in his background?"

"I emailed you what I have, but there isn't much. Thirty-one years old, single, parents both deceased. Looks like he was an only child."

"Has anyone interviewed his boss, beyond verifying that he wasn't with Spencer at dinner Saturday night?" JD asked.

"I'm working on that next. Can you start on a deep background? Maybe Hadley can give more insight about family and friends."

"I can do that." JD ended the call and opened the attachment, reading through the information his coworkers had compiled: born in New York City, graduated from Albany University, his past six months spent at Opinions Matter in DC.

He read the information again, his suspicions humming. The résumé was good. Maybe too good.

JD did a search for the first company Spencer worked for after graduation. An outdated website provided a telephone number that belonged to someone else. He had the same results with his next attempt. The final company proved to still be in business, but their personnel office couldn't locate any record of a Spencer Andrews working for them.

Going backward, JD contacted the university. After being transferred four times, he was finally able to confirm that they had indeed had a student named Spencer Andrews who graduated nine years prior. JD went through the protocols to request that his photo be sent to him.

His stomach grumbled, and he looked at the time on his computer. 12:35. Ready for a break, he pushed back from the desk. He hadn't heard anything from Hadley since he had left her in the kitchen over two hours earlier.

Feeling bad that he had abandoned her when Noah had called, he headed down the hall. The scent of grilled cheese greeted him before he turned the corner and found Hadley standing at the stove.

"Hey," he said.

The spatula Hadley held clattered onto the counter, and she whirled to face him. Her hand lifted to her heart as though to hold it in place.

"Sorry. Didn't mean to startle you."

"It's okay." She took a deep breath and picked up the spatula. "I wasn't sure what you wanted for lunch, but I made some tomato soup and grilled cheese, if you're interested."

"That sounds great. Thanks."

Hadley transferred the sandwiches from the griddle to the two plates she had set out. JD picked up both and carried them to the table while Hadley ladled the soup into bowls.

As soon as they were seated, Hadley asked, "How has your morning gone? Did you have any success?"

"It's slow going so far." JD ate a spoonful of soup and swallowed. "What do you know about Spencer? Where's he from?"

"New York."

"Any brothers or sisters?"

"No. He's an only child." Hadley picked up her sandwich. "I guess his parents died a few months after he graduated from college, so he's been on his own since then."

"Do you know anything about his being involved with the jewelry trade or investing in raw stones?"

"No." Her eyebrows drew together. "Why?"

"We found a stash of diamonds hidden in his condo. The value has to be in the millions."

"What?" Hadley set her sandwich down and stared. "Where would he get that kind of money?"

"I don't know." JD motioned to his lunch. "This is good."

Hadley was not easily distracted. "You think he was doing something illegal, don't you?"

"It would explain his wealth and the hidden diamonds," JD said. "I'm doing a deep background on Spencer. Want to help me with the internet searches?"

"Yeah, I'd love to help." Hadley took a bite of her sandwich.

JD followed suit, the two of them eating in companionable silence. Funny how even when they weren't talking, JD enjoyed having Hadley around. When he finished eating, he pushed back from the table. "Thanks for lunch."

"You're welcome."

CHAPTER 11

SEARCHING FOR SPENCER ONLINE PROVED to be a time-consuming and frustrating task. Who knew there were so many Spencer Andrewses? Hadley knew Spencer didn't personally maintain any social-media accounts. He always said it was hard enough to keep up with everything he needed to do for business that it wasn't worth it.

Hadley had thought that claim odd, especially since his business was dealing with the public, but she had never thought to question his explanation. Until now.

She searched for hours on Facebook, Instagram, Twitter, SnapChat, and a dozen other social-media platforms without success. A couple times, she thought she found him, but in each instance, the personal information lined up but the photos weren't of Spencer, and the pages hadn't been active in years.

Hadley swiveled her office chair around so she could see JD more clearly. "I'm not finding anything for Spencer on social media."

"I had a feeling that might be the case," JD said without looking up from where he had set up at the credenza behind her.

"What do you want me to look at next? Google searches?"

"I think I found something." JD motioned to a photo on his screen. "Look at this."

Hadley rolled her chair closer so she could get a better look at the image. Three people were pictured: a couple in their late forties and a man who appeared to be in his early to midtwenties. "Who's that?"

"That is the real Spencer Andrews."

"What?"

"I'm pretty sure the man you knew as Spencer Andrews was living under an alias." JD pointed at the photo's caption. "The real Spencer was killed in a car accident with his parents three weeks after graduating from Albany."

Hadley leaned closer. The dates indicated the man in the photo was around the same age as her Spencer. "Is it possible there were two Spencer Andrewses who graduated together?"

"No. I checked." JD switched screens and pulled up another image, this one a younger version of the man in the family photo. "This is the photo Albany sent me from Spencer Andrews's ID card. He's the only one they had in attendance in the years listed on your Spencer's résumé."

"If that's the real Spencer Andrews, who is the man I was dating?"

"We're still trying to find out," JD said. "I already sent in a request to the coroner to run the fingerprints. Hopefully, he'll be in the system."

"How long until you get the results?"

"I thought I would have heard by now." JD picked up his phone and sent a text. "Are you about ready for some dinner? I thought we could grill some hamburgers tonight."

"That sounds good."

"Come on. We can go get dinner started so everything is ready to go on the grill when we quit for the night." JD led the way into the kitchen. He pulled the hamburger out of the refrigerator and retrieved a bowl and a few spices. "You don't have to keep searching if you don't want to."

"I want to help. I prefer to feel useful." Hadley retrieved a plate from the cabinet. "Do you have any plastic wrap?"

"Yeah. It's in the second drawer to your left."

Hadley found it and set it on the counter. "What do you like on your hamburger? Lettuce, tomato, pickles?"

"Yes."

Hadley chuckled. She found the desired items and went about slicing a tomato and tearing leaves of lettuce into hamburger-sized pieces. She arranged the produce on the plate and covered it before returning everything to the refrigerator. "This is a great house. How much longer are you house-sitting?"

"Kelsey's folks get back sometime in August." JD transferred the hamburger patties onto a plate and slid them into the refrigerator. "They said I can stay here longer if I want, but I don't want to take advantage of them."

"It's already April. Have you started looking for a new place?"

"I looked online a couple times. Does that count?"

"It depends. Did you find anything you liked?" Hadley asked.

"I found plenty that I liked. Finding something I like and can afford is another issue."

"I know what you mean."

The doorbell rang. The instant JD opened it, Noah walked inside and closed the door behind him. "You're not going to believe what I found."

"You found out that Spencer Andrews is an alias."

"Yeah. How did you know?" Noah asked.

"I found the real one."

Noah looked up and saw JD's houseguest. "Oh, hi, Hadley."

"Hi."

JD motioned them all into the living room. "We might as well get comfortable while we compare notes." Noah glanced skeptically at Hadley again. As though answering an unspoken question, JD said, "She's been helping me all afternoon. I think we can trust her."

Noah took a seat in an armchair, leaving the couch for Hadley and JD. Hadley sat in the corner, noting that JD sat closer to the middle than the other end.

"Any idea who this guy really is?" JD asked.

"The fingerprints didn't come up with a match." Noah leaned forward and rested his elbows on his knees. "We're still trying to find out his real identity, but look at this." Noah stretched out his hand to give JD his cell phone. "That's what he looked like when he applied for his passport a few years ago."

Hadley noted the way JD's eyebrows lifted. "Can I see?"

JD turned the screen toward her. The eyes were the same, but Spencer's face was covered by a thick beard and mustache. Instead of being cut short, his hair was halfway to his shoulders. "Except for his eyes, it doesn't look anything like him."

"I'm sure that was on purpose," JD said. "Did Mitch find anything on his phone and bank records?"

"Nothing."

"Spencer always paid cash when I was with him," Hadley said.

"Which is odd in this day of plastic," JD said.

"Exactly," Noah agreed. "As for his cell records, we couldn't find a phone listed in his name. We backtraced the number Hadley gave us for him and found a burner phone, but she is the only person he ever called."

"He must have had a second phone he used to talk to everyone else."

A light of awareness lit Hadley's eyes. "He did have another phone for work."

"And we didn't find a cell phone on him when we found him," JD said. "What I want to know is why he took on a new identity and changed his appearance."

"I do have a theory," Noah said. "I don't know if you remember it, but about a year ago, a huge stash of raw diamonds seized by the Afghani government disappeared. They were valued at anywhere between twenty-five and fifty million dollars. Intelligence tied the theft to Rabell's group, but no one ever found the diamonds."

"Do we have an estimate yet on how much the diamonds in Spencer's apartment were worth?"

"With the additional stones we uncovered in the book safe, best guess is around fifteen million."

"If he had a partner . . ." JD trailed off.

"The amount would be in the range, assuming they split the diamonds fifty-fifty," Noah finished the thought. "It's not much to go on, but it's a place to start."

"Every day, there's a new place to start," Hadley said. "What are the chances we'll find a place to end?"

"We'll get there," JD said. "It might take some time, but we'll get there."

CHAPTER 12

JD took the opportunity to talk to Noah once they were alone on the deck outside. "Any hits on facial recognition yet?"

"Not yet." Noah leaned against the rail. "Angie wanted to see if you would bring Hadley in tomorrow morning to see if they can come up with a sketch of the third guy."

"Oh man. I totally forgot she was supposed to take care of that today."

"I told Angie it would have to wait," Noah said.

JD set the plate of raw hamburger patties on the patio table and leaned down to turn on the gas for the grill. "Did you talk to Spencer's boss today?"

"I have an appointment with him at ten o'clock tomorrow morning."

"Maybe I'll bring Hadley around nine to meet with Angie so I can come with you."

"Sounds good. How's she doing anyway?"

"Surprisingly well, considering she's been on a roller coaster since I found her in the hotel restroom."

"I think staying here has been good for her." Noah pushed away from the rail. "I should get home. Kels should be home in a few minutes."

"Are you sure you don't want to join us for dinner?" JD asked.

"I'm sure. Have a good night."

"You too. I'll talk to you tomorrow."

JD watched Noah walk back into the house and say something to Hadley. Something stirred inside JD as he watched Hadley say goodbye and then go about setting the table. He still wasn't quite sure what had possessed him to bring Hadley into his home. He should feel some sense of invasion or awkwardness with her here, shouldn't he? What was it about Hadley that made things feel so natural, so normal? Neither of their lives had been either of those things since the moment they'd met.

He flipped the hamburgers, the door opening behind him.

"I think everything's ready inside," Hadley said, joining him on the deck. "Those smell good."

"Yeah, I didn't realize how hungry I was until I started cooking."

Hadley handed him a clean plate to put the burgers on. "You worked hard today."

JD took it from her. "I could say the same thing about you."

"I think it would be more accurate to say I tried to work hard. Every time I thought I found Spencer online, it turned out to be someone who hadn't been active in years . . ." Her voice trailed off, and JD could see the moment her words caught up with his suspicions. "Oh my gosh. The person I thought was him was really the man who died, the man Spencer was impersonating."

"I think so." JD transferred the hamburgers onto the clean plate. "Come on. Let's take the rest of the day off."

Hadley picked up the dirty plate and led the way inside. "What do you want to do tonight?"

"It's still pretty early. Do you want to go for a walk? Or we could head over to Government Island and go for a short hike."

"I'd like that."

* * *

Birds chirped overhead, and the breeze caused Hadley to shove her hands into the front pocket of her hooded sweatshirt. With the sun lowering in the sky, the temperature had cooled several degrees over the past hour since she and JD had started their hike around Government Island.

Hadley reached a bluff overlooking the Potomac River and stopped to enjoy the view.

JD stepped beside her. "I love this spot."

"I can see why." Hadley watched a boat pass. "Do you hike here often?"

"Not really. I usually don't have time," JD said.

"It looks so peaceful out on the water."

"If you stick around until next weekend, we can break out the kayaks. There are a couple back at the house."

"I'd like that." Hadley started back down the trail. "Do you think it will be safe for me to go home by then?"

"I always prefer to err on the side of caution." JD fell into step beside her. "If you're willing, I want to take you with me to the office tomorrow. Noah and I have an appointment in the morning, but while we're in our meeting, you can work with the sketch artist."

She fought against a shudder as she thought of Saturday night and everything that had happened since then. "I'm not sure what good I can do, but I'll try."

"That's all anyone can ask."

"What happens if you can't find the men behind this before I go back to work next week?"

"I'm not sure." JD took her elbow when they reached a particularly steep part of the trail. He waited until they were back on even ground before he continued. "You're welcome to stay at the house as long as you need to. There's plenty of room. As for going back to work, I can do a risk assessment this weekend based on what we know by then."

The idea that a risk assessment would be necessary at an elementary school was uncomfortable enough that Hadley focused on the other part of his comment. "Have you ever noticed how you never talk about the house as being yours?"

JD sidestepped a large boulder and glanced at her. "It's not. I told you, it belongs to Kelsey's parents."

"Yeah, but it's yours for now."

"I guess, but this isn't my normal. I don't want to get too attached to someplace that's only temporary."

"How long have you lived here?"

"Nine months. I moved in right after Noah and Kelsey got married." JD started back down the path. "Kelsey knew I was trying to save for a down payment for my own place. When I got laid up with some medical issues, she asked her parents if I could house sit for them. They liked the idea of having someone in the house, and paying utilities is a lot cheaper than paying rent, so it helped me out too."

"What kind of medical issues did you have?" Hadley asked. When she noticed the way JD's body tensed, she quickly added, "I'm sorry. I don't mean to pry."

"It's okay." He seemed to gather his energy before speaking the words. "I was shot in the line of duty last year. It took a while to get back to 100 percent."

"That's terrifying." The memory of the woman at the hospital popped into her mind. "Wait, that lady in the emergency room. Is that how she knew you?"

"Yeah."

"You saved her life." Hadley's thoughts jumped to JD hauling her out of the hotel. "You saved my life."

"That's my job."

"I didn't realize FBI agents made a habit of rescuing damsels in distress."

"We don't." JD reached the open space beneath a cliff of granite. He stopped, his expression serious. "We train for moments like what happened to you last weekend. We have to make sure we can put aside our fears to do what we can to protect others, but the truth is, much of our work is investigative. We research; we ask questions; we look for patterns. Most of the time, the public never hears about our successes because they result in nothing happening."

"When nothing happens but something could have."

"Exactly."

"I, for one, am very grateful you're good at your job."

His cheeks flushed, and she found it endearing. Realizing she was making him uncomfortable, she asked, "Do you think we've hiked far enough to justify a bowl of ice cream for dessert when we get home?"

He grinned. "I think so."

"Any chance you have any hot fudge?"

"I think I might have some in the fridge."

"If you do, you really will be my hero."

JD laughed. "I didn't know you were so easy to please."

"I'm not. Hot fudge is serious business."

"I can handle that kind of serious anytime."

* * *

JD watched Hadley drizzle hot fudge over her ice cream, followed by whipped cream and a spoonful of sprinkles. She held out the sprinkles. "Do you want some?"

"I haven't put sprinkles on my ice cream since I was a kid."

"You're missing out." Hadley spooned a bite of ice cream into her mouth. "Mmm. That's so good."

Amused by her reaction, JD followed her example and finished building his sundae. The memory of a winter day with his mom and brother surfaced, the innocence of childhood. Sprinkles equaled sunshine, she used to tell him. He took a bite, savoring the contrast of warm and cold sweetness. "That is good."

"The sprinkles make all the difference," Hadley said. "It's like eating a little bit of sunshine."

JD stared at her, startled by how Hadley's words echoed his mother's sentiments. "My mom used to say that."

"Really?" Hadley took his comment in stride. "Smart woman. Where is she now? Still in California?"

"Yeah. My folks live in Bakersfield."

"What do they do?"

"Mom works for the city planning office. Dad's a police officer. Supposedly, he retired last year, but I'm not buying it. It's hard to imagine him walking away from law enforcement." JD let the memories of his childhood wash over him, and he shared them without censure. "Dad was constantly teaching us different skills, like self-defense and how to shoot. He even taught us what to do if anyone ever tried to follow us home or duct tape our hands together."

"Those are some interesting lessons to teach a kid."

"Yeah, but they've come in handy, especially for my brother."

"Why? Is he a cop too?"

"No. He owns a security company." At her confused look, he added, "My dad also taught us how to pick locks. Nothing better for someone who's trying to protect a house than to know how to break into it."

"You must have had some pretty interesting discussions around the dinner table."

"That we did." JD took the last bite of his ice cream. "Have you ever had any self-defense classes?"

"Once in college. They taught us things like how to use our keys as a weapon and to be aware of our surroundings."

"Maybe we should give you an advanced course tonight."

"What do you mean?" Hadley gave him a suspicious look.

"Do you know what to do if someone grabs you from behind?"

"I think so," she said without conviction.

"What if someone locks you in the trunk of a car? Or binds your hands together?"

"No." She drew the word out as though she wasn't sure she wanted to admit the truth.

"Come on." JD stood and picked up both of their bowls, then set them on the counter. "Time to learn."

"I don't know about this."

JD took her hands and tugged until she stood. "Trust me. It's better to gain a skill you'll never need than to not have it and find out you should have learned."

"Okay," Hadley said. "What do I do first?"

"Follow me."

CHAPTER 13

JD HAD TO GIVE IT to Hadley. She was a quick learner. He had a nasty bruise the size of her elbow along his ribs to prove it.

Despite the growing confidence she had gained during their time together, this morning, she had been more distant, especially once they'd gotten in the car to drive to the office. Guessing that she was nervous about trying to remember Saturday night, he had kept their conversation light, talking about simple things like what to have for dinner and the possibility of inviting Kelsey and Noah over to join them.

He walked Hadley to Angie's office and gave her shoulder a squeeze of encouragement before heading to the conference room, where Noah was wait-ing. "Has Spencer's boss arrived yet?"

"Security called and said they're bringing him up," Noah said.

Down the hall, two men approached, one wearing a visitor badge.

Noah stepped forward and extended his hand. "Mr. Hernandez, I'm Special Agent Cabbott. This is Special Agent Byers. Thank you for coming in."

"You didn't give me much of a choice." Begrudgingly, he shook Noah's hand and repeated the process with JD before following them into the confer-ence room. After they all sat at the table in the middle of the room, Carlos said, "I don't have a lot of time. News of the bombing on Saturday night has my staff understandably busy."

"Then we'll get right to it," Noah said. "Tell us about Spencer Andrews. How long has he worked for Opinions Matter?"

"Is he in some kind of trouble?" Carlos asked.

"Just answer the question please," Noah said.

"I'd have to check with personnel. If memory serves, we hired him as a temp last fall."

"When did he become full-time?" JD asked.

"He didn't." A crease formed between his brows. "He worked for two months. Then we picked him up again for another temp assignment in February. That job ended last Friday."

"Any idea what he was doing when he wasn't working for you?" Noah asked.

"Not a clue." Carlos drummed his fingers on the table. "Honestly, if he wasn't so gung ho about always offering to help, I probably never would have known his name."

"What do you mean?"

"Most of our temps are hired on for a specific project, but Spencer was always coming up to my office, trying to find more work to fill his time."

"What kind of things did he help with?" JD asked.

"Press releases, making dinner reservations for clients, taking calls, that sort of thing," Carlos said. "I think he was trying to make a case for himself that we should hire him on a permanent basis."

Noah pulled a paper out of the folder in front of him. "Can you tell me if any of these people are clients of yours?"

JD glimpsed at the list, recognizing it as the names of those who were present the night of the bombing.

"Yeah, we represent a few people on here," Carlos said. "Congressman Burke, Adam Pratt, and Senator Nichols."

"Anyone else?"

Carlos looked over the list again. "No. This is an impressive list of names though."

"Any idea what they were doing at The Waterfront Resort on Saturday?"

"Congressman Burke and his wife were holding an engagement party for their daughter," Carlos said, confirming what they already knew. "We also had a dinner party for Adam Pratt."

"Do you know why the congressman held his daughter's engagement party in Occoquan?"

"His house is only a few miles from there," Carlos said. "If memory serves, the party was at the same hotel where he gives his acceptance speeches every time he wins. I think he's friends with the owner."

"Have you heard of a company called Voice Today?" JD asked.

"I can't say that I have."

"What else can you tell us about Spencer Andrews?" JD pressed.

"Like I said, I barely knew the guy," Carlos said. "Can you please tell me what's going on? Why are you asking all of these questions about Spencer? Where is he?"

"He's dead. His body was found Sunday morning."

Carlos's jaw dropped open, but no sound came out.

"We have an eye-witness who claims Spencer was at the hotel the night of the bombing and that he left the facility shortly before the bomb detonated."

Now Carlos's hands came up in a defensive position. "Whoa. I don't know anything about that."

"We'll need a copy of his personnel file and the names of anyone who worked with him regularly."

"I'll have my assistant get that to you this afternoon."

JD stood and extended his hand. "We appreciate your time."

Carlos shook JD's hand and nodded at Noah.

JD escorted him to the door. With a wave at one of the administrative assistants, he said, "Theresa will take you back downstairs."

JD watched him disappear down the hall before returning to the conference room table. "What do you think?"

"I think he doesn't have a clue about what Spencer Andrews was involved in or why he was killed."

"I agree," JD said.

"I'll follow up with Spencer's coworkers," Noah offered. "Why don't you see if you can trace his money. He had to get it from somewhere."

"True."

"Hadley should be done in an hour or so. Do you want to work from home again this afternoon?"

"Actually, I thought I might order in some lunch for us and see if Angie would be willing to give her a tour of the office," JD said. "That will give me time to do some digging that would be hard to do from home. Did we ever hear back from the lab about Spencer's DNA?"

"It came in this morning. He wasn't in the system."

"It sure would help to know who this guy is."

"Hadley could know more about him than she thinks she does," Noah suggested.

"She hasn't been able to give me much so far. Maybe on our way back to the house, we can swing by Spencer's condo, see if she notices anything out of place or missing."

"Do you think she's up for it?"

"Only way to find out is to ask." JD pushed back to a stand. "I'll catch you later." Leaving Noah behind, JD headed for the elevator. Time to do a deep dive into the fake Spencer Andrews and find out what he was really up to.

* * *

In her office at CIA headquarters, Kelsey studied the images on the screen, a half-dozen figures gathered in the expansive courtyard of a large estate. Several vehicles obscured her view of the front of the house, but she knew precisely what it looked like. She had lived there for nearly two years.

Head scarves hid the features of the men, and Kelsey noted there weren't any women or children visible.

"You wanted to see me?" Eli asked from her doorway.

"Come take a look at this." Kelsey waved him closer.

He circled her desk and came up beside her. "What am I looking at?"

"Satellite imagery from the southern tip of Abolstan." Kelsey rolled her chair to the side so he could take a closer look.

"Looks like a supply caravan," Eli said. "Based on the number of vehicles, I'd guess we're dealing with someone moving in or moving out."

"Or the delivery of cargo going in and out."

Eli straightened. "You think this is Rabell's new headquarters."

"I think it's a possibility," Kelsey said. "Can you pull the last few weeks of images for this site? I want to see what other movement we can pick up."

"Doesn't it seem odd that these guys would be outside when the satellite passed overhead? Usually, these terrorist groups know the schedule of our satellites better than we do."

"We retasked several satellites for exactly that reason."

"I'll see what I can find." Eli headed for the door as Kelsey's secretary approached.

"I have someone here to see you," Lauren said.

When Noah stepped into the doorway, Kelsey fought the urge to cross the room and give him a proper greeting. "Thank you, Lauren."

Noah walked inside and closed the office door.

Kelsey bit back a smile. "You know I have a policy of not being in a closed room with a man I'm not married to."

"Good policy." Noah met her in the center of the room and leaned down to kiss her cheek. "Now, what do you know about Rabell and his operations?"

Kelsey took one of the two seats that faced her desk, waiting for Noah to sit beside her. "Rabell popped up on our radar about three years ago. He was operating as a broker for any number of deals, primarily for clients in the Middle East and in north Africa."

"What kind of deals?" Noah asked.

"He started with weapons and mercenaries." Acid churned in her stomach when she added, "He's since graduated to human trafficking."

The horror on Noah's face confirmed that his feelings mirrored her own. "Slavery?"

"Primarily, but he's also been tied to organ harvesting. A single kidney can bring in a million dollars."

"It makes me sick even thinking about what men like Rabell do to these people."

Kelsey took his hand in hers. "I know."

"What do you know about his involvement in Saturday's bombing?"

"We picked up some intel about an assassination attempt."

"Do you know who the target was?"

"We know it was someone working with Congress, but we don't have a specific name."

"We had three senators and eleven congressmen at the party on Saturday night," Noah said. "Not to mention at least a dozen aides."

"I know, and so far, all of Rabell's associates who we had identified as being involved ended up dead."

"So we're back at square one."

"Not exactly." Kelsey's fingers tightened on his hand before she stood and paced around her desk. She turned to face him, leaning against the front corner. "I think I know where Rabell has set up his new headquarters."

"Where?"

"Abolstan."

* * *

Noah let the single word sink in. He noted the quiet way Kelsey kept her gaze on his without elaborating. A sense of unease rose in his chest, transforming into a sharp blade of panic. "No." Noah shook his head. "You aren't going back there."

"I know the area. I know the language—"

"So do a dozen other people," Noah cut her off.

"But they don't know the compound."

"Wait. Are you saying Rabell—?"

"Has taken over Nassar's old headquarters." Kelsey crossed to him and sat once more. "Noah, I'm the only westerner alive who has ever been inside those walls."

"Listen to what you're saying. You're the only westerner *alive* who's been inside," Noah said. "Others have been there, and they're all dead. And let's not forget that the last time you were there, you were shot, and the Navy SEALs had to bring you home."

"I know."

"Kelsey, I'm not okay with this."

"Noah, we chose these careers so we could make a difference. Can either of us sit by and watch women and children being snatched from their homes, knowing they are being tortured and abused . . ." She trailed off, drawing a deep breath before continuing. "I have to do this. I'm the only one who can."

"Then I'm coming with you."

"I appreciate the sentiment, but we both know that isn't possible."

"You aren't going into a hostile country without backup."

"You're absolutely right." The expression on her face spoke volumes.

"You've already planned the mission."

"My backup is looking over the specs right now."

Noah's jaw tightened as he fought against the sudden helplessness that joined the ball of fear and concern already festering in his stomach. "When do you leave?"

"My go bag is in my car."

Noah leaned forward for a kiss, but this time, he didn't settle for her cheek. His hand lifted to the slender column of her neck, his fingers sensing the tension she carried there.

His heart swelled with emotion, his love for Kelsey rising within him even as he tried to separate that precious part of her that belonged to him from the woman who would soon face danger most Americans could barely fathom.

"I love you," she said in a lowered voice when he pulled back.

"I love you. Be safe."

Kelsey nodded and pushed to her feet. "I'll get word to you as soon as I can."

Noah rose as well and gathered her into his arms. "Be safe," he repeated.

"I will," Kelsey said hoarsely. "I won't be gone long."

Resting his chin on top of her head, Noah prayed that her words would be true.

CHAPTER 14

KADE READ THE UPDATED MISSION plan and the Saint Squad's part in it. In the trailer of his semi that had been converted into a mobile home, he moved from his workstation to the kitchen.

"Do you want a brownie sundae?" he asked Renee without looking at her.

"You don't really think bribing me with dessert is going to keep me from worrying, do you?"

"Worrying about what?"

"About you going with the Saint Squad to Abolstan."

"I'm not exactly going with them." Kade couldn't explain why he felt the need to go on this mission, but he knew he wouldn't rest easy unless he was close by to provide support.

"Going with them, shadowing them. Whatever you want to call it."

"I probably won't leave the supply depot we set up by the border," Kade said. "I told Brent I would make sure they have the vehicles and supplies they need."

"And you want to be close in case there's trouble."

No point in denying it. The woman knew him too well. "Something like that."

Renee crossed to him and wrapped her hands around his waist. "When do you leave?"

"Tonight." He lowered his head, his lips touching hers. "Will you be okay staying here with the Whitmores for a few days?"

"Yeah. I want to be close by in case something breaks on the bombing."

"I love you, you know."

"I know. Which is why I expect you to come home as soon as you can."

He lowered his lips to hers again, deepening the kiss. His fingers slipped into the silkiness of her hair, and a familiar warmth washed over him. When he pulled back, he stared at her flushed cheeks, memorizing every feature. "I'll be home as soon as I can."

* * *

Hadley watched the various FBI employees pass by from where she sat in Angie's office. With the battery on her cell phone nearly dead, she had little choice but to people-watch.

For the past twenty minutes, she had made a game of identifying the agents from the support personnel. Most of the men and women moved about with a sense of purpose but without the frantic urgency that she had seen after the bombing.

A pregnant woman moved down the hall at a surprising speed, followed by a man in his forties. The two stopped at a cubicle in the center of the office, their voices muffled as they discussed something.

The elevator doors opened, and the scent of Chinese food overrode the lingering odor of stale coffee. Someone must be planning to work late.

Two men headed for the elevator, apparently leaving for the day. Hadley watched the doors slide open and JD step out.

She stood when he approached.

"I'm sorry I took so long," JD said. "Are you ready to go?"

"Yeah." She slid the strap of her purse over her shoulder. "Although I'm not looking forward to sitting in traffic on 95."

"Actually, I was hoping to make a stop on our way back."

The way he said it, with a hint of wariness, left her uneasy. "Where?"

"Spencer's condo."

Her chest constricted. "Why?"

"Noah and I searched it, but I'd like to see if you notice anything missing or out of place," JD explained as he escorted her into the elevator. "We know someone was there after he died. What we don't know is if they took anything."

"Do you think it's really that important?"

"It could be."

Though everything in her demanded that she say no, she managed to nod. "Okay."

JD escorted her to his car and opened her door. Neither of them spoke until they were out of the garage and JD had turned onto the main road. "What did your parents think of Spencer?"

"They never met him."

"Really?"

"I've only seen my parents once since Spencer and I started dating, and that was when I went home for Christmas."

"Spencer didn't go with you?"

"No. He had to work."

Hadley expected JD to start his typical questions about Spencer, but instead, he put his hand on hers. "Are you sure you're up for this? We don't have to go."

"I want to get this all behind me. If you think I can help make that happen faster by going to his place, let's do it now."

"Okay." He withdrew his hand and Hadley's sense of comfort with it.

Silence filled the car. JD parked in a visitor spot beside an Audi sedan next to Spencer's building. Not for the first time, Hadley wondered what the people who lived here did for a living to make so much money.

"How are we going to get inside?" Hadley asked when she climbed out of the car.

"I have Spencer's key." JD's gaze swept over the rest of the parking lot and the surrounding area.

Together they went inside, Hadley's steps slowing as they approached Spencer's door. A heaviness came over her, one she couldn't explain.

JD unlocked the door and entered first, then Hadley followed behind him. Something thudded against the floor, and Hadley's heart jumped into her throat.

JD's weapon was in his hand so fast Hadley wondered if he had been carrying it the whole time. He reached out with his other hand and pushed her back against the wall.

A flash of color appeared in the hallway that led to the bedrooms.

"Federal agent! Freeze!" JD shouted, his aim on the man who now stood motionless, his face and hair largely hidden by the ball cap he wore. The man raised his hands slowly.

"Who are you?" JD demanded.

He didn't answer. He held his position for a fraction of a second longer before his gaze lifted to meet Hadley's. Then his hands dropped back to his side, and he sprinted into the bedroom.

"Stay here," JD ordered and took off after him.

Hadley leaned back against the wall, trying to make herself invisible. Who was that man? And why did he look familiar?

"Stop!" JD's shout echoed from the bedroom, and Hadley could hear the balcony door open.

The floor to her left creaked, and she whipped around to see another intruder, but this time, she recognized the face.

"Where is it?" Keith asked, his voice low. He lifted his hand, and Hadley's throat closed when she saw the gun. "Where did he hide it?"

Hadley couldn't take her eyes off the gun, the shiny metal barrel pointing directly at her.

"Where did he hide it?" he asked again.

"Hide what?" Hadley managed to ask. She was so focused on the gun and the possibility of it being used against her that she didn't hear JD until his words sounded from her right.

"Drop it!"

The next few seconds passed in slow motion. Keith swung his gun toward JD. Hadley screamed, her voice merging with the sound of a gunshot. Keith's gun dropped to the floor an instant before he did.

Time sped up when JD hurried to his side and kicked the gun away from him. JD holstered his own weapon and retrieved his phone to dial 9-1-1.

While passing on the necessary information to the operator, JD used his shoulder to hold the phone while grabbing a glove from his pocket. Once he put it on, he leaned down and pressed his hand to the wound he had just inflicted.

Setting the phone aside, he asked, "Who are you working for?"

Trembling, Hadley edged forward. "He's looking for something."

JD glanced at her, a look of respect and appreciation on his face. Speaking again to Keith, he asked, "What were you looking for?"

Keith opened his mouth but only managed to make a gurgling sound.

Sirens sounded in the distance.

"Should I go wait outside for the ambulance?" Hadley asked.

"No. I don't want you unprotected. This guy's friend got away." JD looked up at her. "He knew you. How?"

"That's Keith. He was with us at dinner on Saturday."

The sirens grew louder and then ceased. A minute later, footsteps sounded in the hallway, and the paramedics entered.

"Single gunshot wound to the chest," JD said, moving aside as soon as one of the paramedics knelt to relieve him.

"I've got a pulse," the first paramedic announced.

JD pulled the glove off his hand and avoided any contact with Keith's blood. After disposing of it by sealing it in a plastic bag one of the paramedics gave him, he turned his attention to Hadley. He put both hands on her arms, his eyes meeting hers. "Are you okay?"

"It seems like I'm hearing that question way too often lately."

"I know. I'm sorry."

"Do you have to stay?" Hadley asked.

"I'll need to give a statement to the police."

"But you're FBI."

"It doesn't matter. I discharged my weapon, and I'm the reason that man is bleeding on the floor over there."

Hadley heard the slight waver in his voice, her awareness of JD's emotions elevating. "You did what you were trained to do," Hadley said. "I don't suppose that makes it any easier being in the position to have to pull the trigger."

Surprise reflected on his face before melting into acceptance. "No, it doesn't."

"Do you still want me to look around?" Hadley asked. "After what just happened, I'd rather not have to come back here."

"Let's start in the bedroom."

"I've never been in his bedroom."

"The kitchen, then."

JD led her to the doorway Keith had appeared through only minutes before.

Hadley walked inside, noting the junk drawer was hanging open. "Obviously, that's not normal. Keith must have been looking in there when we arrived."

"He asked if you knew where something was," JD said.

"Yeah."

"That means he didn't find whatever he was looking for." JD approached the open door and studied the contents.

Hadley slowly circled the kitchen, letting her gaze travel as she went. She opened the cabinet beside the refrigerator to find the contents neatly in place. The same was true for the other cabinets.

After a quick search of the pantry, JD escorted her through the other living areas of the condo, but nothing appeared out of place.

"I know you said you haven't been in his bedroom before, but I want you to take a look anyway. You would at least know what clothes he wore and if anything in the bedroom doesn't look like something he would own."

"I guess that's true." Hadley followed JD down the hall into the spacious master bedroom. Her eyes were immediately drawn to the photo on Spencer's bedside table. "I didn't know he had that photo of me."

"He didn't take it?"

"No. That was taken before I met him." She and JD walked through the closet and bathroom and circled through the office before returning to the living room.

A police officer greeted them. As JD recounted what happened, Hadley moved across the room so she wouldn't have to watch the paramedics working on Keith.

She looked out the window without seeing.

When the paramedics finally left with Keith and JD finished with the policeman, JD stepped beside her. "We can go now. Are you ready?"

"Yeah." Hadley crossed the living room, walking past the fresh blood stain on the floor. When JD opened the door for her, she stepped through, determined not to look back.

CHAPTER 15

KELSEY STEPPED OUT OF THE cab in front of JFK Airport, a plain blue carry-on in one hand and a leather handbag in the other. Within moments, she was swallowed by the crowd of people coming and going. Businessmen and -women carrying nothing beyond briefcases and purses, parents hauling children, car seats, and luggage, couples on holiday. Kelsey identified them as she passed, quietly watchful of the people who didn't fit the typical categories.

She noted two men with concealed weapons on her way to security, but the way they veered off indicated they were either air marshals or off-duty FBI agents who would go through their own security checkpoint.

It wasn't the armed men who concerned her but rather the unarmed variety, the ones who waited at airports and quietly watched. The ones who spent their time looking for people like her, people who were invisible.

Shortly after meeting with Noah, one of the CIA drivers had dropped Kelsey off in DC near the World War II Memorial. She had blended in with the tourists on her way to the subway and used her Metro card to take a short trip from the Smithsonian station to Gallery Place. She had exited and paid cash for a quick lunch at a food truck before walking the few blocks to another station, this time entering using the Metro card for another alias to complete her trip to Reagan National Airport.

The flight from DC to La Guardia had gone without incident, as had her rambling trip through New York City to get to JFK.

Keeping her gait steady, Kelsey approached security. She would soon be Taja Al-Kazaz, a nanny who had worked for families all over the world, but for now, she was still Kelly Park, American citizen. She had nothing to hide, no reason for her heartbeat to quicken or for her gaze to falter when the TSA agent called her forward.

She handed over her boarding pass and the correct ID. The agent scanned the passport, glanced at Kelsey's face, and scribbled his initials on her boarding pass. He handed them both back to her. "Next."

Relieved, Kelsey proceeded through security. She glanced at the overhead signs, opting to go the wrong direction in her search of a restroom. She passed one and continued until she reached a second. Then she entered, choosing a stall at the end.

She locked herself in, listening, waiting. Fifteen minutes passed before she was certain everyone who had seen her enter had already left. Her heartbeat quickening, she unzipped her suitcase and traded the small purse she carried for a larger one. She then pulled out a travel pouch that separated one outfit from the others.

Slowly, she unzipped the pouch and drew out her jilbab and niqab so she could dress in the traditional Muslim robe and veil. Fighting back memories of the last time she had worn such clothing, she slipped off her shoes and changed them so they wouldn't catch the attention of anyone who might have noticed her.

A bubble of anxiety rose within her, but she swallowed it. Completing her final transformation of the day, she donned the traditional Muslim clothing and changed her identification one last time.

After securing her Kelly Park passport into the hidden compartment of her large purse, she retrieved a thin cloth covering and closed her suitcase. She stretched the cover over the top of her suitcase, effectively changing it from blue to black. Once she was satisfied that nothing about her appearance could tie her to her previous identity, she flushed the toilet and exited the stall.

Approaching the sink to wash her hands, she glimpsed at the mirror, but she didn't recognize the woman staring back at her.

* * *

Rush-hour traffic had thinned by the time JD and Hadley headed out of DC, dinnertime long past.

Hadley had been remarkably calm when they'd given their statements to the police. She had barely said anything while he'd logged the evidence they'd collected at Spencer's house and turned it over to forensics. She appeared calm and collected, but JD knew she was shaken to the core.

He didn't speak for the first thirty minutes, giving her time to process through her shock and hopefully come to terms with her current reality. When they passed into Stafford county, he glanced sideways and saw her hands in her lap, her fingers laced together. She stared straight ahead, her posture rigid.

"Hadley, I can't apologize enough for taking you to Spencer's house. I never thought those guys would come back."

Silence.

JD changed lanes to take the next exit before repeating the sentiment. "I'm so sorry."

More silence.

Not sure what else he could do, he followed instinct and reached over to lay his hand on top of hers. She didn't react, but after several seconds, JD could feel her relax slightly.

He exited onto Garrisonville Road and tried another tactic. "You have to be starving. Do you want me to pick up something on our way?"

She shook her head.

"Okay. Home it is." Her head turned now, and JD could feel her gaze on him. He glanced her direction to discover she was indeed staring at him. "What?"

"You said *home*."

It took him a moment to recall her observation of how he typically referred to his current living situation. "I guess I did."

* * *

Hadley ran on the treadmill, her mind racing every bit as quickly as her feet. So many questions, so few answers. She wasn't ever going to find normal again. She was sure of it.

Sleep had come in patches all night, and by five o'clock, she had given up on pretending she could hide in her dreams. Instead, she had opted for a more physical release for her pent-up emotions.

She hadn't seen JD yet this morning, but she had accepted his offer to make herself at home by taking advantage of the home gym in the basement.

Footsteps sounded on the stairs, and she reduced her speed to start her cooldown.

"Hey there." JD continued to the bottom landing. "I was wondering where you were."

"I couldn't sleep," Hadley said.

"That's understandable." JD positioned himself in front of the treadmill. "How are you doing?"

"I don't have a clue how to answer that question." Hadley reduced her speed to a slow walk. "I keep trying to figure out how I landed in this nightmare, but nothing makes sense."

JD remained silent for a moment before he asked. "Have you had any breakfast?"

"Not yet." Hadley hit the stop button. "I was going to make a smoothie. Do you want one?"

"It depends on what kind you're making. I'm not eating anything green. Spinach belongs in salads, not in drinks."

"I was thinking strawberry and banana."

"I can do that." JD waved at the treadmill. "Are you done down here?"

"Yeah." She followed him upstairs and set about gathering ingredients while JD retrieved his blender from a lower cabinet.

He set it on the counter. "You mentioned that you went out with Spencer every other weekend in DC."

"That's right." Hadley retrieved the milk from the refrigerator.

"Can you make a list of people you went out with up there?"

"We didn't go out with anyone else."

"Ever?"

"Ever," Hadley confirmed. "Looking back, I guess I should have realized how odd that is that we never went out with any friends."

"Did any of your friends meet him?"

"No, but it isn't like I have a lot of friends here," Hadley said. "I have friends at work, but once the weekend came, I didn't really hang out with anyone except Spencer."

"I thought you've lived here for a few years."

"I have. I had a couple of good friends I used to hang out with, but one was a Marine and got transferred last summer, and the other one moved to Pittsburgh to go back to school for her master's degree."

"That's tough."

Hadley added ice to the blender and hit the On button, effectively silencing their conversation. She retrieved two plastic tumblers from the cabinet and poured the smoothies into the cups.

"Here you go."

"Thanks." JD's phone rang, and he checked caller ID. "Sorry, but I've got to take this."

"It's fine." Hadley watched JD pick up his smoothie and head toward the office before he answered the phone.

She took a sip of her breakfast and contemplated what to do with her day. A shower was next on her list, but maybe once she came back downstairs, she could find a way to help JD. Otherwise, she might not have to worry about someone finding her. She would already be dead from boredom.

* * *

Noah didn't look at the clock on his desk until after he had dialed JD's number.

JD confirmed the early hour when he answered, "Hey, Noah. Is everything okay?"

"Yeah. Sorry to call so early. I came into the office and wasn't looking at the time."

"Noah, it's six fifteen in the morning. Why are you already at the office?"

All too aware that he was on an unsecured phone, he said, "One of my neighbors had to leave town on a business trip, so I decided to come in early."

The brief silence that answered him indicated JD knew exactly which neighbor he was talking about and that Kelsey's trip hadn't required an early-morning trip to the airport.

Noah continued. "I checked in with the hospital. We still don't have an ID on the man Hadley called Keith. His IDs are fake, and his fingerprints didn't flag."

"I'm getting tired of not knowing who we're dealing with."

"Me too," Noah said. "If I don't have anything new up here, I'll probably head your direction early this afternoon."

"My current roommate mentioned making lasagna. Want to join us for dinner?"

"I'm not sure I'll be up for making conversation tonight, but I wouldn't object to you sending a piece or two over for me."

"I can do that," JD said. "I'll talk to you later."

"Yeah. Later." Noah hung up and checked the time again. He didn't know what path Kelsey had taken to get to Abolstan, but his stomach churned with his current situation. She had been gone long enough to be in the Middle East by now, and he wasn't going to rest easy until she was back on American soil.

* * *

Kelsey faced the four men standing in the parlor of the safe house in Istanbul. She hated relying on others, but in truth, she couldn't accomplish this mission without their support.

Patrick, the CIA operative who would pose as her *mahram*, or family member, had worked with her before. She also recognized the three Navy SEALs, only the last time she had seen them had been when they dropped her off at a military base after rescuing her from a hospital in Abolstan. They and the four men currently standing guard outside had saved her life. She hoped they wouldn't have to repeat that performance on this mission.

Brent Miller, the commander of the Saint Squad, motioned to her niqab. "It's safe to unveil your face. My men will alert us if anyone approaches."

Rather than remove her head covering completely, Kelsey unfastened the veil portion of her niqab, opening it so her face was exposed. Fresh, warm air flowed over her skin, and she breathed in.

"What exactly is the plan?" Patrick asked.

"We've looked at the different options, and if we want to get into Abolstan without being noticed, driving over the border is our best bet."

"It would take a whole day to drive that far," Patrick pointed out.

"We have a helo standing by." Brent motioned to the enormous dark-skinned man to his left. "Seth arranged to have three vehicles waiting for us when we arrive."

"Arranged with whom?" Patrick asked. "We can't afford to have locals involved."

"They aren't," Seth said now, his voice carrying both a sense of calm and the lilt of the South. "We have resources available for exactly this type of mission."

Brent retrieved a folded paper from his pack and opened it, spreading it on the kitchen table. "Let me show you what we have in mind."

Everyone gathered around the table, and Kelsey listened to the men explain the details of her insertion and Patrick's role in maintaining her cover.

When Brent's briefing concluded, Patrick motioned to Kelsey. "I still don't like Taja going in unprotected. She won't have any way to communicate with us if she runs into trouble."

Brent patted his backpack. "We have a plan for that too."

CHAPTER 16

JD HUNG UP THE PHONE for the third time in less than an hour. The man Hadley knew as Keith had survived the night but was still in critical condition.

A local jeweler had examined the diamonds discovered in Spencer's apartment, confirming that they were consistent with the gems that had been stolen from the Afghani government. The value came in at a shocking $29 million.

Leaving his work for the moment, he headed for the back of the house and discovered Hadley in the living room. She sat on the edge of the couch, a pen in one hand and a small pad of paper in the other. JD's gaze was drawn to the long wall in front of her.

Sticky notes. Everywhere.

"What's all this?"

"Questions." Hadley tapped the pen against her lips twice before scribbling another note down. She removed the top sticky note and added it to the wall.

JD moved closer and began reading Hadley's notes. Each colorful square listed a separate question. Who is Spencer? Why was my laptop stolen? What was the purpose of the bombing? Who was the bomb meant for? Where did the diamonds come from?

The questions went on, all of them ones JD had asked himself multiple times. "Why are you putting questions all over the wall?"

"So much has happened so quickly, I thought it might help to be able to see the questions so we don't forget anything."

"You have some good ones here."

"I'd rather have good answers."

"Wouldn't we all."

* * *

What was she thinking? Kelsey had asked herself that question already, when she'd boarded the helicopter in Istanbul and again when she'd crossed the border into Abolstan.

Patrick sat beside her as he drove their borrowed car through the rugged desert in the isolated region of southern Abolstan.

Like Kelsey, Patrick was traveling under a false name, not only to protect his true identity but also so his surname would support the claim that he was her brother. Traveling without an escort would have drawn too much attention, and Kelsey doubted Patrick was any more comfortable with being in enemy territory than she was.

The private road that led to Nassar's former compound came into view, and Kelsey pointed. "You can let me off there."

Speaking in Arabic, Patrick said, "Maybe I should accompany you all the way to Nassar's estate. You don't even know if his wives and children are still there."

As much as Kelsey wanted to give in to his suggestion that he accompany her, the memory of her previous handler being executed in front of her held her back. "If they don't live there, I will return to our hotel."

"What will you do if they are home?"

Though they were alone, Kelsey recognized the wisdom of maintaining their cover at all times. The possibility of listening devices was too great in this war-torn country. "I will see if they will permit me to visit for a few days."

"You'll send word if you decide to stay for a visit?" Patrick asked.

"I will let you know before sunset."

The car rolled to a stop. Kelsey gathered her things, her luggage now reduced to a large satchel. Mustering courage from deep within, she uttered a silent prayer and climbed out of the car. Nightmares bloomed of her last moments at Nassar's mansion, and she instinctively rubbed the scar on her thigh.

She took several deep breaths, willing her heartbeat to steady. Any sign of discomfort could be deadly.

She was armed with a carbon-fiber knife strapped to her thigh and a pistol hidden in an inner pocket of her jilbab. She forced her feet into action and started down the dirt road.

Though she didn't look behind her, she knew Patrick watched her until she disappeared over the rise. When silence continued around her, broken only by her footsteps, she suspected Patrick wasn't going anywhere until he was certain she was safely inside.

The sun beat down on her, and she could be grateful it was only April instead of midsummer. A bead of sweat dripped down the center of her back.

She forced herself to continue forward as she scanned the surrounding terrain, the fabric of her niqab obscuring her view to either side. The Saint Squad was hidden somewhere in the rocky ridges that flanked her previous home, but she couldn't see any sign of them.

She reached the bend in the driveway a few yards before the house came into view.

Moving cautiously, she took cover behind a large boulder. No reason to expose herself any sooner than necessary. She peeked out at the familiar scene before her.

A scatter of desert brush lined the path to her left; several more large rocks were nestled against the base of the cliffs to her right. She adjusted her position and looked out over the top of the boulder. Memories flashed, and she fought them back. Salman Nassar wasn't here. She was sure of it.

Kelsey evaluated the scene in front of her—four vehicles near the front entrance, two men with assault weapons standing guard. Another man patrolled the gardens where two women dressed in traditional Arabic garb worked.

Bars on the first-floor windows. Those were new, as were the two large huts to the west of the main house. Something gleamed in the sunlight. Were those padlocks on the doors?

Movement rustled in the bushes to her left. Kelsey ducked back out of sight, her heart leaping into her throat. What should she do? If found hiding, the men at the compound would be suspicious of her, but she wasn't a fan of walking into danger without knowing the situation.

The sound repeated, this time accompanied by a faint whimper.

Kelsey peeked out to the side of the rock again, this time catching a glimpse of black fabric. Now able to identify the other person as a woman, Kelsey called out softly in Arabic. "Who's there?"

The woman's head whipped around to face Kelsey, fear and terror evident in the eyes peeking from behind the veil. Not a woman but a teenager.

"I can't go back. Don't make me go back. Please."

The eyes, the voice. "Mahira, is that you?"

The worst edge of fear receded in her eyes, and Kelsey sensed her former student was working through her own confusion. "Taja?"

"Yes." Kelsey glanced at the compound again, noting the guards changing position. While the guards' attention was elsewhere, Kelsey waved at Mahira to join her behind the boulder. "Come here."

As though Kelsey had thrown her a lifeline, Mahira scrambled from the bushes and darted across the path to take the spot beside her former tutor. "Why are you here?"

"I came to see you," Kelsey said gently. "I wasn't sure if you were still here. I heard your father was arrested."

"Papa is gone. I do not know where." She tilted her head toward the house. "The bad man came and took over everything."

"What is the bad man called?"

"Rabell." Mahira whispered the name as though saying it at all might cause him to materialize in front of them. "He wanted to do business with my father, but Papa sent him away."

Kelsey's stomach turned. For all the evil Nassar had been involved in, the one thing he had never participated in was human slavery.

"What does the bad man do?"

"People are always coming and going. Children, women. They are locked up, treated like animals."

"What about you and your family?"

"Our mothers are forced to work in the house and gardens."

"And your brothers and sisters?"

"At first, we helped our mothers, but last week, four of my sisters and one of my brothers disappeared." Tears shone in Mahira's eyes. "I heard the guards talking. I'm next."

"I'm not going to let that happen." Kelsey reached up and activated the tiny transmitter hidden in her ear. "I can help you, but first, I need you to tell me everything you know about the guards and the changes they've made to the house since I lived there."

"I'll tell you everything," Mahira said. "But don't send me back."

"I won't send you back."

CHAPTER 17

NOAH STRUGGLED TO FOCUS AS he picked up the phone to call Senator James Whitmore. The request for a teleconference had come from the senator's chief of staff shortly after Noah had hung up with JD a second time this morning, but Noah couldn't deny that his thoughts had been on his wife since meeting with her yesterday.

He had known what she was when he'd married her, but he thought dangerous missions were a thing of her past. He was all too aware of the scar on her leg left from a bullet wound, an injury that had taken Kelsey months to recover from.

Noah dialed the senator's number. It rang only twice before the senator answered and greeted him by name. "Agent Cabbott, thank you for making time to talk to me."

"I should be thanking you for your help. Your message said you have information for me?"

"Yes and no," the senator said. "I checked with my sources, and they couldn't find any indication that I was the target of Saturday's bombing."

"What about the program you mentioned?"

"Their anonymity appears to still be intact."

"And if no one knows about the program, it can't be the target," Noah said.

"Right." He lowered his voice. "My sources also indicated this might be related to a smuggling ring. Have you ever heard of Rabell?"

"Intel mentioned him as the likely person behind the bombing."

"Intel hasn't changed their stance. I was told the same thing."

"But we still don't know why he planted the bomb," Noah said.

"Have you been able to tie the suspects who were killed to Rabell?"

"Not directly, nor do we have any idea why Rabell would bother himself with a target in the United States," Noah said. "From everything I've seen, his targets are people he perceives as obstacles in his business ventures."

"And since Rabell has been known to smuggle everything from weapons to people, we have no idea what part of his business is being threatened by someone here in the States."

"At this point, Senator, we're in the stage of uncovering more questions than answers in our investigation."

"Knowing the right questions to ask is half the battle."

"What questions should I be asking that I haven't already considered?"

"My source has traced Rabell to Abolstan."

Noah swallowed before responding. "I received the same information."

"I thought you probably had." Senator Whitmore hesitated. "But did you know he has a yacht currently docked at Occoquan?"

"That I didn't know."

"I thought it might be of interest."

"Yes, sir. It most certainly is."

* * *

Kelsey checked on Mahira; the girl was now asleep on the floor of the cave the Saint Squad had chosen to use as their temporary shelter.

Leaving the traumatized girl to rest, Kelsey returned to where Brent, Seth, and Patrick sat on the floor, a terrain map spread out before them.

Two more men entered—Tristan, the tall, sandy-haired man with the Texan drawl, and Quinn, the dark-eyed sharpshooter.

"The area's clear for now," Quinn announced. "Jay is on lookout, and Damian and Craig are guarding our flanks."

"Any sign of Rabell?" Brent asked.

"Not yet."

"According to the girl, he was there as recently as yesterday," Patrick said.

"What's the call?" Seth asked. "Do we risk going in after him without a positive sighting, or do we wait?"

"Our extraction is scheduled for tomorrow night," Brent reminded them. "And I don't know about any of you, but it doesn't sit well with me to leave here knowing the man responsible for trying to kill my in-laws is likely down there, not to mention those poor women and children who are being brought in and out of there."

Kelsey keyed in on Brent's words. "Your in-laws?"

"Senator James Whitmore. He and his wife were at the restaurant the night of the bombing," Brent explained.

Seth spoke in his quiet, thoughtful way. "Whether Rabell is inside or not, I think we have to help the hostages get out of there."

A weight lifted off Kelsey's shoulders. "According to Mahira, most of the women are being held in these two huts." She tapped her finger on the map. "Children are in these rooms here, but the windows have bars on them."

"You used to live here. Where is our best entry point?" Brent asked.

"The huts are new, but it looks like the locks are standard padlocks." Kelsey tapped a finger on the map. "Two guards are stationed here and here."

"We could go in, take out those guards, and free the captives without anyone being the wiser," Quinn said.

"What about the women locked in the house?"

"How many of you speak Arabic?" Kelsey asked.

"Seth and I do," Brent said.

Kelsey drew a deep breath, an emotional battle waging within her. "I think I can get the three of us in through the side entrance."

"We aren't in the habit of taking civilians with us on our operations," Brent said. "Even if you have been trained."

"I know, but I can lead you through the house to where you need to go. And you may need a woman to help with the hostages. They may be too traumatized to trust men they've never seen before."

"She's right," Seth said.

Recognizing Seth as an ally, Kelsey continued. "If you can dress like guards, I think we can get inside without anyone realizing they're being invaded."

"We'll need someone who speaks Arabic to communicate with the hostages in the huts," Seth said.

"I can go with your men to the huts," Patrick offered.

"No. I want you standing by with the vehicles to make sure we have a way to get these hostages out," Brent said.

Seth's gaze fixed on Kelsey, and he stared for a long moment. Finally, he spoke. "Craig and I can escort Taja into the house while the rest of you free the other hostages."

Relieved and terrified to have Seth's support, Kelsey faced Brent once more. "I know the blind spots coming into the compound. I can get us inside."

Brent fell silent for a moment before nodding. "I'm listening."

* * *

JD rubbed the back of his neck, the tension building from sitting at a desk for the better part of the day. The preliminary autopsy reports on the bombing suspects had come back, but they hadn't revealed anything of significance. The tax records on Spencer Andrews didn't exist, and the records on Voice Today revealed a tangle of shell companies without any evidence of who the real owners were.

Hadley knocked on the open door, a plate in her hand. "I made you some lunch. I figured you must be getting hungry."

"Thanks. Come on in."

Hadley crossed to the desk and set the plate on the empty space beside his right elbow. "How's it going?"

"Still more questions than answers," JD said. "Spencer wasn't filing taxes, and even though his house and car are both titled in his name, his company car was registered under some sort of shell corporation."

"I don't know anything about shell corporations, but wouldn't someone in the government notice that Spencer wasn't paying taxes?"

"They would if he'd been making income somewhere, but the only employment we know about that would have sent him a W2 was Opinions Matter, and this is the first year he would have filed."

"So no one would have noticed yet."

"Even then, with what his boss said, he was likely under the filing limit."

"He must have been making a good income from somewhere."

"I agree. My best guess is that his money is hidden in a company somewhere, or he's getting it through illegal sources that we haven't uncovered yet."

"I still can't get my head around Spencer being involved in something illegal," Hadley said.

"I know. It's never easy finding out someone you thought you knew well was hiding things from you."

"Let me tell you, he was one heck of an actor."

"We'll get to the bottom of this." JD glanced at his computer screen to see he had a new email. He opened it.

"What is it?" Hadley asked.

"The catalog of what was found in Spencer's apartment."

Hadley circled the desk so she could read the computer screen. Her hand lowered onto JD's shoulder, warmth emanating from the simple touch. "I still don't understand how he got that photo of me. He could have just taken one of me, but it looks like he downloaded that one off Instagram."

"I don't know." JD's cell phone rang, Noah's name illuminating the screen. "Hey, Noah. What's up?"

"I got a tip that Rabell has a yacht docked in Occoquan," Noah said. "Can you meet me there?"

JD looked at Hadley, uneasy at the thought of leaving her alone. He calculated the driving time for this time of day. "Give me forty-five minutes."

"It'll take me that long to get there too," Noah said. "I'll see you in a few."

"See you then."

CHAPTER 18

HADLEY SAW THE CONCERN ON JD's face. "You have to leave."

"I do." JD opened the bottom drawer of the desk, and Hadley glimpsed a gun safe inside. JD punched in the code to retrieve his weapon. He pushed back from his desk and stood before holstering his weapon. "I don't like the idea of leaving you here by yourself, but I can't take you with me."

Hadley swallowed. Fear bloomed. Fear for JD, fear for herself. She mustered her courage. "No one knows I'm here, right?"

"No one except Noah and Kelsey."

"Then there's nothing to worry about," Hadley said with forced confidence. "And you have a security system."

"Yeah." JD closed the distance between them, and her heartbeat quickened. "Come on. I'll show you how to use the alarm."

A twinge of disappointment surfaced when JD continued by her without making any physical contact. Where had that come from?

She followed him into the hall where the security system control pad was located. JD gave her the code and showed her the panic button.

"The sheriff's department always has deputies nearby because of the school down the street. If you have a problem, they'll be here in two to three minutes."

"That's good to know, but I'm really hoping not to need their help," Hadley said. "Do you have any idea how long you'll be?"

"I don't know. I should be back by five."

"I'll plan dinner for six," Hadley said, searching for a sense of normalcy. "Making lasagna will give me something to do while you're gone."

JD put both hands on her shoulders, and the undercurrents between them sparked. "You have my number."

"Yeah."

JD stared down at her, his eyes serious. Several seconds ticked by before he finally dropped his hands and opened the hall closet door. He grabbed a backpack from the floor, armed the security system, and headed for the door. "See you later."

"Be careful," Hadley said, not sure what else she could say.

JD glanced over his shoulder and nodded. "You too."

* * *

Dressed in sand-colored fatigues, Kelsey free-climbed the fifteen-foot rock face to reach the cliff where Quinn was on lookout duty. The rest of the Saint Squad was currently finalizing their mission plan for tonight, but she wanted another look at the compound before going back inside.

She reached the top of the ridge and ducked to stay behind the brush. Moving silently, Kelsey approached Quinn. The dark-haired man stared through the scope of his sniper's rifle, not so much as flinching when Kelsey took position beside him.

"Anything?" Kelsey whispered.

"You shouldn't be up here."

"I beg to differ." Kelsey didn't peek over the outcropping of rocks, all too aware of how risky such a move could be. "What do you see?"

"Still four vehicles. The one on the far right appears to be disabled."

"How can you tell?"

"Flat rear tire." Quinn scooted sideways, still holding the rifle in place. "Take a look."

Kelsey moved into his spot and steadied the weapon. Looking through the scope, she studied the terrain. As Quinn mentioned, the box truck parked to the far right was tilted slightly to the left, the rear tire completely flat. The other three appeared to be the same make and model, the cargo doors complete with padlocks.

"You're right. The one truck doesn't have a lock on the cargo door either. Probably broke down, and they haven't fixed it yet."

"Or they need to dispose of it in a way that no one will be able to pull any evidence out of it."

"Does that mean planting an explosive beneath it to take out all the trucks would be a bad idea?"

"We both know we aren't going to be given permission to bring a forensics team in here," Quinn said. "But before we do anything to disable their vehicles, we need to take out their communications."

"That's not going to be easy. Cell coverage is nonexistent here, so I'm guessing they're using satellite phones."

"I already saw one guy with one."

A rumble sounded in the distance, and Quinn tapped her shoulder to have her trade places with him again.

Kelsey relinquished her position, surprised when Quinn pulled a pair of binoculars from his vest and handed them to her. He pointed to the spot to his right where a gap in the rocks would give her a window into what was going on below.

Kelsey belly crawled around him until she too could see the road. Within seconds, a cloud of dust arose, a large van appearing from its center. Two more box trucks followed, moving slowly down the dirt road leading into the compound.

The first vehicle came to a stop, the honk of a horn repeating three times. The front door opened, and a half-dozen men walked out, each carrying an automatic rifle.

Her hands tightened on the binoculars, and she watched the driver of the van climb out and circle to the back. He glanced at the armed men as though making sure they were ready. Then he pulled the doors open.

Kelsey stared in horror as the driver reached in and grabbed a little girl who couldn't have been more than nine years old.

The little girl lifted her arm to shield her eyes as though the brightness of the sun was too much. One by one, more children were deposited by the first, sixteen in all, ranging from about eight years old to twelve.

"They're so young," Kelsey whispered.

Two women were summoned from the house. They escorted the children inside, two of the guards accompanying them.

The same scene replayed with the other two vehicles, only these occupants ranged in age from teenagers to women in their twenties, and instead of going inside, the guards took them around the house to the shacks near the garden. The last group was nearly to the rudimentary shelters when one woman tried to make a run for the road. She made it only a handful of steps before a guard grabbed her and threw her to the ground.

Kelsey clenched her teeth as the woman cried out and the guard kicked her in the ribs twice before dragging her back to a stand. Another guard lifted his weapon, aiming at her until she subsided, a trickle of blood visible on her forehead.

"There must be forty of them," Kelsey said under her breath.

"Forty-three." Quinn spoke into his communication headset, relaying the new information to Brent.

"How can we possibly get them out of here?" Kelsey asked as soon as he finished.

"We'll figure something out," Quinn said with absolute certainty.

"How can you be so sure?" Kelsey asked.

"Because none of us can live with any other option."

"I wish I had your confidence," Kelsey said.

"You can borrow some of mine," Quinn offered. "I have plenty to spare."

"Thanks."

* * *

Hadley moved to the window and watched JD climb into his car. She stared after him for a full minute before she stepped back out of sight. She was alone. For the first time in days, she was truly alone.

Fear pressed in on her, and she fought against it. She took a deep breath and let it out slowly. No one knew she was here. The alarm was on. JD would be back soon. She was safe.

Determined to take advantage of her time alone, she made her way upstairs. Might as well get her laundry done while she had the chance. She opened her door, and immediately, a thump sounded, followed by a mournful meow. Hadley's hand lifted to her chest, her heart pounding.

Lucy emerged from the bathroom and darted toward the door.

Hadley quickly entered the room and closed herself in. "No, you don't. You need to stay in here."

In response, Lucy rubbed against Hadley's leg and purred. Hadley leaned down and scratched behind her ears. Hadley's phone rang, and she snatched it up off the bedside table to find it was her mom calling. She nearly ignored the call, still not ready to talk about the events of the past five days, but reminding herself that she didn't have to reveal everything to her mom, she accepted the call. "Hi, Mom."

"My long-lost daughter." Humor laced her mother's voice. "I was wondering if I was ever going to get you on the phone again."

Not wanting to lie to her mother, Hadley chose her words carefully. "I've been trying to get a bunch of stuff done while I'm on spring break."

"I was hoping you would take it easy this week."

"I'm planning to go kayaking this weekend."

"That sounds fun."

"Yeah, it does." Hadley began sorting her dirty clothes into piles as she chatted with her mom. As soon as she completed her task, she said, "Mom, I need to get going. My laundry is waiting for me."

"Okay, honey. Good finally catching up with you."

Hadley got off the phone, surprised at how much talking to her mom had taken her mind off the stress of being alone. Scooping up the first load of laundry, she headed downstairs. A little over three hours until JD expected to be home. Time to get some housework done and get dinner started.

* * *

JD stood on the dock and stared at the empty boat slip, one of the only unoccupied spots in the harbor.

"According to the harbormaster, Rabell's yacht should be right here," Noah said.

"Maybe he caught wind that we were coming."

"I don't know how."

JD studied the vessel to his left, a sleek, white yacht he estimated could sleep at least eight people. The one beyond was even larger by at least five feet in length. "Judging from the size of these slips, I have to think it was a thirty- or forty-footer." JD looked out over the few vessels coming and going, most of them sailboats taking advantage of the gorgeous day. "I don't see anything that fits the description out there."

"Me neither." Noah motioned to his left. "I'll see if I can find anyone who's seen him lately."

"I'll go this way. Meet you back here in a bit." JD headed to the right. The first vessel didn't have anyone on board, but a man stood on the deck of the second, a rag in one hand as he polished the brass trim.

"Excuse me, sir," JD called out. "Can I speak with you a minute?"

The man lifted a hand against the sun, despite the ball cap he wore. "What do you want?"

"Just have a few questions." JD reached into his pocket and held up his credentials. "FBI."

"Come on up."

JD stepped aboard and climbed the steps to the upper deck.

The man set his rag aside. "What can I help you with?"

"Are you the owner of this vessel?"

"Yes. Chester Elliott."

"I'm Special Agent Byers." JD shook the man's hand. "Have you seen a boat in the slip two over from you?"

"Yeah. Forty-foot yacht, white with black trim."

"Do you know the owner?"

"Can't say that I do," Chester said. "He only docks here a few times a year, and even then, it's only for a couple days at a time."

"Can you describe the owner?"

"I'm not sure which of the guys is the owner. One is about five-ten, gray hair, probably around fifty."

"What about the others?"

"He usually has two or three other guys with him. They're all younger, ranging from late twenties to early thirties."

"Descriptions?"

"Dark hair. Two are around six feet tall, and one is a bit shorter. He's the youngest of the bunch."

JD pulled his cell phone out of his pocket. "Did you ever see any of these men?" JD showed him photos of Rabell and the three bombing suspects, Chester shaking his head on each one. "What about these?" JD retrieved the photo of Keith.

This time Chester pointed and nodded. "Yeah, he was one of them."

Moving on to the sketches by Angie, JD showed him the next image.

"He looks familiar too."

"And this one?" JD asked, showing him the third.

"Yep, him too."

"When did you see them last?"

"Let me think." Chester scratched behind his right ear. "Must have been Friday morning. They put in as I was leaving. I took the family up to DC for the weekend. Didn't get back until Sunday night, but by then, the slip was empty again."

"Thank you for your time. You've been very helpful." JD pulled a business card from his pocket. "If you see the yacht dock here again, can you please give me a call?"

"Should I be worried about these guys? Is it safe for me to stay here?"

"We believe so." JD turned to leave, another thought popping into his head. Facing Chester again, he said, "I have one more photo I want to ask you about."

JD showed him the photo of Spencer and again asked, "Have you ever seen him?"

"Come to think of it, I think I have, but he wasn't on the boat with the others."

"Where was he?"

"Can't remember exactly. Somewhere at the marina."

"Thank you again," JD said. "If you do see that yacht again, call me immediately. Any time. Day or night."

Chester lifted a hand in response and picked up his rag once more.

JD continued down the dock, finding most of the boats unoccupied. When he finally returned to his starting point, Noah was waiting for him.

"Did you find anything?" JD asked.

"Someone said they saw the yacht dock on Friday but that it was gone when they woke up Sunday morning."

"That's consistent with what I found," JD said. "Not only that, but the guy two spots down identified Keith and the two men in Hadley's sketches as being on the boat."

"The yacht could have been their getaway vehicle."

"That's what I'm thinking. Spencer was killed sometime Saturday night."

"They would have had plenty of time to take him out and still get out of here before anyone woke up on Sunday morning," Noah said.

"There's one more thing," JD said. "My witness said he'd seen Spencer around the docks but that he wasn't one of the men he'd seen on the yacht."

"Maybe that's because Spencer was their driver."

"Maybe. The guy also said the yacht typically shows up a few times a year."

"Sounds like this lead may need a while before it warms up again."

"I'm afraid so." JD motioned toward the harbormaster's office. "Come on. Let's see if we can get any more info out of the harbormaster. Maybe the Coast Guard will help us track these guys down sooner."

"It's worth a try."

CHAPTER 19

KELSEY ENTERED THE CAVE TO find Brent, Seth, and Patrick looking over the map again. "Did Quinn tell you what we saw?"

"Yeah." Brent glanced up. "We're redoing the mission plans right now."

"How are we going to get all of those people out of there?" Kelsey asked. "From what Mahira said, I think they already had another fifteen to twenty people locked up."

"We have three vehicles of our own, each of which can carry five adults," Brent said.

"If we pile some kids in there too, we can probably get eight or nine people in each of our vehicles," Seth said.

"And the helicopter can take another eight, plus two of us," Brent added. "That should be enough to get us out of here if we take their trucks too."

"Which means we can't explode the trucks as a decoy," Patrick said.

"We can't explode all of them," Kelsey corrected. "Is it possible to take out the one on the far side without damaging the others?"

"Why would we do that?" Patrick asked.

"Because it's not drivable anyway. Quinn noticed it has a flat tire, and it looks like it hasn't been used in a long time."

Excitement crept into Brent's voice. "That might work."

Seth spoke into his communications headset, asking Quinn for details on the vehicle's position. A moment later, he spoke again to Brent. "Quinn said it's possible, but he doesn't recommend it. He can't guarantee the flames wouldn't spread to the other trucks."

"What's our best alternative for a distraction?" Brent asked.

"We have to take out their communications first anyway. I say we go after the satellite dish on the east side," Seth said.

"We'll have to put the jammer on the northwest corner to make sure it doesn't get damaged by the blast." Brent nodded his approval. "Send Jay up to relieve Quinn. I want his input on where to set up our snipers."

"Will the jammers prevent us from being able to communicate with the headsets?" Kelsey asked.

"It shouldn't. We're on a closed circuit that won't be affected by the signal we're using to jam satellite access, and these guys are too far away from a cell tower to use regular cell service."

"What can I do to help?" Kelsey asked.

"For now, go get some sleep. We have a long night ahead of us."

Though Kelsey didn't know how she could possibly rest, she nodded. "I'll try."

"One of us will wake you two hours before go time."

"Thanks." Kelsey took a few steps toward the back of the cave before she hesitated. "Your squad is all LDS, right?"

"Pretty much. Why?"

"I was wondering if one of you would be willing to give me a blessing before we start out," Kelsey said. "I didn't get a chance to ask my husband before I left."

"We always pray before we leave on any mission, but we're happy to give you that extra protection." Brent motioned to a rock about the height of a standard chair. "Take a seat."

Kelsey sat, and Brent and Seth stood.

"Who would you like to say it?" Brent asked.

Kelsey started to say she didn't care, but when she looked up at the two men, a distinct answer came to her. "Seth, could you do it?"

"I'm happy to."

The two men took a moment before they laid their hands on her head. "What's your full name?"

The answer lodged in her throat. Could the Lord bless her if she used her alias? She couldn't give her real name to these men.

As though he heard her inner struggles, Seth leaned down and whispered in her ear. "Whisper it to me. I'll whisper it back when I start the blessing so no one else will hear."

Though reason told her to withdraw her request for a blessing, the warmth that spread through her confirmed that Seth could be trusted. She turned her head and whispered, "Kelsey Weber Cabbott."

Seth's hands joined Brent's on her head once more, and he leaned down, whispering her name in her ear before straightening and continuing the blessing at normal volume. The gentle words spoken with the lilt of the South flowed over her, bringing her comfort that hadn't been present before. Seth promised her protection and inspiration during the mission to come, as well as the ability to lift up those within her sphere of influence. The words of the blessing buzzed in her head, and her own thoughts circled into possibilities.

When Seth concluded the blessing, she stood and shook hands with him and Brent. "Thank you."

"You're welcome." Seth waved toward the deeper section of the cave. "Better go get some rest."

"I will." Kelsey found a spot a short distance away, the cave floor cool against her. She replayed the blessing again in her mind, and her gaze landed on Seth. He had known she was using an alias, but how? How had this Navy SEAL she had met only once before known her secret?

Despite her curiosity, she closed her eyes. If the Lord was going to give her the extra protection she needed tonight, the least she could do was be ready for whatever came her way.

* * *

JD drove toward the house, anxious to see for himself that Hadley was okay. He had managed to stay on task while he'd been at the marina, but the moment he'd gotten back in his car, all thoughts had been about her.

Even though he had put a blocker on her cell phone, he still preferred to avoid electronic communication between them in case anyone involved had managed to link him to the case. That thought alone caused him to increase his speed.

He turned the corner into his neighborhood. The light breeze carried fallen cherry blossom petals off the various lawns and onto the pavement. Mrs. Henderson from down the street walked on the sidewalk, her golden retriever trotting beside her.

JD continued forward, grateful to see his house exactly as he'd left it.

His house. He'd done it again. Why now, after living here for almost a year, was he finally thinking of it as his? At the end of the summer, Kelsey's parents would return from their mission, and he would have to find someplace else to live.

He parked in the driveway and hurried up the walk. He unlocked the door and called out the moment he pushed it open. "Hadley?"

The scent of tomato sauce wafted toward him. Footsteps sounded in the kitchen, and Hadley appeared at the far end of the main hallway.

"Hey." Hadley waited for him to join her in the kitchen.

JD walked in and took in the scene before him. The table was already set for two, and Hadley was in the process of making a salad. A loaf of Italian bread sat on the counter beside the parmesan cheese and garlic powder.

"How did everything go?" Hadley asked.

"We didn't find what we were looking for, but we think we know where Keith and his buddies were staying before the bombing on Saturday. Looks like they came in on a yacht Friday night." JD inhaled deeply. "Something smells good."

"Hopefully it will taste good." Hadley glanced at the clock. "It should be ready in about fifteen minutes."

"That's what I call perfect timing."

"Do you want to invite Kelsey and Noah to join us? I can set a couple more places."

"No, that's okay. I think Kelsey had to work late, but I promised Noah I'd bring him some," JD said. "Let me go secure my weapon, and then you can put me to work."

When JD returned, Hadley was putting the salad in the refrigerator. "What can I do to help?" he asked.

"I think I've got it." She opened the bread and pulled out five slices. "How many pieces of garlic toast are you going to want? Two?"

"That'd be great." JD retrieved a pitcher from a high cabinet and filled it with ice and water. "What did you do today while I was gone?" He waved toward the oven. "Besides the obvious."

"I talked to my mom today."

"And?" JD asked.

"I didn't tell her about Saturday," Hadley admitted. "Or Sunday."

"Or Tuesday," JD added.

"Or Tuesday," Hadley confirmed. "It was good talking to her though. It made me feel normal again."

"That's good." JD set the water pitcher on the counter. "Have you considered when you're going to tell her everything?"

"I was thinking about it after I got off the phone with her." Hadley set the butter knife down. "I think I want to wait until this is all over. I'm not sure I can handle my mom's questions when we still have so few answers."

"The answers will come."

"Yeah, but how soon?"

"I wish I could tell you, but I don't know."

"My spring break is already half over. What do I do when Monday comes?" Hadley asked.

"I know it's not ideal, but you can commute from here."

"I figured you'd be ready to get rid of me by now."

The familiar warmth spread through him, and JD let himself speak the truth. "Not at all."

* * *

Hadley rinsed her dish and slid it into the dishwasher, repeating the process with the pan she had used to make the garlic toast.

"Let me do that." JD approached, carrying his plate and both of their cups. "You made dinner. It's only fair you let me clean up."

Hadley didn't argue. She stepped aside and watched JD as he finished the rest of the dishes.

"What do you want to do tonight?" JD asked.

"I don't know. Do you have more work to do?"

"There's always more work to do, but there isn't anything that can't wait until tomorrow."

"I'd kind of like to go outside and get some fresh air."

"Want to go for a walk? It's not dark yet."

"Are you bringing your gun?" Hadley asked.

"I usually carry it with me when I'm out of the house."

"Then I'd love to go on a walk with you."

JD loaded the last few dishes and started the dishwasher. "You ready?"

"Yeah. Let me grab my shoes." Hadley went upstairs and slipped on a pair of Keds. When she returned to the main level, JD was waiting by the door. He set the alarm and escorted her outside.

Hadley stopped on the front step and soaked everything in: A little girl giggling across the street while playing tag with her dad. The delicate scent of spring blooms hanging in the air. An older woman walking a golden retriever. To Hadley's surprise, the woman stopped at the end of the drive.

"Come on." JD put his hand on her back and nudged her forward before calling out to his neighbor. "Hey, Mrs. Henderson. You had quite the long walk today."

"Oh, I stopped in on Cynthia down the street and got to talking. You know how it is." Mrs. Henderson turned her attention to Hadley. "I don't think I've met your friend."

"This is Hadley. She's visiting for a few weeks."

"Oh, really? Where are you from, dear?"

Not sure she wanted to explain the reason for visiting from fifteen miles away, Hadley offered a different version of the truth. "I'm from Wyoming."

"You came quite a ways. Have you two been together long?"

Uncertain how to respond, Hadley looked at JD.

"Now, Mrs. Henderson, if I told you everything, you wouldn't have any fun trying to get the details from Noah," JD said.

Mrs. Henderson chuckled, and she once again spoke to Hadley. "Don't you listen to him. The way he talks, you'd think I spend all my time snooping about the neighborhood."

"When it comes to investigative skills, you put me and Noah to shame."

The dog tugged on his leash, apparently ready to move on. "It was nice to meet you, Hadley. I live in the blue house two doors down. You come by for a visit any time."

"Thank you, Mrs. Henderson."

As soon as the older woman continued down the street, JD guided Hadley in the other direction. "She means well, but it drives her crazy when she doesn't know what's going on."

"You realize she thinks we're dating," Hadley said as they started down the walk.

"I did take you to Noah's for dinner."

"That's true."

"What do you say we go for a second date tonight?"

Hadley's emotions somersaulted. She couldn't deny the growing respect she had for JD or the flare of attraction she'd experienced earlier, but only a week ago, she had been in a committed relationship to someone else. Even as her mind raced, Hadley managed to ask, "What did you have in mind?"

"Want to Netflix something?"

After another brief internal debate, Hadley nodded. "Yeah, I'd like that."

"Great." JD reached out and took her hand in his.

"The question is, What movie?" Hadley asked.

"I'll leave that up to you."

She smiled. "You really do like to live dangerously."

"Apparently so."

CHAPTER 20

KELSEY WAITED BEHIND THE SAME boulder she had used as cover hours earlier, once again dressed in traditional Arabic garb with a knife strapped to her thigh and a pistol hidden in the pocket of her robe.

The Saint Squad had spent all afternoon and evening taking turns watching the compound, analyzing the change of the guard, the movement of people in and out. So far, the only vehicles they had seen were those that had brought the new arrivals.

Two members of the squad had gone into the compound three hours earlier. According to Brent, they had successfully planted an explosive under the disabled vehicle in the event that an extra distraction was needed.

Now that she was closer to where the vehicles were parked, Kelsey hoped they could sneak in and out without incident, at least until they were ready to drive those trucks out of here with the hostages inside.

Jay and Quinn had counted fifteen guards so far. She hoped their numbers were accurate. The element of surprise was in their favor, but she and the Saint Squad were still outnumbered nearly two to one.

Kelsey adjusted the communications headset Brent had given her. "In position."

"Go." Brent's simple command spurred everyone into motion. Though Kelsey couldn't see the other squad members, she knew from the mission plan that Quinn maintained his position above the cave, where he could cover them with his sniper rifle.

"Follow me," Seth said quietly.

He emerged from the shadows to her left, his footsteps inaudible as he pressed against the cliffs to her right. Kelsey fell in behind him, using her jilbab to blend into the darkness.

Tristan's Texan drawl came over the headset. "One guard down."

"Make that two," Brent corrected. "Who has the third?"

"Got him," Jay answered. "External guards neutralized."

"Communications?" Brent asked.

"Disabled," came the reply. "We'll blow the charge on your signal."

"Hold for now," Brent ordered. "Let's see if we can get some of these hostages out of here first."

"Standing by."

"That's our cue," Seth said. He led Kelsey to the bottom of the drive. Using the trucks for cover, they continued forward until only open space existed between them and the door.

"Wait here," Seth whispered, his voice only audible through her earpiece, even though he was only a few feet away.

Kelsey nodded, squatting down beside the truck nearest the front door. Seth melted into the darkness, only a flicker of movement occasionally visible beneath the sliver of moonlight. Feeling vulnerable and exposed, Kelsey recalled her years of training to keep her breathing steady, her body still.

"Door is clear," Seth announced.

Recognizing her cue, Kelsey pushed aside her past nightmares and followed the path Seth had taken moments earlier. Another SEAL, Craig, approached from the opposite side, his weapon in hand.

Craig motioned her forward, placing Kelsey between him and Seth. As soon as they reached the entrance, Seth reached out and took her arm, guiding her to the spot behind him.

Using hand signals, Seth counted down from three. Kelsey half expected them to kick down the door when the countdown concluded, but they moved silently forward once more, this time with Craig taking the lead. The two SEALs entered first. Kelsey heard the displacement of air, then recognized it as tranquilizer darts being fired.

When she entered a moment later, two men lay on the ground unconscious while Craig zip-tied their hands together.

Realizing Seth was waiting for her to guide them to the hostages, she pointed to the dark hallway on the left. Using military hand signals, she indicated the possible danger of guards around the next corner.

Again, the SEALs took the lead, and again, Kelsey heard the firing of tranquilizer guns, only this time the victims didn't fall silently.

A shot rang out, the bullet impacting the ceiling. Someone called out from somewhere deep in the house, a shout echoing in the previously still night.

Kelsey urged the SEALs forward, rounding the corner behind them as they reached the heavy doors that separated the women and children in the compound from the men. At least, it had when she had lived here over a year ago.

Seth reached the door first. "It's locked."

Craig retrieved a tool from his vest.

Footsteps pounded against the tile floor and headed their way.

Kelsey was rounding the corner behind Seth when a voice called out. "Who's there?"

With half of her body shielded by the corner of the wall, Kelsey waved at Seth and Craig to remain hidden from view. If she could buy them some time, maybe they could break through the locked door so they could get to the children.

Adopting the meek posture she had used during her time living in Abolstan, she lowered her eyes. "It's Taja."

"What are you doing out of your room?"

Her memory flashed to a similar scene, one that preceded the bullet wound to her leg. Determination welled up inside of her, but again she spoke softly. "One of the little ones is sick. She needs water."

"Where is your guard?"

Kelsey reached her hand toward Seth, her hand flexing open and closed in an attempt to signal him. Relief flowed through her when the grip of his tranquilizer gun pressed into her hand.

"He's sleeping." Kelsey stepped out from behind the wall, aimed the gun at the newcomer, and squeezed the trigger.

Shock illuminated the man's face, and he slumped to the floor.

Kelsey thought they had averted discovery, but shouts sounded outside, and more footsteps pounded toward them.

Brent's voice came over their headsets. "Blow the satellite dish."

Kelsey didn't know which SEAL complied, but instantly, she heard the blast and felt the rumble of an explosion.

Craig straightened from where he had been working on the locked door and replaced the tool in his vest.

Seth pushed the door open. "Come on. We don't have much time."

Kelsey entered the women's quarters, her old room the first one on the left. She picked the lock and pushed open the door, her eyes widening. Inside the space, eleven children slept on mats, several huddled together for warmth.

Two of them stirred, and Kelsey squatted inside the doorway in case either of them opened their eyes. Neither did. She closed the door with a quiet click.

"I've got eight in here," Seth said, his voice low.

"There's nine in this room."

"How many rooms are there?" Seth asked.

"Seven."

Seth immediately spoke into his headset. "Brent, status on the hostages?" Seth asked.

"The doors are booby-trapped. We're still working on them."

Kelsey moved to the next room to find another ten children. One sat up, a terrified look on her face. "It's okay," Kelsey said in Arabic. "I'm here to help."

"Stay away," the little girl said in French.

Though she understood the child, Kelsey fumbled for the right words to respond. She needn't have bothered. Seth appeared beside her and replied for her. "We're here to help."

Craig worked down the other side of the hall, tallying a final count of hostages inside the house. "I've counted sixty-eight kids."

"We can't take all of them out together," Kelsey said. "There are too many."

His weapon now aimed at the door they had come through, Seth spoke into his headset. "Brent, we've got a problem."

"What kind of problem?" Brent asked.

"We have sixty-eight kids in here," Seth said. "There's no way we're getting all of them out of here unnoticed."

As though to punctuate his words, a shout sounded, followed by another. An instant later, a burst of gunfire pierced the night.

CHAPTER 21

THE GROUND SHOOK BENEATH HER, and Hadley's eyes flew open, her mind dazed from sleep, her heart racing.

An arm tightened around her shoulder. "Hey, it's okay."

Hadley turned her head to find JD's face close to hers. The ground shook again, the sound of artillery overshadowing the movie playing on the TV.

"It's just the Marines at Quantico." JD trailed his hand up and down her arm in a soothing motion. "They must be doing a night training exercise."

Hadley took a moment to get her bearings and tamper her rapid pulse. "Do they do this a lot?"

"Every couple months or so. I'm sorry it woke you."

"What time is it?" Hadley asked.

"About ten."

"I'm sorry. I didn't mean to fall asleep."

"It's fine. I'm sure you're exhausted after the week you've had."

"I could say the same thing about you." Hadley sat up and ran her fingers through her hair, pushing it behind her ears. She glanced at the television in time to see the final scene cut to the credits. "I guess I missed the end of the movie."

"You can always watch the rest of it tomorrow."

"What do you have planned for tomorrow? Another day at the office?"

"Noah and I need to follow up on a couple leads, but we're both planning to work from home as much as possible. Friday traffic is a nightmare, and we'll get a lot more done from here in Stafford."

"You're hoping to question the man in the hospital," Hadley said.

"Yeah. With any luck, the Coast Guard will have something on Rabell's yacht by tomorrow too."

"I don't know how you do it."

"Do what?"

"Figure out which of a dozen leads to follow."

"Since we struck out on finding Spencer's real identity, we don't have a lot of good leads left, at least not until some of the other agencies chime in with what they know."

"I didn't realize other agencies were involved."

"When it comes to fighting terrorism, it's all hands on deck."

* * *

Children stirred. Whimpers sounded. Kelsey homed in on the direction of the gunfire, the same direction where the rest of the hostages were being held.

"We've got live fire coming from the northeast corner," Tristan said, his normal Texan drawl erased by his clipped tone.

A single shot rang out, followed by Quinn's voice. "One down, but you've got three more behind the garden wall."

As the squad members outside continued to communicate, Kelsey asked, "How are we going to get them out of here?"

"Our best bet is to get them to the trucks and drive them out of here," Seth said. "We'll go room by room, starting with this one."

"Seth, once we get the kids loaded in there, we're going to need to get them out right away. No telling what a bunch of traumatized kids will do if we try to leave them there while we get the others," Craig said. "I think we should try for two rooms at a time."

Seth debated briefly before nodding. He spoke to the French girl, the other girls in her room now awake.

Though hesitant, the girl stood and joined Kelsey at the door. When a few didn't respond, Kelsey spoke in Arabic. "Come with us. We're going to take you home."

Two more stood. Noticing the blonde hair and fair skin of a girl in the corner, Kelsey repeated the words in English. This time she got the desired response from the remaining children.

"Craig, you lead the way. Taja, take the center, and I'll bring up the rear," Seth said. "As soon as we get outside, Taja, you need to get the kids into the truck while Craig hot wires it. Then we'll have you drive them out of here."

Kelsey nodded in agreement. They ushered the frightened children into the hall, cajoling and comforting them as they went. Two terrified little girls about nine years old grabbed Kelsey's hands, a third one following right behind her.

Craig took position by the door separating them from the rest of the house, his hand on the latch. He looked back at Seth, waiting.

Leaving the other five rooms secure, Seth gave Craig the signal to move. Craig's weapon came up immediately, the familiar swish of air sounding.

Kelsey bit the inside of her cheek to keep from gasping. If she showed fear, she would only make things worse for the kids.

Muttering soft words of encouragement, Kelsey moved forward, the children in front of her instinctively falling back and clustering around her.

When Kelsey entered the main living area, Craig was leaning over an unconscious man and securing his hands. He straightened and waved Kelsey and the children forward.

Kelsey made a beeline for the door, stopping when they reached the entrance. "We're going to get into the truck so I can take you out of here," Kelsey said, first in English and then in Arabic.

Seth took position behind her and spoke in French, repeating her words.

Something in the air stirred, and both Kelsey and Seth turned to see two more men rushing in from the opposite hallway.

"Look out!" Kelsey shouted, her hand reaching for her concealed pistol.

Seth already had his weapon aimed, the tranquilizer dart impacting the wall where one of the targets had been a moment before. Both new arrivals jumped back the way they had come and took cover in the hall.

"Get them out of here," Seth said, crouching behind a chair.

Kelsey hurried the girls forward, her weapon still in her right hand. Her eyes swept the area, relief pouring through her when she saw Damian standing at the back of the truck, waiting to help while Craig climbed into the driver's seat.

"He's a friend," Kelsey said, repeating the words in multiple languages. "He's here to help."

A gunshot sounded behind her, and Kelsey turned to see the two men at the hallway entrance trying to take aim at her.

Seth had abandoned his tranquilizer gun, his assault rifle now in his hand. He squeezed off a round to give her cover, several squeaks of alarm ringing into the night, along with a piercing scream.

"Shhh!" Kelsey scooped up the noisiest of the children with her free arm and hurried forward, boosting her into the back of the truck. Then she turned back to see three more who were still in between the house and the truck. Kelsey raced toward them, circling behind them as though herding frightened livestock. She glimpsed the back of the truck, where the children were trying to squeeze into the space that was far too small.

Another exchange of gunfire sparked in the darkness, but this time it was from near the garden. When Kelsey saw three more guards round the corner of the house, she spoke into her headset. "Three men heading toward us."

She took aim, hitting the first one in the leg. He stumbled and fell to the ground, his two companions taking cover behind the corner of the house.

Damian loaded the last three children into the cab with Craig.

Kelsey saw movement from the enemy and darted behind the pillar by the main entrance.

With only a brief debate, she said, "Craig, go. You need to get them out of here now."

Damian apparently came to the same conclusion Kelsey had. They didn't have time for Kelsey to traverse the twenty feet to the truck and trade places with Craig. "Go, Craig. I'll cover her."

The moment his teammate spoke, Craig put the truck in reverse. An instant later, he shifted into drive and gunned the engine, little girls crying out.

The truck sped away, and Kelsey watched them go. The first twenty were free, but how many more could they save before they had to retreat?

CHAPTER 22

RAPID GUNFIRE SPARKED AGAIN, THIS time coming from near the disabled truck. Damian turned and fired. "Take cover!"

Kelsey hurried back toward the entrance. "Seth, is it clear?"

A burst of gunfire sounded inside before Seth answered. "Clear."

She darted inside, immediately ducking beside him.

"Let's go." Seth motioned her forward. "Damian, you'll need to hotwire the next truck for us."

"I'm a little busy," Damian responded. "Quinn, can you get a shot at this guy? He's got me pinned down."

"Negative. Jay?"

A single shot rang out. When Damian uttered his thanks, Kelsey guessed Jay had taken care of the problem.

"What's our body count?" Brent asked.

"I have five inside, all neutralized," Seth said.

The other members reported in, the number adding up to sixteen.

"That's more than we thought," Kelsey said. Another exchange of gunfire sounded. "And they're still shooting."

Quinn's voice broke into the conversation. "Damian, you've got five more heading your way."

"Need a little help," Damian said.

"Take shelter inside with Seth," Brent ordered. "Signal when you're clear."

"Roger."

More gunfire. Fifteen seconds later, Damian burst through the door. "Clear."

"Blow the truck," Brent ordered.

The blast was immediate. Through the window, Kelsey could see flames spearing into the dark sky. Deep in the house, children cried. Outside, men shouted. Women screamed.

A second blast rocked the ground, followed by a third. More flames burst from the driveway.

Quinn confirmed Kelsey's fears when his voice came over her headset. "We lost the other two vehicles."

"Now what?" Damian asked.

"Kelsey, are there any hidden tunnels or other ways out of here?" Brent asked.

"No, at least, not that I know of."

"Then we don't have a choice," Brent responded. "The only way we're getting everyone out of here safely is if we neutralize Rabell's men."

"Where do we start?"

"Quinn, take out whoever is in your scope," Brent said. "Seth and Damian, clear the house. Tristan and Jay, help me secure the perimeter."

"Do you want me to bring the truck back down?" Craig asked as soon as Brent finished giving assignments. "I have the children secure with Patrick."

"Negative. With so many of them, I want you to keep an eye out up there in case anyone gets past us. And make sure they don't get any reinforcements."

"I'll put the truck across the road to make sure no one shows up unexpectedly," Craig said.

The SEALs fell silent, and Kelsey watched Seth straighten and cross to the door. He pressed himself against the wall to one side and peeked out with his weapon in the ready position. After confirming that none of Rabell's men was heading their way, he closed the door.

"What do you want me to do?" Kelsey asked.

"Come with us. We'll clear the women's hallway first." Seth led the way, and this time, Damian remained in the common area to protect them against any unexpected visitors.

Kelsey followed Seth, and they reached their destination without incident.

"Don't unlock the kids yet," Seth said. "We can't take the chance that they'll try to run out into the conflict."

Kelsey tried to visualize the task the man in front of her was about to undertake. Though she had given the SEALs a basic layout of the complex, she repeated the most critical information over the cries coming from the occupied bedrooms. "Don't forget about the hidden security room across from the kitchen."

"We won't." Seth pointed at the doorway. "Don't let anyone through."

Kelsey watched him disappear before turning her attention to the children who remained captive until safety could be assured. "It's okay," she called to them, repeating the words over and over in every language she could manage.

Another burst of gunfire rang out, and Kelsey prayed her words were true.

* * *

JD stared at the dark-haired man in the hospital bed—the man who had tried to kill him and Hadley. He forced himself to look past the pale face and bandages. "Who were you after? Who was the bomb meant for?"

Keith turned his head to avoid JD's gaze, choosing to stare at the wall instead.

"You help us, we can help you," Noah said, stepping into the man's line of sight.

Again, Keith turned his head, this time fixating on the blank television screen.

"Was Rabell with you on the yacht?" JD asked.

The flash of awareness was brief but unmistakable.

JD pressed on. "Did Rabell come with you? Or did he send you and your friends to do the job alone?"

Nothing.

JD and Noah continued to ask questions, but even after another half hour, the man refused to speak or so much as look at them.

When they finally left the hospital room, Noah lowered his voice. "I don't see him giving us anything."

"Me neither," JD said. "We don't even know the guy's real name."

"I'm going back to the office to do some more digging," Noah said as JD and Noah headed for the elevator.

"Any word from Kelsey yet?"

"No."

"Anything you can tell me?"

"Not really, but if you decide to discover religion, prayers are appreciated."

"I may not go to church as much as you do, but I've got the praying thing down," JD said. "You can count me in."

"Thanks. I have a feeling Kelsey can use all the prayers she can get right now."

* * *

"Perimeter secure," Tristan drawled, his easy cadence giving Kelsey more comfort than the words themselves.

"House is clear," Seth added. Three knocks sounded at the door separating the women's wing from the rest of the house. "Kelsey, it's me. Don't shoot."

The door opened slowly, and relief flowed through Kelsey when Seth's six-and-a-half-foot frame filled the doorway.

"Craig, can you bring the truck back down here to help us transport? Or do you need to stay with the kids?"

A pause ensued before Craig said, "Patrick said he and Mahira can handle the kids for now. I'll be right down."

"How many hostages do you have out there?" Seth asked.

"Forty-three. Six aren't going to be able to walk out of here."

Kelsey closed her eyes against the horrors these women must have endured.

"Jay, turn off the jammer so we can check in," Brent said.

Seth pulled his comm gear from his vest. As soon as Jay confirmed that he had completed his task, Seth changed frequencies.

"This is Scorpion Seven. Location and hostages secure. Request status on the area."

Kelsey couldn't make out what the person on the other end said; the voice was too muffled.

"One hundred eleven."

This time, Kelsey heard the response clearly. "What? Confirm. Did you say one hundred eleven?"

"Affirmative." Again, Seth said, "Request status of surrounding area."

Silence stretched for the next minute while Seth listened to the report. When he signed off, he switched frequencies to communicate with the rest of his squad. "We're clear for now, but intel is seeing military movement to the north that could interfere with a land exit."

"I'm heading your way," Brent said.

"Should we let the kids out of their rooms and check them for injury?" Kelsey asked.

"Not yet. We need to make a plan before we deal with the chaos of transporting ninety more hostages out of here."

Kelsey did the mental math. There were too many of them. With the three SUVs and the truck they had commandeered, it would still take at least three trips to drive everyone out of Abolstan. And the border was two hours away, assuming they didn't run into any trouble. Military movement could definitely cause trouble.

Brent joined them in the wide hallway of the women's wing. Brent and Seth both adjusted their mouthpieces so their conversation wouldn't be transmitted. Kelsey followed suit.

"How do we get all of these people out of here?" Kelsey asked.

"This is a new problem for us," Brent admitted. "I've never even heard of so many being held in one place."

Kelsey tried to let logic override her emotions. "They must be using this compound as a warehouse."

"And we got lucky to be here on a day a shipment came in," Brent said.

"Back to Taja's question: How do we get everyone out of here?" Seth asked.

"Signal our ride to push off another night."

She couldn't be hearing Brent right. "But you could have the helicopter take some of these girls to safety."

"Doing so would risk giving away our location." As though a solution clicked into place, Brent adjusted his mouthpiece and spoke to his squad through his headset. "Jay and Damian, move the wounded women into the truck." He put his hand over the mouthpiece and asked Seth, "How many kids did you get out of here already?"

"Twenty-one, if you include Mahira."

Brent pondered for a moment. "It'll be tight, but I think we can fit them into the three SUVs we have near the cave."

Tristan approached. "We're moving the wounded women into the truck, but who else do you want us to take?"

"See if any of the women out there have any medical training. It would be helpful if we could let one of the hostages help care for the wounded since we're shorthanded."

"We already found two," Tristan said. "They were already treating the injured women who were locked up with them. Apparently, they're both nursing students from Baltimore."

"Get them settled in the truck with the wounded." Brent spoke into his headset again. "Jay, how many more do you have room for?"

"Kids or adults?"

"Two more adults, the rest kids."

"With the wounded in here, probably only another ten, if they're small."

"Stand by."

"Which room has the youngest kids in it?" Brent asked Kelsey.

She pointed across the hall. "That one."

"How many?"

"Eleven."

"Then we'll take everyone in there," Brent said. "I want to get as many out of here now as possible, the younger the better."

Seth unlatched the door, opening it to reveal eleven girls who appeared to range from seven to ten years old. "We're here to take you home," he said in Arabic and then French and English.

The sight of a man his size didn't give the children the comfort he'd intended. They cowered back against the wall, unwilling or unable to move.

"It's okay," Kelsey said gently. "We're here to help."

Hearing a woman's voice did the trick. As she had before, Kelsey repeated her words in English and Arabic. "We're here to take you home."

Pleas and whimpers sounded from the nearby rooms, and Kelsey's chest constricted at the thought that the other children would have to wait to leave. A few more minutes, she assured herself. In a few more minutes, they could return and unlock their doors.

Kelsey motioned for the kids in the current room to follow her. When three of the girls headed for the door still clinging to their blankets, she said to the rest of the children, "Bring your blankets. It's cold outside."

She scooped up several more blankets as she passed an empty room and carried them with her, Seth leading the way. Brent took up the rear, the children clustering around Kelsey.

Kelsey, Seth, and Brent took them outside to the truck, fear illuminating the children's eyes. "These men are friends. They're going to take you someplace safe."

Kelsey lifted one of the children into the back, glimpsing for the first time the women already sitting inside. One of them lay unconscious, her head partially covered by a bandage. Another woman sat with both arms holding her leg steady, a blood-stained cloth wrapped around her calf.

A blonde woman around twenty years old moved toward the children. Her own face was bruised from where someone's hand had made contact with her cheek, her Baltimore T-shirt ripped at the bottom. "I can help."

"Here." Kelsey handed her the armful of blankets. "You can decide who needs these."

Kelsey helped one of the smaller girls into the back, several others climbing in on their own. While Seth and Kelsey helped the rest inside, Brent spoke through his headset. "Quinn, you and Patrick load the kids up there into the SUVs. You, Craig, Damian, and Patrick are going to drive these kids out of here."

"Then what?" Quinn asked.

"We'll radio ahead and have someone meet you at the border. As soon as you drop off these hostages, double back and come pick up the next load."

"Roger."

Seth made sure everyone was safely inside before he closed the back of the truck to secure the passengers inside. "You realize it's going to take us three trips to get everyone out of here, right?"

"And that's assuming the military doesn't make a move that will block us off," Tristan added.

"I know, but that's the best option we've got at the moment." Brent banged on the back of the truck to signal to Craig that it was safe to move. The engine roared to life, and Damian climbed onto the running board to hitch a ride to where the other vehicles were parked. The truck pulled away.

"What do you want the rest of us to do?" Kelsey asked.

"We need to move the rest of the hostages inside so they have better shelter. Some look like they could use some food and fresh water too," Brent said.

"And after that?" Tristan asked.

"We hold our position and wait for them to come back to get us."

CHAPTER 23

AFTER CHECKING ON THE CHILDREN and assuring them that they were safe, Kelsey relented to Brent's insistence that the kids be locked into the women's wing to ensure none of the children went running off. At least they no longer had to stay in their rooms.

On a new mission to provide sustenance, Kelsey led the way into the kitchen, Seth following behind her. She opened the pantry, relieved to find it reasonably well stocked, and pulled out a bag of flour.

"What can I do to help?" Seth asked.

"Grab the rice for me. That's something we can feed a lot of people with." Kelsey opened a lower cabinet and retrieved a large rice pot. After she set it on the counter, she opened the drawer on her left and pulled out a measuring cup.

"Here you go." Seth set the rice next to her.

"Thanks." She measured the rice and water, opening the spice cabinet to retrieve the salt. She used the palm of her hand to measure the salt, tossed some in, and turned on the cooker. "How many people do we still have here?"

"Besides the five of us, nine prisoners, and seventy-one freed hostages."

"I don't know how they were managing to feed so many people."

"I don't think they were," Seth said. "At least, I doubt they were giving them more than minimal food once or twice a day."

He opened the refrigerator and pulled out a paper-wrapped package of meat. "I think I found what the guards were planning to eat for dinner tonight."

"Might as well cook it up." Kelsey started lining ingredients on the counter, along with a large mixing bowl.

"You weren't kidding about knowing this house."

"I lived here for two years. It looks like the new residents didn't change anything in here."

Female voices sounded in the living room.

"I saw a box of figs in the pantry. Do you want to give those to the women?"

"We'd better wait until we have enough food to go around. Undernourished people can turn violent if we don't handle this right," Seth said.

"Maybe you should slice the meat and grill it. It will cook faster and be easier to hand out."

"I don't want any of us to expose ourselves outside."

"You won't have to. The grill is in the inner courtyard. Nassar had the same concern."

"In that case, cutting board?" Seth asked.

Kelsey pointed.

They worked for several minutes in silence, Kelsey starting a second pot of rice and preparing the dough for fry bread.

The memories of the day's events surfaced in her mind: the many times people had tried to shoot the Saint Squad and failed, the successful extraction of the first hostages, her own moment facing a gun. "Does your squad always have so many miracles happen as we did today?"

"What do you mean?" Seth asked.

"Had we come one day earlier, forty-three of these people would still be captive. A day later, and some of them might have already been shipped out to wherever they were destined to go."

"The Lord was certainly watching over us today," Seth said. "It didn't hurt that you asked for a blessing or that we prayed before we set out."

"I've been meaning to ask you about that blessing. How did you know?" Kelsey asked.

"Know what?"

"About my name."

"Let's just say you aren't the first deep-cover operative I've worked with."

Brent walked into the kitchen. "How's it going in here?"

"I was getting ready to grill some meat," Seth said.

"The first batch of fry bread and rice will be ready in ten or fifteen minutes," Kelsey added. "If we cut the bread into strips, everyone can have at least a piece while they wait for me to make more."

"I'll give them some water."

Kelsey retrieved two pitchers from a high shelf and handed them to Brent. "I saw some paper cups in the pantry, but there aren't enough for everyone. They'll have to share."

Seth picked up the platter of sliced meat. "Brent, do you want to grill or call into intel for an update?"

"I'll make the call."

* * *

JD followed Noah into their office, debating how many hours he should try to put in before heading home. Even though Hadley assured him she would be fine on her own, he wanted to be there for her. And as much as he didn't want to admit it, he had enjoyed their time together last night and was hoping for a repeat performance. Whether it was a movie, a walk, or sharing a meal, he enjoyed being with her. How odd to think that he had come to look forward to her company after such a short time.

They reached their desks as Mitch approached from the other direction.

"Hey, Mitch. What's up?" Noah asked.

Mitch held up a file. "We got some of the forensics back from the lab."

"And?" JD asked.

"You're going to love this." Mitch handed him the file. "The lab ran fingerprints on the diamonds you found in Andrews's apartment, and they got some hits."

"Whose prints were on them?"

"Our fake Spencer Andrews's, along with Rabell's and one of our dead guys'."

"Then Spencer was working with Rabell," JD said.

"Working with or stealing from. Either way, they both handled those diamonds," Mitch said. "They also found a partial they were able to trace to Salman Nassar."

"How is that possible?" Noah asked. "I thought these diamonds were the ones stolen from the Afghani government?"

"Rabell might have been responsible for that, but it looks like these were in his possession before then," Mitch said.

"If they aren't the stolen diamonds, maybe Rabell received them in payment for some business dealings with Nassar."

"Possibly," Noah said, "but I think it's more likely that he took over whatever was left of Nassar's business after Nassar was arrested."

"It's very possible," JD agreed, suspecting Noah had some inside knowledge of the subject.

"From what I've read in the reports on Nassar, diamonds were a common form of currency for him," Noah said.

JD held up the forensics report to Mitch. "Was there anything else of significance in here?"

"Mostly a lot of dotting I's and crossing T's," Mitch said. "The handgun you bagged in Andrews's apartment was registered to a ninety-two-year-old man who claims he hasn't seen it in years, but the weapon was wiped clean, so we have no idea who might have handled it since it was last in the guy's possession."

"We think someone had already searched the apartment before we got there," Noah said.

"Were there any new prints in the apartment?" JD asked, knowing a full forensics team had gone in after the altercation with Keith.

"A few belonging to Andrews were found on some household items, dishes, silverware, that sort of thing."

"But no one else."

"No. Even the engagement ring didn't have prints on it."

"That's odd," JD said. "Why would someone wipe down a ring?"

"Maybe whoever was there before us handled it to see if the stone was one of the missing diamonds."

"Maybe."

"The rest of the report is in there, but so far, all we have is a whole lot of nothing," Mitch said. "Any luck with our John Doe at the hospital?"

"He's not talking," Noah said.

"What about chatter from the CIA side of the house?" Mitch asked. "They obviously had some kind of source to tip us off about the bomb."

"I think that was a one-timer," Noah said. "But I'm keeping my fingers crossed they find a new source soon."

JD heard the way Noah's voice tightened. He put his hand on his coworker's shoulder. "I think we all share that sentiment."

CHAPTER 24

SETH HADN'T BEEN EXAGGERATING WHEN he'd said Rabell's men hadn't been feeding their captives. Kelsey worked in the kitchen for nearly three hours, several of the women helping her cook and serve.

The SEALs had assigned each of the children to one of the adults present, a buddy system of sorts. After serving the first bit of food, the Saint Squad had left Kelsey in charge of the interior of the house and all of the occupants while the remaining four SEALs patrolled the perimeter and searched the house for any information that might be useful.

Though Kelsey itched to interview the women to gain human intelligence, she knew she wouldn't get far until everyone's basic needs were met.

Mariana, a woman from Romania, entered carrying an empty platter.

"How much more food do you think we need out there?" Kelsey asked.

"I think everyone is fine for now."

A petite woman with long, brown hair followed Mariana into the kitchen, her eyes dropping to the floor before she lifted her gaze. "Can I help?" she asked in English.

"You're American?"

"Yeah. I'm Robyn Clark from Maryland."

"How did you end up here?"

"I was on a cruise. I went into town when we docked. I stopped for dinner and woke up in the back of a truck."

"How terrifying. How long have you been here?"

"I'm not sure. Maybe two weeks," she said. "Can you really get us out of here before they come back?"

"Before who comes back?"

"The traders." Apparently sensing Kelsey's confusion, she said, "The men who buy and sell women and children."

"Are they different people from the ones who were already here?" Kelsey asked. "There were three trucks that came in yesterday."

"Those were delivery trucks," Mariana said, joining the conversation in her heavily accented English. "The traders always come the morning after new women arrive. They come in smaller vans. They take people away, a few at a time."

"How many vans usually come?" Kelsey asked, alarmed.

"A lot. Probably five or ten."

"Any idea how many guards they bring with them?"

"A couple trucks full."

"What?"

"They look like they're in military uniforms, but that doesn't make sense," Robyn said. "What government would openly engage in human trafficking?"

Two and two slowly equaled four. The unexplained build-up by the Abolstani government and the CIA's inability to trace the funding.

Seth poked his head through the door. "Taja, Brent wants to talk to you."

"I'll be right there." Kelsey turned to Mariana and Robyn. "Gather whatever food we can carry. We'll want to take what we can with us on our journey."

Not waiting for a response, she joined Seth in the hallway.

Seth kept his voice low. "The others should be heading back to pick up the next group in less than an hour."

"Where's Brent?" Kelsey asked.

"In there." Seth waved toward the room next to the kitchen that had once served as Nassar's office.

"Let's talk in private." Kelsey led the way inside, Seth closing the door behind him.

Brent didn't mince words. "We may have a problem. Intel detected military movement in the area. They could pass by us, but we need to be ready to hold up here for longer if we can't safely transport everyone out of here."

"By any chance, is this military movement a couple of troop carriers accompanying a bunch of smaller vehicles?"

Brent's eyebrows drew together. "Two military transports and eight vans."

"How did you know that?" Seth asked.

"Two of the women were telling me about the traders who come after every shipment. They described them as a bunch of vans with a military escort."

"This is their intended destination," Brent said. "Seth, what's the convoy's ETA?"

"An hour and fifteen minutes."

"And our guys?"

"They're getting ready to head this way, but they'll have to take an alternate route to avoid the convoy," Seth said. "Best guess is it'll take them at least three or four hours."

"Seth, let our guys know they've got to get their hands on a couple more trucks. We need to get everyone out of here in one trip," Brent said. "For now, we've got to get these women to a safe rendezvous spot before the military gets here."

"The cave?" Kelsey asked.

"It's big enough, but the tracks would lead them right to us," Brent said.

"Taja, you know the area. Where else can we hide them? It needs to be somewhere we can get trucks in."

"If we want to avoid leaving tracks, we want to take the trail to the south. After the first quarter mile, the whole path is rock."

"Is there shelter?"

"It's a good two or three miles, but there's a cluster of caves along there," Kelsey said. "Beyond that, it would be another mile and a half to hike everyone to where a vehicle can pass."

"Seth, have everyone top off their supplies. Taja, pass out whatever food we can carry with us," Brent said. "You're leading the way."

Seth relayed Brent's order through his comm set. Brent loaded the two laptops on the desk into a collapsible duffel bag.

"We should take fingerprints of the men we encountered here."

"Jay already scanned them." Brent activated his comm unit before he spoke again. "Seth, take point. Tristan and Jay, have the women circle the house before we start up the trail. We need to have footprints going in every direction."

"Got it," Tristan replied.

"Let's move out."

Trying to adjust to the speed in which the Saint Squad changed their plans, Kelsey left the office and stopped in the kitchen, where five women were now loading food into canvas shopping bags.

Kelsey spoke to the two women closest to her. "Go pass food out to anyone who is willing to carry it. Make sure they know we'll need to ration it."

"What can we do?" one of the other women asked.

"Fill containers with water." Kelsey pointed to the cabinet above the refrigerator.

Mariana opened it, handing two water bottles to Robyn, who started filling them. Four more water bottles and three water bags were all they had time to fill before Brent's voice sounded in Kelsey's earpiece.

"Taja, it's time."

She grabbed the remaining stack of canvas bags, five in all, and opened the refrigerator. She loaded the four cartons of juice into the bags, along with the grapes someone had left in the crisper drawer.

Balancing the bags on either shoulder, Kelsey motioned to the women. "Let's go."

"Go? Now?" Mariana asked.

Kelsey sensed her confusion and fear. Certain she would want to understand the situation if their positions were reversed, Kelsey said, "The traders are coming. We're taking you somewhere else until our trucks return."

The chatter on the comm units continued. "Jay, get a count for me. Make sure we have everyone."

"Roger."

"Do any of you have a buddy?" Kelsey asked.

"I do." Robyn pointed at the eleven-year-old standing nearby.

"Bring her with you. Let's go." Kelsey ushered them out the rear exit and moved through the darkness to the path at the edge of the mountain. She did a quick head count. "I have six with me."

Seth approached, leading a group of women and children. He spoke to the women with Kelsey. "Distribute the water to the others so no one is carrying too much."

Kelsey helped them divide the remaining supplies, her heart going out to these women who already looked exhausted. A little girl took one of the water bottles, eager to help.

"Stay ten yards behind me," Seth told Kelsey.

Kelsey nodded and glanced at her watch. Another fifty-nine minutes and the convoy would arrive. She stared at the steep path in front of her, the morning glow already visible over the horizon. Could they get everyone out of sight before the traders arrived? And if so, would they be able to stay in front of them long enough to get these women and children to safety?

* * *

JD tried several times to leave the office, but to no avail. The universe was conspiring against his plan to work half the day at home, where he would be close to Hadley.

A meeting with his boss, several phone calls from the police and fellow agents, and a stream of forensics and autopsy reports kept him tethered to the office. Unfortunately, despite the constant flow of information crossing his desk, nothing was shedding any new light on the bombers or their targets.

JD's most recent attempt to leave had been thwarted when Noah had enlisted his help in going over the suspect list. If Hadley had indeed met all of the men involved with the bombing, there were two more out there besides the intruder at Spencer's apartment who got away and Rabell. The thought that perhaps Hadley had come into contact with the leader of the group popped into his mind. Was it possible she knew the man behind it all without realizing it?

Turning to his computer, he pulled up the handful of images the FBI and CIA had managed to gather on Rabell. The man was known for being elusive. The only photos they had of him had resulted from some surveillance video the bureau had managed to capture of him when he'd been in Boston six months ago. The photos were grainy, none of them giving a clear view of his face. The most useful image thus far was an artist's sketch that had come from one of the CIA's undercover operatives. Since the intel on Rabell had stopped around the same time Kelsey had come back to the United States, JD had his suspicions that Kelsey was the unnamed operative, the only American intelligence agent known to have seen him in person.

JD attached the files to an email and sent them to himself so he could show them to Hadley when he got home. He stood only to have the phone ring once more. Letting out a sigh, he lifted the receiver. "Byers."

"Agent Byers, it's Officer Crandall from the Prince William Police Department. I wanted to let you know we finished processing the evidence from the break-in at Hadley Baker's apartment."

"Anything new to report?"

"No, sir, but I wanted to let you know the pendant you wanted me to run prints on is ready to be picked up at the station whenever it is convenient for Miss Baker."

"I'll swing by and pick it up on my way home this afternoon."

"I'll email you the crime-scene photos as well."

"Thank you." JD hung up, collected his weapon from the locked drawer in his desk, and headed for the door before anyone else could stop him.

He made it to his car, anticipation humming through him at seeing Hadley, but the thought that he would be arriving home with a piece of jewelry given to her by another man dampened his spirits. Today just wasn't his day.

CHAPTER 25

KELSEY TRUDGED UP THE PATH, her legs burning. She had mapped this area before going undercover in Nassar's home, but she had only walked the trail herself once when she had taken her students on a hike.

A scar along her left shoulder blade was the reminder Nassar had given her for leaving the compound without his permission. At least that lesson had been taught with a whip rather than a bullet.

Kelsey glanced behind her, the light now peeking out over the horizon enough that she could see the steady trail of weary travelers struggling up the hill behind her.

They had been walking for the past forty-five minutes, the early-morning quiet broken only by the sound of footsteps and an occasional hushed voice. The compound had disappeared from view fifteen minutes earlier, but Kelsey knew from experience that it wouldn't take long for trained men to catch up to their ragtag group.

A woman stumbled on a rock, barely catching herself before falling.

"Seth, they need to rest."

"Another few hundred yards," Seth said. "We would be wise to be still when the military arrives."

"How far until we reach the first caves?" Brent asked through the headset.

"I'm not sure. Maybe a half mile," Kelsey said.

"Then we need to keep pushing," Brent said. "Once the sun is up, we won't be able to move without exhausting our supply of water."

Kelsey knew Brent was right, but she didn't have to like it. No one had managed much sleep last night, and nearly half the women were malnourished.

Reminding herself of the alternative of what these women would have faced today had the Saint Squad not arrived, Kelsey kept moving.

They reached a small valley, the path evening out for the next few hundred yards. To the left, a narrow path rose farther into the hills. Seth started down the easy path before backtracking several steps.

"Taja, which way?"

"That way leads back toward the city," Kelsey said, pointing at the easy trail. "There are a handful of caves a few hundred yards to the left."

"And that one?" Seth asked.

"More caves, but it goes away from the city. Both paths circle to where the rest of the squad can bring trucks in."

"We'd be best to avoid the city. Have you been up that path?" Seth asked, pointing to the steeper route.

"Yeah. It's rough for about a hundred yards, but we would reach the caves sooner."

"Then we'll go this way." Seth pressed forward, putting his hand on a rock to help maintain his balance as he climbed a particularly steep part.

Kelsey followed suit, stopping to make sure the others were following. When she saw Mariana struggling forward, Kelsey reached out and offered a hand, helping pull her up. She repeated the process with the next ten women and children until Brent hiked up.

"I'll help them. You catch up with the others."

"Okay." Kelsey continued upward, following the women she had assisted. When she reached the top of a rise, only two women and Seth were visible. "Where is everyone?"

"We found our resting spot." Seth motioned to a wide cave opening across from him and then to a narrow crack in the rock face barely big enough for her to fit through. "And our water."

Kelsey joined him, looking through the narrow opening into the deep cave. Seth had given them a glow stick, because she could see the faint illumination and hear the trickle of water.

Mariana emerged from the cave, holding one of the water bottles. "I refilled our water."

"Good." Kelsey motioned to the other cave. "Go ahead and rest over there for now."

"Okay." Mariana led the way, a few others following her lead.

Seth reported his find to the other members of his squad. Brent arrived a moment later and did his own analysis.

"I say we stay here for the day and have our guys meet us tonight. Much safer than trying to travel in the middle of the day," Brent said.

"My thoughts exactly," Seth said. "Jay and I can scout the rest of the trail and pick a rendezvous spot."

"Get some rest first," Brent said. "Taja, how much farther do you think it is to the nearest road?"

"I think we're about halfway there, but we'll be going downhill for most of it."

"Seth, radio Craig and tell him we'll meet him three hours after sunset," Brent said.

"Will do."

* * *

Hadley paced the length of the kitchen and living room, stopping by the french doors leading onto the deck. Through the glass, she could appreciate the fading blossoms on the dogwood in the backyard and the full foliage of the ornamental pear tree, but at the moment, she stared without seeing.

Despite the peaceful setting and the security she had found while staying with JD, today her mind had been plagued with memories of last weekend and the days and months leading up to her final date with Spencer.

The questions that had annoyed her when JD had first asked them had replayed over and over today, a new clarity emerging with each passing minute.

A car approached, and the garage door rumbled open. When JD walked inside, Hadley was waiting for him.

"I've been thinking about all the questions you asked me," Hadley said.

JD ran a hand through his hair. "I'm sorry you felt like I was hounding you. I was just doing my job."

Recognizing the weariness in his voice, Hadley reached out and put her hand on his arm. "I know you were, but I think I was giving you the wrong answers."

"What do you mean?"

"Remember when you asked if I normally went to business dinners with Spencer?"

"Yes."

"Saturday night was the only time I went with him when it was planned," Hadley said.

"What about the other business dinner you mentioned?"

"Spencer took me out to eat, and we ran into three guys he worked with," Hadley said. "They saw us together, and I think Spencer was trapped into introducing me. The man, Wyatt, insisted we join them so they could get to know me better."

"So it's possible the men with you on Saturday night wanted you along to keep Spencer in line," JD said, summing up Hadley's suspicions.

"I keep wondering if that's what happened, but it seems so farfetched."

"Not if Spencer went to such great lengths to keep his professional and private lives separate," JD countered. "He might have known the men he worked with would use you against him."

"But I don't understand why," Hadley said. "Why would it make a difference if those men knew me? It's not like any of them told me what they were planning."

"No, but if Spencer was having second thoughts on whatever his involvement was, they could have used you as a pawn to make sure he didn't back out or tell anyone what they were up to."

"I guess that makes sense." Hadley slid onto the stool beside the kitchen counter. "I still can't wrap my mind around the idea that Spencer would be involved with trying to kill people."

JD didn't respond, as though debating what to say.

"What?" Hadley asked.

"We got the forensics report back today. The diamonds we found in Spencer's apartment had both Spencer's fingerprints and the man's we believe to be in charge of the terrorist group behind the bombing."

"Every time you tell me more about evidence against him, I wonder how I could be so stupid to have not seen any signs of who he really was."

"When you look for the best in people, it's hard to see the secrets they keep."

"I guess."

"By the way, I stopped at the police station on the way home." JD pulled a plastic bag from his pocket. "They were finished with this, so I thought you would want it back."

Hadley looked down at the heart necklace Spencer had given her for Valentine's Day. "I don't even know if I want to keep anything he gave me now that I know what he was involved in."

"Keep the necklace and the good memories." JD opened the evidence bag and drew out the chain, offering it to her. "Let everything else sort itself out."

"That may be easier said than done."

"Give it time." JD pressed the necklace into her hand, his fingers lingering on her palm.

Hadley curled her fingers around the piece of jewelry, surprised by the shiver JD's touch caused. "I think for now, I'll put it away. Maybe when all this is behind me and I find a new place to live, I'll be ready to face the memories."

"You're planning to move?"

Hadley nodded. "I was thinking about it today. There's no reason to stay where I am. I had already started looking a bit before Spencer . . . before last weekend."

JD tugged at his tie. "Sounds like we both need to do some house hunting."

"It could be our next date."

The weariness in JD's expression faded. "I'd like that."

* * *

Kelsey stood at the edge of the large cave and rubbed at the spot where a knot had formed along her right shoulder blade from carrying grocery bags for the past two-and-a-half miles. Those grocery bags were nearly empty now. The juice had been consumed along the way, only the trash remaining, and the hostages had eaten the rest of the food when they had settled into the cave.

Knowing there was little food to go around, Kelsey had opted to eat a piece of the protein bar she had brought with her.

Seth approached from the path they had traversed two hours earlier.

Kelsey waited for him to join her in the shade. "Any sign of pursuit?"

Before he could answer, a rumble sounded above them. Seth grabbed her arm and tugged her deeper into the cave, speaking into his headset at the same time. "Take cover. Choppers inbound."

Several of the women in hearing distance sat up, and Kelsey turned to face them, lifting a finger to her lips to signal them to remain quiet.

"Do you think they're equipped with heat sensors?" she asked, lowering her voice.

"Probably, but the rock should mask our presence."

Kelsey sent up a silent prayer that Seth's assumption was correct. "Was there anyone on the path behind us?"

"Negative. It looks like they gave up when they reached the spot where the path split off," Seth said, his weapon in his hands despite his words.

"Which is why we have helicopters circling overhead," Kelsey concluded.

"They're impatient," Seth agreed. "They don't want to waste time marching troops in when they might not ever find us. It's easier to send up a spotter first to narrow down the search area."

The helicopter grew closer, the sound blasting into the cave and echoing from deep inside. A few of the children whimpered; women gasped.

Seth tugged on her arm, leading her even deeper into the cave.

The helicopter seemed to take position right above them but finally moved on to hover a short distance away.

Seth motioned for her to sit, waiting until she did so before he settled beside her, his weapon lying across his lap. Minutes dragged out, stretching into an hour before the helicopter finally passed overhead again. This time it didn't slow as it made its way back the way it had come.

"Now what?" Kelsey asked. "If the helicopter comes back when we try to move everyone out, they could intercept us or our transportation."

"We have at least another ten hours before sunset," Seth said. "Plenty of time to get organized."

"I wish I had your confidence."

"You're welcome to borrow some of mine."

"You know, I think I had this exact same conversation with Quinn."

"Now, that's a scary thought." Seth scratched behind his ear. "I must be hanging around him too much."

"It could be the other way around," Kelsey suggested. "Maybe you're a good influence on him."

"Now, that's taking positive energy to a whole new level," Seth said. "But I like it."

CHAPTER 26

"What about this one?" Hadley pointed at JD's laptop screen. "It looks like a great neighborhood."

JD studied the traditional colonial with the blue shutters. "That's a pretty big yard."

"Most people like to have their space," Hadley said. "Unless you want to reconsider and look at townhouses."

"No." JD shook his head. "No more sharing walls with people."

"I don't blame you on that," Hadley said. "I am so tired of apartment living."

"What made you decide to move?"

"Besides not feeling safe there anymore, the neighborhood isn't the greatest. I had started looking into places here in Stafford or even as far as Fredericksburg."

The thought that such a move would have put more distance between her and Spencer popped into his head, but JD didn't have the heart to bring up any reminders of Hadley's former boyfriend a second time tonight. Instead, he asked, "Would you switch schools?"

"I've thought about it, but I really love my kids."

"The school year is almost over," JD pointed out.

"I know, but I feel like I can make a real difference where I'm at," Hadley said. "Most of these kids come from pretty bad situations. They don't always know where their next meal is coming from or even if their mom or dad will remember they exist, much less go grocery shopping."

"Addicts?"

"A lot of them. Some have wonderful parents, but they're often single moms trying to make ends meet."

"That's tough."

"I know. That's why in spite of everything, I really want to go to work tomorrow."

"We haven't seen any indication of someone tracking you since you came down here," JD said. "Maybe whoever broke into your place realized you don't have what they want."

"Maybe. I still can't figure out why they stole my computer though. It's not like it's new or anything."

"I haven't been able to figure that one out either," JD said.

"If you would catch these guys, you could ask them their reasons."

"Yeah, I'll get right on that."

Hadley's lips twitched into the beginnings of a smile. "I don't think you've worked less than a twelve-hour day since I met you."

"That's not true. I only worked eight hours today."

"So far."

"So far." JD's eyebrows drew together, and he swiveled in his seat to face her. "How did you know I planned to work some more tonight?"

"Because you've been home for over an hour and you haven't asked me any questions yet," Hadley said, her expression confident. "I assume you have updates on the case you want to talk about."

"Yeah." Seeing no reason to put it off any longer, he pulled up his email and retrieved the images of Rabell. "Have you ever seen this guy before?"

She leaned closer, and he could smell the scent of his soap on her skin. "It's hard to say. Do you have any with a better view of his face?"

JD slowly clicked through the photos until the sketch finally appeared on his screen. "Anything?"

"There's something familiar about him." She shrugged. "It's kind of like when you see someone in the grocery store but don't really know them. Who is he?"

"We only know him as Rabell. He's the man we believe is behind the bombing."

"And you still don't know why the bomb was planted?"

"No. We think he was after at least one member of congress," JD said. "For all we know, he could have chosen the engagement party because of the easy access rather than a specific target."

"It certainly would have made a lot of headlines. Members of congress, actors, news reporters. If the bombing had been successful, the impact would have rippled far beyond the Washington social scene."

"That's true," JD conceded. "As it was, the story only lasted a couple of news cycles."

His brow furrowed, and his mind caught up with Hadley's comment. "Wait a minute. What news reporter was there?"

"Richard Lincoln. He's on Channel 9 News."

"I don't remember seeing his name on the witness list." JD switched screens and pulled up the file of attendees at the restaurant. Sure enough, Richard Lincoln wasn't listed.

"I'm pretty sure I saw him outside the hotel when I was sitting in the ambulance," Hadley said. "Does he go by a different name when he's not on camera?"

JD did a search on the TV station's website. "It doesn't mention it here. Who was he sitting with? Could you tell if he was part of the engagement party?"

"I'm not sure. He was sitting at one of the smaller tables with a woman. She looked familiar, but I don't know why."

JD glanced at the time on his computer. "I'm going to call Noah to see if he can do a deeper background on him."

JD dialed Noah's number. "Hey, can you run something for me?" JD asked. "Hadley said the newscaster Richard Lincoln was at the restaurant the night of the bombing, but his name isn't on the list."

"Yeah, he was cataloged under his legal name, Richard Linderberger," Noah said.

"Okay. Thanks," JD said disappointedly.

"I gather you haven't had any more luck on finding a motive either."

"No, and I'm tired of hunting for needles in haystacks."

"I know what you mean."

JD heard the frustration in his friend's voice and guessed it was due more to Kelsey's absence than their current case. "Any other updates?"

"Nothing yet."

"Want me to save you some dinner?" JD asked.

"No. I think I'm going to stay late tonight. Thanks though."

"I'll talk to you later."

"Is everything okay with Noah and Kelsey?" Hadley asked as soon as JD hung up.

"They've just got a lot going on right now."

"Maybe we should invite them to go kayaking with us tomorrow. It sounds like we could all use a diversion."

"I'd like that," JD said. He didn't mention that at the moment, Kelsey Cabbott didn't exist.

CHAPTER 27

THEY STARTED AT DUSK. WITH their trash carefully hidden deep within the cave and their water bags and bottles topped off, Kelsey fell into step behind the last of the hostages.

After the helicopter had departed, Tristan and Jay had hiked the rest of the trail and selected their meeting spot for tonight.

Jay was on point now, leading the way, with Kelsey and Tristan bringing up the rear.

They made it half a mile before Kelsey came around a corner to find the group resting inside a shallow cave.

Brent signaled to Jay, who set out again, this time with five women and five children, all of whom appeared to be moving well on their own.

To Kelsey's surprise, when the next few started to move forward, Seth stopped them.

She approached Brent. "What's going on?"

"Possible air traffic heading our way. We need to break down into smaller groups so we can take cover quickly if a helicopter passes overhead." Brent waited for Tristan to join them. "Tristan, you take the next group. Take cover a quarter mile up and wait for me to bring the next group."

Tristan continued forward, Seth instructing the next ten women to follow him.

"If we only send ten at a time, the last group is going to have forty women in it," Kelsey said.

"Seth and I will take turns doubling back."

"That's an awful lot of walking," Kelsey said. "Do you want me to take a group too?"

"I don't know . . ."

"It'll go faster if we have a third," Seth said in his quiet way.

"Okay. Seth, you take the next bunch. Taja, you take the ones after that."

Kelsey nodded, the gravity of what she had just volunteered to do pressing in on her. She was trained to be invisible, not rescue hostages. Reminding herself that the men with her did this for a living, she watched Seth disappear around the corner, a single line of women following behind him.

Brent selected ten women, all of whom were adults, to go with Kelsey. Stepping beside her again, he said, "When you get to the next stop, wait there with them so Seth can come back to help me get the rest."

"Whatever you say."

"I'll see you in a few minutes."

Mustering confidence she didn't feel, Kelsey spoke to the women with her. "Let's go." She started up the path, checking behind her to do a quick head count. She reached the peak of the hill, then started her descent. The light was fading, but she proceeded at a moderate pace, careful to make sure everyone was keeping up.

They trudged up another short rise before they reached a steep drop-off. Kelsey slowed, walking sideways to maintain her footing. When Seth came into view halfway down the hill, relief flowed through her. One step closer to getting home.

* * *

Noah leaned on the conference room table, studying the images in front of him. Photos of the aftermath of the bombing, driver's license photos of three missing coeds from the University of Maryland who were believed to have been abducted by Rabell's men while visiting Thailand, a seating chart for Makenna Burke's engagement party. Somehow, all of this fit together, and Noah needed to find the missing piece to show him how to stop Rabell and how to do it once and for all.

JD walked in and closed the door behind him. Despite being alone, JD lowered his voice. "Have you heard from Kelsey yet?"

"No."

"I'm sorry," JD said. "I can't imagine how hard it must be having her in the field again."

Noah swallowed hard. As much as he respected the need to keep intelligence strictly guarded, he also needed someone to bounce ideas off of. Since JD was the only other FBI agent aware of his wife's true background, he stepped onto the bridge of trust. "I met with her right before she left on Tuesday."

"And? Did the agency have any insight on Rabell's group?" JD asked.

Noah dragged both hands through his hair. "They think Rabell took over Nassar's compound in Abolstan."

"Wait." Awareness filled JD's expression. "Kelsey went to Abolstan?" When Noah didn't respond, JD asked, "What else did she know?"

"They didn't have anything more than we do about who might have been the target. Their source was dating one of the bombers and overheard a conversation."

"So we're not getting any more intel from her."

"No. From what the agency has gathered, Rabell took over Nassar's pipeline and has been using it to expand into selling everything that can bring a price," Noah said. "Arms deals and human trafficking appear to be his bread and butter."

"Wait a minute. Didn't you say Congressman Burke was introducing new legislation to increase our funding to combat human trafficking?"

"Yeah. That's one of his big stances, along with immigration and school safety," Noah said. "I have a hard time believing a criminal from Abolstan would single him out for that though. It's not like he was the only one backing the bill."

"But how many backers of that bill were at the party?"

"I'm not sure. I can check though."

"It's worth looking into," JD said. "Besides, you could use the distraction."

"That obvious, huh?"

"Oh yeah."

"How are things with your distraction?" Noah asked.

"Hadley's hardly a distraction. She's a witness."

"Yeah right." Noah's mood lightened. "I saw the way you kept trying to leave the office early yesterday. I haven't seen you try that hard since you had a date with Miss Virginia two years ago."

"Whatever." JD glanced at his watch. "Do you need help with your research, or are you cool with me taking off?"

"It's noon."

"On Friday. You know how bad traffic gets going into the weekend," JD said. "Burt said I could work at home with Hadley on our seating chart this afternoon."

"Go." Noah waved toward the door.

"Let me know if you find anything."

"I will." Noah watched JD leave, his own cubicle closing in on him. Maybe it was time for him to get out of the office too.

* * *

Kelsey reached the last stop before their rendezvous point. This time, instead of finding a cave for shelter, the Saint Squad had chosen a cluster of boulders that created a natural barrier between them and anyone else on the path.

After her group reached their hiding place, Kelsey took position beside Seth, who was standing guard at the edge of the trail. "It shouldn't be much farther."

"Another quarter mile," Seth said.

"Has the rest of your squad arrived yet?"

"Haven't heard from them, but they'll maintain radio silence until they're in position."

"We're going to be sitting ducks if they can't make it through."

"They'll be there."

Tristan emerged from the darkness. "I'm ready for the next group."

"Is there any place down there to conceal so many people?" Kelsey asked.

"We have everyone staggered along some outcroppings of rocks," Tristan said. "It's the best we can do for now."

More women and children came into view, this time with Brent trailing behind them.

"Tristan, I want you to take this group next," Brent said. "One of the women sprained her ankle, and it might take them longer to make it down."

Though surprised that Brent would want them to continue on with so little rest, Kelsey kept her thoughts to herself.

Brent motioned the injured woman forward, leaning down to check the ace bandage wrapped around her ankle and shoe. He spoke quietly to her in Russian before signaling for Tristan to proceed.

"Any word from Craig?" Brent asked Seth after they disappeared around the bend.

"Negative."

"Jay, what's our status down there?" Brent said, speaking into his headset now.

"Thirty ready for transport," Jay responded.

"How many more can you handle?"

"Ten. Anyone beyond that will be exposed."

"Travel time from last rest area to pick-up zone?" Brent asked.

"Five to seven minutes."

"We'll hold the last two groups until our guys arrive."

"Roger."

Brent flipped off his microphone. "As soon as the trucks get here, we'll take everyone as a single group."

Craig's voice came over Kelsey's headset. "ETA one minute. Prepare cargo."

"Roger," Jay answered.

"Let's go." Brent motioned to the women and started forward.

Kelsey fell in line in the center of the pack, between two teenagers.

The familiar rumble of a helicopter sounded in the distance. Kelsey's heart dropped into her stomach. "Oh no."

* * *

Kade pulled the Humvee to a stop behind the three cargo trucks that would transport the rest of the hostages out of Abolstan. He wasn't sure why he'd felt the need to accompany them into hostile territory. After all, this was a military mission, one that would be classified and buried, unless the powers that be decided to share the results. Successful results, he hoped.

Kade jolted at the buzz of the warning on his radar. He glanced at the monitor mounted to the dash, then spoke into his comm headset. "We've got an incoming aircraft."

"ETA?" Brent asked.

"Two minutes." Another blip popped up on his screen. "He's got a friend. Looks like they're in a search pattern."

"Tristan, get ready with the MANPADS," Brent said, referring to the anti-aircraft missiles they had brought with them.

"On it."

"We only have one missile," Damian announced. "It's all we could get our hands on."

"That's a problem," Tristan said.

The rumble of the helicopter approached from the west.

"As soon as the first one is in range, take it out," Brent ordered. "We'll deal with the other one when we have to."

A broad-beamed spotlight came into view. A second later, the trail of the missile lit up the sky. The helicopter veered right, but it was too late. The missile tracked it and found its target, and a thundering explosion and raining flames replaced the beam of the spotlight.

CHAPTER 28

THE GROUND JOLTED BENEATH HER, and Kelsey prayed the tremor was the result of Quinn's successful shooting.

With nothing but the darkness to protect them, she quickened her pace. She wasn't the only one. Several women in front of her broke into a run, Brent leading the way at a jog.

The teenager beside Kelsey stumbled and cried out as she fell to the ground. Kelsey stopped and reached down to help her. The moment the girl put weight on her left leg, she cried out again and immediately clutched Kelsey and lifted her foot from the ground.

"Hold on to me." Kelsey slipped her arm around the girl's waist to support her weight as they hobbled forward together.

Seth sprinted toward them. "Let me take her."

To Kelsey's surprise, he offered her his assault rifle. "Take the rear. If the helicopter circles back around, shoot off one round and only one."

"Are we sure we don't have any friendlies in the sky?"

"Yeah. Brent couldn't get anyone to sign off on air support because of the military movement in the area. Our government wants us invisible," Seth said. "And you can bet that if you see a searchlight, they aren't friendly."

"Got it." Kelsey gripped the weapon and checked the safety.

Seth leaned down and picked up the injured girl in a fireman's carry. He moved forward as though the extra weight didn't bother him in the least.

The rumble of the helicopter increased in volume, a swath of light cutting over the nearest ridge and shining onto the ground only a few yards from the trail.

Ensuring the others were in front of her, Kelsey continued forward a few steps before turning and lifting her weapon. She took several deep breaths, released the safety, and aimed at the top of the ridge.

Ten seconds later, the white glow of the spotlight burst through the darkness, the entire beam now unobstructed. The helicopter emerged a second later.

Kelsey squeezed off a single round, bullets sparking overhead as they made contact with something metallic on the aircraft.

Immediately, the helicopter veered away.

Kelsey turned and hurried forward, jogging as quickly as the rocky trail would allow. The air in her lungs burned, and her chest tightened. She could see the last three women on the trail as they pushed through a narrow pass that forced everyone to go single file.

Another fifty yards and she would catch up with the others.

Engines echoed through the stillness, followed by the cry of a frightened child.

Brent's voice came over Kelsey's headset. "Quinn, if the helicopter gets over us, aim for the pilot."

"Roger."

The light crested over the ridge again. Kelsey lifted the weapon but then remembered Seth had told her to fire off only one round. Afraid her interference might cause Quinn to miss his opportunity to down the helicopter, Kelsey pressed herself against the side of the rock wall to her left, praying she would remain hidden by the night.

The helicopter appeared overhead, and the light found the trail and remained fixed to it. The beam passed within inches of her position, and Kelsey struggled to breathe.

Concern for the others helped her find her voice. "Inbound," she said into her microphone.

"Get everyone in the vehicles," Brent demanded. "Quinn?"

"Ready."

* * *

Noah fought through Friday traffic, not sure what had compelled him to make another appointment with Senator Whitmore. He could have spoken with any number of witnesses about the accuracy of the seating chart and possible targets, but the senator's openness with him during their first interview made Noah think that the older man was as interested in helping as Noah was in stopping a future attack.

He walked into Whitmore's outer office, and the woman behind the reception desk showed him into the senator's private office.

The older man stood upon his entrance and circled his desk to greet Noah. "Good to see you again, Agent Cabbott."

"You too, Senator." Noah shook the outstretched hand. "Thank you for fitting me into your schedule."

"Please sit." Senator Whitmore waved at one of the two chairs facing his desk, opting to sit in the one beside Noah rather than the one across from him. "So, you're still trying to piece together the puzzle from last weekend."

"We are."

"I've only received highlights on your investigation. Why don't you fill me in on what you know so far."

Noah hesitated briefly, reminding himself that the man beside him sat on the Senate Intelligence Committee and held a top-secret clearance. "We're aware of four men who were at the restaurant Saturday night and left shortly before detonation."

"Why would the people involved go inside right before a bomb went off?" the senator asked. "They had other men outside, correct?"

"Yes. Best we can figure, the inside men were there to ensure the target was in the building."

Senator Whitmore tapped his finger on his thigh. "Then it's unlikely Congressman Burke or any of his family was the primary target."

"I agree. If they were, it wouldn't have been necessary to have anyone scouting out the party."

"So we're still looking for who they were after."

Noah pulled a file from his briefcase. "Would you look this over and tell me if you see anything out of place?" Noah handed him the seating chart he had created using the party planner's notes.

Senator Whitmore studied the three pages that had been taped together to make a fold-out chart. "This looks pretty accurate. The bride's and groom's families were moving around a lot, visiting the different tables, so they weren't ever sitting for long, but the rest of it looks right."

"What about the others there that night?"

"I honestly wasn't paying much attention. The only person I recognized outside the engagement party was Richard Lincoln. I remember wondering how he knew the bride and groom," Senator Whitmore said. "Turns out he didn't. He was sitting right over here with a woman."

Noah verified that the senator's statement coincided with what they had already pieced together. "Any updates on the program you mentioned?"

"Every indication is that it is secure. Since I haven't had any new security being thrown at me, I assume you also didn't find anything to indicate a breach about my future candidacy."

"No. Nothing." Noah slipped the seating chart back into his briefcase, snapping it shut. "Every lead we follow comes up a dead end."

"What else do you know?"

Noah proceeded to tell him about Spencer's death, the diamonds discovered in his condo, and the run-in with Keith. "Everything we have so far supports the idea that Rabell is behind this. His yacht was spotted in Virginia, but so far, the Coast Guard hasn't found it."

"It's probably docked somewhere and covered."

"If that's the case, he's likely still close by."

"I guess we have to pray the current mission in Abolstan will shed some light on the situation."

"How did you know . . . ?"

Now Senator Whitmore hesitated before speaking. "I don't normally tell people this, but my son-in-law is a Navy SEAL."

"I didn't realize that. And he's involved with the current mission?"

He nodded. "It's hard when you don't know if your loved ones are in harm's way or when you'll get word that they're coming home, but I don't have to tell you that."

"I don't know what you mean."

"I'm sure my son-in-law and his squad are doing everything they can to get back home to their families," Senator Whitmore said. "And they'll bring your wife back to you. Have faith in that."

A lump formed at the back of Noah's throat, and he was unable to form any words.

The senator stood. "In the meantime, why don't you bring that seating chart of yours over to my house tonight. You can join Katherine and me for dinner, and she can tell you if she sees anything out of place."

Noah stood as well. "I don't want to impose."

"No imposition at all. Besides, the distraction will do us all good." A hint of worry crept into the older man's expression. "Not to mention that Katherine has quite the memory when it comes to social events. If anyone can help you fill in the blanks, it's her."

Noah found himself nodding. "In that case, I accept."

* * *

Kade rushed to Seth's side, helping him lower the teenager he carried into the back of the truck. "How many more?" Kade shouted over the roar of the approaching helicopter.

Seth glanced behind him, where three more women ran toward them. "Those should be the last of them, except for Taja."

Taja Al-Kazaz. Or rather, Kelsey Cabbott.

"Where is she?" Kade asked at full volume.

"She was covering our six. She should be right behind them."

The helicopter came around the edge of the mountains, a new spotlight streaming over several of the stragglers.

A rapid succession of gunfire sparked from the helicopter. A woman fell to the ground as several members of the Saint Squad returned fire. The helicopter evaded, bullets sparking off it.

"Damian and Craig, get that first truck out of here," Brent said. "Jay and Patrick, take the second."

Truck engines came to life as the helicopter circled for a better angle.

"Quinn, when he circles around again, take the right side. Tristan, take the left," Brent said. "I'll aim for the fuel tank."

The ground vibrated, the telltale sign of the approaching aircraft. Kade helped Brent settle the last of the women in the back of the truck, the first two vehicles starting forward, the headlights off to avoid the helicopter's notice.

Kade had no doubt both of the drivers were making good use of their night-vision goggles to guide them down the dirt road.

"Taja, what's your ETA?"

"Two minutes. I had to take cover when the helicopter flew overhead." Her voice cut out. "It's coming around again."

The helicopter engines filled the valley once more, but this time, gunfire sparked the moment the craft appeared over the ridge. The response was immediate, three weapons firing in tandem.

Kade couldn't tell whose shot made contact first, but the helicopter jerked hard to the right an instant before one of the rotors impacted the side of the rock face. The helicopter immediately bounced off the rock and spun downward over the trail Kelsey was supposed to be traversing.

"Take cover!" Brent shouted.

The helicopter hit the side of the mountain a second time and ricocheted off it before it dropped straight down. To Kade's horror, it exploded only a few yards from the trailhead. The fireball burst in every direction, and the earth shook.

"Taja!" Kade called out, racing forward. The three SEAL team members who had seen the crash echoed her name as well.

Footsteps sounded behind him, but Kade didn't turn to see whose.

"Quinn, Tristan, get that last truck out of here," Brent ordered.

"Roger," Quinn responded tersely.

"Taja," Brent repeated. "Status?"

Again, no answer.

Kade reached the edge of the flaming debris and circled to the left in the hopes he could find a path around the narrow entrance to the trail. He didn't know if Kelsey had survived or not, but he wasn't leaving without her body, dead or alive.

CHAPTER 29

By the time Kade reached the flames, Seth had caught up to him. Kade let the SEAL take the lead, knowing Seth had come through this area moments before.

They picked their way over rocks, skirting past patches of fire. Brent brought up the rear, again attempting to communicate with Kelsey.

"Taja? Do you read me?" Brent asked. "We're coming to you."

With the path blocked, Seth opted to climb over one of the enormous rocks to the side of the trailhead. Kade followed suit, his foot slipping more than once as he tried to follow the taller man's lead.

When they reached the top, Kade straightened and scanned the terrain in front of him. The trail was little more than a narrow walkway worn through the side of the steep mountain, cliffs to one side and a steep drop to the other side. Despite the aid of the light from the fire, Kelsey wasn't anywhere in sight.

"I don't see her," Seth said.

"Could she have been caught under the wreckage?" Brent asked.

Seth didn't answer; instead, he continued his forward progress by climbing down the far side of the ridge.

Understanding the unwillingness to accept such a possibility, Kade retrieved one of his inventions from his pocket.

Brent stepped beside him. "What's that?"

"A tool for sensing intruders. It picks up body heat."

"Will it work this close to the fire?"

"We're about to find out." Kade opened the scan and followed Seth, grateful the downward side was traversable without using his hands. He looked at the small screen, the location of the fire filling the right side.

"Anything?" Brent asked.

"Nothing yet."

"Taja!" Seth shouted.

Again, no response.

Kade reached the trail and jogged forward, trying to put more distance between his scanner and the heat of the fire. An alert popped. "I've got something!"

He started down, extrapolating the location. He looked at the steep cliff to his left, confused. "It says someone is right down there."

* * *

Kelsey gripped the edge of the cliff, her fingers cramping, her body dangling in midair. Her heart pounded, and she didn't dare look at how far she would fall if her grip faltered.

The warning to take cover had given her just enough time to drop to the ground behind a boulder that resembled a beach ball, but the impact of the explosion had bounced her right off the trail, down a steep embankment, and over the edge of a sharp drop.

She had been lucky enough to grab onto the edge as she'd slid over, preventing her from plummeting down the mountain. Her headset hadn't been so lucky.

Panic clawed at her, and she fought against it. *Think*, she ordered herself.

She lifted her right leg, her foot connecting with the cliff. Pressing her toe against the rock, she searched for a foothold, finally discovering a tiny ledge. Using it to relieve some of the weight of her body, she attempted to repeat the process with her other foot without success.

Her arms trembled with exertion, and she closed her eyes. Even if the Navy SEALs could get past the wreckage, how would they ever find her?

The glow of a fire gave her some perspective, enough so that she could see she had slid at least twenty feet from the trail. Unfortunately, the sheer volume of the blaze was enough to drown out any calls for help.

Her right pinkie slipped. She gasped.

Frantically, she tried again to find a second toe hold. Why had she come back to Abolstan? What had she been thinking? She had everything in Virginia. A home, a husband she adored, friends.

Desperate to get back to that life, the one she had spent the past year building, she closed her eyes and sent up a silent prayer.

She dug her fingers in harder, her errant pinkie finding a grip. Seconds ticked by as she fought for calm, still searching for a resting place for her left foot.

Hallelujah! An indentation several inches wide, as well as deep, helped support her weight further.

The blaze seemed to grow in volume, the dull roar forming into words. "Taja!"

"Down here!" she croaked.

She couldn't see who the voice belonged to, but she heard the words grow louder.

"Hold on! We're coming!"

Kelsey closed her eyes once more. She would hold on as long as she could, but would it be long enough?

* * *

The surge of relief Kade experienced when he heard Kelsey's voice plummeted when he looked over the edge of the cliff and saw for himself where she had ended up.

Beside him, Seth hammered a climbing anchor into the rock. Apparently, these SEALs really did prepare for everything.

With impressive speed, Brent pulled a rope from his pack, fed it through the anchor, and looped it around himself. Seth secured a second anchor, looped a second rope through, and handed it to Brent. A moment later, Seth took hold of the tails of both ropes, wrapped them around his waist, and braced himself to give extra support to his teammate.

"Ghost, shine your light down there," Brent said.

Kade complied in time to watch Brent step off the edge of the cliff and literally walk down a vertical wall. One step at a time, he lowered himself down. In the beam of his flashlight, Kade stared at Kelsey again. How she had managed to catch hold of the narrow ledge was beyond him.

He saw her fingers slipping, but she clawed at the rock until she once again found a hand-hold. He was watching a miracle. He only hoped the miracle would last long enough for the SEALs to bring her to safety.

* * *

A light shone overhead, but Kelsey didn't dare look up, for fear her delicate balance would shift and she would tumble down the mountain. The fingers of her left hand cramped again, and she tried to readjust her hold. Pain registered in the back of her mind when she grasped onto a sharp edge.

Blood oozed from her fingertips where the rock cut into them, her grip slipping. Every muscle in her body vibrated with exertion, and Kelsey tried not to think about her bleeding fingertips and the effect the moisture would have on maintaining her grip.

She pressed her fingers down harder, fighting against gravity and the now-slippery rock only to have the edge cut deeper into her skin. She yelped in pain, her hold faltering. The change in her balance caused her to lose her toeholds, and her left hand fell away, sending her heart plummeting.

"No!" she cried in alarm, her body dangling from the rock, only her right hand preventing her fall.

"Hold on!" A man's voice shouted from above.

Two seconds later, a hand gripped her left arm.

"I'm here," Brent said, his voice reigniting her hope. He reached around her, looping a rope around her middle. "Grab the rope with your left hand."

Kelsey followed his instructions, her bleeding fingers grasping it.

"Now press your feet against the rock."

Again, Kelsey complied, grateful for the extra stability.

"Now, we're going to climb up together."

Kelsey hesitated, not quite ready to give up the hold she still clung to with her right hand.

"We've got you," Brent insisted. "Trust us."

Kelsey closed her eyes and sent up another silent prayer. With a leap of faith, she let go of the rock and grabbed the rope.

"Good. Now, do what I do. One step at a time."

Mimicking Brent's actions, Kelsey worked her hands up the rope, her feet pressing against the mountainside for purchase. Together they climbed upward until hands reached down and grabbed Kelsey's arms. An instant later, her feet were on solid ground.

Her legs collapsed beneath her, and she would have fallen had it not been for Seth and another man holding her up. She took a moment to find her voice. "I didn't think you would find me."

"Having Ghost here sped up the search," Seth said.

"Ghost?" Kelsey repeated.

"Consider me your guardian," Ghost said.

"Thank you," Kelsey's gaze shifted to Seth and Brent. "All of you."

"You're welcome," Brent said. "But I vote we get out of here."

Seth nodded. "I think that vote is unanimous."

* * *

JD couldn't believe it took him so long to get home. Nearly three hours to drive what should have been an hour or less. That was what he got for trying to make it through rush hour on a Friday in April, especially during spring break.

He had expected the favorable weather forecast to increase the volume of beach traffic, but he hadn't counted on three accidents, one of them requiring a medivac.

He had stopped to give assistance on that one, all the while wishing he were home.

When he finally got back on the road again, the realization that Hadley's spring break was coming to an end surfaced, along with the problems her work schedule could create for her safety. Rabell's yacht still hadn't been found, nor had any hits come back on the BOLOs his office had sent out on the men Hadley had described to the sketch artist.

By the time he pulled into his driveway, his mind was churning with possibilities and his stomach was grumbling. Seven thirty. And he had hoped to be home by two. Life wasn't fair.

He made his way inside and was greeted by the glorious scent of something baking. Instantly, his mood brightened. Were those chocolate chip cookies he smelled?

He walked into the kitchen to find Hadley sitting at the kitchen table, a scatter of colored paper spread around her, a marker in one hand. On the counter, several dozen cookies were spread out on a cooling rack.

She glanced up. "Hey. I was wondering when you would get here."

"Sorry I'm so late. Traffic was a bear."

"I saw on the news. They showed a picture of 95. It looked like a parking lot."

"That's pretty accurate." He moved to the stove. "Are these for anyone?"

"Yeah. Help yourself." Hadley pushed back from the table. "Have you already had dinner?"

"I'm about to." JD stacked three cookies in his hand.

"Maybe you should consider some real food."

"This can be my appetizer." He popped a cookie into his mouth. "Mmm. That's good."

"Glad you like it." She opened the refrigerator. "I made some tuna salad, and there's still some leftover chicken in there."

"Have you already eaten?"

"I had a sandwich a while ago." She motioned to the cookies. "I had a sweet tooth though, so I decided to do some baking. I hope that's okay."

"Are you kidding? What guy wouldn't want to come home to a house smelling like this?"

"One on a diet?"

"Okay, that may be true." JD popped another cookie into his mouth.

"Do you want me to make you a sandwich or something?"

"That's okay. I can do it." He opened the refrigerator and pulled out a package of sliced cheese and another of ham. He nodded in the direction of the table. "What's all that?"

"Oh, I was trying to get organized for next week. My class will be starting a new geography project. With everything going on, I'm a bit behind."

"How much longer are you going to be at it?"

"I'm almost done. It'll probably only take me another fifteen or twenty minutes."

"Anything I can do to help?" When Hadley didn't answer him right away, he turned to look at her, noting the concerned expression on her face. "Hadley? What's wrong?"

"Will it be safe for me to go to work on Monday?"

He wanted to give her the assurance she so clearly needed, but he opted for the truth instead. "I'm still not sure."

"What do I do?"

"I had a lot of time to think about this case on my way home," JD said. "How would you feel about my coming in with you on Monday?"

"You? Come to school with me?"

"Yeah." JD leaned back against the counter. "I figure best case, I can come and make sure no one is still looking for you."

"And worst case?"

JD set his dinner aside, his gaze meeting hers. "I'm not going to let anyone hurt you."

Hadley reached out and put her hand on his shoulder. "I know I've said it before, but thank you for letting me stay here."

"This may sound corny, but you've made this house feel like home." JD's hand lifted to cover hers. "I've enjoyed having you here."

"I've enjoyed being here. I'm going to miss you when all of this is over."

"You don't have to." His gaze dropped to her lips before his eyes met hers. "Being with you, spending time together—I don't want it to end."

Her expression softened. "Neither do I."

For days, JD had kept his distance, all too aware that she was struggling with the loss of her boyfriend and the turmoil of emotions the threats against her had caused. The barriers he had tried to keep in place crumbled, and the connection between them pulled him closer.

Unable to resist, JD leaned toward her. The kiss was whisper soft, a teasing sample of what he craved. She tasted sweet, like the cookies she had baked, her lips soft against his. His fingers tangled in her hair as his lips met hers again.

Images of her cartwheeled through his head: the way she curled her legs up underneath her when she sat on the couch, the shyness that came over her the first time they went to Noah's house, the animated expression she got when she talked about her students.

She was generous and kind. And in this moment, she was his.

He deepened the kiss, and something softened inside him. When he pulled back, he found himself intrigued by the way her eyes fluttered open, her gaze dark and mysterious.

Her lips turned up slightly. "We'd better make sure we don't do that in front of my class."

JD couldn't help but laugh. "It would get their attention."

"I don't think that's the kind of attention you want from a bunch of third graders."

"Maybe not." His heart light, he slipped his arms around Hadley's waist. "Why don't you finish up your work while I eat, and then we can watch a movie together?"

Hadley slid her arms around his neck. "Is this another date?"

JD leaned down for another kiss. "Absolutely."

CHAPTER 30

NOAH WASN'T SURE WHAT HE expected when he arrived at the Whitmores' house for dinner but sitting at the kitchen table, eating chicken the senator had grilled himself, certainly hadn't been it.

The meal was simple and made him feel at home.

"Thank you for having me tonight. Dinner was wonderful," Noah said after their meal concluded and the table was cleared.

"It's our pleasure." Senator Whitmore motioned to where Noah's briefcase rested beside him. "Why don't you show Katherine that seating chart of yours."

This was why he was here, Noah reminded himself. While Katherine helped her husband clear the table and put food away, Noah retrieved the seating chart from his briefcase.

Katherine wiped off the table and motioned for him to show her. "Let me see what you have." She stepped beside him and looked over the sketch of tables.

Silence stretched out while Katherine read through the names, the only sound coming from the running water as the senator rinsed the last of the dishes. The water shut off, and Senator Whitmore retrieved a hand towel from the front of the oven. "What do you think, Katherine? Can you think of anyone they're missing?"

"Everything looks right, except these two people switched seats." Katherine looked up. "Ellen Tremont has a severe seafood allergy, so Sue traded places with her to keep her from sitting next to someone who was eating salmon."

"Anything else?" Noah asked.

"Just that this name doesn't look right." Katherine tapped her finger beside a table with two names. "I remember Richard Lincoln sitting with a woman, but this says the woman's name was Jane Smith. I can't recall her name, but I'm pretty sure that isn't it."

"Where do you know her from?"

"I think I saw her on television, maybe as a news consultant, but I don't remember when it was or what she was talking about."

"But you're sure she was the woman sitting with the newscaster?"

"Yes. I'm sure."

"I can reach out to the studio to see if Lincoln can identify her. If she's worked as a news consultant in the past, it's likely she was there to discuss some future project."

"Why would she give a fake name to the authorities though?" Katherine asked.

"I was wondering the same thing," Senator Whitmore said. "It sounds like she's already a public figure."

"It's a question I look forward to finding the answer to," Noah said. "Thank you, Mrs. Whitmore. You've been very helpful."

"Good luck, Noah." Katherine laid her hand on his arm. "And feel free to drop by any time. In fact, next time, bring your wife. I'd love to meet her."

Noah swallowed, taking a moment before responding. "I'm sure she'd love to meet you too."

* * *

How had everything changed so quickly? Last Friday night, Hadley had been talking with Spencer on the phone to make their final plans for their date on Saturday, and here she was a week later dating an FBI agent. Should she feel guilty for moving on so quickly?

The movie continued on the television in front of her, JD's arm warm around her shoulders. She shifted her feet underneath her, struck by the simplicity of the moment. How long had it been, she wondered, since she had been able to have this kind of comfort with someone, spending time together day after day with no expectations for her to be anything other than herself? She hadn't had that with Spencer, she realized now.

JD's fingers trailed along her bare arm. "What are you thinking?"

"I don't know. Just about how much has changed lately."

"Your whole life has been turned upside down. I'd say you've taken change to a whole new level."

"True, but I was thinking in more basic terms."

"You're talking about us." JD hit the pause button. "Is this moving too fast for you?"

"No, it's not that." Hadley shook her head. "Not exactly."

"What is it, then?"

"Shouldn't I be feeling guilty or something? I mean, a week ago, I thought Spencer was the person I would build a future with, and here I am now with butterflies in my stomach every time you look at me."

"I give you butterflies?" Amusement and delight filled his voice. "That's good, isn't it?"

The tension that had been building inside her evaporated. "How do you do that?"

"What?"

"You make life seem so simple." Hadley turned so she was facing him, now sitting cross-legged. "I mean, you're an FBI agent. You have to stare at the worst part of humanity every day, yet sitting here, it's like you don't have a care in the world."

"I care about you." Heat bloomed on her cheeks, and he reached out and took her hand. "I care enough that if this is too soon for you, I'll wait."

The sincerity in his voice touched her in a way she couldn't describe. Determined to leave the past behind, to give herself the freedom to step into a new future, she forced herself to admit the truth to JD and to herself. "I'm embarrassed to admit that I think I wasn't so much in love with Spencer as I was with the idea of me and Spencer."

"You were hoping for the fairy-tale ending," JD said. "There's nothing wrong with that."

"There is when you spend six months searching for it with the wrong person." She linked her fingers through JD's. "You know how I kept getting annoyed that you were always asking me questions when I first met you?"

"Yeah. What about it?"

"You stopped asking questions." Hadley squeezed his hand. "I mean, sometimes you do, but mostly when we talk, I feel like you're interested in me, not in your case."

"That's good."

"It is," Hadley agreed. "I never realized it before, but Spencer never stopped asking questions."

"What do you mean?"

"We went out once a week, and the first thirty minutes of every date was spent with him asking about everyone else."

"Like who?"

"My students. Their parents. Even the other teachers and administrators at my school." Hadley shrugged. "I'm not sure why I looked forward to spending time with him when we pretty much had the same conversation every week."

"What did you talk about when you spoke on the phone?"

"When and where we were going to meet. I could have been a business appointment rather than his girlfriend," Hadley said. "The crazy thing is that I didn't recognize it."

"People don't always see clearly when they're in the middle of a situation," JD said.

"Yeah, but I should have. Feeling like I was being interrogated isn't exactly a new thing for me. It's exactly the reason I broke up with my previous boyfriend."

"Who was that?"

"I think you met him, actually. Chad Hicks. He manages my apartment complex."

"I didn't realize you two dated."

"It only lasted a few weeks. The guy didn't like kids, but he was always talking about my students as though he cared. It wasn't hard to see through the insincerity."

"Whatever the past, I'm glad you're here now."

She leaned forward and pressed her lips to his. "Me too."

* * *

Noah parked his car in the garage and immediately headed for the house two doors down. He didn't consider that it was nearly ten o'clock at night or that most of the lights were off when he rang the bell.

Movement stirred inside, nearly a minute passing before footsteps sounded on the tile floor and lights flicked on in the entryway.

JD pulled the door open, his eyes squinting as though not yet adjusted to the light. "Noah, what are you doing here this time of night?"

Noah glanced at his watch. "Sorry. I assumed you were still up."

"Yeah, we're still up." JD pulled the door open wider. "Come on in."

"Thanks." Instead of heading for the back of the house, Noah moved into the office to his right. "I just finished having dinner at the Whitmores' house, and I might have something."

"What?" JD flicked on the overhead light.

"Katherine Whitmore pointed out a woman who was sitting with Richard Lincoln, but she's quite certain the name didn't match the person."

"What was the name given during the witness interviews?"

"Jane Smith."

JD shook his head. "That's about as obvious an alias as you can get. Who missed that one?"

"One of the local cops conducted that initial interview. I tried to follow up on the contact information, and none of it checked out."

"Any idea who this woman is?" JD asked.

"Mrs. Whitmore thinks she's seen her before on the news as a correspondent or media consultant."

"Have you already called the studio?"

"Yeah. It looks like Richard Lincoln is on vacation this week."

"I was really hoping to get this thing closed out before Monday."

"What's on Monday?" Noah asked.

"Hadley starts back up at work again." JD leaned against the front of the desk. "I'm planning to ask Burt for permission to escort her that day."

"You're going to spend the day at an elementary school?"

"That's my plan," JD said. "If someone is trying to find her, it's our best chance at figuring out who and why."

"Does Hadley know you're planning on using her as bait?"

"I'm not using her as bait. I'm making sure she's safe," JD corrected. "But to answer your question, yes, we've discussed the risks."

"Sounds like you're falling for this girl."

"Can you blame me?" JD asked.

A flash of memory surfaced, the moment Noah had learned who his wife really was. He supposed he couldn't have stopped himself from falling in love with Kelsey any more than he could expect JD to guard his heart. "I'm happy for you."

"Thanks." JD lowered his voice. "Any word yet from Kelsey?"

"Nothing yet." The helplessness swamped over him. "I should have heard something by now."

"We both know that sometimes no news is good news."

"I'd rather skip to the good news." Noah took a step toward the door. "I'll talk to you tomorrow."

"Sounds good."

Noah walked outside and started across the lawn. He was nearly to his front door when his phone vibrated. He pulled it free, relief pouring through him when he saw his wife's name illuminated above the text message.

The two words were simple and direct, but they told him everything he needed to know. *Coming home.*

CHAPTER 31

KADE SAT BESIDE KELSEY ON the military transport plane that would carry them from Frankfurt to Norfolk. He had acted as Kelsey's mahram from Istanbul to Frankfurt, where she had shed her Taja Al-Kazaz identity and slipped into her Kelly Park persona again.

He had to give it to her. The woman was a chameleon and did an exceptional job changing her appearance right down to the color of the suitcase and handbag she carried. Impressive.

They had left the Saint Squad behind in Turkey in case extra support was necessary with the hostages and so they could prepare for the possibility of extracting Rabell from Abolstan. Assuming they could find him.

Personally, Kade doubted Rabell was anywhere near Abolstan. Something was brewing in the U.S. If Rabell held true to his pattern, he would want to be somewhere close to see it go down.

Kade opened his laptop and checked for any new messages from his fellow operatives. When he found nothing that pertained to his current case, he opened the photos the Saint Squad had taken at Rabell's compound. He supposed it would have been too easy to find a set of blueprints or an address to focus on. As it was, the intelligence gained at the compound consisted more of what Rabell had been up to rather than what he had planned. They also still had no idea why he had chosen to plant a bomb in the first place.

"Can I see?" Kelsey asked.

Kade adjusted the laptop so she too could view the images. Even though the other passengers of the plane were too far away to overhear their conversation, Kade lowered his voice. "You know this compound better than anyone. What changes have been made since you lived there?"

Kelsey stiffened, her eyes darting up to meet his.

"Yes, I know your file," Kade said, confirming the question illuminated on her face. "I know everything."

"How is that possible?"

"I'm a ghost."

"You said that before, but I don't understand what that means."

"A ghost," Kade repeated. "Some people know us as guardians."

"When I was going through my training, I heard rumors about the guardians, something about secret operatives who watched over agents and came to the aid of those in trouble," Kelsey said. "I thought it was a wives' tale."

"We're very real," Kade said. "I've been your guardian for some time."

Awareness dawned. "Wait. Were you responsible for my rescue last year?"

"I put in the orders for the Saint Squad to come in after you," Kade said.

"How did you even know where I was?" Kelsey asked. "I've always wondered how the SEALs found me."

"The guardians have had a man working his way into Rabell's group for some time. He discovered your whereabouts and fed me the information."

"I'd very much like to thank him."

"I'll pass your thanks along," Kade said before adding, "assuming I can find him."

"What do you mean?"

"Not long after Nassar was arrested, our man went deep under cover. We haven't heard from him in months."

"That's odd." Kelsey shot him a speculative look. "I didn't realize guardians worked as operatives."

"We don't. This man is an exception. He didn't adjust well to living in the shadows and ultimately chose to take on an alias to enter the intelligence world again. We're hoping to hear from him soon. With any luck, he knows who the targets of the bombing really were."

"If guardians normally operate in the shadows, why did you come with the SEALs this time?"

"I don't know. It seemed like a good idea." He patted the black backpack at his feet. "Turns out it was."

"Seth said that if you hadn't been there, they might not have found me in time. Maybe you are my guardian angel."

"No one has ever called me an angel, but guardian is true enough." Kade motioned to the screen. "Speaking of which . . ." He retrieved a cell phone from his pack. "This is for you."

"What's this for?"

"That's how you can get ahold of me if you ever need me. My number is programmed in," Kade said. "Now, what can you tell me about Nassar's old compound before Rabell moved in?"

Kelsey stared at the photos. "The main structure hasn't changed except that the locks on the doors were reversed in the women's quarters and bars were put on the windows."

"Anything else?"

"Go through the photos, and I'll see if anything stands out."

Kade clicked through the photos of the common areas, Kelsey indicating that both the living room and kitchen hadn't changed since she had lived there. When they reached the photos of the office, she edged forward in her seat.

"A file cabinet used to sit in the corner there."

"It was confiscated after Nassar's arrest," Kade said. "Anything else?"

"Nothing significant. The desk has been moved, and there are a few more chairs in the room." Kelsey pointed to a photo of the wall beside the window. "That bulletin board is new."

Kade flipped to another image, this one a close-up of the bulletin board. His stomach churned at the sight—photos of children, teenagers, and women lined the board as though creating an advertisement for prospective clients. A small piece of paper hung below each one, notes scrawled in Arabic. "Can you read these?"

"Zoom in."

Kade did as she asked, noting the way her face paled as she read.

"These are price lists and information about the victims. It appears some of them were being sold as slaves. The ones with rare blood types were being listed as a source for kidney transplants."

"That's sick." Kade refocused the image, now zooming in on a square piece of paper that didn't appear to be attached to any particular photo. "What about this?"

"It's a hit notice."

"Who's the target?"

"It doesn't say. One is listed as traitor. The best translation for the other one would be one who knows too much."

"You're saying he had two targets?"

"Yes. That's what I'm saying."

* * *

Early-morning sunlight shimmered off the water, the current of the Rappahannock River sweeping by. The scent of eggs and bacon wafted from a nearby restaurant and overshadowed the scent of the water.

JD unloaded the kayaks from the trailer Kelsey's parents had left at the house. Together they carried the kayaks one by one to the water's edge. As soon as they had them positioned to launch, he strapped his pack into the mesh netting that covered the storage compartment in the stern, then he returned to the trailer and retrieved their paddles.

"Are you all set?" JD asked.

"I think so." Hadley slid her kayak into the water, balancing on the seat before accepting the paddle JD offered her. She pushed off, holding her position a short distance away while she waited for JD to join her.

"Which way?" she asked as soon as he pulled up beside her.

"Let's head upstream a ways first, then we can drift back down here," JD said. "There's a little island on the other side of the bridge where we can stop for a snack."

"Lead the way."

JD started upstream, pleased to see Hadley keeping pace beside him. He had chosen this area of the river because of its gentle currents so they would be able to avoid hiking several miles back to their vehicle. Maybe next weekend, he should consider a more challenging run.

"What a cool building." Hadley pointed at a historic mansion that sat on a rise along the riverbank.

"Yeah, it is. That one dates back to before the Civil War."

"There's so much history in this area. It's nothing like Wyoming. Everything there is still so spread out."

"I can imagine."

They chatted as they pushed against the current, finally banking their kayaks on the beach of a sandy island in the middle of the river.

JD pulled a couple water bottles from his pack and handed one to Hadley.

"Thanks." She took a sip and stared out over the water. "And thanks for bringing me here. I needed this."

"Are you nervous about going back to work on Monday?"

"A little. I'm more nervous about what I'm going to say when people ask what I did this week. I doubt they'd believe me if I told them I was trying to help identify terrorists."

"Probably not. It would be comical to see their faces though."

"True." She smiled and took his hand. "I think it might be easier to say I went kayaking with a really great guy."

"That could work," JD conceded, his heart lifting at her words.

"Of course, since you're planning to come with me on Monday, my friends will be more interested in asking about you than how I spent my week."

"I'm sure everyone will be too busy wrangling kids to worry about my presence," JD said. "You really have twenty-four kids in your class?"

"Twenty-four." She reached up and kissed his cheek. "And they're all going to love you."

"I don't know about that."

"Oh, I do. Trust me."

* * *

Noah startled awake from the rumble of the garage door. He bolted up from where he lay on the living room couch and reached the kitchen as Kelsey appeared in the doorway. The sight of her caused his breath to rush out of him.

She barely managed to set her suitcase down before he had her in his arms. "I was so worried."

Her fingers dug into the fabric of his shirt, a telltale sign that things hadn't gone as smoothly as she had hoped. Noah clung to her, giving both of them a moment to control their emotions.

"I wasn't sure you would still be up," Kelsey finally said.

"I fell asleep on the couch, watching TV." Noah pulled back, studying his wife's face. He could see the fatigue there, the redness in her eyes, and the faint shadows beneath them. "Are you okay?"

"Yeah." Kelsey pulled free and moved to the cabinet to retrieve a glass. She filled it with water from the refrigerator dispenser, and Noah caught sight of her fingers.

"What happened to your hands?" he asked.

She lifted one as though she had forgotten her fingertips were wrapped in white gauze. She took a sip of water. "I had a little trouble extracting."

"How much trouble?"

Kelsey took another sip.

"Kelsey?"

"I'm home," she said. "And I'm fine."

"You're avoiding." Noah crossed to her, taking her free hand in his. "What happened?"

She drew in a deep breath and let it out in a rush. "A helicopter crashed near me. I got knocked off the path. My fingers got torn up when I fell."

Noah searched her face again, both annoyed and impressed by her ability to give a piece of the truth while not offering the information he was looking for. "I'm going to assume you're holding back because you don't want me to worry."

"That would be a good assumption."

"My question is, Who do I have to thank for saving your life?"

"Let's just say I have a new guardian angel." She set her glass aside. "It's late. I think I'm going to head upstairs and go to bed."

Noah fought against the resentment that national security was once again creating secrets between them. Determined to keep their jobs out of their personal lives, he closed the distance between them and scooped her into his arms.

Her breath caught before she managed to ask, "What are you doing?"

"Helping you upstairs." He lowered his mouth to hers, reveling in the connection between them. His lips twitched into the beginnings of a smile. "You're exhausted."

"Is this your chivalrous streak coming out again?"

"Maybe. Do you mind?"

She reached up and kissed him, her fingers linking behind his neck. "Not at all."

CHAPTER 32

KELSEY SET OUT THE INGREDIENTS for dinner, not sure exactly how she was going to fix it with her fingers bandaged. Noah had offered to grill, but she needed the routine, the simplicity of cooking in her own kitchen, knowing she was in her own home.

Noah had already indulged her when they'd gone to church this morning. They had deliberately arrived late and left the moment sacrament meeting had ended to avoid anyone noticing her injury.

The doorbell rang, and a moment later, she heard Noah talking to someone. When footsteps sounded in the hall, she glanced up to see Hadley walk in.

"Hi, there. I thought maybe I could help with dinner. Noah said you injured yourself."

Hadley held up her hands. "Yeah. I let some friends convince me to go rock climbing. It didn't end so well."

"I don't think I could go rock climbing. I'd be too afraid that I would fall and break my neck."

"I guess if you put it that way, I'm lucky it was only my fingers that got messed up."

"What can I do to help?" Hadley asked.

Though Kelsey's instinct was to refuse the help, the truth was she needed it. "First thing we need to do is cut this chicken into bite-sized pieces."

"That's easy enough." Hadley picked up the knife and set about her task while Kelsey poured some oil into a pan.

"How have you been holding up this week?" Kelsey asked.

"Lots of ups and downs," Hadley said. "JD has been so great through everything, but it still doesn't seem real that Spencer is dead."

"Noah mentioned he was living under an alias. Any idea why?"

"None at all. It's like I was dating a ghost. Everything I thought I knew about him turned out to be a facade."

Hadley's choice of words resonated with Kelsey. "What do you know about him?" she asked.

She noticed the way Hadley hesitated, recognizing her awareness that she was privy to classified information.

"Don't worry. Noah already gave me the highlights of what happened Saturday."

"I guess being married to an FBI agent, you hear all sorts of confidential information."

"Not as much as you'd think, but he and JD wanted me to know what happened because they thought you might need someone to talk to."

"Oh." Hadley finished cutting the chicken and slid it into the hot oil. "Do you need me to stir?"

"No, I can do it." Kelsey pointed at the bag of carrots to her right. "But you can peel those for me."

Again, Hadley set about her task, the two of them working in silence for several minutes.

"I keep thinking about something I told JD the other night about Spencer," Hadley finally said.

"What was that?"

"Looking back, I realize Spencer almost never talked about himself or his own work, except in the most basic ways."

"That makes sense if he was living a lie."

"Yeah, but what doesn't make sense is the way he was always asking me questions. He asked about my students all the time, but not once did he ever ask to come visit me at school or attend a school event." Hadley set the peeler aside. "And he never wanted to meet my friends."

"What did you do together, then?"

"He liked waterfront restaurants. We almost always went out to eat at someplace along the Occoquan when he came down to visit me, or when I went up to DC, we would eat someplace overlooking the Potomac."

"Did you ever meet any of his friends?"

"Everyone I met appears to have been some sort of terrorist," Hadley said with disgust. "Apparently, he didn't have a very good track record when it came to friends."

"Apparently not."

"Until we ran into his friends at the restaurant in Occoquan, I wouldn't have had any idea that he knew anyone else but me. I think some of my friends even thought I'd made him up."

"He kept himself invisible," Kelsey said quietly.

"That's exactly what he did."

* * *

Kade sat beside his wife, both of them focused on the computers in front of them. Rather than return to their home in southern Virginia, they had opted to stay on the Whitmores' property until they tied up the loose ends on the investigation into Rabell and the bombing.

Kade wasn't sure what Renee was working on at the moment, but his entire day had been spent searching for a way to contact the operative who had been working in Rabell's organization for the past two years.

Unlike the others operating in the guardian program, Brody had stepped away from his anonymity to reenter society as an undercover operative. A former Secret Service agent who had been targeted by a counterfeiting ring connected to a Mexican drug cartel, Brody had struggled with the lack of connection with people on a daily basis. When he learned his seventeen-year-old cousin had disappeared in Belize and was suspected to have been a victim of human trafficking, he had volunteered to infiltrate Rabell's group.

Unfortunately, in breaking away from the guardians, Brody had created a shield around himself that even Kade couldn't penetrate. While Brody had originally been given access to the guardian message board, that access had been lost when the guardian database had needed to be reset last year.

Still, Brody knew the location of several of the guardian safe houses. He could have left a message at one of them. The memory of a compromised safe house last fall came to mind. Maybe he had tried to get a message to them but had chosen the one location they no longer owned. With the old safe house now under new ownership, there was no way to be sure if Brody had tried to contact them by leaving a message there.

Kade's cell phone rang, and he looked down at his newest contact. "Is everything okay?" he asked by way of a greeting.

"I'm not sure," Kelsey said. "I wanted to see if you would check something out for me."

"Guardians are not in the habit of doing intel work for our clients."

"I understand, but this has to do with one of your people."

"I'm listening."

"A man was murdered shortly after the bombing last Saturday in Occoquan," Kelsey said. "We were operating under the assumption that he was working with the terrorists, but a few things haven't been adding up."

"Such as?"

"He took his girlfriend with him to dinner at the restaurant that night but then promptly pushed her into a breakup. His apartment had several concealment devices in it, millions of dollars in diamonds hidden inside. Rabell's fingerprints were found on some of the diamonds, but we have no idea what the man was doing with them or how they came into his possession."

"Anything else?" Kade asked.

"We confirmed that he was living under an alias for at least the past six months."

Kade's fingers tightened on his phone. "What was his name?"

"Spencer Andrews."

Kade didn't recognize the name, but he had trained Brody well. If he had decided to take on a new alias, he certainly had the skills to do so.

"Like I said," Kelsey continued, "it's possible he really was one of the terrorists, but if he was, why was he killed? I thought he might be your missing man."

"I'll look into it."

"I know you don't normally funnel information to analysts, but I'd appreciate if you could make an exception on this one. We're spinning our wheels and going nowhere."

"I'll let you know what I find." Kade ended the call and turned to his wife. "We need a deep dive on the name Spencer Andrews. Kelsey Cabbott thinks this guy could be Brody."

"Where is he?"

"If she's right, he's in the morgue." Kade set his phone aside and began his own search.

"Kade, you've got to see this," Renee said, her eyes still on her computer screen.

"What is it?" He rolled his chair closer until he could see an image of a passport. The face was hidden beneath a thick beard, but Kade recognized the eyes. Brody. He read through the personal information on the ID. The name: Spencer Andrews.

"It's him."

"I'll run facial recognition to be sure, but it sure looks that way."

"I'll do that. I want you to hack into the FBI files and see what they've got on him," Kade said. "Kelsey said they haven't been able to make any progress with who he is or why he was killed. Maybe we can."

They both fell silent, Kade's fears confirmed when the facial comparison between the passport and Brody's file photo matched. "It's him, all right."

"It looks like he's been very busy since you heard from him last," Renee said. "I'm getting red flags all over the place."

"What kind of red flags?"

"He was driving a car that was supposedly destroyed during a flood after the hurricane last fall in Florida. His car and house are both owned under his alias, but he was staying under the filing limit for taxes. His second vehicle was owned by a shell corporation that is showing a break-even for the past two years."

"He was using all the tricks we taught him."

"Yes, he was."

"Rabell must have found out who he was."

"Or Brody tried to stop the bombing and was punished for it."

Renee swiveled in her chair to face him. "I guess we're spending our evening looking through the rest of the file."

"I'm afraid so."

CHAPTER 33

JD FOLLOWED HADLEY DOWN THE hall, little bodies pressing in all around them. His steps slowed.

Hadley was three steps in front of him before she stopped and turned to see him lagging behind. Amusement lit her face. "They won't bite."

"Promise?"

"You realize you're the one with the gun, right?"

"Yeah, but there's only one of me."

Hadley reached for his arm. "Come on."

JD's idea to escort Hadley to work on her first day back had been born out of concern for her safety. He hadn't considered the hit his sanity might take in the process.

It wasn't that he didn't like kids. Individually, they were fine. Even two or three at a time, he could handle. But twenty-four? In one place? Overwhelming.

Eight children sat outside Hadley's classroom, leaning against the wall. A little girl jumped up when she saw them approaching.

"Miss Baker! I missed you."

Hadley's face lit up. "I missed you too, Emma."

Two more girls joined Emma, temporarily blocking JD and Hadley's path.

With a skill JD couldn't help but admire, Hadley continued down the hall, the munchkins trotting along with her and holding their own individual conversations with her.

"Okay, everyone. Grab your backpacks and go start on your morning work."

Hadley waited in the hall until the children had filed inside. She put her hand on JD's arm once more and guided him into her classroom.

JD stared. Brightly colored posters covered the walls, the desks clustered in groups of four. A tall bookcase beside the window held clear plastic bins, each of them neatly labeled. Every inch of the classroom served a purpose, from the cubbies and coat hooks on the wall to the oversized neon beanbags in the corner beneath a sign that read "Chill out zone."

A boy with dark eyes and even darker hair tugged on JD's jacket. "Who are you?"

"This is Special Agent Byers," Hadley said. "He works for the FBI."

"The FBI?" The boy's eyes widened. "Cool."

"Why are you here?" another boy asked.

"He came to talk to all of us about how to stay safe," Hadley said. She shooed both boys toward the desks. "Go sit down. You'll have plenty of time to talk to Agent Byers later."

Another little hand tugged at his jacket. JD looked down at the darling little blonde, her green eyes bright, a dimple in her left cheek flashing when she smiled. Her shirt was a size too small, and her big toe poked through the fabric of her tennis shoe.

JD's heart ached as he recognized the signs of neglect. He forced himself to look past it and offered the little girl a smile.

"I'm Cammie." She held her hand out as though she didn't realize she was eight instead of eighteen.

JD took the little hand in his and shook it as his insides melted. "Nice to meet you, Cammie."

"Are you really an FBI agent?" she asked.

JD squatted down so he was looking up at her instead of the other way around. "I am."

"Do you carry a gun?"

"Sometimes."

"Guns are scary," Cammie said.

"They can be," JD admitted, afraid her comment came from exposure to the real-life variety. "My job is to make sure people don't use guns to hurt anyone."

Cammie nodded her approval. "That's a good job."

"I think so." Enchanted, JD asked, "What do you want to be when you grow up?"

"I want to be a teacher, like Miss Baker."

"That's a good job too."

Cammie leaned closer. "Miss Baker is really pretty."

JD couldn't stop the grin from forming. Smart kid. "Yes, she is."

Apparently oblivious to the fact that she had become the topic of conversation, Hadley chatted with some students, directing others as they came into the room.

"Cammie, you need to put your things away."

"Yes, ma'am." Cammie took a step toward the cubbies before turning back. "You can sit with me at lunchtime if you want."

"Thank you, Cammie." He straightened, reminding himself he had a job to do.

JD crossed to the window. Hadley's room looked out over the back corner of the school, the edge of the bus ramp visible on the right, the grassy area beyond it stretching out until the school property ended at a wooded area.

A woman in her twenties entered the room a few minutes before the first bell rang.

"Abby, this is Agent Byers. He'll be talking to our class this morning." Hadley turned to JD. "Abby is my paraprofessional."

"Good to meet you." JD extended his hand.

"You too," Abby said.

The chaos of the morning routine continued around him until finally all of the students took their seats and the morning announcements came on over the television in the corner of the room.

JD remained by the window, his attention now on the class. Twenty-two students sat at their desks, ten girls and twelve boys.

Hadley took attendance, noting the names of the children who were missing. Once her task was complete, she stood at the front of the class.

"Okay, everyone. I'd like to introduce you to Special Agent Byers from the FBI," she said, motioning to where JD stood by the window. "Who would like to hear about his job?"

All twenty-two hands shot up.

Hadley gave him a sweet smile and patted his arm. "They're all yours."

A new wave of terror crested, and he swallowed hard. "Thanks."

* * *

Kelsey stared at the mansion in front of her, trees lining the property along the road. Ghost had sent her a message to meet him here and to bring her husband. Though she had come to trust the man, despite not knowing his real name, she didn't know what to think about his request to meet him at a senator's house.

"I don't know about this," Kelsey said.

"What?"

"This." Kelsey waved toward the house. "I've never even met Senator Whitmore, and now someone I barely know is telling me to meet him here. I'm starting to wonder if I'm being set up. I don't need someone on the Senate Intelligence Committee blowing my cover."

"I doubt that's going to happen." Noah climbed out of the car and circled to open her door. "The senator and his wife are good people."

"I know you interviewed them after the bombing, but that doesn't mean they're going to be thrilled about having us show up on their doorstep."

"I guess I didn't mention that they also had me over for dinner one night while you were gone."

Kelsey's eyes widened. "What?"

"They're good people," Noah repeated.

The cell phone Ghost had given her chimed. She looked down and read the message. *Are you going to stand outside all day?*

Kelsey held it up to show Noah. "I guess they're waiting for us."

"Come on." Noah took her hand, and together they walked up the driveway. He rang the bell, and a moment later, an older man with gold and silver hair opened the door.

"Noah. Good to see you." The senator waved them inside.

"You too, Senator. This is my wife, Kelsey."

"Good to finally meet you." He motioned to the door to their right. "We'll meet in here. If anyone asks, my wife and I invited you over for breakfast."

Kelsey walked through the open door to find a tray of muffins, grapes, and bananas on the desk. Ghost stood to the side of the door.

As soon as Noah and Kelsey were inside, Senator Whitmore closed the door.

"My wife is upstairs. I thought it would be best if she didn't connect that both Noah and Kelsey have access to classified information."

Relief flooded through her. Kelsey didn't know how the senator had managed to access her full file, but she appreciated his understanding that her cover needed to be maintained.

"Please have a seat. And help yourself to something to eat."

Noah focused on Ghost. "So, you're the reason we're here?"

Kelsey made the introductions, or at least as much as she was able. "Noah, this is Ghost."

"Have a seat," Senator Whitmore repeated.

Noah and Kelsey sat across the desk from the senator, Ghost choosing to remain standing. "What did you find out?" Kelsey asked Ghost.

"You were right about Spencer Andrews. He was the operative we inserted into Rabell's organization."

Noah perked up beside her. "He was an agent?"

"Of sorts. We hadn't heard from him in over nine months."

"Isn't that odd? To have someone drop out of contact for so long?"

"It is, but we knew he was going deep. We didn't expect him to try to contact us unless he had something that would allow us to either make arrests or inform us of a situation that needed preventing."

"But he didn't tell you about the impending bombing," Kelsey said. "Our intel on the bombing came from a girlfriend of one of the other men."

"That may be, but I have a feeling he's the one who spurred the conversation that was overheard. It might have even been what got him killed."

"Why wouldn't he have simply contacted you directly?"

"I don't know. Maybe he had someone watching him, or at least, he thought he did," Ghost said. "I didn't find a computer when I went to check out his condo, which is how he would typically contact us. I didn't see any mention of one in the FBI files either."

"We didn't find a computer. In fact, his girlfriend's laptop was stolen a day later."

"They were probably looking for evidence of who might have known about their organization," Ghost said. "My guess is that someone knew he was the source of the leak, and they were trying to make sure it was completely plugged."

"There's one thing I don't understand," Noah said. "I realize I don't have as much experience with deep-undercover operatives as you do, but why would your agent develop a relationship with a third-grade teacher? We did a deep background on her, and the woman is about as far removed from criminal activity as you can get. She didn't even live near him."

"That's another piece of the puzzle we don't understand," Ghost said.

"And the diamonds we found?" Noah asked.

"I think I can speak to that," Senator Whitmore said. "In an investigation by one of our specialists in human trafficking, she discovered that diamonds were being used as currency."

"That would make sense. Raw diamonds are easy to transport and hard to track," Kelsey said.

"It would explain why Rabell's fingerprints were found on some of the gems," Noah added. "Of course, that's assuming your man didn't flip to the other side. You said you hadn't heard from him in a long time."

"No way he would join forces with Rabell," Ghost said. "He volunteered to go undercover after his cousin disappeared. Fighting and stopping human trafficking was his obsession."

"I had to ask," Noah said.

"I know." Ghost's posture relaxed. "My guess is that Brody intercepted some of the diamonds and was trying to disrupt the flow of payment to either destabilize Rabell's human trafficking ring or to keep someone from being paid for services about to be rendered."

"Like someone who built a bomb," Senator Whitmore said.

"Exactly."

"This helps us see the picture of how Spencer Andrews played into this whole operation, but it doesn't give us any indication of who Rabell's target was or if and when he will try again," Noah said.

"We're working on that," Ghost said.

"What can we do to help?" Kelsey asked.

"The same thing you've been doing. Keep trying to identify the target. That will help us narrow down possible future threats." Ghost focused on Noah. "Do you have any new leads on who Rabell was after?"

"We're still grasping for something that makes sense," Noah said. "One theory is that Rabell was trying to wipe out Congressman Burke since he's preparing to introduce new legislation cracking down on human trafficking and giving aid to the UN to help police problem areas in other countries."

"That wouldn't really make sense. Even if the bomb had successfully killed all the members of congress present at the party, a terrorist attack would only strengthen the resolve of the others pushing the bill to get it through. If anything, it would make it more likely to pass the new legislation."

"I agree with you, but so far, that's the only theory that makes any sense."

"Any sighting of Rabell or his yacht?" Ghost asked, changing the subject.

"Rabell's in the wind," Noah said. "No one has been able to locate him or the boat we believe he came in on."

"If you find anything, let me know," Ghost said. "Kelsey knows how to get in touch with me."

"And you'll tell us if you find something new?" Noah asked.

"The guardians typically operate in the shadows, but one of our jobs is making sure the various intelligence agencies are sharing pertinent information with one another," Ghost said. "Having the two of you working together makes my job easier, but you can count on me giving you anything that will help you stop another attack."

"Thank you," Noah said. "That's what I wanted to hear."

CHAPTER 34

HADLEY STOOD ON THE SIDE of the playground, her class actively engaged in the impromptu soccer game on the near field. Even the kids who normally preferred to sit in the shade or climb the playground equipment had decided to join the game.

In the center, JD alternated between playing for the two teams, encouraging the kids as he went. He still glanced around the playground at regular intervals, scanning for newcomers, but she doubted any of her colleagues noticed. Her students certainly hadn't.

Tucker, one of the smaller boys, who tended to avoid sports, stood on the side of the field, looking too intimidated by the other kids to engage.

JD gained control of the ball and had a clear line to the goal, but instead of pushing forward, he dribbled to where Tucker stood. JD passed the ball to him and took position beside Tucker to keep the other kids from crowding him.

With JD jogging beside the young boy, Tucker moved toward the goal and took a shot. He missed, but JD gave him a high five as though he had scored the winning goal.

JD said something in the boy's ear, and Tucker's laughter rang out. Hadley's heart simply melted.

Sharon, one of her fellow third-grade teachers, stepped beside her. "It looks like your guest speaker is a hit with your class."

"Yeah. The kids love him," Hadley said. "They were so good when he was talking to them about his job. He even taught them some basic self-defense."

"That sounds dangerous. What does he do?"

"He's an FBI agent," Hadley said, remembering the rest of the cover story she and JD had created. "He was supposed to come in for career day next month, but a conflict popped up, so he offered to spend a day or two here helping with my civics unit."

"If he sticks around too long, the PE teachers might put him to work too. I can't remember the last time Tucker voluntarily participated in physical activity."

"It's good to see him laugh like that."

"Yes, it is."

Hadley's face brightened at the thought of JD's effect on her students. "You should have seen him with Cammie this morning. The expression on her face was priceless when she untied herself."

"Untied herself?"

"Yeah. JD taught them how to use their shoelaces to get loose if their hands were tied together. Cammie and Emma were the queens," Hadley said. "It was pretty amazing."

"I would have liked to see that." Sharon fell silent for a moment. "How long have you been dating this guy anyway? When we left for spring break, you were dating someone else."

Hadley had braced for when someone would ask the question, but it didn't lessen the impact. Choosing her words carefully, she said, "Spencer and I broke up on Saturday. I ran into JD the same day."

"Rebound?" Sharon asked suspiciously.

Hadley offered the whole truth now. "No, not at all. JD is an amazing guy. I'm lucky to have found him."

"Then I'm happy for you," Sharon said. "I have to admit, he's an improvement over the last boyfriend."

"What do you mean? You never met Spencer."

"Exactly. Any guy who cares enough about you to come to your work after only a week is someone worth keeping around."

Hadley let her gaze linger on JD once more. "You could be right."

* * *

JD waited until Hadley had her class safely inside before he walked the perimeter of the school property. After searching the wooded area surrounding the playground, he walked along the bus ramp and headed for the main parking lot under the guise of retrieving his lunch.

His cell phone in hand, he hit the record button as he walked the length of the lot, keeping the camera aimed downward to pick up the license plates. After retrieving his lunch, he returned the way he had come, this time taking video of the cars on the other side of him.

He noted the white Altima and red Jeep parked on the road but was unable to read the plates. Not wanting to draw attention to himself, he headed for a side door and used the keycard Hadley had loaned him to gain entrance.

When he reached Hadley's classroom, she was sitting at her desk, and her students were actively working on an assignment she had given them. Not wanting to distract them, JD continued past her room, glancing into the various classrooms as he passed. He circled the entire school before stopping in the corner where two hallways intersected.

JD pulled his cell phone from his pocket again. Though he would have preferred to call Noah, he didn't want to chance being overheard. Instead, he texted. *Can you have a black-and-white do a drive-by for me? I want the plate numbers for the vehicles parked on the road outside the school.*

Will do.

JD then retrieved the video he had taken and sent it to Noah with another message. *And I need you to run the plates on these cars in the parking lot.*

Oh. Joy.

Thank you.

I'll let you know if anything flags.

Satisfied that everything was being done to ensure Hadley's safety, he returned once more to her classroom. The calm he had observed before had been replaced by scurrying bodies lining up at the door, lunch boxes in hand. He started to back away, afraid he would get cornered into reliving his childhood in an elementary school cafeteria. The kids were cute and all, but he was ready to have some time alone with Hadley.

Cammie was too quick and grabbed his hand. "You can eat lunch with me."

JD waffled. If any of the kids could make school lunch worth going back in time, it was Cammie. The kid was seriously adorable.

Hadley saved JD from making an excuse. "I'm sorry, Cammie, but Agent Byers has to do some work during lunch so he can stay with us this afternoon."

"But . . ."

"No buts." Hadley's gaze darted to JD's before she continued. "I bet I can convince him to come with me to pick you up from the cafeteria though."

JD nodded his agreement. "I can do that."

Abby stepped forward. "I'll take them down to the cafeteria."

"Thanks, Abby."

JD watched Abby walk out into the hall, and the kids followed in a single line. As soon as they cleared the room, JD joined Hadley inside.

"Thanks for that," JD said.

"I figured you'd need a break." Hadley returned to her desk and retrieved her lunch from the bottom drawer. "Besides, it wouldn't have been fun seeing the kids fight over who got to sit with you. You're quite popular with them."

"I don't know why." JD joined her at her worktable on the side of her room. "They are cute kids though. I can see why you love what you do."

"I always seem to get the best class."

"I think it would be more accurate to say you create the best class," JD countered. "These kids are lucky to have you. You're very good at what you do."

She looked up at him, and JD read the surprise reflected in her expression. "Thank you."

JD put his hand on hers. "You're welcome."

* * *

Dismissal time had come and gone, the children all safely on their way home. Hadley scanned through her emails and clicked on one from the school counselor that informed her that her two missing students had both withdrawn from school over the break. So sad. The twin girls, Saige and Sara, had been doing so well, especially considering their background. Their mother had managed to avoid the social workers for the past few years, despite her chronic drug habit and history of neglect, and Hadley could only guess the move was yet another attempt to stay ahead of the law.

Trying not to think about what she couldn't control, she looked over her lesson plans for tomorrow, unsure how she would adjust them if JD once again accompanied her to school.

JD had left shortly after school ended to do a security check of the parking lot and surrounding area, but he appeared in her doorway now and leaned one arm against the doorjamb. Her heartbeat quickened at the mere sight of him.

"Are you about ready to go?"

"I think so." Flustered by her reaction to his presence, Hadley focused on the scatter of papers on her desk. She gathered the ones she would need at home tonight and slipped them into her oversized purse, then looked up at him. Home. The image that flashed into her mind wasn't of her apartment or even of her temporary residence but, rather, of sitting beside JD as the sun faded. She wasn't sure why her definition of home kept changing, but it terrified her that she was beginning to associate it with a person rather than a place.

She was losing her mind. There was no other explanation. All of the stress and adrenaline over the past week had caused her to exaggerate her feelings for JD. She needed time to know how she really felt, time to find a new normal.

"Is everything okay?" he asked.

Her cheeks colored when she realized she'd been staring at him. Hoping he didn't notice, she said, "I guess so." She waved at her computer. "I just found out my two missing students transferred out of this school. I'm sorry to see them go."

"That's too bad."

"I assume everything looked okay outside," she said, trying to push the negative thoughts aside.

"So far, so good." JD straightened. "By the way, Noah texted me a while ago. We thought we could grill some hamburgers over at his place tonight."

"That sounds good. Why don't you text him and tell him we'll pick up the side dishes? Kelsey doesn't need to cook for us again."

"I could go for some potato salad." JD retrieved his phone and texted Noah. "Okay. Message sent."

"Good." Hadley joined him in the hall, and together they walked to the side door. Fear bubbled within her when he walked outside first and held a hand up to keep her from following. She noticed the way he looked around before giving her the signal to join him.

He does this for a living, she reminded herself. If JD said he could keep her safe, she wanted to believe that.

They walked the short distance to his car, both of them silent until they were safely inside.

"What happens now?" Hadley asked. "I can't imagine your boss will let you come with me to work every day."

"No, but I did talk to your school safety officer today." JD slid the key into the ignition and started the engine. "He'll be doing an extra ID check on visitors, as well as running perimeter checks during the day."

"Maybe we should run by my apartment so I can pick up my truck. I'll need some way to get to work tomorrow."

"Actually, I'm going to adjust my schedule so I can drop you off and pick you up. Better safe than sorry."

"Do you really think someone is looking for me?"

"I honestly don't know." The muscle in JD's jaw twitched, and Hadley suspected he was holding something back.

"What aren't you telling me?"

"It's always worried me that your apartment was broken into while your truck was outside. I don't know if that means the intruder wanted to find you home or lucked out that you weren't there."

"I wondered about that." Hadley glanced out the window before returning her gaze to JD. "I guess I really do need to look for a new apartment."

"I've been thinking about that. How would you feel about house sitting for someone for a couple months?"

"Who?"

"My neighbor, Patty Henderson. She has this big trip planned to visit all of her children. She leaves in three weeks. Noah and I agreed to keep an eye on her place while she's gone, but I think she'd love having someone staying there."

"I guess that would work, but would she be okay with me having Lucy?"

"I doubt she would mind. I barely even know Lucy's in the house most of the time." JD reached over and laid his hand on hers. "And it would be nice to have you so close."

She smiled. "I would like that."

"I'll talk to Mrs. Henderson when we get home." JD gave her hand a squeeze. "When is your lease up for your place?"

"July 1."

"You know, if I manage to find a house before Mrs. Henderson gets back, you could always come over and house-sit for Kelsey's parents. That would get you through the end of your lease. Her folks don't get back until August."

"I'm hoping to sublet my apartment so I can get out early."

"Chad mentioned that Spencer talked to him about that," JD said.

"Spencer never talked to Chad." Her eyebrows furrowed. "I don't think they ever even met."

"That's not what Chad said. He told me Spencer came in and asked about the details of your lease and what you'd have to do to break it."

"That's weird. When I talked about breaking my lease to Spencer, he kept encouraging me to stay."

"That is odd." JD fell silent.

"What are you thinking?" Hadley asked.

"I think I want to talk to Chad again. If Spencer really did come in to see him, I'd like to know why."

"Maybe he was asking about my lease in the hopes that I wouldn't be able to get out of it," Hadley said. "After all, I was planning on moving another thirty to forty minutes farther away from DC."

"Could be, but I still want to look into it," JD said. "Anything we can find out about Spencer at this point is a good thing."

Memories of her time with Spencer surfaced, competing with the new ones she had made with JD. A cloud of despair and confusion settled over her. The chapter of her life that included Spencer was over, but she still didn't understand the truth of that relationship. Her friendship with JD was so new, so vibrant, so real. How could she feel an attraction for him so quickly after believing herself to be in love with someone else?

The familiar questions filled her mind, and once again, she wondered if she would ever truly regain control of her own destiny.

CHAPTER 35

JD ENTERED NOAH'S BACKYARD THROUGH the side gate, the scent of meat on the grill indicating where his friend was currently located. Sure enough, when he rounded the corner, Noah stood beside his grill, spatula in hand.

"Did you make enough for four?" JD asked.

"Depends. Did you pick up potato salad on your way home?"

"Potato salad, green salad, macaroni salad." JD shook his head. "Once Hadley got started, I couldn't get her to stop."

"I know what that's like."

Kelsey walked outside. "Are you two talking about me again?"

"Not this time." Noah nodded toward JD. "Our friend here is learning what it's like to be in a relationship."

"I see. And how is that going?"

"It would be going better if we didn't have to check over our shoulders, wondering if someone is looking for her," JD said. "I got your text. What did you need to talk to me about that couldn't wait ten minutes?"

"We had a breakthrough today," Noah said.

"What?"

Noah exchanged a look with Kelsey before answering. "Spencer Andrews was an undercover operative."

JD stared at his partner before looking at Kelsey for confirmation of the unlikely statement. "Seriously?"

Noah nodded. "He infiltrated Rabell's group two years ago. Unfortunately, his handler lost contact with him and didn't realize he was living under the name Spencer Andrews until Kelsey made the connection."

JD readjusted the facts in his mind, sorting through dozens of details. "Hadley was right, then. Spencer did back her into a breakup to try to get her to leave the restaurant that night."

"It would make sense if Rabell's men were using her presence as a way to keep him under control." Noah reached into his pocket and produced the ring box JD had found in Spencer's apartment. "Evidence turned this over to me. Since Spencer had no next of kin, it goes to Hadley. I thought you might want to be the one to give it to her."

JD took the box, wrapping his fingers around it rather than opening it to view the contents. "I'm not sure how to begin that conversation. How much can I tell her?"

"She can know as much of the truth as we do," Kelsey said. "It isn't much anyway."

JD slipped the ring box into his pocket. "If it's all the same to you, I think I'll wait until after dinner to talk to her."

"That would probably be best," Kelsey agreed.

Noah flipped the burgers, grease sizzling in the flames of the grill. "I'd better go help Hadley haul all those side dishes over here."

"Hey, JD?" Noah said before he could leave. "We'll understand if you want to cut our evening together short."

"Thanks. I think I might want some extra time at home after dinner."

"I figured as much."

* * *

Hadley didn't know what had come over JD, but he hadn't been himself all evening. He'd said the right things and chatted with her, Noah, and Kelsey over dinner. He had helped Noah clean up after dinner, had complimented her on the brownies she had made for dessert. But something was off.

It wasn't until JD had opened the door at home for her and escorted her inside that she had realized what it was. The little touch on her back to guide her inside was missing. Now that she thought about it, he had been physically distant from her all night.

She waited until he disengaged the alarm before she asked, "Is everything okay?"

"Yeah. Why?"

Hadley didn't know how to describe the strained connection between them and chose not to try. Instead, she simplified her question. "What's wrong?"

JD flipped the lock on the door and walked into the living room. Hadley followed.

"JD?" Hadley tried to pinpoint the moment things had changed but couldn't think of anything in particular she might have done to upset him. Unless his mood didn't have anything to do with her.

He stood facing away from her for a moment, then glanced at her and motioned to the couch. "Maybe we should sit down."

The seriousness of his tone sent her stomach plummeting. *He's breaking up with me.* An ache tore through her, more painful than she had thought possible. Had she really thought she could build a future with JD? She barely knew him. Or did she?

His kindness and sensitivity, his ability to make her feel safe, even the sensation of his hand in hers or his arm around her shoulders. So many little things that made up the whole of the man she had come to admire in such a short time.

JD swallowed hard, making Hadley brace for what was to come. She sat on the couch and noticed the way JD's hand went to his pocket before he sat beside her. "I got some news about Spencer today."

Her thoughts took a left turn. "What about Spencer?"

"We still don't have a lot of details, but your instincts about him were right. He wasn't trying to kill anyone."

"I don't understand."

"Spencer was an undercover agent. He was trying to help people."

Hadley's mouth dropped open, but no sound came out.

JD pulled something from his pocket and held it out to her. "You should have this."

Though the box remained closed, the shape and size of it left little doubt as to what it contained. "Where did that come from?"

"I found it in Spencer's apartment. I have to assume he bought it for you." JD pressed it into her hand.

The idea that Spencer had really planned to propose hit her like a brick. They had dated long enough that she had started to wonder if their relationship would end up with a proposal, but until now, she hadn't been sure what her answer would be. Her voice was low and husky when she managed to respond. "It doesn't seem right for me to take it."

"Why not?"

Her eyes lifted to meet his. "Because I wouldn't have accepted it if he had offered it to me while he was alive. It isn't right for me to have it because he's dead."

JD stared at her. "You wouldn't have said yes?"

"No." Hadley looked down at the closed box. "I wanted to think I could make a future with him, but the truth is part of me was relieved when we broke up."

"I didn't expect you to say that."

Curious, Hadley opened the ring box to see what she was giving away. The enormous diamond set in a platinum band caught in the light and represented everything she wasn't. A new thought crept into her mind. "Are you sure this was supposed to be for me? Maybe Spencer was dating someone else too."

"Why would you think that?" JD asked.

"Spencer and I talked about jewelry a few times. I mentioned that I prefer yellow gold to silver and platinum, and I'm also not a big fan of diamonds, especially large ones."

"Not even for an engagement ring?"

Hadley shook her head. "I've always preferred stones with color. Diamonds are okay, but I've always liked them best to accent another stone than to be the main focus," Hadley said. "Doesn't it seem odd to you that he would know that and still go out and spend a ridiculous amount of money on a ring I wouldn't like?"

"What's your favorite gemstone?" JD asked.

"Amethysts are my favorite."

"Spencer knew that?"

"Yeah, he did." Hadley stared down at the ring a moment longer before snapping the lid shut. She handed it back to JD. "You said yourself he was working undercover. Maybe the reason I only saw him once a week is because I wasn't the only one he was seeing."

"I can look into that possibility, but when I searched his apartment, the only photograph in his bedroom was of you."

CHAPTER 36

JD STOOD IN THE CONFERENCE room, evidence photos and forensics reports covering the table. With the new information about Spencer's true role with Rabell's group, he needed to readjust his thinking and see the situation from a new angle.

If Hadley was right, that Spencer had been dating someone else, JD hadn't been able to find any evidence of it.

Noah knocked on the open door and walked in. "How's it going?"

"Nothing new is jumping out so far," JD said. "I was looking through the apartment photos to see if there was anything to show he might have been dating someone else."

"Hadley thought he was cheating on her?" Noah asked. "The guy bought her an engagement ring."

"She doesn't think the ring was for her."

"Why does she think that?"

JD explained Hadley's observations. "If she's right, it's possible Spencer really was involved with someone else. Even though we didn't find any other photos or evidence of a second girlfriend, we know someone beat us to Spencer's apartment."

"Which means they could have removed any trace of the other person he was dating," Noah said, following JD's train of thought. "But you said Hadley had been to Spencer's apartment before. If he really was dating someone else, I'm not sure he would have risked bringing a girlfriend to his place."

"With as much money as he had, he could have had a second apartment."

"I suppose it's possible." Noah laid both hands on the table and looked at the photos. "Let's assume there was another woman. What was the purpose of dating Hadley?"

"What do you mean?"

"If he wasn't genuinely interested in her, why would he have dated her?" Noah asked. "She isn't involved with Rabell's group. She doesn't have anything to do with human trafficking or terrorist activities. Why her?"

JD could think of a thousand reasons why a man would want to date Hadley, but not one for why he would date her and then cheat on her. "I don't know."

"An undercover operative chooses his relationships deliberately. Hadley doesn't serve a purpose for him," Noah said. "Unless he fell for her and was willing to risk his safety to be with her."

"Which doesn't add up with him buying a ring that wasn't intended for her," JD said.

"Maybe Spencer didn't pay attention to what kind of jewelry Hadley liked."

"The necklace he gave her for Valentine's Day was exactly her style."

"I hate to say it, but when it comes to Spencer, all the questions seem to come down to one thing," Noah said. "Why was he dating Hadley?"

"Even Hadley has been asking that question lately." JD ran his fingers through his hair. "You know, she even mentioned that almost all of her dates started out with Spencer asking about her work and the kids in her class, but he never once took the time to visit her there or meet anyone she worked with."

"Wait a minute. I'll be right back." Noah hurried out of the room, returning a moment later holding two files. "Do you remember the case on the three coeds who disappeared in Thailand?"

"Yeah. They were supposed to go on a cruise and never showed up. No one has seen them since."

"A witness placed them at the marina an hour before they were supposed to board," Noah said. "Which has always made me think they ended up on the wrong boat."

"Or were forced onto the wrong boat."

"Right."

Noah opened the top file and set it on the table. "Do you have the list of dates Rabell's yacht was in port?"

JD dug through a stack of papers to his left. "It's incomplete, but here's what we've got."

"Any chance it was docked at Occoquan on March 23?"

JD used his fingers as he scanned through the dates, stopping on March 23. "How did you know that?"

"A twenty-six-year-old woman and her eight-year-old daughter disappeared that day. They were last seen in Woodbridge, Virginia." Noah slid the file in front of JD to reveal the photo of an attractive woman with blue eyes and her daughter, a younger version of the mother, blonde ringlets hanging past her shoulders. "What's their story?"

"Single mom, had some drug problems in the past, but was trying to get clean. She had just started working for a restaurant when she disappeared," Noah said. "Supposedly, she sent an email to the school to withdraw her daughter. Had it not been for the woman's boss, no one would have ever known she was missing."

"What school did the girl go to?" JD asked.

"Osborne Elementary."

"That's only a few miles from where Hadley teaches." The light dawned. "Hadley said most of her students are from single-parent, underprivileged homes."

"If Rabell has an inside track on knowing which of these kids and parents don't have a support system . . ." Noah said.

"He could be snatching them up without anyone ever knowing they are missing."

"Yes. If I'm right, Rabell is using his yacht to transport victims out of here."

"And Spencer could have been dating Hadley to try to identify who might be next."

"Wait a minute." JD reached out and grabbed Noah's arm. "Hadley said something on our way home last night about twin girls who had withdrawn from her class. She was really upset because they were doing so well despite their home environment."

"If they were kidnapped, Rabell or his men could be in the area." Noah gathered his files and headed for the door. "I'll run missing-persons reports for the area for the last few weeks."

"And I'll contact Hadley's principal to see if he can get me a list of kids who have withdrawn from school."

"Start with the names of the twins from Hadley's class. They're the ones who might still be in the area."

"I will." JD pulled out his cell phone and called the front office. If he and Noah were right, he wanted to give Hadley the news face-to-face.

* * *

The energy in the Washington field office was palpable. Noah tacked another photo to the bulletin board where he had created a time line of potential kidnappings and Rabell's sailings. The numbers terrified him. Twenty-three children so far. He had several fellow agents trying to locate them to see how many had truly transferred to different schools, but so far, only two had been found.

JD approached with a stack of paper in his hand. "Here are the school photos of the kids who were listed as transfers. I narrowed the search to those whose parents informed the school by email."

"Help me put them up here. Maybe you can help me find a trend."

JD proceeded to pin photos on the board, each child's name, transfer date, and school written across the top of each image. When he was finished, both men stepped back and studied the board.

Twenty-one children, all girls. The ages ranged from eight to fifteen. When they added children listed as runaways, the number skyrocketed to forty-seven.

There were six sailing dates scattered throughout the year, each one with five to ten names and photos listed beneath them.

"These are all from this year," JD said. "If Spencer went undercover two years ago, who knows how long this has been going on."

"And we can't be sure how many of the mothers might have been taken with their children," Noah added. "These dates appear completely random. One in September, two in October. Two more in March, and the one we think is happening this month."

"Warm weather."

"But we don't see any trends in the summer, not even with the missing-person and runaway reports," Noah said.

"What time is it?" JD asked, glancing at the wall clock to check for himself. "Two thirty. I think I'm going to head out and pick up Hadley. If I bring her back to the office, maybe she can help us make some sense of this."

"All of this is happening a lot closer to home than to here. I'll make up a new board for us to work with at home," Noah said. "I'll try to get down to your house by four thirty."

"See you then."

Noah turned his attention back to the board as Mitch approached. "Anything new?" Noah asked.

"Actually, yeah. Apparently, there was a rescue mission in Abolstan last weekend. One of the hostages was Ruby Norton." Mitch tapped the photo of a dark-haired girl who had supposedly been withdrawn from school last month.

"She was kidnapped at the beginning of March."

"Burt is trying to pull some strings to see if we can get an interview with her. If she can tell us how she was transported—"

"We might be able to stop it from happening to the latest victims," Noah finished for him. "I'll see if any of my contacts with the CIA can help us shake some information loose."

Noah left Mitch and crossed to his cubicle. Determined to use every available resource, he picked up his phone and called Kelsey on a secure line. After giving her a brief update on their progress, he said, "We've been able to identify one of the victims as one of the people who was rescued last weekend. What are the chances you can help us get an interview with her?"

"I might be able to get some questions answered. What specifically do you want to know?" Kelsey asked.

"Anything that will help us know where she was taken from, by whom, and especially how she was transported out of Virginia," Noah said. "We still haven't found Rabell's yacht, but I don't want to assume that's how he's getting these girls out of here when he could be using another transportation method."

"I'll see what I can do," Kelsey said.

"Also, is there any way you can get me a list of names of the hostages who were rescued from Rabell's compound?"

"I can, but that's not something I can send you electronically. With the press clamoring for the story, the agency is being very protective of the hostages' identities."

"I'm meeting JD at his place at four thirty. Think you could bring it with you then?" Noah asked. "You don't even have to show it to me. I just need to know if any other missing persons cases ended in that rescue."

"I'll find a way to make it happen."

"Thanks. I'll see you in a couple hours." Noah ended the call and grabbed a camera. Time to make sure he could recreate his work to take it home tonight. When he stepped in front of the bulletin board again, his eyes were drawn to the three photos in the last column: twin eight-year-olds and an eleven-year-old. If their hunch was right, all three girls were still being held here in Virginia. Somehow, they had to find them before it was too late.

CHAPTER 37

THE BLOOD DRAINED OUT OF Hadley's face. She couldn't be hearing JD correctly. "Sara and Saige were kidnapped? They're victims of human trafficking?"

JD took her hand and led her to the couch. "We're doing everything we can to find them."

Tears threatened, and Hadley blinked against them. "They're only little girls. Their lives are just beginning."

"I know." JD rubbed his thumb back and forth over the back of her hand. He sat and tugged on her hand so she would sit beside him. "I need your help though. What do you know about where they lived and where they spent their time when they weren't at school?"

"The school should have their address, but I don't know much about what they did when they weren't at school."

"We already checked out their apartment, but the manager said he had to evict them six months ago. Was it possible they were living in a shelter?"

"I don't know." Her mind continued to reel.

"Think with me. Your students tell you things all the time. When these girls walked in on Monday mornings, what did they tell you?"

Hadley fought against the terrifying images of what her students could be going through right now and concentrated on JD's question. "I think they were staying near the mall. I remember a couple of times the girls talking about things they got when they went dumpster diving with their mom."

"What kind of things?"

"Food that was still in the wrappers, paper, and school supplies. Staples was one of their favorite places to get stuff because they said the dumpsters were always clean."

"I know there are quite a few homeless people who set up tents in the woods not too far from there," JD said. "How did they get to school?"

"They rode the bus." A lightbulb flipped on in her head. "It was bus 246. The driver would probably know their stop." Hadley pulled her cell phone from her pocket. "Do you want me to call transportation?"

"Give me the number, and I'll do it."

Hadley retrieved the number from her phone and held it up for JD. The doorbell rang.

"That'll be Noah," JD said, his phone pressed to his ear. "Can you let him in?"

"Sure." Hadley went into the entryway and checked through the side window to make sure it really was Noah before opening the door. "Come on in. JD's in the living room."

"Thanks." Noah walked inside, a large bulletin board in one hand and a stack of files in the other.

"Here. Let me take that." Hadley reached out and relieved him of the bulletin board. "I assume you want it in the living room?"

"Yeah. Thanks."

Hadley leaned it against one of the kitchen chairs. "What can I do to help?"

"We have photos of the kids we think may have disappeared. I need you to help us look for patterns. The dates are clustered in the spring and fall, but we aren't sure why."

Noah opened one of his files. One by one, he tacked photos in six different columns.

Her throat closed when he put on the last two, her two students.

JD finished his phone call. "Transportation gave me the intersection where the bus picked up the twins. I have the cops checking out the area for me."

Noah picked up the bulletin board and propped it on one of the bar stools so it would be closer to eye level. "This is what we've got. Now we have to figure out if there's a pattern we can use to stop Rabell from abducting anyone else."

"These dates are so random," JD said. He put a hand on Hadley's shoulder. "Do you have any idea what would make these times more advantageous than other times of the year?"

"You make it sound like a business deal," she said, annoyed at the calm way JD asked the question.

"To these people, it is a business. We need to think like them if we're going to stop them."

Hadley forced herself to look at the photos, even in the face of the horror of someone kidnapping these young girls pictured in the photos. A familiar face stared back at her—brown eyes, her hair pulled back in a messy braid. Hadley's hand lifted to her mouth to control the sob that rose within her.

"Hadley, it's okay," JD said, his hand slipping around her shoulder. "It's going to be okay."

Hadley shook her head, tears spilling over. She pointed at the image of the little girl, the second photo from the left. "That's Ivy. She was in my class."

"I'm so sorry." JD turned her and wrapped her in his arms, Hadley clinging to him as though he could make the nightmare disappear. So many children, so much tragedy.

"Hadley, I know this is hard," Noah said gently, "but you know more about the schools in Prince William County than the rest of us. We need to find a pattern here, something that will help us figure out where they might strike next."

A breath shuddered out as she tried to stem her emotions. Noah was right. Hiding in JD's embrace wasn't going to help these girls. She couldn't fathom what Ivy might be going through, or if it was even possible to find her after so many months of her being gone, but she might still be able to help Saige and Sara.

With some effort, she turned away from JD and faced the display Noah had created. So many smiling faces. She doubted any of these children had had any idea that their school photos would be used like this.

Hadley stepped closer to the board. "These are all school photos."

"That's right." Noah put his hand on top of the bulletin board. "I had the company that takes them send the images we needed."

"School photos," Hadley repeated. She pointed to the dates on the top of the board. "We take them twice a year. They start around the second week of September and go through the first week of October."

"And the second time?"

"March and April."

"Someone is using school photos to screen who they want," JD said.

"But how would they know which children could be kidnapped without being missed?" Noah asked.

"They do what Spencer did. They date someone who works at the school." Hadley pointed at the first column. "The kids here all came from three schools." She pointed at the next one. "These were from two."

"So two or three guys start dating teachers in underprivileged schools. They somehow tap into the school photos and basically handpick their victims," JD said.

"And then they send emails to the schools saying the kids are being transferred out of state so they won't be reported missing," Noah finished for him.

"How do we stop them?" Hadley asked. "If Spencer really was trying to stop them, he wouldn't have told them about the kids in my class."

"No, but you and the other teachers talk about your students," JD said. "It could be any of the other teachers."

"Or administrators," Noah added. "Which teachers are dating someone right now? Maybe someone they've only been dating for a couple months?"

"I can't be sure about everyone, but I can make a list of the people I do know about."

"It's got to be someone you are close to. Otherwise, they wouldn't have known about the twins."

Hadley mentally went through the list of teachers and faculty members she worked with, the ones she confided in. "It has to be Abby. She started dating someone about two months ago," Hadley said. "She's my paraprofessional, so she knows all about the kids in my class."

"Do you know her boyfriend's name?"

"His name is Donnell."

"Can you describe him?" JD asked.

"I only saw him once when I saw Abby at a restaurant. Spencer was in a hurry to leave, so I didn't even get the chance to talk to her." Hadley tried to bring the image into focus, that brief glance she'd had of Abby's boyfriend. Her hand reached out and gripped JD's. "Oh my gosh. I think he was the man you chased out of Spencer's apartment."

"That was Donnell?"

"I think so." A new awareness came over her. "Not only that. Chad introduced Abby to him."

"Chad? Your apartment manager?"

Images flooded her mind. "How could I have been so stupid?" Hadley's hand tightened on JD's. "Chad started asking me out right after school started. As soon as our class photos came in, we broke up."

"When was that?" JD asked.

"First weekend in October. It was on a Saturday."

Noah picked up a file from the table and flipped through pages. "The email requesting Ivy be withdrawn from school was sent on Friday, October 2." Noah looked at Hadley. "When did you start dating Spencer?"

"I met him the next weekend." Again, the memories of her past took on new clarity. "He was dating me as part of his investigation."

"Did he ask you about Chad?" JD asked.

"No, but he did ask about the kids in my class and the people I worked with."

"He didn't know who he was looking for, but somehow, he had connected the disappearances of these kids to Rabell," JD said.

"We found fingerprints on the diamonds that belonged to both Spencer and Rabell," Noah said. "He must have infiltrated the top end of the organization without gaining access to the supply chain."

JD turned to Hadley. "You said you were the one who talked to Chad about breaking your lease, right?"

"Yeah. Why?"

"Chad said it was Spencer. He also mentioned that he thought Spencer was about to propose to you."

"There weren't any fingerprints on the engagement ring you found," Noah pointed out. "Do you think Chad planted it to back up his story?"

"Making it look like he was serious about Hadley would explain why he was at her apartment the night he was killed and deflect any suspicion that Spencer was investigating him," JD said.

"You think Spencer knew Chad was involved?" Hadley asked.

JD nodded. "I think that's what got him killed."

Hadley drew a shaky breath. "So, not only did Chad use me to get to an eight-year-old, but he's also a cold-blooded murderer?"

JD stepped in front of her, waiting for her gaze to lift to meet his. "Chad took advantage of you." JD pulled his keys from his pocket. "And now I'm going to stop him."

"I'll come with you." Noah reached for his suit coat.

"No. I don't want Hadley to be alone."

"Then let me go."

JD glanced at Hadley, and she saw the determination in his eyes. "No. I need to do this. I'll call Mitch and have him meet me there."

"Be careful," Hadley said, not sure what other words she could offer.

"I will." He leaned forward for a kiss before turning to Noah. "Keep her safe. I'll call you as soon as I have Hicks in custody."

"Good luck."

With a last look at Hadley, JD nodded and walked out the door.

CHAPTER 38

KELSEY HURRIED UP THE FRONT walk of her parents' house, where JD was staying. She knocked twice before she let herself in. This was no time for formalities.

Noah appeared from the living room and closed the distance between them before she could enter. He lowered his voice. "Hadley's here. She's trying to help us figure out where they might strike next."

"The girl you asked about wasn't able to give us much, but she did say she rode in a big boat and then took a bigger boat."

"That tracks with the patterns we're seeing," Noah said. "Any idea if she was held somewhere first?"

"'Metal walls' is all she could remember. My guess is Rabell has a warehouse or storage unit someplace where he keeps his captives until he's ready to transport them out of the U.S."

"I'll call the office to see if some agents can search for possibilities."

"I also called Ghost. He's tapping into the Coast Guard resources as well as local police agencies. Everyone is searching for that yacht and the missing girls."

"Come on into the kitchen. Even though Hadley's in there, you can run the comparison of the lists without her finding out who you are."

Kelsey debated briefly. She could just as easily do the comparison at home, but the truth was she wanted to be where the brainstorming was happening, to be present in case her insight could make a difference. "Put me to work." Kelsey followed him into the kitchen.

Hadley sat at the table, files and notepads spread out in front of her. A project board had been propped on a bar stool to face them.

"Hi, Hadley." Kelsey looked around the room. "Where's JD?"

"You just missed him."

"He and Mitch are on their way to bring in a suspect," Noah said. He turned to Hadley. "I told Kelsey what was going on. She wanted to help too."

"Who's the suspect?" Kelsey asked, appreciating the way her husband managed to make the reason for her presence believable.

"Chad Hicks. He's my ex-boyfriend," Hadley said. "JD is going to find him now."

Understanding the worry reflected on Hadley's face, Kelsey put her hand on her new friend's arm. "He'll be careful."

"How do you manage to stay calm when you know your husband is out looking for danger every single day?"

"He isn't looking for danger," Kelsey said, choosing her words carefully. "He's trying to stop it."

"Speaking of which, I was hoping you could help with a project." Noah flipped through several papers, finally coming up with the one he wanted. He handed it to Kelsey. "Can you compare this list with the other one I gave you?"

"Happy to." Kelsey chose a seat in the living room corner that faced everyone else. She retrieved her secure tablet from her purse and pulled up the necessary file.

She was vaguely aware of Noah calling his office to enlist some of his coworkers' help with ownership records for local warehouses. Before she had made it through the first dozen names on her list, her husband sat across from her on the couch and opened his laptop. She had no doubt he too was joining the search.

* * *

Rage and disgust boiled inside JD. The look on Hadley's face when she had learned her students had been kidnapped would haunt him for the rest of his life.

Chad had used her. Spencer had used her. The last seven months of the woman's life had been based on lies, lies she'd known nothing about, lies that had played on her emotions in every possible way. She deserved more than that. So much more.

JD gripped his gun and approached the corner of the building that housed the office of Hadley's apartment complex. He could see now that the surveillance cameras had been positioned more to protect the office than the residents.

"I'm in position," Mitch said, his voice sounding through the earpiece JD wore.

JD checked the camera aimed at the front door. Chad would see him coming, but with Mitch's help, he would make sure Chad didn't get past him.

JD gripped his gun again and prepared to move. "Go."

The single word propelled both men into motion. JD sprinted to the office door, slowing only long enough to check for possible explosives before bursting through the entrance.

A woman sat at the reception desk, saw JD's gun, and screamed.

"Federal agent." JD scanned the room, but the woman was the only occupant. He shifted his aim to Chad's office door. He hurried forward and pushed the door open to find the lights off and the room empty.

Mitch appeared from the back. "Clear."

JD turned to the woman. "Where is Chad Hicks?"

"I don't know." Her voice trembled. "He took a few days off."

"When did you see him last?" JD pressed.

"Two days ago." She looked from JD to Mitch and back again. "What's going on?"

"I need Chad's employee file."

"I don't have that here." The woman waved a hand helplessly through the air. "Those files are held at the corporate office."

"Do you know where he lives?"

"Yeah." She motioned across the parking lot. "Apartment 274." Her hands trembled, and she pointed at her drawer. "If you promise not to shoot, I'll give you the key."

JD lowered his gun. "Deal."

* * *

Hadley jumped out of her seat when she heard the garage door open. The moment JD walked through the door, she threw her arms around his neck. "I'm so glad you're back."

JD pressed his lips to her forehead before continuing inside.

"What happened?" Noah asked.

"He wasn't there. We checked both his office and apartment, but we didn't find anything to tie him to Rabell," JD said.

"Could we be wrong about him?" Noah asked.

"I don't think so." JD stopped in front of the bulletin board. "I had his employer pull his vacation time for the past year. Every time Rabell's yacht was in the area, Chad took between three and five days off."

"When is he supposed to be back to work this time?" Noah asked.

"Day after tomorrow."

"Then whatever is happening is going down in the next two days."

"I'm afraid so." JD tapped the board. "We have three possible victims here. All of the other dates had at least five. We have to assume there are more to come."

Hadley stared at the board, her notes creating a comparison of children taken from each school. "They usually take two to three per school," Hadley said.

"Then we concentrate on the two schools we know about," Noah said.

Hadley stepped between the two men, staring at the notes on each photo rather than the faces staring back at her. "Do you think Chad and Donnell are dating multiple women at the same time, or do you think there's someone else out there?"

"Most likely, he's working with the men you know as Drake and Carlos."

"That would make sense. Then we're dealing with a crew of three or four," Noah said.

"I think we know all the players," JD said.

Kelsey rose from where she had been sitting in the living room. "Noah, I finished comparing those names."

"Let me see," Noah said.

Kelsey handed Noah a piece of paper that listed the suspected victims.

"What were you comparing?" Hadley asked.

"There was a rescue in Abolstan last weekend. Several victims of human trafficking were recovered," JD said.

"And you think some might be from here?"

"I found five," Kelsey said.

"Was Ivy Bellman one of them?"

Kelsey shook her head. "No. I'm sorry."

Hopelessness and helplessness spiraled inside Hadley, an ache settling deep within her stomach.

Kelsey picked up a highlighter and marked the photos of the girls who had been recovered. She picked up a sticky note, then wrote a name on it before pressing it onto the board beneath the March 23 column. "This woman was from here as well. She's Ruby Norton's mother."

"Mother and daughter." Hadley shook her head. "I can't begin to comprehend the horrors they must have endured."

"They're safe now," Kelsey assured her.

"But Sara and Saige aren't." Hadley forced herself to look at the photos of the twin girls. "And we have no idea how many more will be in danger before tomorrow ends."

Noah and Kelsey exchanged a look that held hidden meaning before Noah spoke. "I'll get a message to our people with the hostages to see if they can get any more details of where the victims were held before they were shipped out of here."

Kelsey crossed back into the living room and slipped her tablet into her purse. "It's getting late. I think we should quit for the night and start first thing in the morning."

"She's right," Noah agreed. "We've got a dozen agents searching for where the girls are being held, and the authorities have the marina staked out."

"But—" Hadley started to protest.

JD stepped between her and the photos. "Hadley, I know it's hard, but driving ourselves into the ground isn't going to help. It will only hurt our efforts."

"I can't stand knowing someone could be hurting these girls, that we're helpless to stop them."

"We aren't helpless," JD said. "We've had one breakthrough after another today."

"Have faith that we'll get the information we need when we need it," Kelsey said gently.

Noah reached for the project board. "I'll take this home. I think you two can use a break from the reminder for a while."

"Thanks." JD escorted them out and returned a moment later. He slid his hands around Hadley's waist and held her loosely in front of him. "Are you going to be okay?"

"I don't know." Hadley blew a strand of hair out of her face. "I thought worrying about someone looking for me was bad. Knowing Saige and Sara are missing is so much worse. And I can't even think about what's happened to Ivy."

"I know." He pulled her close. "And I'm sorry you have to see the dark reality of what happens in the criminal world."

"Can you stop it?" Hadley asked. "Can you stop these men?"

"I hope so," JD said. "Over a hundred victims were rescued last weekend. If I have my way, we'll add to that count before the sun goes down tomorrow."

"I'll pray for that."

"That makes two of us."

CHAPTER 39

JD COULDN'T SLEEP. NO MATTER how many times he had told Hadley that she needed to step away from the things she couldn't control, he was having a hard time taking his own advice.

For hours, he had tossed and turned. Every time he dozed off, the worry would surface, not only for the victims he hoped to rescue but also for the ones who would be affected in the future if he and his coworkers weren't successful in finding and stopping Rabell.

He glanced over at the clock. 4:12 a.m. Giving up, he grabbed his cell phone off his night table and pulled up his work email to read the latest updates. Since he had checked last night, two searches had been conducted by fellow agents. One raid had uncovered a meth lab and led to several arrests. The other had resulted in the discovery of a forty-seven-year-old veteran who was living in a storage unit with all his belongings.

Frustrated that the FBI had yet to find the correct location, JD headed for the shower. Fifteen minutes later, he padded downstairs to find Hadley sitting on the living room couch, the soft glow from the television washing over her, and Lucy curled up on the couch beside her.

"You couldn't sleep either, huh?"

"No." She stroked the cat. "I hope you don't mind my bringing her down here. I was afraid she would wake you if I left her alone in my room."

"It's fine." JD reached out and scratched between Lucy's ears. "Mind if I join you?"

"Of course not." Even though the volume was already low, Hadley muted the TV.

JD took the spot beside her. "What are you watching?"

"The news. I know it will sound silly, but I was hoping I would see something that might help us find Saige and Sara."

"It's not silly. We've received a lot of great tips from the news."

Lucy stood and stretched before padding across Hadley's lap and climbing onto JD. JD stroked the cat, amused when she turned a circle and proceeded to lie on his chest.

"If she's bothering you, I can take her."

"She's fine." JD continued to pet the animal, Lucy's purrs now vibrating against his chest. "How long have you been up?"

"An hour or so," Hadley said. "Every time I fell asleep, I started dreaming about my students, terrified that another one will disappear."

"We'll do everything we can to prevent that," JD said.

"All of this is so surreal." Hadley raked her fingers through her hair, letting it fall to curtain her face. "A bomb one weekend, kids disappearing the next. It's hard to fathom that the two things are even connected."

"So far, the only connection we have is that the man who is running the organization is responsible for both crimes."

"Did you ever figure out why the bomb was planted?" Hadley asked.

"We still aren't completely sure," JD admitted. "The theory that he was after Congressman Burke to stop the stiffer legislation against human trafficking only makes sense if he doesn't realize that the bill will likely go forward even if something does happen to one of the sponsoring congressmen."

"Would the law even matter to him? I would think he would be more concerned about avoiding getting caught than what would happen if he's arrested."

"The new legislation is more focused on funding prevention and enforcement efforts than prosecution," JD said. "A task force has been working for the past couple years to find solutions on how to disrupt the flow of victims across borders and to finance sting operations to recover those who have already been taken."

Hadley's gaze landed on the television again. "It's hard to fathom that Saige and Sara could be locked up somewhere, terrified, and the newscasters have spent the last hour talking about weather, sports, and politics."

"I wish that's all they ever had to talk about," JD said.

Hadley straightened beside him and pointed at the television. "That's her."

JD looked up at the screen where a photo of a woman was on display. The face was vaguely familiar, but he couldn't place the name. "Who?"

"She's the woman who was eating dinner with Richard Lincoln."

"She was there the night of the bombing?"

"Yes."

JD shifted the cat off of him and grabbed the remote. He turned on the sound and hit the rewind button to back up the live stream to when the segment first started, *Breaking News* flashing across the bottom of the screen.

The newscaster's voice filled the room. "The woman's body, discovered in Westmoreland State Park yesterday, has been identified as Georgia Archer, a senior analyst with the Department of Transportation. Recognized for aggressive strategies in the prevention of human trafficking, Archer was heavily involved in planning the implementation of the funding bill that is set to go before Congress in July."

The newscaster paused briefly before continuing. "Congressman Burke said her loss is a heavy blow to this country and referred to Archer as 'a pioneer in protecting human rights.'"

"She was the target," JD muttered.

"But why plant a bomb that would have killed so many?" Hadley asked. "Obviously, they knew enough about her to find her without waiting for a dinner party."

"But if the bomb had been successful, we never would have known who they were after," JD said. "And all but one of the sponsors of the human trafficking bill would have been killed."

"Which might have killed its progress."

"She must have known her life was in danger if she was using an alias with the reporter."

"But I don't know why she looked familiar to me. I know I've seen her somewhere before."

"Let's see if we can find out more about her." JD stood and reached for her hand. "Come on."

Hadley, who had become Lucy's new resting place, stood, still holding the cat. "I'd better go put her back upstairs."

"She'll be fine." JD waited for Hadley to set Lucy down before he led the way into the office. He sat at the desk and turned on his laptop.

"What are you doing?"

"I'm going to pull her personal information off her background check." JD completed his task, then adjusted the screen so Hadley could see it. "Look at this and see if there is anything you have in common with her."

"She's ten years older than me; we didn't go to the same college or anything; she lives in DC." Hadley shook her head. "I have no idea where I would have seen her before."

"Could you have seen her at a restaurant somewhere? Or maybe passed her on the street when you were with Spencer?"

"Wait a minute." She waved at the computer. "Can you check her address?"

JD punched a few keys to pull up the right screen. "This address looks familiar." Awareness dawned, and Hadley confirmed the truth.

"That's Spencer's address. They lived in the same building."

* * *

Hadley remembered the encounter clearly now. "I saw her in the hall outside Spencer's apartment. She gave me an odd look, like she didn't approve of me. That's probably why I remembered her. I normally don't get that kind of reaction from a complete stranger."

"It's possible she was working with Spencer, trying to identify Rabell's methods. On the surface, it could have appeared that you or another teacher was helping Rabell."

"So Spencer was dating me, trying to find out information."

"I'm afraid so. At least partially," JD said. "It wouldn't have taken him long to realize you weren't involved. If he only cared about his case, he would have cut ties way earlier."

"Thanks for trying to make me feel better, but we both know he was still using me for information."

"Whatever his reasons for being with you, he was trying to save lives."

"I know." Hadley circled to the other side of the desk and sat in the chair opposite him. "I assume that since Rabell succeeded in killing this woman, there shouldn't be any more bomb threats."

"I hope not."

"Now what?"

"Now we keep looking for the missing girls," JD said.

"You said there were other agents who were looking for Rabell's warehouse. Any news on that?"

"They checked out a couple places, but no luck so far."

"With all the research you and Noah have done, there has to be something we're missing," Hadley said. "Not that I'm an expert on this stuff."

"You're becoming one pretty quick."

"I doubt that. I don't know how I'm going to be able to work today. Maybe I should call in."

"Don't do that."

"Why not?" Hadley asked. "I can't imagine trying to keep up a good face in front of my students, knowing that they're going to ask why Saige and Sara aren't back from spring break yet."

"Even though there isn't any clear-cut pattern that tells who the next victim might be, most of the days kids went missing, there were more than one from each school."

"There are already two kids missing from my school."

"But only one household," JD pointed out. "If you're at work, you can be our eyes and ears if anyone is absent or another withdrawal notice is sent in."

"I never thought I would pray so hard for all of my students to be at school."

"I know what you mean."

CHAPTER 40

KELSEY LISTENED TO THE TAPPING of Noah's fingers against his cell phone screen, the faint glow not quite hidden by his body. She leaned up on one elbow and put her free hand on his shoulder. "Did you even try to sleep?"

"I tried." He sat up and gave her a kiss. "I'm sorry. I didn't mean to wake you."

"I didn't have the best night's sleep either," Kelsey said. "Seeing the pictures of those kids is almost as bad as knowing what happens to them if they are sent overseas."

"I know. If the pattern holds, Rabell should be transporting the victims today."

"I thought he normally docked his yacht for a few days before he left again."

"He does." Noah threw the covers off and climbed out of bed. "If he knows we were looking for him after the bombing, he might have traded out what boat he's using."

"It's possible."

"I'm going to grab a shower and get this day started."

"I'm going to check out the project board again." Kelsey stood. "I keep thinking that if we can figure out who the next victim might be, we have a chance of catching Rabell and his men in the act."

"Sometimes there are two kids from one class who disappear at the same time," Noah said, turning on the water.

"You have Hadley to give you intel on her school," Kelsey said. "Do you want me to get the other teacher's info?"

"Yeah, that would be great."

"I'll see what I can do." Kelsey grabbed her laptop from her dresser and climbed back into bed. Today was the day, she decided. She wasn't going to stand by and watch more people fall prey to Rabell and the horrors he could inflict.

* * *

JD was debating how to start his day when his phone rang. He picked it up, half expecting to see Noah's or Mitch's name illuminated on his screen because of the early hour. Instead, he saw a 703 number. "Agent Byers."

"Agent Byers, this is Chester Elliott. Sorry to call so early, but that yacht you were asking about is back."

"Where? In Occoquan?"

"That's right. I passed it coming into the harbor when I left this morning for a day trip."

"So you aren't there now?"

"No, but I passed it a few minutes ago."

"Thank you for your call, Mr. Elliott. I appreciate it."

"No problem."

JD hung up and immediately called Noah. "Hey, we have a sighting of Rabell's yacht. A witness just saw it at Occoquan."

"Call Mitch and have him get us a search warrant. We can head up there as soon as you're ready."

"I'm ready now," JD said. "Do you mind driving though? I'll need to let Hadley use my car so she can get to work."

"Yeah, no problem. I'll see you in a minute."

Twenty minutes later, JD hung up again and glanced at Noah in the driver's seat. Both men had foregone their typical suits, instead opting for casual wear that would help them blend in at the dock. "That was Mitch. He said they didn't turn anything up in the warehouse district."

"What about storage units?" Noah asked, turning off the freeway and heading toward the marina.

"Nothing. They went through the surveillance feeds for everything within a ten-mile radius of the harbor and didn't find anything out of the ordinary."

"I'd have to think they'd be holding the girls nearby. Otherwise, it would be too risky to move them to ship them out."

"I agree," Noah said. "My guess is the metal walls were from some sort of shed, or maybe even the back of a tractor-trailer."

"So many options. I have a feeling this is going to be a long day."

"There's a cooler in the back seat with some cold chicken," Noah said. "There's some fry bread and cookies back there too."

"I really love your wife."

"From what Kelsey said, Hadley is the one who made the cookies she packed for us."

The mere mention of Hadley's name warmed him. "Okay, so I may love Hadley too."

"I was starting to wonder. You two have been pretty tight this last week," Noah said. "I can't remember you ever lending your car to someone before."

"She didn't have another way to get to work."

"I'm not complaining," Noah said. "Just observing."

"And what are you observing?"

"You and Hadley seem to be well suited for each other." Noah turned into the marina parking lot. "And she's not a bad cook."

"True." JD motioned to his left. "The yacht should be docked over there."

"It'll be at least a half hour before Mitch gets here with the warrants." Noah parked in the shade on the far side of the lot. "Let's take a look around."

Both men climbed out of the car and headed for the docks.

"I'll start on the east side. You can start on the west," Noah said.

"Meet you back here." JD's hand went briefly to his weapon in his waistband, a confirmation that it was there if he needed it. With the breeze coming in off the water and the sunlight shimmering across the gentle waves, he continued forward until the yacht he was looking for came into sight.

He fixed his gaze on the boat, eager for any sign of the missing girls. Were the victims being held somewhere else until Rabell deemed it time to move them, or were they already on board? JD hoped it was the latter so their search could end and he could stop this man once and for all.

* * *

It was like an itch he couldn't scratch. For the past two hours, Kade had reviewed the latest intel and witness reports on Rabell's operation, searching for something, anything that might give him a hint of what he could do to help. The missing girls from Woodbridge and the FBI's assumption that something was going down had tugged at him throughout the night until he had finally given up on sleep.

It was time to leave the Whitmores' property and move closer to the action.

Kade exited the trailer through the trap door in the center of his living room and proceeded to disconnect the water and electrical hookups. He had to give it to the senator. When undergoing some repairs last year, he had extended both the water and electricity lines past his barn to create the hookups for him, even though he and Renee only came to visit a handful of times a year.

When Kade finished his task, he reentered his home, where he had left Renee sleeping. To his surprise, she was up and dressed now.

"Are croissants okay for breakfast?" she asked. "We can eat them on our way."

"How did you know we're leaving?"

"When I woke up and saw my digital clock had no power, I figured we were getting ready to move."

"Gorgeous and smart." Kade leaned forward for a kiss. "No wonder I married you."

"What can I say? You're a very smart man."

Kade appreciated the playful tone but fought against the distraction. "We'll continue this discussion another time. I want to get on the road."

"Then, croissants it is." Renee grabbed their breakfast and a couple of water bottles from the fridge, then made her way to the cab. "Where are we going?"

"I'm not sure, but everything seems to be happening in Prince William County, so I thought that would be a good place to start." Kade started the engine.

"There's RV parking in Prince William Forest Park."

"Make us a reservation. I think that's about to become our new home base."

Renee glanced at the clock. "You realize we're going to be fighting through rush-hour traffic until we hit 95, right?"

"Nah. We'll go the back way through Manassas."

Renee clicked her seat belt into place. "In that case, I'm ready when you are."

* * *

Kelsey wasn't about to sit at a desk all day and wait to find out what happened. She had managed to get the contact information for the middle-school teacher who had a student withdraw via email yesterday, but the woman wasn't answering her phone.

Kelsey supposed having a strange phone number show up on the screen at seven in the morning could be cause to reject the call, but she wasn't going to let that stop her. Armed with FBI credentials she had received on a previous undercover assignment, she parked in a visitor's spot in front of the school and made her way into the main office.

"May I help you?"

"Yes. I need to speak with Olivia Wilkins, please."

"She's already in her classroom. The first bell rang three minutes ago."

"Where is her classroom?" Kelsey asked.

"I'm sorry. We don't allow visitors during school hours. Can I leave her a message?"

"It can't wait." Kelsey flashed her badge. "I need to speak with her now."

A man around forty approached from a back hallway. "I'm Principal Vargas. Perhaps we can chat in my office, and you can tell me what this is about."

Recognizing this man was her fastest way to the information she needed, she nodded and stepped around the reception counter to follow him back the way he had come.

As soon as the door closed, he turned to face her, waving her into a chair. "Now, what is this about?"

Kelsey remained standing. "Yesterday, you received an email that Courtney Rivera was transferring to another school."

"How did you know . . . ?"

"We believe she may have been abducted," Kelsey said.

His face paled, and he lowered into his seat. "Abducted?"

"I don't have time to go into details, but I need to know if you have received any other withdrawal notices in the last two days. And I need to speak with Courtney's teacher."

Principal Vargas picked up the phone. "Desiree, please send someone down to Miss Wilkins's room to watch her class. I need her in my office immediately. And I need to know if we received any withdrawal or transfer requests since yesterday."

"Well?" Kelsey asked as soon as he hung up.

"Lani Brenlin. Her mother sent an email late last night, asking for us to forward her transcripts to a school in California."

"Does she have Miss Wilkins for a teacher?"

He turned to his computer and typed a few keys. A few seconds later, he nodded. "Yes. She's in her fourth-period science class. How did you know?"

"Lucky guess. I need Lani's address, her mom's work information, and any emergency contacts."

He pulled up another screen and jotted down the information. "Her mother was unemployed, and she never provided any emergency contacts, but here's her address and phone number."

A knock sounded on the door.

"Come in."

A stocky brunette entered the room, a diamond bracelet winking from her left wrist. "You asked to see me?"

"Yes. Please sit down."

She did so, her eyes darting to where Kelsey stood beside the desk.

"This is an agent with the FBI. She needs to ask you a few questions."

Kelsey got right to the point. "I assume you have a boyfriend right now."

She nodded, bewilderment evident on her face.

"I need his name, address, and phone number," Kelsey said.

"Why do you want to know?" Miss Wilkins asked.

"Because I believe he's been using you to find out which of your students are easy targets for a human trafficking ring."

"Drake would never be involved in something like that."

"Let me guess. You've been dating for a few months but didn't meet him until after Christmas. When you see him, he always asks about your students, but he's never visited you at school," Kelsey said, laying out the facts Hadley had given her. "He has money, but you've never visited him at work. In fact, you probably only have his cell phone number."

"How did you know all of that?"

"Because I know the pattern. I believe Lani Brenlin and Courtney Rivera have been abducted. If we don't find them today, they may never be seen again," Kelsey said bluntly. "Now, I'm going to ask you again: What is your boyfriend's name, what is his phone number, and where can I find him?"

CHAPTER 41

THE NEXT VICTIM. THOSE WORDS kept rolling through Hadley's mind, her thoughts consumed with the idea that another of her students could be at risk.

Though she would have preferred to avoid the two empty desks in her classroom, the knowledge that her presence at school might make a difference for the safety of her students pushed her to get ready for work.

Not looking forward to the drive from Stafford to Woodbridge, she adjusted the seat of JD's car so she could reach the pedals. Once she pulled out onto the road, she considered the kids in her class. Knowing the girls were the most likely to be targeted, she concentrated on them, going over the seating chart in her room.

She tried to think like a criminal; she evaluated the home life of each child. Two had attentive stay-at-home moms, and another lived with her grandparents, who were retired. Four others arrived each day from a reputable daycare center.

Of the remaining three girls in her class, Shantell came from the worst situation, with a mom who had been in and out of jail, but she had been placed in foster care three weeks earlier. Based on her appearance yesterday—clean clothes, a full lunch box in hand, her hair pulled back into a neat ponytail—Hadley guessed she was still living with the foster parents.

Madelyn also came from a less-than-ideal living environment. Her mom was constantly taking off with various boyfriends and leaving her three kids alone to fend for themselves. Hadley didn't know if Madelyn's mom was in town at the moment, but ever since Madelyn's older brother had gotten his driver's license, the girl had been on time for school.

Abby would know that too, Hadley thought, which meant Donnell probably would as well. Which left Cammie.

From what she had seen, Cammie's mom didn't do much more than provide her a place to sleep and free rein of whatever food was currently in the house. Cammie's packed lunch for their field trip last month had consisted of a pocketful of Fruit Loops and a stick of gum.

Yet despite it all, Cammie walked the half mile to school every day, always eager to come and learn, anxious to have those six hours of normal before she had to go back to the dreary little townhouse where she lived.

The memory popped into Hadley's mind of a day last winter when she and Abby had walked Cammie home. An unexpected snow storm had prompted the school district to dismiss school early. Concerned about Cammie making it on her own and not allowed to drive her because of school policy, Hadley had opted to escort her home. Abby, more familiar with the area than Hadley, had insisted on coming with her.

Afterward, Hadley had understood why. Drug dealers on corners, a busy intersection, and an active construction site had been only some of the daily obstacles the poor kid had had to deal with.

An accident on I-95 slowed Hadley's progress a mile before her exit. Anxiety built with each wasted minute. When she finally crept past the fender bender, she checked the dashboard clock. If she went straight to school, she would make it on time.

Hadley reached the intersection where she needed to turn right. She turned left.

Though district policy didn't allow teachers to drive students, except with advanced approval under very specific circumstances, Hadley wasn't going to let that stop her. The rule was put in place to protect the students, and today, Hadley couldn't think of a better way to protect Cammie than to drive her to school.

* * *

Kelsey tried both Noah and JD without success. What a time for them to be out of contact. With no way to run a background check remotely without their help, Kelsey started to call her office to see if anyone was in yet who could do it for her. Then she remembered that she wasn't exactly operating as herself at the moment. The last thing she needed was her CIA counterparts digging into the aliases they weren't cleared to know about.

Opting to use another source of information, she dialed the number for Ghost.

Ghost's greeting came in the form of a one-word question. "Yeah?"

"It's Kelsey. I think I've identified another suspect in Rabell's organization. I need a background check on him, but . . ."

"But you're not FBI and don't want to raise any red flags."

"Exactly," Kelsey said, relieved. "I have an address for him, but I wanted to verify it before I call in the cops."

"I'd rather you not make that call yourself," Ghost said. "Tell me what you've got."

"The man's name is Drake Jeffries." Kelsey proceeded to give Ghost the man's address and phone number, along with the information about the latest victim.

Ghost repeated them, but Kelsey couldn't tell if he was saying it back to her to verify the accuracy or if he was giving them to someone else. "Okay, it looks like the cell phone is a burner. The only contact he talked to on it was Olivia Wilkins."

"That's his girlfriend. She said she hasn't seen him since Friday. He said he had some work obligations that were going to keep him busy through the weekend and into this week."

"Which is consistent with what Donnell's girlfriend said."

"How did you know that?"

"It's in an FBI report," Ghost said. He fell silent for a moment before he added, "The address you gave me for Jeffries checks out. I'll send a black-and-white unit out to bring him in."

"Do you think he's even there?"

"I doubt it," he said. "Did the girlfriend give you any info on what he drives?"

"A silver Lexus. Virginia plates. Not enough to run a check unless it's registered in his name."

"It's not."

"Why does that not surprise me?"

"Because you've been doing this for a while," Ghost said. "I'll let you know if I get any hits or if the cops find this guy or the missing girl."

"Thanks."

* * *

Noah turned at the sound of the approaching car; it was Mitch pulling into the parking lot.

"Finally," Noah said.

Mitch parked beside him, climbed out, and held up a folded piece of paper. "The warrants just came through—an arrest warrant for Rabell and a search warrant for the boat and any other vehicle or property he owns."

"Sounds like the judge was in an agreeable mood this morning."

"No one wants to get in the way of finding missing kids, even if someone does show up at his house at seven thirty in the morning," Mitch said. "Any movement?"

"Nothing yet," Noah said.

"We don't know if anyone is even on board," JD added.

"Let's go find out." Noah opened the back door of his car and retrieved his bulletproof vest, the letters FBI written in white across the back.

The other two men donned their vests, and all three drew their weapons. Noah contemplated the best way to approach the vessel. Like the other boats in the marina, the one in question had been backed in so the stern was closest to the dock. A strip of dock also extended along the right side, giving the occupants access from that side as well.

"I'll take the starboard side. You take the rear," Noah said, motioning to JD. "Mitch, cover us from the dock. Make sure he doesn't get past us."

"You got it."

"And call in the Coast Guard in case they try to make a run for it," Noah said.

"I already asked them to be on standby," JD said. "A rescue boat should be here any minute."

"In that case, let's go." Noah led the way, taking position on the far side of the boat, JD stopping when he reached the rear corner of the port side.

As soon as Noah signaled he was ready, JD stepped onto the low platform in back, the boat immediately swaying beneath his weight. The click of a latch carried over the gentle waves.

Noah barely had time to identify the man who emerged from the cabin before he saw the weapon in his hand.

"Gun!" Noah shouted the warning. "FBI! Drop it!"

The fake Carlos Hernandez didn't heed the command. Protected by the high side railing, he took aim at JD, but JD dropped and took cover behind the rear of the boat, the bullet whizzing over his head and splashing into the water behind him.

Carlos quickly adjusted his aim, shooting instead at Noah. This shot missed Noah, impacting a neighboring boat. Noah shifted to his left to get a better angle for a shot, but Carlos dove for cover between the boat cabin and the port-side railing.

JD popped up and scrambled aboard in pursuit, both men disappearing from sight.

Still positioned on the open dock, Noah charged forward. He came to a sudden stop when a second man emerged from the cabin, dragging a girl with him. Noah didn't recognize the child, but she appeared to be around twelve or thirteen. Another victim. The new arrival held the girl in front of him like a shield. Terror shone in her eyes, but a gag in her mouth prevented her from crying out.

"Let her go." Noah steadied his gun with both hands and aimed at the part of the man's head that was exposed to him.

"Back off, or she dies." He moved to the side, taking away any chance of Noah having a shot.

"Federal agent. You're under arrest," Noah called out, trying a different tactic.

"I don't think so." His weapon rose, and Noah read his intent.

With no place to hide, he sprinted forward again and ducked down to take away the angle of a potential shot. Another shot rang out. Wood splintered behind him.

Noah reached the edge of the dock, the top of the boat providing him his only shelter. Squatting, he aimed his gun upward. He glanced toward the shore, where Mitch took position beside the boat behind him. Not sure where JD had gone, Noah waited for his fellow agents to make their move.

CHAPTER 42

JD STRUGGLED TO KEEP HIS balance as the boat swayed beneath him. He pressed his body against the side of the cabin, footsteps sounding on the bow.

His hand flexed, gripping his pistol. He edged forward until he reached the curve where the cabin gave way to the open space over the bow.

Leading with his gun, he swung around the corner to face the man standing a few feet away. Carlos held an automatic pistol in his right hand. Without hesitation, JD kicked out with his left leg. His foot connected with Carlos's wrist. The man's weapon dropped to the deck and skittered several feet along the bow until it came to rest along the edge of the railing.

Carlos leaned down to retrieve it, but JD charged him before he could grasp it. He pushed Carlos down, and the momentum of the impact knocked Carlos to the left of the fallen gun.

Apparently recognizing that reaching his weapon was unlikely, Carlos kicked out instead, his foot barely missing JD's ankles.

The boat rocked, and JD fought to keep his footing. Before JD fully regained his balance, Carlos scrambled up and rushed toward him.

With Carlos too close to use a weapon accurately, JD struck out with his fist but found nothing but air.

Carlos ducked out of the way, his own fists flying. JD managed to dodge the right hook, but the left jab caught him in the chin. He stumbled, once more struggling for balance.

Carlos saw JD's vulnerability and charged him again, but JD flattened himself against the front of the cabin and used the solid surface for leverage. He then kicked out his right leg, connecting solidly with Carlos's midsection.

Carlos stumbled back, and his arms windmilled, his hands grasping at air as he tried to remain upright. JD struck out again, this time using his hands. One good push sent Carlos overboard into the water.

Satisfied that Carlos was no longer a threat, JD secured the man's weapon, engaged the safety, and tucked it into the holster in the back of his waistband.

A girl cried out, fear and anguish carrying through the air. JD circled to the back of the boat in time to find a new threat and the innocence he was hiding behind.

* * *

Noah heard the splash, followed by JD's negotiations with the man still on the boat. Knowing he couldn't get a good angle on their target from the dock level, he opted to make sure Carlos couldn't cause any more trouble.

Staying close to the hull of the yacht, Noah made his way forward until he saw the man treading water a few feet from the boat's bow.

Noah aimed his weapon and motioned for Carlos to swim toward him. Carlos turned and headed the other way. With no interest in taking a swim fully clothed, Noah spoke quietly into his communications earpiece. "Mitch, we've got a suspect swimming to the next dock over. Can you intercept?"

"I've got him."

Noah caught a glimpse of Mitch making his way toward the main dock, where he could traverse the path to the next row of slips.

Footsteps carried toward him, along with another muffled cry.

With his partner's safety and the safety of the hostage in mind, Noah reached for the railing above him. It was barely out of his reach.

Noah moved halfway down the vessel's length and tried again. This time when he stood on his toes, his fingers could grasp one of the metal railings.

Noah holstered his weapon and reached up with both hands. Using his upper body strength, he pulled himself halfway up.

"Hey! What are you doing there?"

The unfamiliar voice halted Noah's progress, and he dropped back onto the deck and turned to face a man in his sixties standing on the vessel on the opposite side of the narrow deck running from stern to bow.

"Federal agent. Return below deck."

"How do I know . . . ?"

Noah pulled his ID, held it up, and ordered, "Now!"

The commanding tone had more effect than the words, and the man opened the door leading to the cabin of his cruiser.

Reaching up again, Noah started the process over, hoping he could get aboard before Carlos's buddy reached the helm and decided to make a run for it.

* * *

Big blue eyes stared at JD, a silent plea evident, along with the fear. JD looked past the girl, focusing instead on the gun pointed at her temple and the man holding the weapon. Drake. The last of Hadley's dinner companions the night of the bombing.

"Drop your gun, or she dies," Drake demanded, backing toward the steps that led to the upper deck.

The question of why the man didn't try to shoot him surfaced in JD's mind, but with the way Drake's hand shook, JD suspected handling weapons wasn't typically part of his everyday business.

JD held his hands out, adjusting his grip on his gun to show he wasn't a threat. "There's no need for anyone to get hurt," JD said, his voice calm. "Just let the girl go."

"Drop the gun."

"Okay." JD held his gun out farther to his side. "If I put it down, will you let her go?"

He took a jerky step back and shouted, "Drop the gun!"

"Okay. I'm doing what you asked. No need to get upset." JD lowered his right hand to his side as he squatted and put his weapon on the deck.

"Not on the deck. Drop it over the side."

"Okay." Keeping his eyes on Drake, JD used two fingers to lift his weapon. Taking a step to the port side, he dropped it into the water.

"Now stay back." Drake reached the steps, the girl still held in front of him. When JD didn't move, he amended his request. "Get off the boat."

A quick glance at the dock revealed a new component to the equation. The line previously tethering the boat to the dock had been cast off, the yacht's anchor the only thing keeping it in place.

"Give me the girl, and I'll leave you alone," JD said. "You can cruise out of here, and I won't be able to do anything about it."

"Not until I'm at the helm."

"I'll wait here," JD said calmly. "As soon as you send the girl down, she and I will get off the boat together."

He didn't agree or disagree. Without saying anything, Drake started up the steps, his hostage remaining between him and JD.

* * *

Hadley did her best to look past the drug deal going down on the corner three blocks from Cammie's house. Seven thirty in the morning. Where were the cops when you needed them?

She continued along the route she assumed Cammie would take, her eyes sweeping the area in search of the petite girl with her faded blue backpack. Hadley's cell phone rang, pulling her concentration away from the cluster of men standing at the construction site to her left. She nearly ignored the phone, but the thought that it might be JD caused her to fumble in her purse with her right hand.

She answered it without looking at the caller ID. "Hello?"

"Hadley, it's Kelsey. Where are you?"

"I'm on my way to school."

"Noah asked me to have you give him or JD a call once you take attendance and let them know if you have any students missing."

Hadley stopped at a red light a block from Cammie's house. "Actually, I'm going to swing by and pick up one of my students to bring her to school. I'm almost there."

"Is that going to get you in trouble?"

"I honestly don't care," Hadley said. "When I was thinking about who would be the most likely target out of my students, Cammie topped the list."

Hadley drummed her left hand on the wheel, impatiently waiting for the light to turn. She looked past it to the strip of townhouses to her left, where Cammie lived. Her breath caught when she saw Chad Hicks buckling someone into the back seat. He straightened, slammed the rear passenger door of his SUV, and circled to the driver's seat. "Oh no."

"What?"

"I might be too late. Chad is in front of Cammie's house. It looks like someone is in the back seat." Brake lights illuminated, and Chad's car started forward. "He's pulling away."

"Is he coming toward you or away from you?" Kelsey asked.

"Away." The light turned, and Hadley pulled forward. "I'm following him."

"Where are you?"

Hadley gave Kelsey the cross streets.

"I'm going to call Noah and tell him what's going on. I'll call you right back," Kelsey said.

"Okay."

"And, Hadley?"

"Yeah?"

"Don't get too close to this guy. If you think he's onto you, get out of there."

Hadley hung up and set her phone on the seat beside her. She passed by Cammie's house, no sign of Cammie anywhere. Fear for her student combined with adrenaline to send her heart into overdrive.

What if Chad noticed her? How could she help Cammie without putting both of them in danger?

Her fingers gripped the wheel tighter. This was JD's car. Chad wouldn't know it was her.

A white sedan merged into the open space between her and Chad.

She could do this, she told herself. All she had to do was follow behind until Noah and JD sent help, preferably heavily armed help.

Chad signaled left and changed lanes. A Jeep on Hadley's left prevented her from following. Anxiety welled up within her. She couldn't lose sight of him.

A moment later, Chad changed lanes again, this time not bothering to signal as he crossed through the right lane and made a right turn.

Gathering her courage, Hadley sped up, signaled, and made the right turn behind him.

CHAPTER 43

KELSEY HUNG UP HER PHONE. No answer again. For the past several minutes, she had tried calling both her husband and JD but had been unable to reach either of them. She could only assume they had their phones off and were in the middle of something important. But she needed to talk to them. Now.

The thought of a third-grade teacher following a kidnapper prompted Kelsey to punch Hadley's last location into her GPS. Kelsey started on an intercept course, not sure how she could request help without blowing her cover.

Since Hadley hadn't actually seen anyone take her student, the police weren't likely to help without going through a methodical investigation, an investigation that would likely take too much time.

With both of Kelsey's contacts with the FBI out of reach, she grabbed her second cell phone and dialed.

"Yeah?" Ghost answered in what appeared to be his usual greeting.

"I need some help." Kelsey gave him the latest updates and added, "Do you have the ability to get this information to the FBI?"

"I'll put it through. Give me Hadley's phone number so I can track her GPS signal."

"JD put a blocker on it to keep her from being found."

"What about her car?"

"She's in JD's car." Hope rose within her. "You should be able to track the GPS signal on it. His full name is Jacob Devin Byers."

"I'll pull it up. In the meantime, call Hadley and ask her where she is now. Put both of us on speaker phone so I can hear everything."

"Okay." Kelsey did as he asked, putting him on speaker while connecting to Hadley through the Bluetooth on her car.

Worry and rising panic carried over the line when Hadley answered. "Kelsey, are JD and Noah coming?"

"They aren't picking up. Where are you now?"

"I just turned east." She hesitated a moment before giving the street name. "What do I do? This is a residential road. There's hardly anyone on it."

"Can you tell me Chad's license plate number?"

"Mud's covering part of it," she said. "The last four digits are 8914. It's a Virginia plate."

"What kind of car is he driving?"

"A black Honda Pilot. He bought it new last year."

"Hadley, hold on a minute." Kelsey muted her call with Hadley and spoke to Ghost. "Can you look up the vehicles?"

"I've got Byers's car, and I put an alert into the FBI switchboard on a possible kidnapping with his car listed as belonging to a witness."

"What about the Honda Pilot?"

"I'm running through them, but I've still got too many possibilities."

"Narrow your search to addresses in Woodbridge."

"I'm not finding it," Ghost said. "Best guess is the plates are phony or the vehicle's registered to a company." He fell silent for a moment. "I think I've got it. I've got one registered to a company called Host Central. The address is in Alexandria, but everything else matches."

"It would make sense if he's really involved in human trafficking that he would take precautions to keep his anonymity," Kelsey said. "Can you see where it's located?"

"Nope. Looks like it's got a GPS scrambler on it."

"Then it probably is him. What do I tell Hadley?"

"Tell her to keep following him, but if he turns into any kind of driveway or parking lot, have her keep going and give you the address."

"I hate involving civilians."

"We all do, but she's the only one who knows where this guy is. And don't forget, she thinks you're a civilian too."

* * *

JD retrieved Carlos's confiscated weapon from his waistband holster as soon as Drake climbed out of sight. The hope that the hostage would be sent back down the stairs died quickly, but JD had figured it wouldn't be that easy. It rarely was.

He debated whether to follow Drake up the stairs but decided against it. He'd make far too easy a target. Instead, he started along the starboard side, able to see Mitch jogging down the dock, parallel to them, toward where Carlos was hanging on the edge, trying to climb out of the water.

JD reached the point where the cabin gave way to the bow and stopped. If he continued forward, he would be visible. He peeked around the edge to find Noah positioned across from him.

With his partner able to cover Drake from the front, JD headed back the way he had come. He reached the stairs and pressed himself against the starboard side so any bullets aimed downward would miss him. "Come on, let the girl go," JD called out. "I just want the girl."

He had no idea what the response would have been because when a Coast Guard rescue boat came into view, a string of curses punctuated the air.

The boat engines came to life, along with the motorized anchor.

JD approached the stairs and looked up from the right side and then from the left to ascertain Drake's position. Only able to see the girl's legs in front of him, he started upward, adrenaline pumping through him.

The boat started forward, and JD's grip tightened on the stair railing to keep him from losing his balance. The boat increased speed, and the momentum knocked JD's feet out from under him, his body now held in place only by his grip on the rail.

When he once again regained his footing, he looked up, but the girl's legs were no longer visible.

With the boat now in motion, JD guessed that Drake had taken his spot at the helm, and the girl was likely beside him.

"Get off the boat!" Drake shouted. For a split second, JD froze, debating whether to rush up the steps or jump down off of them. When the command was repeated, he realized Drake must be talking to Noah and not him.

Sure enough, Noah responded. "FBI. Let the girl go, and I'll leave."

They were sounding like a broken record, JD thought to himself. And he was tired of getting the same results. Praying that Drake didn't have his gun trained on the stairs, he took a deep breath and sprinted upward onto the deck.

As suspected, Drake stood with a hand on the wheel, his other hand aiming his pistol at Noah. The girl had been shoved into a seat behind the helm with nowhere to go and still in the line of fire. JD took a step to his right so he could aim without fear of hitting the girl.

"Drop it!" JD ordered.

Drake immediately jerked the wheel, sending JD stumbling and making the turn faster than would be deemed safe. Below, Noah skidded across the bow, barely catching himself on the railing to keep from going overboard.

With little room for error, JD grabbed the side of the captain's chair to his right and took aim. As Drake lunged forward to grab the girl again, JD squeezed off a single shot.

The bullet caught Drake in the stomach. The gun dropped, and he fell against the control console, his elbow knocking into the boat's throttle. The wheel turned; the boat increased speed.

JD went skidding backward, barely catching himself before stumbling down the stairs. Fighting the movement of the boat, he leaned down and collected the weapon. He then checked Drake's condition and confirmed he didn't have any other weapons before reversing the throttle to bring the boat to a stop.

JD turned to the girl, who was still sitting in a nearby chair, a gag in her mouth, her hands tied in front of her. She scooted away from JD as he approached.

"It's okay now." JD untied her and took the gag out of her mouth. "Can you tell me what happened? How did you end up here?"

Her eyes teared. "I was leaving my house to go to school, and this man said my mom told him to drive me. I tried to say no . . ."

"When did this happen?"

"Today."

"What about the other girls?" JD asked.

"What other girls?"

CHAPTER 44

HADLEY'S KNUCKLES TURNED WHITE FROM the constant grip she kept on the steering wheel. For nearly fifteen minutes, she had followed Chad's car, not once seeing any sign of Cammie or anyone else in the vehicle.

Hadley was already late for work and had yet to call in. Attendance wouldn't be taken for another twenty minutes, so until then, she couldn't be sure if Cammie was even absent.

"Where are you now?" Kelsey asked, still on the phone.

"It looks like we're heading toward the Potomac River."

The road had gone from four lanes down to two, a canopy of trees curtaining the sky so that sunlight dappled down between the leaves. It was exactly the kind of place she loved to search for on weekend drives, the countryside a vibrant green that exuded a sense of peace. But today's drive was anything but peaceful.

Chad's brake lights illuminated. "Wait. He's slowing down."

"Where?"

Hadley glanced at the break in the trees where a long driveway met the road. "It looks like a farm entrance."

"Keep going," Kelsey said. "Pass by as though you're going somewhere down the road."

Knowing she wasn't trained or equipped to pursue Chad on her own, she battled against her concern for Cammie and followed Kelsey's advice. "Okay." She watched Chad's car make the right-hand turn. "What do I do now?"

Hadley's phone beeped twice and went dead. She glanced down to see the call had dropped. She slowed briefly and watched the black SUV continue through the trees and wind out of sight.

Not sure what to do next, Hadley passed the paved driveway and went another fifty yards before she pulled to the side of the road. She left the car idling and picked up her phone to find she had no service. "Great," she muttered under her breath. "Just great."

Hadley put the car back into drive and pulled forward another fifty yards, finally able get a weak signal. She pressed the button to redial Kelsey, several seconds passing before the phone started to ring. The call connected, but Hadley could hear only garbled syllables cutting out. Trying again, Hadley hung up and pressed the redial button.

This time Kelsey's voice came over the line clearly. "Hadley?"

"Sorry, there's not a good cell signal here, but I can hear you now." Hadley started to ask what she should do next, but a flash of movement appeared outside her driver's-side window, and the door yanked open.

Before Hadley could utter a word, her cell phone was ripped out of her hand, and she found herself facing the man she had once called her boyfriend.

* * *

Kelsey heard a gasp of surprise before the phone went dead. She immediately tried calling Hadley back, but this time, no one answered.

Kelsey pressed on the gas pedal, increasing her speed. If she was right, she was within five minutes of where Chad Hicks had turned off the main road.

Her phone rang, and Kelsey snatched it up before the phone could display the caller ID. "Hadley?"

Instead of her friend's voice coming over the line, the ringing continued. It took her a moment to realize it was the cell phone from Ghost ringing rather than her personal one. She answered. "I think Hadley's in trouble."

"I'm on my way," Ghost said.

Kelsey approached a sharp turn in the road and hit the brakes, slowing enough to keep her car under control. "Can you tell me where JD's car is now?"

"You're almost on top of it," Ghost said.

Kelsey rounded the bend to find JD's car parked two hundred yards ahead. "I see it."

"Be careful. I don't have to tell you how these men treat women."

"No, you don't."

* * *

Two Coast Guard seamen boarded the yacht, one of them making his way to the controls.

"I assume you can get us back to the dock," JD said.

"Yes, sir," the one at the controls said, then went about his task, his counterpart securing the vessel.

JD saw Noah disappear from sight and assumed he would take care of searching the cabin. JD turned back to the girl. "What's your name?"

"Lani." Her gaze darted to where her former captor lay sprawled on the deck, the life drained from him. "Is he . . . ?"

"Yes, he's dead." JD reached out a hand. "Let's go downstairs."

JD escorted her to the lower deck, led her to a bench in the rear section, and waited for her to sit. "Did these men take you anywhere other than here?"

She shook her head.

"Did you hear them talking about anywhere else?"

Again, she shook her head. "The man . . ." She pointed at the upper deck. "He was mad that the other one brought me here. He said it was too risky."

"Do you know why he brought you here?" JD asked.

"I'm not sure. He said something about a roadblock." Her lip quivered. "Can I go home now?"

"An ambulance is going to take you to the hospital to make sure you're okay, but after that, we'll get you home." JD noticed a Coast Guard medic standing on the dock. With a subtle nod, he signaled that it was okay to approach and administer first aid.

Noah emerged from below deck. "I didn't see any sign of anyone else staying on board, but I found a stash of zip ties, and one of the cabins below had the lock reversed."

"Lani said she never saw any other girls and that one of them was mad when the other showed up with her here."

"How long did they hold her here?" Noah asked.

"She was abducted this morning before school. She has no idea where the others are."

"I have to think they're close by, probably somewhere near the water," Noah said.

JD and Noah passed the two paramedics who had come to treat Lani. When JD and Noah reached the end of the dock, Mitch approached.

"Where's the other suspect?" Noah asked.

"I turned him over to the police. They'll take him in for processing."

"Any updates from the office?" Noah asked.

"Yeah. You've got to see this." Mitch led the way past the police cruiser and ambulance in the parking lot.

"What is it?" JD asked.

"Your car."

"What about my car?"

"A bulletin posted with a suspect's vehicle, but it also gave the description of the car following it," Mitch said. "It was yours."

JD's heart sank. His stomach curled. "What?"

"Since you're here and your car isn't, who is driving your car?" Mitch asked.

"Hadley." JD pulled his phone from his pocket and called her. No answer. He dialed again, this time calling the school's front office. As soon as the receptionist answered, JD said, "This is FBI Special Agent Byers. Did Hadley Baker come to work today?"

"No, sir."

"Did she call in?"

"No. Is everything okay? This isn't like her."

JD didn't answer her question but, rather, fired off another of his own. "What about the students in Miss Baker's class? Were any of them absent today?"

"Not that I'm aware of."

"What about anyone who was recently withdrawn from school?"

"One moment. Let me check." The line went silent, worry rising inside him. Thirty seconds later, she came back on the phone. "Miss Baker doesn't have anyone absent, but she did have one student who was withdrawn from school this morning."

"Who?"

"Cammie Seiler."

Cammie. The vibrant little girl with golden curls and a friendly disposition.

JD hung up without bothering to say goodbye. He turned to Mitch. "Run the GPS on my car. Where is it now?"

Mitch complied. "It looks like it's parked down the road from the wildlife refuge."

"That's not far from here." JD started toward Noah's car. "Let's go."

"JD, wait," Mitch called after him. "There's a roadblock up for a construction zone. It'll take at least twenty minutes to circle around to get there."

Beside him, Noah's phone rang, but JD's mind was already racing. The paramedics escorted Lani past them to the waiting ambulance, and another police car pulled into the lot. JD looked away from the now-blocked entrance and homed in on the Coast Guard rescue boat.

JD pointed. "We can get there by boat in half the time."

Noah hung up and spoke to the police officer standing nearby. "Have your men secure the boat and take a statement from the witness. She needs to stay in protective custody until you hear from us."

"Yes, sir."

JD started for the dock. "Come on."

Noah jogged to catch up. "That was Burt on the phone. He received a report that your car has been found."

"And Hadley?"

"She's gone."

No. JD's throat closed up. First Cammie, now Hadley. Not trusting himself to speak, JD broke into a run, racing toward the Coast Guard vessel that had docked to wait for its crew members.

Noah's footsteps pounded beside him, Mitch close behind.

Noah shouted out the words JD couldn't manage. "Cast off! We need a ride."

One of the crew members standing on the edge of the dock lifted a hand to get Noah's attention. "Sir, this yacht is faster than our rescue boat."

"He's right." The commanding officer leaned over the rail of the Coast Guard vessel.

"Can one of you drive it?" Noah asked.

The seaman on the dock spoke again. "I can, sir."

"Then cast off. Let's go," Noah said.

"Go," the captain said, giving his permission. "We'll be right behind you."

The three FBI agents scrambled on board, right behind the two seamen who had docked the yacht. A moment later, they were underway.

Mitch gave the captain the coordinates, Noah called Burt for an update, and JD stared out at the water, unable to do anything but worry and pray.

* * *

"How much farther?" Kade asked, his eyes on the road in front of him. He had turned off the freeway and was closing in on the last position Kelsey had given him.

"We're only a couple miles from where Agent Byers's car is parked. You'll want to take a left at the next light."

Kade approached the intersection, a police car blocking the roadway.

"What's going on up there?" Renee asked.

"Looks like a construction site, but I didn't see it scheduled," Kade said. He turned into a grocery store parking lot. "Isn't today Wednesday?"

"Yeah. Why?"

"The president is supposed to be at Quantico today. The roadblock is probably here to keep traffic from getting too close to the base."

"We need to get on the other side of that barricade," Renee said. "With it in place, we're going to have a tough time getting the police out there if we need them."

"I know." Kade parked his rig along the back edge of a parking lot, where he could unload one of the motorcycles he had stored in the storage compartment in the back of his trailer. "I'm going to take one of our motorcycles."

"I'll come with you."

"No. I need someone to coordinate with all of the agencies involved," Kade insisted, not only because his words were true but also because he didn't want Renee anywhere near Rabell and his men. "Call in a couple of local police units to back us up. That's the only way we'll have them available if we do need them."

She put her hand on his. "Be careful."

"I will." He opened the door and climbed out of the cab. "And let me know of any movement. This has the potential of being a mess, with so many agencies already involved."

"I'll keep everyone in line."

"I know you will." Trusting his wife to use their intelligence database to feed information to the various law enforcement agencies working the rescue effort, he circled to the back of his rig and unlocked the trailer. A minute later, he had his motorcycle unloaded, the back locked again, and was on his way to find the women he had promised to protect.

CHAPTER 45

HADLEY SAT IN THE FRONT seat of Chad's car, her wrists and ankles bound by zip ties, the seat belt holding her in place.

Beside her, Chad spoke as though he were speaking to an old friend rather than someone he had just abducted. "I have to say, I've really missed you, Hadley."

Hadley stared at his profile as he drove down the dirt road, dense trees blocking out the sunlight. "How can you prey on children? How can you live with yourself?"

"Oh, I live just fine," Chad said, apparently unconcerned with her opinion of him.

Hadley glanced in the backseat where Cammie was also restrained, her hands and ankles bound, the strap of the seat belt looped around her arms before being secured so Cammie couldn't raise her arms to signal for help.

"She's only eight years old," Hadley said. "She's just a child."

"She's cash in the bank. That's what she is."

Hadley swallowed hard and forced herself to ask, "And me?"

"A bonus."

Hadley let the implication sink in, unable to speak. The thought of being sold off to the highest bidder, of her students being robbed of their childhood, stirred a survival instinct in her that she had never known existed.

She thought of the many conversations she and JD had shared over the past week, including his insistence on teaching her basic self-defense techniques. She looked down at the zip ties binding her wrists. Freeing herself wouldn't work unless she could get a few seconds alone and enough headroom to lift her hands high above her head.

She could do this.

The river came into view, an old-fashioned wooden dock stretching out into deep water. A pickup truck was parked beside an aluminum shed, and a man stood beside the padlocked door. Hadley stared at him, her breath catching when she recognized the face and connected it to a name. Rabell. The man JD and Noah were looking for, the man responsible for Spencer's death.

Chad parked and climbed out of the car.

"What took you so long?" Rabell demanded.

"Sorry. I ran into a little obstacle on my way here, but I took care of it." Chad pointed at her.

"Who's that?"

"Her name is Hadley Baker. She's one of the teachers," Chad said. "She showed up right after I made my last pickup."

Anger bubbled inside her at the casual way Chad referred to Cammie like she was a piece of produce or a car part. Behind her, Cammie whimpered.

"It's going to be okay, Cammie," Hadley said, trying to force some confidence into her words. "We're going to get out of here."

Rabell circled Chad and leaned down to look at her through the driver's-side door.

Dark-brown eyes met hers, and Hadley struggled to keep from squirming. After a moment, Rabell straightened. "Does she have anyone who will notice she's gone?"

"Her family is out west, and her boyfriend was Spencer Andrews."

"Well, that is something. Maybe Spencer had some use after all."

"If we send in an email to her school saying she's sick, we should have until next week before anyone reports her missing."

"Good. Make sure you have her cell phone, and then put the girl with the others. The boat should be here in about twenty minutes."

"Do you want me to put Hadley with the kids?"

"No. Putting a teacher with children is a sure way to create a mutiny." Rabell shook his head. "Get a photo of her and then lock her in the back seat of the car."

"What are you going to do?"

"We have some auctions to set up." Rabell leered at Hadley. "I think your friend there may be the first one we list. She'll certainly generate some interest."

Disgust combined with fear. Hadley fought against both as Rabell headed for the path that led to a nearby cabin.

Chad opened Hadley's door and yanked her out of the car, nearly tripping her as he pulled her to a stand. Chad pulled out his cell and took a step back. Holding his phone up, he snapped several photos. He then opened the back door and tugged on Hadley's arm, forcing her into the seat beside Cammie. As he had before, he looped the seat belt around her arms twice before he clipped it into place to restrain her.

Chad slammed the door and circled to the other side. Hadley looked down at Cammie's sneakers; one shoelace was untied. Lowering her voice, she said, "Don't forget what Agent Byers taught you about shoelaces. Teach the other kids what you know."

Chad opened the door. "What were you saying to her?"

"I was telling her to be good. That everything would be okay."

He glared at her as though not sure whether to believe her. Then without another word, he retrieved a knife from his pocket and leaned down to cut the bands from Cammie's ankles.

"Come on, kid. Come with me."

Cammie gave Hadley a last look and then climbed out of the car. Chad grabbed her arm and headed across the tall grass toward the metal shed.

* * *

Kelsey debated whether to drive onto the dirt road in search of Hadley and the missing kids or if she should go in on foot. She certainly didn't want to announce her presence, but the idea of being without an escape vehicle didn't sit well with her.

The rumble of an approaching vehicle interrupted her thoughts. A motorcycle came around the corner and pulled up behind her car.

Kelsey's heartbeat quickened, and her hand moved to the gun holstered at her back until the helmet came off and she recognized Ghost.

"Don't shoot." Ghost swung his leg over the bike and hit the kickstand. "I'm on your side."

"Good, because I could use some help developing a mission plan," Kelsey said. "I have no idea how far this road goes."

Ghost pulled a cell phone from his pocket and hit a few keys. "It looks like it goes in about a quarter mile, but if we cut through the woods, it's less than half that."

"How do we make sure they don't get past us?" Kelsey asked.

"My partner is putting in a request for a couple of police cruisers to come and set up a barricade here," Ghost said. "They'll move in if we need them."

"I don't suppose you brought that toy with you that registers heat signatures."

Ghost patted his front pocket. "I did. I figured it might come in handy, especially since we're looking for missing kids."

"In that case, let's go."

Ghost motioned to her left. "Head that way. If I'm right, we'll find them near the dock."

"I hope you're right."

"I usually am."

* * *

Hadley never realized how hard it could be to unfasten a seat belt when tied up. She wiggled and shifted in her seat until she managed to press her thumb against the release button.

Untangling herself from the seat belt took several more precious seconds. With no shoelaces in her shoes to break the zip tie around her wrists, she reached both hands toward the door and gripped the handle. She pulled on it, but nothing happened.

Hadley tried again, using her shoulder to push against the door at the same time. Her third attempt confirmed her suspicion. The child safety locks were on.

Not willing to give up, she inched her way across the center console and climbed awkwardly into the front passenger seat. This time, when she pulled on the door handle, it opened with the help of her shoulder pressing against it.

Then she used her teeth, like JD had taught her, to tighten the zip tie as much as possible. She stood up, raised her hands over her head, and slammed her arms down as hard as she could, her wrists impacting her midsection.

Amazement and relief washed over her when the zip tie popped open and fell to the ground.

Hadley sat back down in the passenger seat and used her fingernails to work at the zip tie around her ankles. After a moment, she released it as well.

The shed door banged closed. Panicked, she raced to the closest tree and ducked behind it. She peeked around the edge at Chad's car, the passenger door hanging open. Chad stood at the doors to the shed, his back to her.

The open car door would scream a warning of her escape, so she darted farther into the woods. Using the thick foliage to mask her movements, she continued forward, only making it twenty feet before she heard a muttered curse and rapid footsteps. "Hadley!"

She froze, pressing her back against a mature maple tree, the leaves above her rustling in the breeze. Should she run? Could she hide? Her foot tilted as a rock the size of a baseball gave way beneath her shoe. Moving slowly, she leaned down and picked it up. It was hardly an effective weapon against a gun, but it was better than nothing.

"Hadley!" Chad yelled again.

Rabell's voice carried to her. "What's going on?"

"I don't know how she did it, but she got away."

"Find her," he demanded. "Kill her if you have to. We can't take a chance of her getting the cops involved before we get our cargo safely out of here."

"I'll take care of it."

"Make sure you do."

Footsteps approached. Hadley's hand fisted on the rock she held. Fight or flee. The choice was hers.

* * *

Kelsey heard the shouts and fought the instinct to break into a full sprint. The element of surprise. That was what they needed.

Thirty feet to her left, Ghost continued on his parallel course. A squirrel scampered up a tree a few yards away. A bird took flight.

Hadley's name was called yet again. Hadley had gotten away. Kelsey scanned the woods with a new purpose.

She caught a flash of movement in the distance but couldn't identify the source. She continued forward, increasing her pace. Across from her, Ghost matched her step for step.

He lifted a hand to signal, indicating he was taking an alternate path. Not sure what he intended, she stopped until he signaled again, this time pointing to a spot to her right.

Kelsey noted the device in Ghost's hand, and suddenly, everything made sense. He was tracking body heat. Someone was in front of her.

Not sure if she was heading for Hadley or one of the criminals, Kelsey approached cautiously, the sound of each footstep getting swept away in the gentle breeze.

Kelsey was nearly on top of her target when she saw the contrast of yellow fabric against the greenery.

Without warning, the owner of that yellow shirt moved suddenly, lifted a hand, and hurled something in the opposite direction from where Kelsey stood.

Kelsey noted the long dark hair and realized it was Hadley only a moment before a gunshot sounded.

Hadley dropped to the ground, as did Kelsey.

"Hadley, it doesn't have to be this way," a man called out. "Come out, and you won't have to die."

Staying low, Hadley backed away, ducking behind a cluster of three trees. When she sensed Kelsey, she startled and whirled to face her.

Kelsey held her finger to her lips, relieved to find Hadley unharmed.

Another shot fired. Both women ducked again.

Not sure where Ghost had disappeared to, Kelsey debated her next move as she approached Hadley's new hiding place.

Though Kelsey could read the questions in Hadley's eyes—primarily, why Kelsey was there—the woman didn't ask anything. Instead she whispered, "I think the girls are locked in the shed by the dock."

"How many kidnappers are there?" Kelsey asked, keeping her voice low.

"I saw two." Hadley's fingers curled around a fallen tree branch the size of a baseball bat. "Kelsey, one of them is Rabell."

"Are they both up ahead?"

"No. Just Chad. Rabell went into the cabin on the hill. I'm not sure, but there might have been someone else up there. He said 'we' when talking about setting up an auction. I don't know if he was referring to Chad or someone else."

"How far away is Chad?"

"Maybe thirty yards."

Kelsey considered the threat to her cover for a fraction of a second before she reached for her weapon. Sure enough, Hadley's eyes widened when she saw the pistol in Kelsey's hand.

"When I tell you, I want you to throw that branch to our right. Let it make some noise."

"What are you going to do?" Hadley asked. "You can't take this guy on alone."

"I'm not alone. I have a friend here, and more help is coming," Kelsey assured her. "Trust me."

Hadley nodded.

"After you throw it, stay sheltered here."

"Okay."

Kelsey positioned herself so she was ready to move, gun in hand. "Now."

Hadley popped up long enough to hurl the branch. Kelsey waited until she heard footsteps before she pushed forward, trying to create a better angle. Movement flashed between the trees, but she couldn't see her target long enough to take a shot. He saw her though.

Changing directions, he darted between trees and ran toward her. Kelsey lifted her weapon and fired off one shot just as he darted to his left.

"What the . . . ?" Clearly surprised by the return fire, he took cover. "Who's there?"

Kelsey didn't answer. She moved to the side in an attempt to circle around him. When she caught sight of Ghost to her left, she read his hand signals and held her ground.

A moment later, Chad appeared ten yards in front of her, his head peeking out from behind an oak tree. "Give it up, Hadley."

Realizing he had mistaken her for her friend, Kelsey called out, "It's over. Hadley already left."

"Who are you?"

"A woman with a gun. Now drop yours, and maybe I'll let you live."

"It doesn't work that way." Chad's arm came up, gun in hand.

Another tree branch came flying toward Chad, thudding onto the forest floor a few feet from him. The distraction Hadley had created was exactly what Ghost needed to approach Chad from behind.

Kelsey saw Ghost's gun hand come up over Chad's head and then thrust down with force. A thump sounded, and Chad went limp as he fell to the ground.

"Got any handcuffs?" Ghost called out.

"I'm afraid not." Kelsey turned to where Hadley had hidden. "Hadley, it's safe now."

She stepped out from behind the cluster of trees and continued past them. "We have to get the kids out of here."

"Hadley, wait." Kelsey caught up to Hadley as they reached a clearing, the river visible to the left, a long dock stretching out from the shore. "We don't want to put them in any unnecessary danger."

"They've been kidnapped. How much more danger can there be?" Hadley asked.

A sleek white yacht came into view as it headed toward the shore.

Kelsey and Ghost exchanged a look before Ghost answered for her. "You don't want to know."

CHAPTER 46

NOAH STOOD ON THE LOWER deck beside JD, no words spoken between them. What could Noah say? Clearly, JD had developed feelings for Hadley, and he knew firsthand how overwhelming it was to be helpless when loved ones were in danger.

The Coast Guard seaman navigated the yacht through Occoquan Bay, the rescue boat now a good half mile behind them. The seaman was right. This yacht had some serious speed. Not surprising, considering it was being used to smuggle women and children out of the country.

Noah's phone rang, and he saw his wife's name on his caller ID. He knew she had stopped by the middle school this morning, but right now, he needed to focus on his immediate goals: getting back on land and finding Hadley and the missing children.

He hit the silence button only to have the phone ring an instant later. He let out a sigh. Better to tell her now that he wasn't available than to have her keep trying to call if things turned nasty. "Kels, I'm going to have to call you back. I'm a little busy right now."

"Where are you?" Kelsey asked.

"Long story, but I'm on Rabell's yacht heading for where we think he's hiding out."

"You're on the boat?" Kelsey asked. "A big white yacht, black trim?"

"How did you know . . . ?" Noah's voice trailed off. "Wait. Where are you?"

"I'm about fifty yards from the dock you're approaching."

"What? How. . . ?"

"I'll explain later," Kelsey said. "For now, the area is clear for you to dock. Hadley said Rabell is in the cabin on the hill."

"Is Hadley okay?"

Beside him, JD reached out and gripped his arm, his eyes alight with hope.

"She's okay," Kelsey said.

"She's okay," Noah repeated for JD's benefit. "What's the situation on shore?"

"We need to get the kids out of here, but now that you're here with Rabell's yacht, I think the easiest thing would be to load the kids onto the boat. It will look like Rabell's men are doing exactly what he wants," Kelsey said.

"And we can get them out of here without him ever knowing they're being rescued."

"Right."

"Two men were on board when we arrived. JD and I will take their places. We'll have the others with us stay out of sight." Noah motioned to JD to have him pass the message along.

"Okay," Kelsey said. "Ghost can play the part of the man we took into custody."

"Let's pray this works."

"I'm already ahead of you on that one."

* * *

They were ready. Kade had left Kelsey with Chad and Hadley. They had zip tied Chad's hands together, but Kade knew that couldn't last for long.

Though Hadley had wanted to come with him to rescue the children, the chance of her being seen by Rabell wasn't worth it. She hadn't liked being kept on the sidelines, but at least the woman had seen his logic.

Kade waited until the yacht was docked before he picked the lock on the shed. The kids rustled inside, and he could smell the fear. "It's okay," he said. "We're here to help."

Kade pulled the door open, and immediately, a girl tried to rush by him. He lowered his arm and snagged her around her waist as another darted past.

"Federal agent," Kade said as the little blonde dashed into the trees. Unable to pursue without the others fleeing, he tightened his hold on the wriggling girl in his arms and blocked the door with his body.

He hated that he couldn't prove to these kids that they were here to help, not hurt.

The girl in his arms kicked at him.

"Stop that. We're here to take you home."

Noah approached with another man. "How many are there?"

"I'm not sure. They tried to escape. One made it past me."

"Where's Hadley?" the other man asked.

"She's with Kelsey."

"Ghost, this is JD," Noah said, offering introductions.

"I'd shake your hand, but this one doesn't believe we're here to help."

JD pulled his badge out of his pocket and held it in front of the girl's eyes. "We really are here to help, but we need you to calm down so we can get you out of here."

At first, JD's words didn't seem to register, but he stood there holding his badge in front of her until she stilled.

"I'll take her onboard," Noah said. "You can try to convince the rest of these kids we aren't going to hurt them."

"Where did the other kid go who got out?" Noah asked.

Kade looked around, not seeing any sign of the little girl. "I'm not sure."

* * *

JD fought against the urge to look up the hill, where a man stood on the deck of a simple wooden cabin. If the information Kelsey had given Noah was correct, that was Rabell himself only a few hundred yards away. He tugged on the ball cap he had found in the living quarters of the yacht. He hoped Rabell didn't look past the clothes to the men wearing them.

Ghost handed the girl over to Noah, who gripped both of her arms as though he didn't trust her to come willingly. When the child jerked to pull away, JD realized Noah was right. Poor kid. She was terrified despite seeing his badge.

JD reached for the shed door. The moment Ghost gave him a nod to signal he was ready, JD cracked the door open a few inches, and immediately, another girl tried to run past him.

Ghost caught her and nudged her back inside before JD pushed the door closed again.

"This isn't working," Ghost said. "We need some way to show these kids we aren't going to hurt them."

Ghost was right, but the only solution JD could come up with was the last one he wanted to entertain. "Hadley."

"What?" Ghost asked.

"If we're right, three of the kids in there are her students."

"You think she can calm them down and get them to cooperate?"

"I think so, but how to do we bring her to the shed without Rabell suspecting something?" JD asked.

"We pretend she's part of the cargo." Before JD could protest, Ghost added, "It's the only way to get her near the children without anyone suspecting anything." Ghost motioned to his left. "She's over there, fifteen yards past the tree line."

"I'll be right back."

"And I'll be holding the door."

CHAPTER 47

HADLEY HEARD THE APPROACHING STEPS, her senses heightened since her escape. Kelsey stood beside her, weapon in hand in the event that Chad tried to break through the zip ties on his wrists. He had regained consciousness within minutes of being knocked out, but by the time he had, they had secured him and placed a gag over his mouth to keep him from warning Rabell of their presence.

The footsteps kept coming, and adrenaline rose within Hadley. Kelsey shifted slightly as though she too wasn't sure who was more of a threat, the newcomer or Chad.

Fear turned to joy when JD stepped into sight. The moment he spotted Hadley, he rushed to her and pulled her into his arms. He didn't speak for a moment, finally drawing her away so he could see her face. "Are you okay?"

"I think so."

"I hate to ask this, but we need your help," JD said.

"What kind of help?"

"The children being held in the shed are terrified. They keep trying to escape. We need you to calm them down so we can take them on the boat to get them out of here."

Kelsey stepped forward. "JD, let me do it. From a distance, Rabell will think I'm Hadley."

"That may be true, but some of the girls know Hadley. They trust her." JD turned his attention from Kelsey to Hadley. "I know it's a lot to ask, but can you do it?"

Fear rose up and lodged in her throat, but she nodded. She had come here to help Cammie. She couldn't stop now when they were so close to bringing the children to safety. "I'll do it."

"We have to make it look like you're my prisoner."

"Do you have to zip tie my hands again?"

"No. Just hold them in front of you like they're tied up."

"Okay. Let's go."

JD looked at Kelsey. "You've got him?"

"Yeah. I've got him, but I'd feel better if you'd lend me your handcuffs to make sure he doesn't break free," Kelsey said.

"I can do that." JD retrieved a set of handcuffs from a spot near his gun holster and handed them over, along with the key.

"Cover me." Kelsey pocketed the key. She then removed the zip tie, forced Chad to hug a nearby tree, and secured both wrists so he had no way to see them, much less try to get away.

"As soon as we get the kids onto the boat, we'll come back and get him."

"I'll be here," Kelsey said. "But yell if you need me."

"I will."

* * *

JD held Hadley's arm to make it appear as though she were his prisoner instead of his girlfriend. He wasn't sure *girlfriend* was the right word for what she was to him, but at the moment, he wasn't going to take the time to analyze his relationship status.

"Did you find Cammie?"

"I don't know. It's dark in the shed, and I couldn't get a good look inside because the kids kept trying to get free," JD said. "Not that I can blame them."

"That may be my fault. I told Cammie to teach the others how to break free of the zip ties."

"That would explain why at least a few of them aren't tied up." JD gave her arm a gentle squeeze. "I'm sorry, but the easiest way to give you time with the children is to put you in there with them."

Hadley didn't say anything at first. Then she said, "I'll be okay."

They neared the shed where Ghost stood guard.

"Open the door and let her in."

"Are you sure about this?" Ghost asked, but JD wasn't sure if he was asking him or Hadley.

"I'm sure," Hadley answered.

"Here." JD pulled his cell phone out of his pocket and handed it to her. "You can use this as a flashlight. It might help the kids calm down if they can see you."

"Thanks." Hadley gripped the phone and gave him one last look before she nodded at Ghost to open the door.

* * *

Hadley stepped into the darkness, Ghost and JD quickly closing the door behind her, so no one would escape. A child whimpered.

She spoke in a soothing tone. "It's okay. I'm here to help you." Hadley pressed the screen on JD's phone and turned on the flashlight feature. She held the light to the side of her so the kids could see her face.

A little voice sounded in the dark. "Miss Baker?"

"Yes, it's me." Hadley turned the light toward the depth of the shed, circling it to see six little girls inside, two of them with identical faces. "Sara, Saige, are you okay?"

Both girls stood and gripped her around the waist. It took a moment before Hadley registered that they had that capability. "Your hands aren't tied up."

"Cammie helped us break the things around them," Saige said.

Hadley held the light up again, searching each face. "Where is Cammie?"

"She got away." Sara's voice wavered. "We tried to follow her, but the bad men closed the door again."

Urgency filled her, and Hadley squatted down so she was eye to eye with her students. "I know bad men brought you here, but the people outside are my friends. They're here to help us get away."

"Are you sure?" another girl asked. "They could be trying to trick you."

"They aren't. They're FBI agents. One of them saved my life," Hadley said. "I need you to trust them."

"If they're good people, why won't they let us out?" a teenager asked.

"Because there are still bad people out there. They want to get you safe before they go after them," Hadley said. "There's a boat at the dock. I need you to pretend that my friends are the bad men. You're going to follow them onto the boat. As soon as you're all on there, they'll take you to safety."

"What if the real bad men come again?" Saige asked.

"My friends will stop them," Hadley said, hoping her words were true. "Do whatever they tell you, and they'll keep you safe. Can you all do that?"

Again, Hadley used her light to look at the faces. She sensed skepticism from the two teenagers. "It's either this or stay here and hope the bad guys don't come back before my friends can rescue you."

The last holdouts nodded.

"Good. Make sure you keep your hands together like you're still tied up. We need to make sure we look convincing," Hadley said. "Now, everyone line up so we can get you out of here."

Hadley noticed how slowly several of the girls were moving, and she couldn't help but wonder how much they had been fed during their ordeal.

She waited until the girls took their positions before she gave a gentle tap on the shed door. "JD? They're ready."

* * *

JD opened the shed door slowly, amazed to find Hadley standing in front of a neat line of girls as though she were preparing to walk them from her classroom out to the playground.

Noah jogged toward him, reaching the edge of the shed as Hadley stepped out. "Mitch has the first girl." His eyebrows lifted when he saw Hadley with the other children, all of them now calm and no longer trying to break free. Noah spoke past JD, his eyes focusing on the children. "I gather everyone else is ready for their rescue now."

"They are," Hadley said.

"Follow me," Noah said. "We're going to walk nice and slow, like a game of pretend, okay?"

The girls nodded.

"You take the lead," JD said with a glance at Hadley. "I'll take the rear."

Noah started forward, and Hadley motioned for the girls to follow. Instead of falling in line with them, she stood beside him and spoke to Ghost. "You said one girl got away. Where did she go?"

"I'm not sure. By the time I got another girl under control and the door closed again, she had disappeared," Ghost said. "Best guess is that she ducked into those trees."

"I have to find her."

"Hadley, we'll find her," JD said gently. He hated playing the odds, but sometimes it was the only way to function when trying to ensure the safety of both agents and victims. "But first, we need to get everyone else out of here and take Rabell into custody. We can't afford to break off and go looking for one girl."

"That missing girl is Cammie."

"What?" JD watched the last of the hostages exit the shed, searching for the familiar face. His eyes came back to Hadley's. Still, he couldn't help the question from forming. "Cammie?"

"I have to find her," Hadley insisted again.

Ghost stepped behind the last of the girls. "I'll help Noah get these kids onboard and come back to help."

"Tell our other agent on board to get everyone out of here," JD said before speaking to Hadley. "You too. Go with them."

She opened her mouth as though to refuse. Before she could, JD squeezed her arm. "Please, Hadley. I need to know you're safe so I can do my job."

"Okay. Please be careful."

"I will." JD watched her step beside Ghost, the other man taking her arm as though keeping her under control.

JD turned his gaze toward the cabin above him. Rabell stood overlooking the progress of his operation, a second man positioned beside him. JD read the body language, the wave of Rabell's right hand, the other man's nod. An order had been given, but for what?

The second man headed for the stairs leading off the deck, and JD made the connection. Donnell. The man from Spencer's apartment.

His pace brisk, JD could only guess Rabell had ordered him to check on the progress of the job or, worse, to see if the men escorting the children were really his own.

JD glanced behind him; Noah was almost to the dock. Hadley, on the other hand, was only fifty yards away.

JD reached for his gun, still debating whether he should announce himself as a federal agent or try to play the part of kidnapper a little longer.

When he turned back to face the man heading toward him, JD caught a glimpse of movement in the bushes only a few yards from the trail between the shed and the cabin. Donnell must have sensed it too because he immediately stopped and turned toward it.

JD's heart stuttered when he caught a glimpse of blonde curls and faded blue leggings. The man darted toward the trees, and in a flash, he grabbed at Cammie.

She screamed, and, in that instant, the decision was made for JD. His gun lifted. "Federal agent. Freeze!"

In a repeat of the scene on the boat, the man grabbed the child and held her up as a shield. Cammie wiggled in his grip, her terrified gaze now fixed on JD.

CHAPTER 48

HADLEY HEARD THE SCREAM. SHE whirled around, even as Ghost grabbed her arm to keep dragging her forward.

"Keep going. Get the girls on board."

"But JD . . ."

"You do this, and I'll help him."

In front of them, Noah waved the children forward as he changed directions. "Keep going!" he told the girls as he rushed back onto shore. "Hadley, help Mitch get them on board."

She noted the gun in his hand and knew the best thing she could do was take over the care of the girls so Noah and Ghost could help JD.

"Go. I've got them." Hadley quickened her steps and caught up to Sara, who was at the end of the line. "Hurry. We need to go quickly."

Sara and Saige tried to run, but they moved like they were wading through molasses. Hadley lifted Sara into her arms.

"Saige, keep coming. I'll be back in a minute to help you." Hadley jogged onto the open dock, passing one of the other girls as the first three climbed aboard one by one. The man Noah called Mitch stood on the edge of the yacht, steadying the girls as they came aboard.

The yacht's engines rumbled to life. Several birds took flight from the nearby trees.

Hadley reached the end of the dock and held Sara out to Mitch. "Here. I'm going back for her sister."

The moment Mitch lifted Sara from her arms, Hadley raced back down the dock to where Saige was still coming toward her. She leaned down and picked her up, her gaze moving to where a man stood holding Cammie, her feet dangling a foot off the ground.

"Come on!" Mitch shouted.

Remembering her responsibility at the moment, Hadley turned back to the yacht and ran forward. She handed Saige to him, surprised when Mitch set her on the deck and immediately jumped off the yacht onto the dock.

"Get on. Keep an eye on the kids. The Coast Guard will help you."

Hadley stepped onto the rear of the yacht and climbed up onto the main part of the lower deck.

The moment she was securely on board, Mitch waved at the Coast Guard seaman at the helm. "Go!"

Only Saige remained in the open space at the back of the boat. Hadley opened the door to the cabin. "Go inside. I'll be down in a minute to check on you."

Eager to see what was happening on land, Hadley climbed the steps to the upper deck to find a Coast Guard seaman who appeared to be in his early twenties. Behind her, a Coast Guard vessel approached, but she quickly trained her gaze on where JD stood, his gun drawn and aimed at the man holding Cammie hostage.

Hadley swallowed hard, not able to fathom the fear the little girl must be experiencing right now. She saw Mitch reach the end of the dock and duck behind the shed. Ghost had disappeared from sight, and Noah crouched behind Chad's SUV, his hands resting on the hood as he aimed at Cammie's captor. Kelsey appeared a short distance away, her weapon trained on the same target.

With the FBI agents and Kelsey, the man wasn't getting away, but would Cammie get caught in the crossfire?

Hadley gripped her hands on the back of the padded chair in front of her, tension filling her. The deck where Rabell had stood only moments ago was now empty, no sign of him anywhere.

When she saw a new source of movement, her heart nearly stopped. Only ten yards from where the man held Cammie, a rifle barrel poked out from the brush.

"JD! Watch out!" Hadley cried, but she was too far away, her voice lost in the sound of the engine and the waves.

The gun barrel steadied, taking aim at JD.

The idea to search for a loudspeaker flashed through her mind, but instead she said, "Sound the horn!"

The seaman didn't ask questions, immediately laying on the horn and sending out a loud blast.

* * *

JD jolted at the sound of the horn and instinctively ducked. He sensed rather than heard the bullet that whizzed by his head.

"Gun!" Noah shouted.

JD dove to the ground and rolled to his side before scrambling to his feet and dashing into the bushes. The man holding Cammie took advantage of the shot and also ran for cover.

JD lost sight of him, but Cammie's whimper gave away their location. A hand came down on JD's shoulder, and he whipped around to find Ghost behind him.

Ghost held his finger to his lips and used hand signals to indicate his intention. JD took a moment to process the silent communication before he nodded his understanding.

Ghost slipped deeper into the brush. JD counted off ten seconds before he shouted, "Come out with your hands up."

Nothing. As expected.

JD edged toward where he had heard Cammie, moving slowly to mask his footsteps. When the white of Cammie's shirt appeared between the leaves, he stopped, holding his position, seconds ticking off in his head. Just thirty more to give Ghost time to get into position. JD squatted down and peered through the underbrush.

Donnell was kneeling, Cammie kept in front of him by the hand he held over her mouth. The girl had paled, and it took only a moment for him to see why. Whether Donnell realized it or not, he was suffocating her.

Ten more seconds for Ghost to get into position, but JD couldn't wait. He pushed up behind the closest tree and took aim. "Let her go!"

Donnell startled, releasing his grip from Cammie's mouth and wrapping his arm around her middle again as he stood.

"You don't have anywhere to go," JD said, repeating words he had said earlier. "Right now, it's only kidnapping. You don't want to bump the charges up to murder."

JD saw the challenge in the other man's eyes, the look that told him he had no intention of going to prison. "It's prison, or I can kill you right now," JD said.

"If I die, so does she." He moved the gun upward, but JD didn't give him the chance to bring it to Cammie's head.

JD aimed and fired, his bullet tearing into the man's foot.

A shout of pain echoed, and his hold on Cammie weakened, her feet dropping to the ground. In a move that made JD's heart soar with pride, Cammie stomped her foot on Donnell's fresh wound.

He cried out again, and Cammie broke free and ran toward JD.

The gun lifted, this time pointed at Cammie instead of JD. Afraid of taking a shot with Cammie running between them, JD aimed, praying she could make it past him in time for him to shoot.

A shot sounded, and Cammie screamed. She stumbled but regained her footing and kept heading for him.

It was then that JD saw Ghost standing behind her, Cammie's captor now on the ground, Donnell's weapon secured in Ghost's hand.

Trusting Ghost to take care of Donnell, JD lowered to one knee as Cammie reached him and threw her arms around his neck. JD hugged her, relief pouring through him. The fear that had consumed him when the last shot had sounded stole his voice, and he struggled to find it. Finally, he loosened his grip and pulled back to see Cammie's face. "Are you okay?"

Her green eyes met his, a plea reflected there. "Don't leave me."

"I won't. I've got you now."

Ghost approached them, Cammie once again tightening her hold on JD.

"Rabell's still out there," JD said.

"I know. Keep her hidden. I'll help the others flush him out."

"Be careful."

Ghost nodded. "Always."

CHAPTER 49

KADE SCANNED THE WOODS WHERE the shots had originated, already convinced the shooter had moved an instant after he'd squeezed the trigger. Rabell. It had to be him. No way Kade was going to let him slip through his fingers, not after what he had witnessed today, not to mention the haunting images that had remained with him since his time in Abolstan.

The device in his hand revealed the location of everyone nearby, seven heat spots, besides himself. He could identify the two that belonged to JD and the little girl, as well as those for Kelsey and Chad. He guessed the one nearest the SUV belonged to Noah. That left the other FBI agent and Rabell. Kade analyzed the two signals. One was fifty yards to the east, near the river, while the other was in the woods near the cabin. Either way, Rabell appeared to be making his escape.

Unsure which was the true target, Kade headed toward the one known quantity. He reached the clearing where the SUV was parked and saw Noah heading toward him. Taking advantage of the cover of the woods, Kade waited for Noah to reach the tree line before calling out.

"Noah. Over here."

"Ghost?"

"Where's your other agent?" Kade asked.

"Mitch is covering the area by the river," Noah said. "Rabell's disappeared."

Kade held out his scanner and pointed to the remaining heat spot. "This must be him."

"Then who is this?" Noah asked, tapping on the screen where a single signal was closing in on Rabell.

Kade went over all of the players again, quickly ascertaining the answer. "Either Chad Hicks got away, or that's your wife."

* * *

Kelsey saw her target clearly. Rabell was slipping through the trees, making his way toward the cabin.

She'd watched his movement ever since she'd seen Rabell dash out of his hiding place after his attempt on JD's life. She didn't want to think about what would have happened had that horn not sounded when it did.

She had waited and watched for Noah, JD, and Mitch to follow after Rabell, but they never had. When Rabell had reached the edge of the woods, where she could see him, she had made the decision to follow him. She couldn't stand by and watch Rabell get away again, not after seeing firsthand what he was capable of. The mere thought of how he had kept women and children locked up like animals was enough to keep her moving forward, even though she didn't know where Noah and his fellow agents were now.

Her pistol warm in her hand, she paralleled Rabell's flight, the woods making it impossible for her to get a clear shot. When he reached the cabin, she expected him to go inside, but instead, he crept around the far side. Did he know he was being followed? Or did he have an escape route already planned out?

Afraid it might be the latter, she quickened her steps, keeping to the woods on the opposite side of the cabin to where she had seen Rabell disappear.

Memories welled up inside her, images of the dozens of girls who had been locked up in Abolstan surfacing with a vengeance. Seeing the children rescued today only fed her fury. Men like Rabell needed to be stopped, and she was determined to make sure he didn't slip away.

Afraid she would lose him, she stepped onto the swath of grass between the trees and the cabin and increased her pace to a jog until she reached the front corner of the structure. Slowing, she pressed her body against the exterior wall and leaned forward. Suddenly, Rabell's motives became clear. He was running to his car.

A full-sized pickup truck dominated the gravel driveway. Rabell reached the driver's side, and Kelsey lifted her weapon, firing off a shot before he could climb in. "Freeze! Federal agent!"

He ducked, swinging his rifle toward her.

Kelsey took cover behind the cabin, a shot splintering into the wood beside her. Why was it that no one ever listened when she said that?

She dropped to a knee, peeked around the corner, and returned fire, hammering out two more shots.

Rabell already had the truck door open and used it for cover. He dropped his rifle on the ground and reached beneath the seat, coming up with a pistol. He fired three times before climbing into the cab.

"Don't do it," Kelsey warned.

Again, he ignored her.

The engine started, Rabell's concentration now on his escape.

Kelsey stood, giving herself an extra second to take aim. Then she pulled the trigger on a single shot. The bullet hit the driver's-side window but didn't appear to go through.

Noah and Ghost rounded the corner as she fired again. This time, Rabell cried out.

Noah rushed in from the passenger side, Ghost taking the front of the vehicle. Kelsey stood her ground, her gun still raised.

"Let me see your hands," Noah demanded.

This time, Rabell listened, his hands coming to rest on the steering wheel.

While she and Ghost covered him, Noah opened the passenger-side door and confiscated Rabell's weapon.

Once he was in handcuffs, Kelsey lowered her gun. "How come he listened to you and not me?"

"He probably figured if he didn't, you'd shoot him again." Noah inspected Rabell's wound, a bullet to the left shoulder. "Nice shot, by the way."

"Thanks."

"I assume you deliberately didn't kill him," Ghost said.

"You've got that right. No way I was going to let him off that easy. I want him alive so we can make sure his operation is shut down for good."

Ghost holstered his weapon. "If you two have this covered, I'm getting out of here. I'd prefer not to deal with too many police types."

"Thank you for your help today. I don't know how I would have managed without you."

"Glad this chapter is behind us." Ghost took a step back. "You have my number. Use it if you need me."

"I will. Thanks again." Kelsey watched him leave, then turned to face her husband.

"Um, I hate to say this, but maybe you should get out of here too. This place is about to be crawling with cops," Noah said.

"Good idea." Knowing an investigation would be conducted because the suspect was wounded, Kelsey offered Noah her gun. "You'd better take this."

"Thanks." He took it. "I guess I'm calling this my spare weapon today."

"Whatever works." Kelsey headed for the woods. "And, Noah?"

"What?"

"Don't work too late tonight. I think you've earned an evening off."

"I think we both have."

CHAPTER 50

HADLEY STOOD IN THE SHADE of the harbor parking lot to combat the overly warm midday sun. An ambulance pulled away to take the last of the victims to the hospital.

Although a few had suffered from lack of food and water, the Coast Guard medic who had first attended to them said they were in overall good health. The man hadn't needed to speak the obvious, that if they had been an hour later, they would have been in anything but good health.

When the yacht had docked at Occoquan Harbor, several FBI agents had met them, questioning everyone as the paramedics started evaluating the girls further. Hadley recognized a few agents from when she had accompanied JD to work, but she had yet to hear from JD. The Coast Guard had relayed the message that everyone was safe, a message that was reiterated by the other FBI agents. Though the words gave her some comfort, Hadley knew she wasn't going to be completely satisfied until she saw for herself that JD and Cammie were well.

She glanced at her watch. She should have heard from him hours ago.

A familiar car pulled in and parked, and Kelsey climbed out from behind the wheel. She approached Hadley and lifted a hand in greeting to the agent standing nearby.

"Hey, Noah called me and asked if I would come by and drive you home," Kelsey said. "He and JD got caught up with some legal matters in the city."

"But they're okay?" Hadley asked.

"Yeah. Noah said they're fine."

Hadley noticed the way Kelsey phrased her response as though her husband had told her of his status rather than acknowledging that she had been present to see for herself how he was doing. She was suddenly grateful the statement she had given to the FBI agent had focused on the criminals and not the people who had come to rescue them. Hadley turned to the closest agent. "Is it okay if I leave now?"

"Yes. I have your statement and your information. We'll call if we have any more questions."

"Thanks." Hadley followed Kelsey to the car. She opened the passenger-side door to find her purse and school bag sitting on the floor.

Kelsey didn't say anything until she had started the car and pulled out of the parking lot. "Did you tell anyone you saw me today?"

"No."

Kelsey's shoulders visibly relaxed. Instead of offering any kind of explanation, she changed the subject and motioned to the floor. "I figured you might want your stuff, so I grabbed it out of JD's car for you."

"Thanks." Hadley stared at Kelsey for a moment before she asked the question that had been burning inside her for hours. "Kelsey, who do you really work for?"

Kelsey didn't respond, her eyes glued to the road in front of them.

"I may be a third-grade teacher," Hadley continued, "but I've been living in Virginia long enough to recognize a government operative when I see one."

"As far as anyone knows, I'm a nanny working in DC."

Kelsey had evaded the question, and Hadley tried to process the conflicting emotions of curiosity, annoyance, and understanding. Finally, she said, "Seems to me, a nanny and a school teacher would make good friends."

Kelsey glanced at her, the beginnings of a smile on her face. "I think so too."

"And while we're where no one can hear us, thank you for everything today. I don't know what I would have done without you."

"You were doing just fine on your own, but I'm glad I could help." Kelsey let the full smile come this time. "And I have just the thing you can do to repay me."

"What's that?"

"I think it would make JD's day if we spent some time in the kitchen and made baklava."

"Baking is a good way to relax."

"I agree."

* * *

JD sat beside Cammie in the back of the ambulance. Besides some cuts on her wrists from the zip tie and some scrapes from running through the woods, she had survived her ordeal remarkably well. At least physically. JD hoped she would be as resilient emotionally.

"Does she have to go to the hospital?" JD asked the paramedic.

"She looks good. If you want, we can take her to the hospital for a complete eval, but as far as I can tell, she doesn't have anything a Band-Aid can't fix."

"Thanks." JD turned his attention to Cammie. "What do you think, Cammie? Should we take you home?"

"I want to stay with you."

"I think your mom will be worried about you." When she didn't respond, JD asked, "Don't you want to go home?"

Her lips pressed together, and tears came to her eyes. One spilled over. "I can't go home."

Though JD's instinct was to reassure her, he found himself asking a question instead. "Why not?"

"My mom gave me to that man."

Nothing Cammie said could have shocked him more. Fighting to keep his own emotions under control, he glanced at the paramedic, nodding his head to ask for some privacy.

"I'll let you two talk." The paramedic climbed out of the ambulance and stepped out of sight.

JD angled his body so he could see Cammie's face. "Can you tell me what happened today?" JD put his hand on hers. "I need you to tell me everything."

Again, her lips pressed into a firm line, but she nodded.

"When did you first see the man who brought you here?"

"He knocked on the door before I left for school. He had a box for my mom."

"What was in the box?"

"I don't know, but he said she could have it if I went with him."

"Then what?"

"My mom opened the box. Then she told me he was going to drive me to school and that I should be a good girl for him." Another tear spilled over. "He was a stranger, so I tried to leave, but he took my hands and put that plastic thing around them. Then he carried me to the car and put me inside."

"And then he brought you here?" JD asked.

Cammie nodded.

"Cammie, does your mom take drugs?"

"I'm not supposed to tell."

"I need you to be honest with me," JD said. "It's the only way I can help you."

She sniffled, then nodded.

Noah approached from the side of the ambulance. The look on his face told JD that Noah had heard enough to understand the situation. "Do you want me to call child services?"

"No, not that!" Cammie cried.

JD suspected he understood the source of the problem. "Did your mom talk to you about child services and foster care?"

Her lips pressed together, and tears sprang to her eyes.

"Cammie, when people like your mom have problems with drugs, they don't always see things clearly," JD said. "There are good people who can take care of you, people who will keep you safe."

"Mommy said they would lock me up."

"No one is going to lock you up. I promise." JD saw the doubt visible on her face. "Tell you what. How about if I come with you to make sure your foster home is okay?"

Cammie blinked back tears. "Will you bring your gun?"

"I'll bring my gun," JD confirmed. "But where you're going, I won't need it."

* * *

JD's car was parked in the driveway when Hadley walked out of Kelsey's house. She broke into a run and burst through the front door. "JD?"

Silence. Where was he? She realized suddenly that this whole ordeal was finally over. When Kelsey had come to take her home, she hadn't considered that she should go back to her apartment instead of to JD's house.

Footsteps sounded from upstairs, and JD appeared on the top landing. Hadley's mouth opened to form an apology, but she struggled to find the right words. What could she say? I'm sorry I love being here with you? I'm sorry if I overstayed my welcome? I'm sorry I'm falling in love with you?

The last thought startled her enough that she remained silent.

JD raced down the stairs and pulled her into his arms. "Are you okay?"

"Yeah. I was worried about you though," she said.

"I'm sorry I didn't get a chance to call you."

"It's okay. You're home now." Hadley pulled back and laid her hands on his chest, checking for herself that he was here and whole. "I was so scared. I saw that gun pointed at you . . ."

"Wait." His eyebrows drew together. "Was that you who sounded the horn?"

"Technically, the seaman did. It was the only thing I could think of to warn you."

"You realize you probably saved my life."

"I don't know about that."

JD's hands lifted to her cheeks, his eyes intense as they stared into hers. "You did. You saved me, and you helped me save Cammie."

"Where is Cammie? Is she okay?"

"Yeah. That's actually why I got tied up today. I went with the social worker to take Cammie to her foster home."

"Was it a good family?" Hadley asked.

"Yeah. She really lucked out. They have a daughter who's only a year older than her. They even said they would drive her to school for the rest of the year so she wouldn't have to change schools if she doesn't want to."

"They sound great."

"Yeah. They are," JD said. "I have a good feeling about them."

"I'm glad. I only wish we could have saved more of the girls who were taken. Every time I think of Ivy and the life she must be living now, I get sick to my stomach."

"We'll keep looking for her and the others," JD promised. "Try to focus on the good you did, not on what we couldn't do."

"I know. You're right."

"You made a difference today. Never forget that." JD pushed a strand of hair out of her face, his gaze on hers. "You changed lives for the better."

Warmth filled her, and her eyes grew moist. "Thanks for saying that."

"It's true." JD stepped back and slid his hands down to take hers. "Can I ask you a favor though?"

"Of course."

"In the future, do you think you can restrict your changing-lives efforts to the classroom?" JD asked. "I don't ever want you to need those self-defense skills again."

Hadley smiled. "I'll do my best."

CHAPTER 51

JD PARKED IN THE SCHOOL parking lot and stuffed the wrappers from his drive-through lunch into the takeout bag. He knew he would see Hadley tonight after work, but he couldn't wait to give her the latest news.

He checked the time. If he was right, Hadley's class should be heading out to the playground for afternoon recess about now.

He signed in with the front office before circling to the back of the school. One of Hadley's coworkers waved when he approached, and JD returned the greeting.

"Hey, Sharon. How's it going?"

"Good. Hadley's class should be out in a minute."

"Great. Thanks."

An argument pulled Sharon's attention away. "Duty calls."

As she moved away, JD looked up the gentle slope leading to the back door of the school. Sure enough, only a few seconds passed before the door swung open and children poured out, Hadley right behind them.

JD's heartbeat quickened at the mere sight of her, along with a warmth and sense of anticipation he now associated only with her. He didn't know how it was possible for her to still have that effect on him.

Hadley had been living in Mrs. Henderson's house for a month now, but even seeing her every day didn't seem to be enough. He was beginning to think no amount of time together would ever be enough.

Hadley's class spotted him, and several of the kids raced down the hill toward him, Cammie leading the way. She made a beeline for JD and hugged him around the waist. "Agent Byers! You're here!"

"I am." JD couldn't help but smile. "How's everything going at your new house? Do you still like it okay?"

Her eyes brightened. "We got a new kitten on Saturday. She's orange and fluffy and likes to play with string."

"Sounds like you have a new friend."

More children reached him, and he was inundated with pleas to play soccer.

"Sorry, guys. Not today. I need to talk to Miss Baker."

Hadley stepped up behind them. "You all go play. I'll see if I can convince Agent Byers to come to our end-of-the-year party next week."

"Yay!" twenty-four voices yelled in unison.

Hadley waited until the kids scattered to various areas of the playground. "What are you doing here?"

"I have news I wanted to share."

"What kind of news?"

"Intel finally figured out what Spencer was up to before he died," JD said. "Apparently, a flash drive was discovered in Georgia Archer's apartment."

"The woman who lived next door to Spencer? The one who was killed?"

JD nodded. "From what we've been able to piece together, the two of them were working together to stop Rabell and save as many kids as they could."

"Save them?" Hadley asked.

"Spencer confiscated the diamonds we found, and he was using them to buy the girls Rabell kidnapped. He saved twenty-two, that we know of."

"Ivy?"

"Ivy was one of them. She's living with a wonderful family in New Hampshire."

The weight she had carried for the past month dropped away. "Ivy's okay?"

"She is."

"I don't understand how Spencer was helping kids while also being involved with Rabell."

"We think he was trying to intercept kids before they ever made it out of the state. From what Ivy and the other girls said, he took them on a boat to a house and then he gave them new names and placed them with families."

"Like his own adoption agency."

"Exactly. The flash drive detailed all the transactions and the locations of the children who were saved," JD said. "For the ones with bad home lives, he put them with foster families. In a few cases, he helped the parent of a missing child relocate to reunite the families."

"This all sounds so complicated. Why didn't Spencer tell the authorities what he was up to?"

"We think he tried," JD said. "I guess whatever messaging system his organization used was compromised, and he was cut off. That's why he started working with Georgia Archer. We think Spencer was trying to find a way to message his superiors through her without alerting anyone who was on Rabell's payroll."

"Do you have any idea why Spencer was working at Opinions Matter if he already had a way to help the kids?" Hadley asked.

"Rabell got him that job," JD said. "The report Ghost sent us mentioned that Spencer didn't know why Rabell wanted him on the inside. Spencer must have discovered the bomb plot but didn't get the chance to warn Georgia."

"And Rabell's men had him bring me along to keep him from causing trouble," Hadley said. "Spencer was a hero."

"Yeah, he was."

* * *

Hadley smiled as she watched her students file out of her classroom to catch their respective buses. JD stood by the door, exchanging high fives and chatting with each one as they left.

Touched by the sweet interaction, Hadley stepped up behind him and put her hand on his shoulder. "I guess you decided a classroom full of kids isn't so scary after all."

"I'm warming up to them." JD turned and took her hand, a serious look on his face. "Just promise me one thing."

"What's that?"

"Promise that when we start having kids of our own, we'll only have one at a time." He waved toward the hallway where several of her students were still visible. "This many at once is exhausting."

"When we have kids?" Hadley repeated. "I think you're getting ahead of yourself."

"You saved my life." JD nudged her a step back so he could close the door. As soon as the barrier was in place, he added, "That means someday you'll have to marry me."

Butterflies took flight in her stomach, but she managed to keep her voice steady. "You saved my life first. Doesn't that make us even?"

"Nah. I like my way of thinking better."

She wasn't sure if she should be amused, flattered, or terrified. "Don't you think we should wait a few more months before you start thinking about putting a ring on my finger?"

"You like amethysts the best, right?"

"Yeah."

He leaned down for a kiss. "Just checking."

ABOUT THE AUTHOR

TRACI HUNTER ABRAMSON WAS BORN in Arizona, where she lived until moving to Venezuela for a study-abroad program. After graduating from Brigham Young University, she worked for the Central Intelligence Agency for several years, eventually resigning in order to raise her family. She credits the CIA with giving her a wealth of ideas as well as the skills needed to survive her children's teenage years. She has gone on to write more than twenty best-selling novels that have consistently been nominated as Whitney Award finalists, and she is a five-time Whitney Award winner. When she's not writing, Traci enjoys spending time with her husband and five children, preferably on a nice, quiet beach somewhere. She also enjoys playing sports, traveling, writing, and coaching high school swimming.